Yukon Winter

By

Vicki Pinkerton
&
Lynn Beau

Copyright © 2024 Vicki Pinkerton & Lynn Beau

Paperback ISBN: 978-1-61929-562-9
Hardback ISBN: 978-1-61929-564-3

Flashpoint Publications First Edition: October, 2024

Printed in the United States of America.

Cover design by TreeHouse Studio

www.flashpointpublications.com

About the Authors

Vicki and Lynn Beau are a mother /daughter team who have been writing together since Lynn was in grade school, although they probably told stories together long before that. When Lynn was in grade 8 they collaborated on a historical fiction novella and both enjoyed it so much they swore to do it again. Just proves you shouldn't swear. Life stepped in and it was years before they both looked at their schedules and said, "No way we could write anything because we are just too busy but…." And they began to write. Their first novel, *Yukon Winter* took them longer than they expected. It is hard to get two busy women, one who lives north of 60 in the Yukon Territory with two children and a big dog, and the other a self-employed grandmother, together to write, but they managed. During the writing of this book, both discovered things about themselves they didn't know…and about each other. They talked about relationships, romance, and sex in ways they hadn't tackled before either. Oh, blush! On the other hand, growing up in a house with four teens, most of those things got talked about at the dinner table, so they didn't have far to go. "We both learned so much," says Lynn, "and we can hardly wait to do it again."

Chapter One

Jackson was almost there.

He should have been elated. The successful completion of an eight-day road trip that no one, other than perhaps his sister, thought he could do should have been immensely satisfying. Instead, Jackson gripped the steering wheel and wondered whether it was safe to do a U-turn on this desolate stretch of the Alaska Highway.

What the heck was he doing here? Hadn't his parents tried to talk him out of this insane drive across the country to house-sit for some woman he'd never met?

Jackson took a deep breath and relaxed his hold on the steering wheel. That was the old-him talking. The new-him was very clear on why he'd left London, Ontario, to travel west across Canada to the Yukon. Almost finished with the last book of a series his publisher had asked for, Jackson was ready to experiment, to find inspiration for topics and genres he could be proud of without the voices in his head telling him he wasn't good enough. The idea of seeing the north had grown. He'd imagined himself driving first over the rocky Canadian Shield, past huge lakes the size of seas in other parts of the world, and then across prairies and into the mountains. It would be inspiring, terrifying, and exhilarating.

It would also give him distance from his family.

"Why do you need distance?" his mother had demanded. "You already bought that condo, even though we told you it was no problem to keep living with us. Now you're going to the Yukon to prove a point?"

"It's a long way," his father had added. "You really think your writer's brain can handle an entire winter up north? It's cold so close to the Arctic Circle. You'll need to remember to feed yourself there to survive."

Jackson's "writer's brain" had resulted in a very successful career as a romance novelist, but he would be the first to admit he could get so involved in his work that he'd forget basic self-care, including proper meals. He'd recently come to the embarrassing realization he'd never had to. His parents, especially his mother, would insist on making them for him. Where she found the time in between her work as a literary scholar, he'd never know. Despite moving out, his parents were still far too involved in his life. They'd invite themselves over at all hours, stocking his kitchen and taking over Jackson's household tasks without asking. He was capable of ironing his own shirts, or assumed he would be if they weren't whisked away the instant they came out of the dryer.

When the house-sitting gig came up, Jackson had jumped at it. Six months in the wilds of Canada would prove to everyone he could stand on his own. He was almost twenty-nine years old and capable of anything he put his mind to, but he needed space. Unfortunately, the amount of space staring back through the windshield was vast. Had he overestimated the amount needed?

Dense, boreal forest crowded the narrow highway. Lush mountains rose beyond the trees. Even in September, they were capped with snow. There wasn't a utility pole or a sign of civilization in sight. Come to think of it, he hadn't seen another vehicle since a grocery truck had blown past him twenty minutes ago, probably also heading to Whitehorse. For the first time in his life, Jackson was truly alone.

No, there had been someone. A hitchhiker, a few minutes ago. A guy with a hopeful expression, wearing a massive backpack. He'd been walking up the middle of the road. Hearing the car, he'd taken a few steps backwards, sticking his thumb out.

Jackson had averted his eyes and kept driving. He'd never seen a hitchhiker before, or even known someone who'd hitchhiked. It was far too dangerous, as was stopping for one. There were enough dangers out here with the bison, moose, and grizzlies. Jackson was not going to risk getting murdered, especially so close to his destination. He'd concentrated instead on the scenery, which was so different than what he would see at home.

A shuddering movement brought him back to the present. He stepped on the gas and his car, an elderly

Ford Sunfire he'd named Sunny, made a sputtering noise. What was that about? Did she need more gas? He pressed harder on the pedal, but it only made the engine cough, then stop.

Using the last of Sunny's momentum, Jackson steered her to the shoulder, ensuring he was safely off the highway. Now what? His trusty Sunny, who'd got him this far without a single problem, had given up. Jackson turned the key in the ignition, just to be sure, but the car didn't make a sound. Jackson took out his phone to call a tow truck, but it showed no bars. "Great," he muttered. He was completely on his own, which was what he'd wanted but not like this. There was a toolbox in the trunk that his father insisted he pack, but Jackson had no idea how to use anything in it. Now he wished he was one of those guys who'd rebuilt motors in their spare time. Still, he had to at least try.

Jackson checked thoroughly through the windows in each direction, including the ditches. Wild animals treated these highways as their own. There had been many deer, elk, bison, and even the occasional bear sightings during his journey, especially through the mountains. A random stranger driving past would be welcome right now. His main concern was bears, though. What if he met one? But the road appeared empty of all life. It should be safe. Jackson pushed the button to unlatch the hood, unlocked the door and stepped onto the road. It was startling to be on a major transportation route and not hear cars whizzing past, only the occasional bird cry and the wind in the trees.

Taking a steadying gulp of fresh mountain air, Jackson walked to the front of his car. "Come on, Sunny, don't give up on me now." Jackson lifted the hood and leaned under it. The aroma of warm steel and oil enveloped him. Tilting his head, he squinted. Nope, Sunny was not about to reveal the mysteries of her engine. "Why do people always open the hood?" Jackson wracked his brain for the slightest bit of car knowledge, but it was all superficial. None of his characters had been a mechanic, which meant he'd had no reason to research cars. Jackson had never even changed his oil. "We're almost there girl, just a few more hours. Please?"

"Need a hand?" someone said.

Jackson startled upright, flailing. His head cracked into the hood, dislodging the support arm, and it crashed closed. Augh, that hurt! He pressed his hand to the back of his head, overbalanced and landed hard on the gravel shoulder. Stars swam, his vision narrowed, and gravel bit into his butt.

"Shit!" said the other voice. "Are you okay? I'm so sorry."

Jackson groaned, settling onto his butt and holding his head to contain the ringing in his skull. As his vision cleared, the disembodied voice merged with a shock of curly blond hair and worried blue eyes.

"Let me look." The baritone was soothing, and the man hunkered down, his gentle hands running through Jackson's short hair. "It's not bleeding but you're probably going to have a bit of an egg there. Let me help you up." He fit a strong arm under Jackson's, bracing him while he scrambled to his feet.

"Thanks." Jackson sidled away and rested against his car. Embarrassment flooded through him, making his palms slick with sweat and his breath fast and shallow. The sharp pain in his head shifted to a dull throb.

"Can I check your eyes?" the stranger asked. "You probably don't have a concussion, but let's be on the safe side." The alarmingly forthright man stepped right into Jackson's bubble and peered intently into his eyes, first one then the other, looking for...what? Jackson had no idea. The heat and confidence pouring off this stranger drove him back, overbalancing him. He would have fallen again if not for the quick hand to his elbow.

"Whoa, no sudden moves," said the man.

"Are you a doctor or something?" The large, dusty pack, worn jeans, and blue T-shirt didn't scream health-care professional, but Jackson was in no position to judge.

"No, just seen my share of concussions. The man's smile was easy. "I did the ski patrol training at the Whistler Resort a few years ago, so I have my Wilderness First Aid Cert. People tumble on those hills a lot. I got some firsthand experience. Name's Wes." He released Jackson's elbow and extended a calloused hand.

Jackson spent a beat too long looking at the hand before reaching out. "I'm Jackson."

"Good to meet you, Jackson. You need to sit down. Let me help you to the car."

"I've got it." Jackson's voice cracked. Why was this guy crowding him? Using the fender for support, he gingerly walked to the driver's side. From there, he slid into the driver's seat pulling the door shut behind him.

Wes rummaged in his pack, then left it leaning against the back door and climbed into the passenger seat. He shoved a battered metal water bottle at Jackson. "Have a sip, it'll help."

Jackson tried not to let his face show his feelings about putting a used water bottle to his lips. "I've got cold bottles." Jackson twisted his body to reach the small cooler behind the passenger seat, grabbed a chilled plastic bottle and cracked the top. "Do you want one?"

"Thanks, mine's good. Single use plastic is bad for the environment." Wes tipped his bottle up.

Jackson didn't know what to say to that, so he ignored the comment and tipped the bottle to his lips. The cold water was bracing as it went down.

Wes gulped a deep drink then turned to Jackson. "I don't think you should be driving?"

"I'm okay. I can drive."

Wes held up a placating hand. "Hear me out. You got quite a knock there. You look fine, but we should make sure it's nothing serious before you get behind the wheel."

That made sense. Jackson felt weak and his heart was still pounding, but he was tired and maybe even a bit lonely after so long on the road. "I can't drive anyway. I'm not parked on the road for sightseeing. It's Sunny. She's not moving."

"Your car's named Sunny?"

"Yeah."

"Ha." Wes jerked his thumb toward the pack. "I thought I was the only one who named things. Meet Shadow. He's been with me longer than anyone."

Jackson couldn't help giving him a brief smile. It was nice to meet someone who thought the way he did. Gathering his courage, Jackson decided to ask for help. Wes was already in the car, and it was probably too late to worry about him being a serial killer. "That's nice. Wes, could I get a lift with you to Whitehorse? I need to get Sunny some help and my phone doesn't have any bars."

"Sorry, I'm on the thumb-plan. I was walking by when I heard you talking to your car." Wes grinned, dimples popping. "Or was it begging?"

"Oh, crap." Jackson hunched over the steering wheel burying his face in his arms. Now he remembered. "You're the hitchhiker I didn't stop for."

"You're stopped now. Maybe we can help each other."

Jackson lifted his head, wincing as the pounding increased. "What do you mean?"

"There's no rides on this road today. I've been on my feet all morning. How 'bout you let me take a look at Sunny and see if there's something I can do?"

"Are you a mechanic?"

"No, but I know a thing or two about engines, and I've had lots of experience helping people on the side of the road."

What choice did Jackson have? "Fine, what do you need me to do?"

"Try starting her up and let me hear what happens."

Jackson turned the key and whispered under his breath, "Please." Sunny wheezed like a long-time smoker but didn't catch. So much for begging.

"Right." Wes stepped out of the car. "Got any tools?"

Jackson gingerly got out and dug through his trunk. Under the pile of supplies his mother had foisted on him, including a now-empty box of homemade brownies, was the toolbox. He hauled it out and handed it to Wes.

"Thanks." Wes placed it on the ground and sorted through it, a slight frown on his face. "Ah, this should do it." He held up some kind of tool and began tinkering with the engine.

Jackson tried to force himself to take deep breaths. His fists were closed so tight his nails were biting into the skin on his palms.

"Try it again," said Wes.

Jackson headed back to the driver's seat and turned the key. Sunny grunted but didn't start.

Wes tinkered for a bit more and then asked Jackson to turn the key again. When that didn't work, he selected another tool and tried something else.

If Sunny didn't start, then what? Jackson would be stuck walking to Whitehorse with this guy, although maybe walking down the road together they would be less likely to end up animal food.

Wes took a hammer from the toolbox. Dropping to the ground, he wriggled underneath and whacked something.

Jackson flinched at the resounding clang. Well, that was the end then, the car was being beaten to death.

Wes popped up. "Okay, try it now."

Jackson turned the key and the engine caught. "I can't believe that worked." He sagged with relief.

"Thanks for the vote of confidence."

Jackson didn't know what to say. Pins of heat pierced him from his chest to his ears. "I—that wasn't what I meant, I mean, thank you, it was just—"

"You're welcome, and I was kidding." Wes was brushing himself off. "I'm filthy. Let me change so I don't get Sunny dirty. Then I'll drive okay?" Walking around the car to his pack he pulled his shirt over his head and used it to wipe the dust from his arms and his neck. Then he shucked his pants on the side of the road.

Jackson's eyes almost popped out of his face. It was broad daylight and there was Wes, wearing only navy briefs and searching through his pack for clean clothes. Jackson couldn't look. He glanced up and down the road, watching for traffic. If a car came, should he yell out a warning so Wes could cover himself? What was the protocol when not watching a near naked man on the roadside?

Finally, Wes opened the back door, pushing some of Jackson's stuff aside on the seat and loaded Shadow in. Slamming the door shut, he walked around to the driver's side. "Okay, I'm ready."

Jackson couldn't do it. He sat paralyzed with indecision, his stomach clenching.

Wes crouched down by the driver's door. "Hey, you just went some eight shades of gray."

Had he? "Maybe I should get to a hospital."

"I don't think it's that serious." Wes inspected Jackson's pupils. "The closest one is in Whitehorse, anyway."

"But if I drive back—"

"The nearest hospital will still be farther away than the one in Whitehorse. You'll probably be fine to drive. If I wasn't here, you'd have to, but I'm here and I can make the next few hours easier for you." Wes's voice softened. "I get it. You don't know me, but hey—" he grinned "—Sunny likes me and I'm sure she doesn't want to sit here on the side of the road. I'll be careful and I know the way."

"I don't know." Jackson could feel the exhaustion dragging at him. "I guess it wouldn't hurt to be a passenger for a bit." The walk around the front to the passenger side was long as he second guessed his decision. Doing up his seat belt he watched Wes adjust the seat and mirrors. Sunny started with what almost sounded like a purr and Wes pulled onto the empty highway.

Wes handled the car confidently. His driving was good, at least out here in the middle of nowhere. It wasn't an eight-lane freeway, so the obstacles were minimal. That was one less thing to worry about. Jackson. He stared out the window at the passing scenery. The brilliant purples and reds of the fireweed blurred together. His eyes burned with fatigue and his head ached. Probably he should be talking but he didn't know what to say. Questions formed in Jackson's mind, but it was too hard to ask them. Driving on his own had been fun. No one to make demands, no one's schedule to keep. But he hadn't noticed until now that the long days and constantly not knowing anything about where he was had been exhausting. His body, being lulled by the road, was ready to shut down. His eyelids were leaning together until a voice startled him awake.

"How are you doing?" Wes asked. "You look like you're fading."

"I'm okay," Jackson mumbled.

"Good to hear," said Wes. "But I'll feel better if you stay awake and talk to me. And I could use the company while I drive."

Jackson shifted in his seat. "I'm not really great company."

"Let me be the judge of that. Why don't we play, I get to ask the new guy why he's here?"

"Talking about me is never my favorite topic, but I have a question? Were you really planning to walk all the way to Whitehorse? What do you do at night?" Visions of hungry wolves filled Jackson's imagination as he watched the dense forests leaning into the road.

"When we're traveling, Shadow and I camp whenever the spirit takes us. The outdoors is big and it's free. Last night though, we stayed in a campground along the road. Every once in a while a shower and laundry is a good thing. We rolled out early this morning but rides were scarce and yes, we did walk a long way but it doesn't matter, I like to walk. It's a great, carbon neutral method of transport, and you really experience the land."

All the walking explained Wes's lean form and muscular legs. Not that Jackson had been looking.

"I get to ask you one now," Wes said. "Sunny has Ontario plates and is packed for a long trip. You moving up here?"

The headache had lessened, and Jackson was starting to relax. "Nope, not moving. I'm coming to house-sit for a woman who lives in the woods near Whitehorse."

"Wow. Seems to me you don't have to travel all the way across the country for a bit of house- sitting. You must really like to drive."

"I've never driven more than across town before. I really didn't know what it would be like, but I think I do like it." It surprised Jackson to say it, but he had been enjoying himself, from the moment he'd told his counselor what he was doing. The packing, the planning, the getting away. It was all new and it represented a fresh phase in his life.

"Your turn," Wes told him. "What do you want to know?"

"Same question. Are you from around here or just passing through?"

"Wes laughed. "A little of both. I was born here but I left when my parents died about ten years ago. It's been like a magnet pulling me back probably because I've got a few ends to tie up, and my bank account is low. It's always a good place to make some quick cash."

Jackson wanted to express sympathy for Wes's loss, but didn't know what to say, especially since Wes had said it so casually. Instead he asked, "Judging by the amount of luggage you're carrying, you're not staying long?"

"No real plans right now. Hey, I've got some trail mix in the top pocket of Shadow. Can you reach it? I'm hungry and we should probably both eat something."

Jackson unbuckled his belt and twisted around. Finding the bag was easy and soon they were both munching the nutty mix. The food settled Jackson's stomach and made the world look just a little better. The only sound was tires turning on the pavement. The scenery rolling by was spectacular: snowcapped mountains, rivers, and lakes. Several times Jackson raised his phone to the window to try to capture what he was seeing. "I'd love to ride my bike here." Then the car began a long climb. "Or maybe not."

"That's where hoofing it has its advantages. You're not pushing a hunk of metal along with you." Wes smiled, glancing in his direction. "It is beautiful, though. I had forgotten how amazing it is."

At the crest of the hill, they saw a river laid out below them with a long bridge over it. "That's the Nisutlin Bay Bridge in Teslin," Wes said. "Its six arches are unique in the Yukon."

The scene before them was breathtaking. The bridge crossing the river, a lake on the other side, the sky purple with mountains in the distance and a small community nestled into the trees. So remote and yet so... Jackson couldn't think of the right words to say, but Wes was clearly okay with being quiet. It was good.

'I'd say we've just under two hours left to get to Whitehorse," Wes said. "How are you doing? Do you need to stop?"

"To be honest, I'd prefer to keep going. I've kind of been procrastinating a bit.

"I'm in a bit of a hurry myself. I'm hoping to get to my friend's place today, so I don't mind but I'm interested. Sounds like a pretty sweet gig, this house-sitting thing. Why aren't you rushing in headfirst?"

Jackson was careful. "I'm kind of putting myself out there, I mean for me." He tried to put his thoughts into words. "I'm a city boy. I've never been out of town. I've always tried to be the person my family wants me to be, and this is not that. It's really random and out of my comfort zone. My mother is freaked out and horrified. I'm telling myself it's going to be great and I kind of believe me, but actually, I am pretty horrified myself. It'll take everything I've got to make it work."

They were negotiating some interesting curves in the road and Wes didn't look at him when he spoke. "That's crazy, but you've made it, you're in the Yukon now and—wow! Look at that!"

There on the side of the road was a large, shaggy, black bear standing on all fours, watching them intently.

Wes slowed the car to a roll. "There's your welcome."

Jackson couldn't believe how close he was to the big-guy and raised his phone to take a picture.

"I'd say it's a good sign for your visit," said Wes. "It can't get much better than that." The car sped up.

"Crazy. A bear greeting me? I've been worried about a bear eating me. What's a city guy like me gonna do if one shows up while I'm house-sitting in the woods?" Possibilities rolled through Jackson's mind, none of them good.

Wes glanced at him. "Bears don't want to meet you any more than you want to meet them. Best case scenario, they smell you and they don't come out of the woods. Worst case, you see the bear and he scares the shit out of you and then he really smells you." Wes laughed at his own joke in a way that made it seem funny. "As far as the cabin in the woods goes, probably the nastiest thing would be if the place is totally heated by wood, and you'll have to learn the ins and outs of a wood burner or freeze to death. It's not rocket science. Don't sweat it. Where does she live?"

"A place called Porter Creek. Is that far from Whitehorse?"

"Technically it's part of the city but it's pretty spread out. More woods than subdivision, but there are some places in the back that are pretty far from the beaten trail. It's within hiking distance of Whitehorse if you like to walk, but it's all uphill from downtown, though. My aunt and uncle have a beautiful place up that way. I've walked it, but you may want to be nice to Sunny so you don't have to do it in mid-winter." Wes patted the steering wheel.

"Are you staying with them?"

"Ah." Wes swallowed audibly. "My Uncle Jeff died a few years ago. This is a great playlist." Wes cranked up the radio.

Jackson shut up, staring out his window, twisting his fingers. God, he was stupid. "I'm sorry. I didn't mean to make it awkward. I'm not good at being social. I usually don't talk, it's less embarrassing."

Wes glanced at him. "It's not you. I've been on edge since I decided to come back. I'm not ready to think about that."

They sat listening to music. Traffic picked up as they got closer to Whitehorse and they started to see signs of civilization off the Alaska Highway. Wes slowed Sunny and pulled off onto the wide gravel shoulder, stopping about a hundred yards before a lonely traffic light. "How are you doing? You feeling better? Your color looks pretty good."

"Why? Do you want me to take over?" Jackson gripped the car door, ready to jump out.

"Nope, this is my stop and I'm wondering if I need to drag you down the hospital?"

It was impolite, but Jackson couldn't help gawping at him. "I'm fine and I'm not letting you out here. It's the middle of nowhere."

Wes waved a hand at the world outside. "Welcome to the Yukon, it's all the middle of nowhere. This is one of the main roads into town. The next is a couple of miles that way."

"At least let me drop you off at your friend's house."

"Naw. I like to walk, remember. There's lots of local traffic now, and Yukoners usually stop for hitchhikers because it's remote and there's no cell service except in town. I'll get a ride unless you feel the need for a checkup."

"I almost feel like my normal self, I'm good." Jackson climbed out and walked around the car, watching Wes pull Shadow out. "Maybe we'll run into each other?"

Wes smiled. "I'd like that. Keep an eye on that bump."

Jackson rubbed his head. It was tender but no longer frightening. "I'm feeling much better. A good night's sleep is all I need now."

"If you have any dizziness, or anything else that worries you, there's a good emergency room at the Whitehorse hospital. Don't second guess yourself. Just go." He shook Jackson's hand, holding it a beat too long. "Will you be okay with my directions?"

"I think so." Jackson slipped his hand into his pocket to wipe the tingles from his palm. "It's straight down this road, past the next light. My phone's got bars again and so if I can't find it, my GPS will get me there."

"Good luck." Wes heaved Shadow up onto his back with a grunt and then he gave a last wave and headed down the hill. There was a bounce in his step.

Jackson watched him go.

Chapter Two

Jackson's phone claimed he'd arrived. Pulling Sunny up on the shoulder, he peered down the laneway, but huge pine trees hid the house from view. There was no turning back now. His heart was beating fast and he was starting to sweat. What had made this seem like a good idea? Deep breathing in situations like this was almost second nature these days.

"I chose this, I chose this," he chanted softly to himself. It was going to work. Having driven without major incident across the continent, through the Rocky Mountains, and along some of the most remote roads in the world, he was capable of anything. He forced himself to breathe deep, right into his belly. The laneway waited for him and Jackson eased Sunny into it.

Sunny's tires crunched on the gravel drive and a log home set in a clearing came into sight. That must be the place. A huge black dog with white and tan markings sat on the front porch. Standing up, the massive animal shook itself and ambled toward the car. Jackson stayed put because the thing was the size of a bear. The dog pressed a wet nose against the driver's side window. It didn't look aggressive. In fact, it looked like it was smiling at him.

Jackson had often been accused of having an overactive imagination. But dogs couldn't smile, right? He glanced at the front door of the house and found a gray-haired woman standing there.

"He's good," she called.

Well, if she said so. Jackson slowly pushed the car door open and took another deep breath. He stood and dropped his hand on the dog's head. The big guy wiggled around him like a puppy. "Good boy."

The woman walked toward them. "He's a Bernese Mountain Dog, loyal and friendly. His name's Kale. I'm Isabelle Grenfield." She held out her hand.

"Um, hi, I'm Eddie—I mean, Jackson. Here to

house-sit." He tried to smile in lieu of shaking her hand, given that his palms were wet and cold.

Isabelle grabbed his hand and shook it anyway, either not noticing or caring about its clamminess. She peered through the car window at the crammed back seat. "Want some help carrying all of that?"

"It's okay," said Jackson. "I only need my overnight bag. I can get the rest later."

"All right. Follow me and we'll get you settled in."

Jackson must have waited a beat too long because she turned around. "Are you okay?"

"Yes, I mean no, but I will be in a minute."

Isabelle's face creased in concern.

"I need a minute. I get anxious in new situations. Meeting people is hard, talking is hard." Jackson had to stop. He was making it worse. "Can I have a drink and sit down for a minute?"

"That's doable." Isabelle's face relaxed and she led him to the kitchen. "I thought maybe you were having a heart attack."

Settled in a wooden chair, Jackson made his face into something he hoped appeared pleasant. "It feels serious inside of me but it's really not that bad." Kale rested his big head on Jackson's lap, looking for pats.

Isabelle handed him a glass of water. "Don't downplay it. I'm watching you get some color back and thinking it was rough."

"I'm okay. It's been a long drive." Jackson patted Kale, the silky fur and huff of the dog's warm breath settling him. "I'm glad to be here."

She gave him an understanding smile. "Okay, well why don't I show you your room for tonight and I'll get dinner on the table. Let's leave the formal showing you around till later. You can settle in and rest up for an early start tomorrow. I want to show you everything before I leave."

Dinner was a hearty serving of mashed potatoes and homemade meatloaf with a colorful salad. Isabelle gave him space and didn't seem to expect much conversation. The house was cozy and warm with lots of raw wood and handmade quilts. Jackson started to relax, even as his emotions swirled in a combination of elation and trepidation. He had made it. This was about as far away from home as he could be and still be in the same country. Tomorrow, he would learn the ins and outs of the property and then he'll truly be on his own.

When Jackson found himself yawning non-stop, Isabelle pointed out the guest room and he headed to bed. It took him a few minutes and some creative pillow stacking to keep his bruised head off the mattress. The sharp pain had retreated, and he was grateful that Wes had been so reassuring about the bump. It gave him peace of mind. More relaxed than he had been in days, he drifted off and slept the dreamless sleep of the truly exhausted.

****

Despite it being mid-September, the room was still dark when Jackson woke up at eight in the morning. He did a mental inventory. No headache. Yes, he could still feel a bit of a bruise but all in all, he was intact. Stretching under the covers, soft flannel sheets wrapped him and held him. It would be nice to linger and enjoy the sensations a little longer but he was sure Isabelle was waiting for him. Jackson slipped out of bed. The chill of the wood floor was startling, so he dressed fast. When he opened the door, Kale was sitting there, wagging his tail and waiting.

"Hi, buddy. What's up?"

Kale whined and offered a paw. Jackson bent over and took it in his hand. "Morning, sir. Good to see you again."

The dog jumped up and danced around as Jackson stepped into the bathroom across the hall from his bedroom. When he was ready to face the day, the dog stuck close to his heels for the walk around the foot of the stairs into a large open concept living area.

Isabelle was carrying a plate of food to the already laden table. "He likes you."

"Yeah. I think animals understand me better than people."

"Isn't that always the way? It's one of the reasons I

live out here away from town."

It looked like Isabelle had been up for a while. She was dressed in well-worn jeans and a sweater with silver wavy hair pulled carelessly out of the way. Her face was creased in lines that made her look like she laughed often. "We have lots to go through today. Are you up for it?"

Jackson nodded, hoping he wasn't lying. Anticipation of the unknown was raising his shoulders towards his ears.

Isabelle indicated the table, and they pulled out chairs. "This won't be hard. I've written everything down in such detail you won't need a tutorial, but it'll make me feel better. I have to say it is weird to be leaving a stranger in charge of my whole life for so long. I'm happy Kale approves."

"Me too."

"First, let's eat. You'll need a bit of weight on you so you won't freeze this winter." Isabelle followed his gaze to the food. "Maybe a bit over the top for two people, but I didn't know what you liked."

"I've been on the road for eight days. I could eat kale for breakfast."

The dog at his feet whined.

"Sorry," Jackson said to him, "I meant the green stuff."

"Come on, Kale, you've eaten. Why don't you go and check who visited during the night." Isabelle got up and opened the door. Kale walked out with a backward look at Jackson.

Jackson loaded his plate with pancakes, eggs, bacon, fried potatoes, and fruit. "Thanks. There's no way I'll eat like this again till you get back. Food isn't my priority."

"I can tell." She smiled, scooping fruit into her bowl.

They ate in silence and Jackson's shoulders came down with every bite. The quiet was soothing.

Isabelle got up and brought a carafe of steaming coffee back to the table. She offered and he reached his empty cup out of for a refill. She sat back down and poured creamer into hers then stirred it, looking at him.

"You really looked done in by the trip yesterday, so I

gave you some space but I'm really curious about something."

The food dried up in his mouth and he wished that Kale was still leaning against his leg under the table.

"I was expecting a guy called Eddie, actually got to know him pretty well by email and then here you are."

"I am Eddie. Well, Edward Jackson Williams. I promise I wasn't lying!" He had been so caught up in finding himself he didn't even think about how it could be perceived showing up here with a different name.

Isabelle laid a hand on his forearm. "I know it's not my business, but there's got to be a story there if you don't mind sharing." She started clearing the table, giving him space and not making eye contact, as if she knew exactly how to handle socially awkward house guests.

He collected his thoughts. "My father's name is Edward, I'm Edward Jr but my family has always called me Eddie. As I drove across the country, I left Eddie behind somewhere in the foothills of Alberta. You're only the second person who is meeting the new me."

How much was safe to tell her? Then again, she'd be trusting him with her whole life for the next few months. Perhaps Jackson could do the same. "I was an anxious kid and the people who love me are always trying to protect me." He brought his plate to Isabelle in the sink and started wiping the table, the mundane acts making his words come easier. "I'm almost twenty-nine years old and my mother still breaks into my place when I'm not looking to deliver casseroles or do my laundry. Finishing university, moving out, having a career... It doesn't seem to make a difference, she still sees me as needing rescuing. That's why I'm here. I'm done being told how to live my life."

Isabelle was silent for long enough that Jackson worried he had said too much.

"I think I understand," she said eventually. "My trip might be for the same reason." Isabelle dried her hands and gestured for him to follow her to the door. "Come on, we can talk while we work."

The work started with donning a pair of rubber boots, or "gum boots" as Isabelle called them, and a flannel jacket "to keep the stink of chickens off his nice things." She gave him the ten-cent tour, which complemented her detailed written guide, pointing out what was needed to manage the house. The massive property was breathtaking. The immediate area around the log house was neatly landscaped. But the rest was wild, with lots of trees, undergrowth, and a small creek snaking back and forth through the property that Isabelle claimed would eventually reach the Yukon River. Kale helped by running back and forth sniffing things, chasing squirrels, and doing doggy things in a way that showed he was serious about his job. Jackson was almost sure the big dog watched them and the woods, making sure nothing they didn't want to meet would walk out of the wilderness. It sounded almost silly, but he knew he was safer under Kale's watchful eyes.

The grandeur of the location lifted his spirits. What a perfect place to write. But could he really handle it all? He took in a breath of fresh air and watching Isabelle' confident steps. She almost wasn't thinking about the job. This place was an extension of her.

The next stop was a neat lean-to filled with stacked wood, located at the side of the house. "Let's try your hand at chopping," said Isabelle. "You'll need to figure that out to keep the furnace humming through the winter."

Wes had said something about learning to use a wood furnace or freezing to death, so Jackson paid attention as Isabelle showed him the ax and something called a maul, which had to be dangerous. She gave him gloves, and then demonstrated the deft splintering of a log into pieces that would fit into 'Big Bertha,' the furnace.

"Now you try," said Isabelle.

The axe was heavy, and Jackson was nervous, but he tried imitating Isabelle's relaxed swing. It wasn't as easy as it looked. He kept trying, though, and before they left the chopping block, the wheelbarrow was filled with wood perfect for burning. They walked the barrow around the house and to a back basement door, stacking what they had chopped in the wide entryway. Despite stiffening muscles, Jackson was filled with immense pride and massive a sense of accomplishment. This must be how a squirrel felt when building its stash in the fall.

"You'll need lots for the whole winter," said Isabelle. "I usually chop a bit every day or two till I fill that hall. You want some inside for those stormy days when you don't want to go out. But as a general rule, frozen wood is easier to chop so you'll enjoy chopping it on cold days too."

As they finished up, Isabelle sighed, leaned against the wall with a faraway look. "You told me why you came here, so I guess I owe you a bit of my story." She gazed into the forest. "My husband died almost three years ago."

"I'm sorry, I didn't know."

"No need to be sorry. You couldn't have known. It's hard and I'm not over it. I don't think you ever get over something like that but I'm coping. It was a heart attack, that's why I was so worried when I saw you go gray yesterday."

"Oh no, I didn't mean—"

"Of course, you didn't, but people have been babying me too." Isabelle snorted in disgust. "Kids whose diapers I changed now think I can't hack it out here because my husband passed. My niece wants me to go and live with them, leave this place." Her voice got quiet. "I can't picture myself in the life she wants for me." Isabelle visibly straightened and the steel came back to her voice. "Time to show you the rest." She walked him past an insulated doghouse for Kale and a couple storage sheds pointing out the snowshoes and ski gear he could borrow. "And now, let me introduce you to my girls."

Her girls were her chickens. The chicken coop was a small but tight wooden building with a fenced-in, covered yard to keep them safe from any wildlife that might come calling. Inside, the smell made Jackson's eyes water. Isabelle noticed and explained at this time of year, the manure was left to pile up and fresh bedding was simply placed on top. The thick layer on the floor was smelly but it generated heat to keep the girls warm.

"In the spring, we'll clean it all down and put it on the garden. It's a big job but makes the garden really grow. Maybe we can do it before you leave. I could use the help." Isabelle smiled at the face he made. "You get used to the smell and the eggs are wonderful. Speaking of which, you need to collect the eggs."

As with chopping wood, Isabelle made collecting eggs look easy. Jackson tried to follow her lead and reached under the terrifying feathered beasts for the nest's precious contents. They immediately flapped their wings at him and pecked at his hands. Jackson pulled away. "I don't think they like me."

"Don't worry, they're protecting what's theirs from a stranger. They'll learn to love you." Isabelle latched the door behind them and they found their way back to the house. "After you emailed me about house-sitting, I Goo-gled you."

"You did?"

"I love your stuff. You've put out a lot of books for someone so young." She walked up onto the porch and sat in a wooden chair, gesturing to the one beside it.

Jackson's face heated and he sat trying to find his nonexistent, suave author self. "I've been writing since I was a teenager for Hanson's Publishing. I'm always try-ing to keep up with their number one author, Simone DeBravé. She's good and she loves going to conferences and schmoozing with her readers. I don't do that, so I have to write harder and faster."

"I know her work. She turns up everywhere, but I've got you on my porch, not her."

"Invite her." Jackson tried to keep the envy out of his voice. "She'll come, do a podcast and a mass signing."

"And you won't?"

"Not a chance, never, no way. Although the agent says it would help my sales. I've thought about it but the idea gives me hives." Jackson chuckled and shook his head. "Then again, this trip is about change so I shouldn't say never. Maybe I will one day. Just don't quote me on that." Jackson remembered the high he felt when he sent Eddie packing and decided on a new name. Right now, he was sitting comfortably on a stranger's porch, looking out on the possibilities of a new life, one he couldn't have imagined as early last spring. The fluttering of his heart was not anxiety. It was hope.

Isabelle's eyes crinkled and she leaned back into the chair. "My lips are sealed."

The view from the porch was distant snowcapped mountains peeking over the trees surrounding the house. The road sounds were distant, almost drowned out by the birds. "I guess I should tell you," Jackson said, "I'm feeling somewhat less confident in my ability to keep this place functioning than I was this morning."

"That's an honest response. All this talking is over-complicating the process, I think, but—" Isabelle looked him right in the eye. "After meeting you, Jackson Williams, I believe you are one hundred percent capable of doing this. Everything we've discussed today, and more, is meticulously detailed in my notebook. I'm sorry if my nerves are making you doubt yourself, I can't help it. Part of me is scared to go and I'm dragging things out."

He stared at her. "You're scared?"

"Nothing is as easy as it looks. Jeff and I talked about taking this trip forever, but he was so rooted to the land, things kept coming up that made us postpone, right up until I lost him. He was going with me for sure, but he was doing it for me. It was my dream. Then he died. The money is still there. I have a good friend who moved to Paris a few years ago. We have so many things planned, and I can't wait to go, but I'm not ready to leave. Do you know what I mean?"

"I think so. It's kind of like me. It was easier to stay in my condo and go to Sunday dinner every week, letting Mom tell me how I'm not living the life she and her book club would choose for me. If I'd taken time to think about what I was doing when I sent you that email, I wouldn't have come. If I hadn't been scared of letting you down, I probably would have changed my mind."

Isabelle laughed. "Well, aren't we a fine pair." She looked out past the front yard over the trees and to the mountains in the distance. "I'm going to miss this. I love winter here, the quiet. I hope you'll love it too. Don't worry about anything I showed you today. You'll be fine. It's easy and if you have any trouble, I left you the phone number for Abby, my niece. She lives about twenty minutes away in the Riverdale subdivision in Whitehorse. She'll help. Or Mrs. Skinner down the road, she's the one who will take the eggs from you so you don't need to bother trying to sell them or eating them all. She can be here in five minutes if you've got problems. Out here you don't see your neighbors much because we all like our space, but we pitch in if anyone needs anything." She waved the notebook in front of him. "It's all here and it's not rocket science. You'll get it. Come on, I'll get dinner started."

Isabelle's faith in Jackson was a balm. Having just met him, she trusted him with everything, her chickens even. He would make sure she did not regret her decision. Now moving around the kitchen and humming, Isabelle seemed pretty calm for someone leaving in a few hours for the trip of a lifetime. But she was pretending. That gave Jackson something to think about. "What can I do?"

"You feed Kale. One cup of kibble. Use the plastic cup that's in the bag. I'll get the soup on."

Kale watched his dish watching, tail swishing.

Jackson carefully measured out the kibble and placed it on the floor. Kale stared at the bowl and back to his server. He cocked his head then sat down glancing between the full dish and Jackson.

"What?"

Kale barked once.

"I don't know what you want."

Two sharp barks.

"What's up?" Isabelle asked, drying her hands on a towel.

"I put his dish down and he won't eat."

"What did you put in the bowl?"

"A cup of kibble, like you said."

"There's the problem. I usually give him a bit of a treat on it, which is a little of what I'm eating. Tonight I've made soup, so that's what he'll get. Don't worry, it's in the notes." Isabelle took the dish to the stove where she splashed a little out of the pot. When she put it back down in front of Kale, with perhaps more of a flourish than necessary. Kale put his head down to eat, first turning, looking long and hard at Jackson as if to say, "pay attention, that's how it's done." Then he dug in.

Isabelle laughed. "You've been told."

He shook his head. "I'll never get it."

"Sure you will. By the time I get home, you'll be doing it with one hand tied behind your back. Besides, I'm leaving in the morning, so ready or not, you'll be taking care of the place on your own. Get used to it." She flashed a dimpled smile and turned back to the stove.

Jackson was setting the table when Kale rushed to the front door. He stared at it for a moment then barked deep and loud, turning to Isabelle and wagging his tail.

"Who could that be? I said my goodbyes yesterday." Isabelle began washing her hands. "Could you get the door, please?"

Jackson glared at the entrance. The last thing he wanted was a meet and great with some random friend of Isabelle's. But he took a deep breath and pasted on what felt like it could be a cheerful smile, and he reached for the knob.

Chapter Three

Wes watched Jackson pull back onto the highway then turn toward town. The way the day started out, he had been pretty sure he'd be sleeping on the road tonight. Finding Sunny stalled on the roadside had been a gift and being able to start her was even better. Things were definitely going his way.

Storming out of town all those years ago, Wes had sworn nothing would bring him back. Yet, lately, there was a dark hole in his center. Maybe coming home and getting some resolution would help. He was also getting to an age where drifting and sleeping on roadsides didn't have the same appeal it once had. To top it all off, just yesterday he got an email from Nick, his best friend in the world, telling him to find a phone and call for good news. It was a sign, getting the message right when he was mere hours from being able to hear the words from Nick in person. Nick would be surprised to find him on the doorstep when he thought Wes was currently in Peru. Now that would have been a long walk.

Speaking of surprises, Jackson had been a nice one, with his beautiful narrow face, huge brown eyes, and cute blushes. His buttoned up shirt and pressed slacks spoke of someone trying to look older, although Wes guessed Jackson was near his own twenty-six years, in spite of the air of innocence surrounding him. After the initial punch of attraction, it was the blushes that had Wes's fingers itching to touch him. But the guy had an air of serious-relationship-or-nothing attached to him. That was fine for some people but Wes was not looking for that kind of complication, especially not on this trip. It would be all business. Repair the relationships he could, dump those he couldn't, and get a job to make enough cash to get outta town.

Speaking of the town, there was the old sternwheeler he'd visited as a kid. The SS Klondike in dry dock at the park was a point of pride for the Yukon's capital city.

Whitehorse loved its gold rush history and there were plaques and relics all over town. Wes's heart leapt at the sight of the boat. It grounded him. He was really here.

Wes crossed the bridge over the Yukon River and stopped in the middle to lean out over the railing. Cold air rose off the glacier-fed water as it raced past. He shivered and kept walking. Although it was still light out, the sun was heading towards the shortest day of the year. Yukoners, very aware of the approaching long dark, would be enjoying every second of the light until it was gone. There was a good chance Nick and Sophie, his wife, wouldn't be home.

Wes got lucky because not only did he make it as the sun was dipping below the horizon, but the lights were on. Number fifteen Green Crescent was a cozy looking duplex with a big pine tree in the front yard and a balcony on the second floor. Warm, yellow light shone from behind a curtain of what he assumed was the living room. They were home.

Wes rang the bell and waited, his fingers tapping against his leg.

Heavy footsteps came from inside and the door opened. There stood Nick, his mouth open and eyes wide. "Wes?"

Wes stood back, drinking in the look of shock on Nick's face. He absorbed his friend's familiar shaved head ("Shut up I like it like this, I'm not going bald") and the unfamiliar trimmed beard that was probably him trying to fit in to the manly beard culture of the Yukon but looked more hipster than local.

Nick snapped his mouth shut before pulling Wes into a bone-crushing hug. "You're here!" He took a step back and turned his head to yell, "Sophie!" before returning his attention to Wes. "That email worked fast I just sent it." Nick pulled him through the door and up a short flight of steps.

The cooking smells from the kitchen made Wes's stomach growl and he dropped Shadow on a low bench at the top of the steps.

"Sophie!" Nick called out again, "Look what the fox dragged in!"

Sophie emerged from the kitchen, drying her hands on a cloth. "Wesley!" she squealed and threw herself at him.

Wes grabbed her and lifted her five-foot frame right off the floor in a hug. He hadn't loved another woman this much since his sister—no, he wouldn't think of her right now. Tonight was for Nick and Sophie. Setting her back on the floor, his smile felt like it covered his face. Their wedding had been four years ago, way too long to go without seeing his two favorite people.

Dinner had been almost ready when he arrived, so they sat down to eat together. Time flew as they chatted and caught up.

"I thought you were in Peru," Nick said. "How'd you get back so quickly?"

"I was already back," Wes said. "I got your email when I was I setting up camp at Watson Lake."

"You're still using that beat-up tablet?" Nick chuckled. "You'll never get a cell phone, huh?"

"My tablet works fine," said Wes. "You know me, I'm not a sheep to be manipulated by corporations or be tied to social media. Besides, it's hard to pay the bills when I don't have an address. But anyway, what's your news?"

The two of them talked over each other in their excitement, but finally Nick paused long enough to allowed Sophie to say, "I'm pregnant!"

Wes would deny his eyes got a little misty when they shared their news of their growing family. It seemed like only yesterday that he and Nick had been kids themselves, bumming around the world. Now they were adults. It was a scary thought.

They lingered around the table, enjoying each other's company for hours. When Nick stood to collect the dishes, Wes took his cue. He got up, headed for the sink and rolled up his sleeves. The small kitchen had no dishwasher and Wes remembered the many times he and Nick stood side by side, doing camp dishes or working in kitchens to pay for meals along the road. Working with him was second nature.

Sophie got up too. "Wesley, you turning up has been

the best surprise. I am sorry but I must go to bed now." Her liquid French accent rolled the consonants. Standing on her tiptoes she reached to give him a kiss on the cheek.

"I still can't believe you're growing a tiny human in there." Wes settled a clean plate into the dish rack for Nick to dry. "You must be exhausted, even thinking about it is making me tired."

Sophie rolled her eyes, lifting her wavy dark hair from her neck. "You have no idea. At first, I thought I had the flu but it turned out to be more." Her smile was mischievous. "Now, I believe Nicholas has an evening project he needs you for, since I can no longer help. Enjoy yourselves. I expect him to call in sick tomorrow."

Nick opened his mouth to protest but she silenced him by grasping his shaved head and pulling him down for a sweet kiss. His lanky six-foot-three frame dwarfed her.

Wes averted his eyes. Like the sun, that kind of love hurt your eyes. Although he'd first met Sophie when Nick invited him to be the best man at their wedding and paid to fly him to Quebec City, they had exchanged enough emails and confidences that they were old friends. Being able to hear about the baby in person was a gift.

"Wesley, you should still be sleeping when I get up for work," said Sophie, "but I expect to see you many times before you leave town. Good night."

"'Night."

Wes passed another dish to Nick. "I believe she gave us permission to get sloppy tonight." Wes didn't know the last time he'd had alcohol, but it would be nice to share a few glasses with his old friend. "Your bride is a true Yukon treasure."

"I don't think the Yukon had anything to do with it. They raise their women right in the backwoods of Quebec—to respect their husbands."

Wes snorted. "Ha, I know respect when I see it. She has you wrapped up and tied down."

"Maybe, but the benefits are delicious. I thank you for driving me into her arms."

Wes shoved the last glass under the water and swirled the cloth past it. "How do you figure? When you two met, I was still in Peru."

"Yes, but when we were tree planting you were so homesick. All those late night talks filled my head with the call of the north. Anyway, don't get sloppy on Sophie's say-so. She always has ulterior motives."

"What? Not our sweet little Soph?"

"Don't let her fool you." Nick got a familiar sly look in his eye and Wes jumped out of the way just in time as Nick snapped at him with the damp tea towel.

Wes laughed. "Seriously. What does she want?"

"It's a two-pronged approach. First." Nick paused, glancing sideways at Wes. "We want you to stay."

"You of all people know why I can't." Wes rinsed the suds from the sink and tugged the cloth from Nick to dry off his hands without making eye contact.

"I know, don't worry about it for now." Nick gestured to the cupboard. "Grab us a couple of glasses?" He stopped and squinted at Wes. "Are you still okay with soft liquor?"

It had been a few years but Wes still remembered their code for beer and wine. "Of course. I'd let you know if anything changed."

Nick nodded, leaning into the pantry.

Wes loved that Nick knew his past and still trusted him to know his limits. He opened the cupboard. "I've been looking forward to trying Yukon beer now that I'm of legal age. All those underage beers didn't count."

Nick laughed, "You're gonna have to wait a little longer for that."

Wes turned to see Nick withdrawing a dark bottle from a full rack. "You've only got wine?"

Nick grimaced. "So that's the second part of those ulterior motives. We made our own wine and got in over our heads."

"Define over your heads?"

"They suggest you go in with friends the first time, but we figured we'd be fine. Then, surprise! Sophie's knocked up. Anyway, that's the project I need help with. It will be a while before she's drinking again and there's way too much for me. It's decent stuff but there's lots more in the basement."

No one could say Wes didn't have his friend's back. "Sure, anything you need. You don't even have to ask." He grabbed a couple of oversized wine glasses.

"I'm going to tuck Sophie in. Be right back, pour some wine and make yourself at home."

Wes made sure the kitchen was tidy then poured from the bottle of red wine on the counter. Heading into to the living room, he met Nick coming down the hall. His shirt was mussed.

"Well, it's good to know the passion is alive and well in your marriage." Wes raised his glass to Nick's red-faced grin.

They moved into the living room. Mixed in with the stylish white furniture were touches of home. Wes touched the ironbound oak trunk they were using as a coffee table. He remembered seeing it at the wedding. Years ago, when Sophie's grandparents were courting, Sophie's grandfather had built to give to his bride. When Sophie was getting married, her family wanted her to have it and Nick had paid the outrageous shipping costs to move it from Quebec to Whitehorse as a token of his love and wedding gift. Wes had helped wrap and drag it to the airport the day before the festivities. "It got here in one piece," he murmured.

"Yeah." Nick watched him as he ran his fingers over it. "It reminds her of home and was worth every penny to get it here."

Wes moved to a wooden mask displayed on the sideboard. It was one he had carved while he was facing his demons in rehab. "I can't believe you still have this or these." There were a surprising number of photographs on the wall. Many were of the wedding festivities, where Wes mostly stood awkwardly beside Nick in a rented tux. There were also quite a few of him and Nick looking tanned and healthy on the sweeping slopes of Whistler Mountain, wearing their ski patrol jackets and big smiles.

Wes turned to look at Nick. "I haven't seen these in years. Sophie has a knack for displaying the past without making it weird. It feels like home."

"It is your home, anytime. You know that."

"Thanks." Wes sat on the couch beside Nick. "It's nice."

"Yeah. I never thought I'd want this, or need it, but Sophie made it real."

"I can see that. You look happy."

"I am. You should try it."

"Not for a million dollars and a male version of Sophie!" Wes took a sip of the robust red wine.

"I knew it! You've always loved her more than me."

"Of course, I do. She smells better, is better dressed, and never tries to tell me what to do."

"Are you sure? That woman is dying for a chance to mother you!"

"Should I be worried?"

"Definitely! She wants to get to know you better, and probably set you up with a local so you'll stick around."

The smile froze on Wes's face. "Nick, I—"

"Hey," Nick soothed. "Don't worry. We're so glad you're here." He grabbed Wes's knee. "We both knew you were never coming back and yet here you are. We'll do anything we can to make this visit easier on you."

"It's fine, there's nothing to help. I'm here to see my friends and maybe reconnect with some family, no big deal. I'll move on when it's time. Now pass the bottle." Wes topped them up and noticed Nick's face. "What?"

"I sent my email yesterday, hoping you would call me and yet here you are, so you were already on your way. What's up?"

Wes let the breath he was holding whoosh out. "You remember when I told you about Miguel, the Andean elder who took me on as a student in Peru? He said I couldn't move forward with my training as long as I was carrying my burdens."

Nick nodded, his face filled with understanding. "Very true."

It was no surprise that Nick agreed. His training as a psychotherapist had taught him that in order to heal those in pain, or the Earth, you needed to work on yourself first. Something he'd told Wes many times before, but it had never stuck until recently.

"You know things weren't great when I ran outta here," said Wes. "I really hurt Abby and Auntie Izzy. I've been a coward. I'm already too late to apologize to Uncle Jeff. I don't want anyone else to die before I make amends. And what about you?" Wes's gaze slid towards Nick. "Maybe I need to make amends with you too?"

"What?" Nick put his glass on the weathered wooden trunk. "No, you and me Wes, we're good. We were together at the bottom and it's worth it to be able to see each other at the top."

After taking off from Whitehorse over ten years ago, Wes had landed rudderless on the lower east side of Vancouver, eager to drown his pain in whatever was cheap and available. Nick had found him and helped get him off the street, reminding him that life was worth living, dragging him through a season of tree planting and several seasons on the slopes at the Whistler Resort. For four years, they'd been inseparable. The fun came to an end when Nick fulfilled his promise to his parents and returned to university. That had been Wes's cue to find his own path. For the next six years, they never lost touch. When he was in remote Peru, Wes's beat-up tablet was a lifeline. Sometimes, the simple act of writing to Nick to tell him what was going on helped Wes know what he was feeling and what he needed. But maybe Wes had done too much taking and not enough giving.

"Come on, you know that's not how this works." Wes nudged Nick with his toe and smiled trying to lighten the mood. "You wouldn't deny me one of my twelve steps, would you?"

"Fine." Nick gave in. "But not tonight, tonight we're celebrating." He held his glass high. "To family, both old—" he gestured to Wes "—and new." He glanced at the stack of parenting books on the coffee table. "God help me. I'm not ready for this." He clinked his glass to Wes's and downed it in one gulp.

Wes laughed and drank a bit slower. "You'll be a great father."

Bedtime snuck up on them. Sitting together, leaning shoulder to shoulder, Nick drifted off first, leaning back and snoring gently. Wes placed his empty glass on the coffee table and carefully extracted Nick's from his limp hand. Then he slumped, exhausted, back into the soft cushions. He would sit a minute longer. He rested his head on his best friend's shoulder and let his eyes drift shut.

****

The morning came early. After a slow wake-up and hitting the shops, Nick insisted on driving him up the hill to his aunt's place. Wes was stretched tight. "God I'm nervous. All those years I've imagined this moment and, here it is."

They sat in the car, parked at the end of the lane. "You've got this, "Nick reminded him. "You've got enough food to soothe a troop of angry bears. And your aunt loves you, remember."

"She used to, but I really hurt her and Uncle Jeff, and now he's gone so I can't even—"

Nick turned off the motor. "Do you want me to come in with you?"

"No, if there's trouble, I don't want you there. It could make things more awkward. I'll walk up. It'll be fine."

"You're right, but don't forget, you've got the keys to the house. It's your place too and you're welcome anytime for any reason."

They got out and walked around the car. "I didn't know the nightmares were still so bad," said Nick. "You woke me up last night. Please promise you'll call if things get too hard."

"That one was bad. I think being here stirred things up. It's good to know you're so close."

"You know it. Any time. Good luck." Nick hugged him. "Should I wait?"

"Naw, if this goes tits up, I'll hitch back to town, or heck, maybe even take the bus. I'll leave the wine with her. It'll be a fitting punishment if she kicks me out."

Nick whacked his shoulder. "Keep in touch. In case I didn't mention it last night I really need you to talk me down when I'm freaking out about this baby thing!"

Wes looked at him. "Good freaking out?"

Nicholas sighed happily. "Yeah, good freaking out." He passed Wes three cloth bags of groceries and two bottles of wine from the back seat, got back in the car, waving as he backed out.

Wes hefted his load and started walking the length of the long drive. He rounded the bend, taking his time. The place hadn't changed. The pines were maybe taller but seeing the log house standing in the grove made him want to shout, "Uncle Jeff, Auntie Izzy, I'm back!" A wave of unexpected grief stopped Wes in his tracks. The man who'd helped him through his childhood was gone. It would be hard to be here without him. How could he now say the things he needed to say?

Wes's legs didn't want to move forward but they did anyway. He reached the steps of the wide veranda and put the bags down. A deep woof sounded from inside and Wes raised his hand to knock. His respite was officially over, it was time for the hard stuff.

The door swung open and there stood— "Jackson? What are you doing here?"

Chapter Four

Kale tangled under Jackson's feet as he reached for the door and pulled it open. He stood stunned for a moment gapping at the tall, slim man with unruly blond curls standing there.

Wes stepped back. "Jackson? Where's my Aunt Izzy?"

Jackson opened the door wide allowing Wes to step into the entrance way. In the commotion of the door opening, Kale's happy door dance, and the flash of recognition, it took Jackson a moment to become aware of Isabelle standing in the living room, still holding a towel, staring at the visitor. Her face was white.

"Wes? Wesley Palmer, is that you?"

And suddenly, they were in each other's arms, in tears.

"Wes, it's really you. Ten years." Isabelle sobbed. "Oh my gosh, I can't believe it."

"Aunt Izzy, don't cry." Wes stroked her hair, his own voice choked with tears. "I'm sorry. I was gone too long."

Jackson didn't need to be here for this. He went to his room and quietly shut the door, allowing the family reunion to happen in private. He flopped onto the bed, trying to lose himself in the erratic patterns of the plaster ceiling. In just a few minutes, he'd returned to feeling completely awkward and unsure of his place here. Isabelle was the long-lost aunt Wes had talked about, the one he was planning on staying with. Damn, after such an intense reunion, Jackson wouldn't be surprised if she canceled her trip.

The house was quiet. When Isabelle and Wes started talking, Jackson tried to muffle the sound by burying his head under a pillow. The cadence of their voices rose, but he couldn't make out what they were saying. One thing Jackson did know was Isabelle didn't need him now. Wes was family and he needed a place to stay. Jackson was some guy, a stranger who was obviously incapable of doing something as simple as feeding the dog. Isabelle hadn't known Wes would be here when she asked for a house sitter. How was he going to deal with this new disaster? Where would he finish his book? Going home, with his tail between his legs was not an option.

Jackson sat up and pulled out his phone. Whitehorse was not a big city. He should be able to find a place to rent at least long enough to finish this book and then who knows what, but he could manage. Jackson grimaced as he scrolled through the listings. Last week he had been so close to conquering the fear his mother was right, that he couldn't survive without her constant nagging and reminders. He had driven across the country, past bears and bison, bighorn sheep, and caribou. He'd navigated through Winnipeg without getting lost. He'd done all that on his own. He was capable and he could live the life he wanted to live without her interference. He was not giving up now.

"Jackson?" Isabelle knocked on his door. "Dinner's ready. Come meet my nephew." She gave him a mischievous smile. "Again."

Jackson gave her a weak smile in return. At least he'd been spared having to explain his chance encounter with her nephew? A glance in the small mirror over the dresser convinced Jackson he didn't look like he was having a meltdown. He followed her to the dining room.

Wes walked in, carrying a stack of dishes to the table. He grinned at Jackson and began setting the table. "Isn't this crazy? Who'd have thought this was the place we were both heading to."

"Yah, crazy." Jackson sat in a chair, avoiding eye contact with anyone.

"Well, I'm not surprised." Isabelle set down a bowl of salad. "The city only has a population of about thirty-three thousand. You could fit everyone here into one of those southern football stadiums."

Wes put a hand on his aunt's shoulder. "You take a seat, I'll serve the soup."

"Thank you." Isabelle sat down.

"When you show up at dinner time, the least you can

do is serve the table." Wes brought bowls of steaming soup, golden tea biscuits and a tossed salad. Isabelle had outdone herself preparing her last meal in the house.

"Sure," said Jackson." What else could he say? It was probably best to keep quiet and eat. After the grueling day, Jackson was starving. He buttered a tea biscuit and bit off a piece. It smelled good and tasted better. Yet it wouldn't go down. He realized Wes was looking at him expectantly and swallowed hastily, almost choking. "What?"

"I said, has she been driving you nuts with the details of working the place?" Wes asked.

"Nuts," Jackson echoed. "Yeah. It's a lot to remember."

"Yah, well, you should have been here when they had the horses, and every other animal Uncle Jeff took a fancy to."

Isabelle laughed and the two started to talk about old times.

The rental prices Jackson had pulled up before dinner were staggering. This wasn't in the budget, but maybe he could find a room for a month or so. There is no way he would show up back home next week. He needed to finish this book before making any decisions. Maybe he could drive farther north to Dawson City—and then it was silent again. He'd been asked another question. "Pardon me?"

"I was wondering if you wanted more." Isabelle gestured to the pot still simmering on the stove.

"No, thanks," said Jackson.

"You were right, this would be a great place to write." Wes balanced a pat of butter on a steaming biscuit. "I haven't been here in years and yet it hasn't changed. It's so peaceful." He shoved the biscuit towards his mouth.

"Yeah, it seems to be." Jackson trailed off. The thoughts swirling around him were overwhelming. It was time to leave the table and start packing. If he ate more, the food was going to start coming back up and that would be past embarrassing. Worse still was sitting here, knowing disappointment was written all over his body.

Glancing at Wes, their eyes met. He was probably trying to figure out a nice way to tell Jackson to shove off.

Isabelle turned to Wes. "What are your plans?"

"I'm planning on getting a job, rediscovering my roots." Wes's tone was hesitant but there was a defiant tilt to his chin.

"Where are you staying?" Isabelle asked. "You should call your sister. I'm sure if you work at it, she'll forgive you and let you stay there."

"I was hoping I could stay here?" Wes's response was both a statement and a hopeful question.

Jackson was rooted to his chair, his breath tangled around his lungs.

"Well, hon, it's like this." Her tone was apologetic as she leaned toward him. "I wasn't expecting you when I planned this trip. I have thirty thousand dollars sunk into it and as much as I'd like to spend time with you, if I don't go now, I never will." Isabelle turned her attention to Jackson. "And I have a house sitter who I'm not turning out in the cold."

Jackson could breathe again. Thank goodness he didn't have to leave. But now he felt guilty. Because of him, Wes had nowhere to go. The table was quiet. Jackson should say something, but what would make it better? Especially since this was all his fault.

Wes pushed his bowl away, face unreadable.

"But I really want you here when I get back," said Isabelle. "I want to hear all your adventures and shake you till your teeth rattle for not calling me in all this time." She took a breath. "I would say you could stay in the spare room, but Jackson needs quiet to do his work, so I really don't have space for you—unless you don't mind moving into the Castle?"

"That's perfect." Wes's body relaxed. "It suits me better anyway. I want to get out on the land. The Castle won't tie me up too bad. Thanks, Aunt Izzy." Wes's smile lit up the room.

Isabelle patted Jackson's hand. "I think I overwhelmed you today, didn't I? This might help you relax about getting through the first few days." She turned to Wes. "I'm hoping you can stay around to help if Jackson has any trouble, especially when it gets cold, and he needs to fire up Big Bertha."

"I can do that." Wes spooned up the last of his soup.

Jackson was trying to keep up. "There's a castle?"

They laughed. "My husband was a good man but not long on patience," said Isabelle. "We didn't have kids of our own but between my brothers and cousins, there was always a pack of 'em roaming around. He couldn't stand the noise, so he built a playhouse. A cabin really, you probably glimpsed it through the trees today when we were out near the pump house. We have two hundred acres of bush and creek land, and in those days, we let them run wild. It's waiting for Abby's kids to take over the tradition, but they're a bit young for it now."

"When we were little," Wes said, "Abby and I thought staying the night out there was the biggest adventure. I wanted to be the knight and she was my princess and I always wanted to rescue her. She hated that." Wes grinned. "I took to calling it the Castle and it stuck."

Jackson processed what he'd learned. This was in theory Wes's place to stay and yet Isabelle had chosen Jackson, and Wes appeared to be happy about it, thrilled even. Maybe it could work. "It sounds like a great place, and I'll be glad to have someone I can get help from if I need it."

"Well, that's settled then," said Isabelle. "You'll stay there, help when needed, and you'll be here when I get back for a real visit. When will you move in?" She began clearing the table.

Jackson jumped up to help, collecting everyone's plates. It was so much easier to concentrate on a job than try to interact.

"I haven't got much stuff," said Wes. "I hitched a ride in. My pack's on the porch."

Once Jackson had collected all the empty dishes, he started washing up, staring hard into the sink. Wes hovered awkwardly by the table.

"Well, I have to finish packing and get to bed," said Isabelle. "It's an early start tomorrow. Do you need a walk to the cabin?"

"Naw," said Wes, "even after all of these years I

think my feet can find the path."

Isabelle gave Wes a long, detailed rundown of the changes in the cabin. Wes patiently listened to her long explanations and eagerly he gave her his email address so they could keep in touch. Even after all these years, the love between them shone and it warmed Jackson from the inside out. This was his kind of happy ending.

Wes turned to look at him but spoke to Isabelle. "Don't worry about a thing. I'll keep this guy out of trouble."

"Wesley Palmer, you will do no such thing," said Isabelle sternly. "Jackson will ask for your help if he needs it. Otherwise, no bullying or pulling rank. This is his place while I'm gone."

"You got it, Auntie." He saluted her then turned to leave.

"Wait." Jackson couldn't leave things like this. Even though he was glad he wasn't looking for a place to stay, by rights this should be Wes's place. Maybe he could do something to make it right. "What about the key. Wes should have a key in case he has to get in when I'm not here or busy?"

His words seemed to hang in the air and then both of them started to laugh. Not the reaction he expected. "There is no key." Was Isabelle speaking slowly, like you might to someone who just didn't understand? "The door is always unlocked."

"Unlocked?" Jackson blinked in confusion. Was he missing something? "What if someone wants to break in.?

"What if someone needed to get in?" countered Wes. "What if a neighbor's car broke down and they were freezing? What if they needed to use the phone, or the bathroom?"

They were still both looking at Jackson as if he'd dropped from the sky. "What if someone wants to hurt you or take your stuff?"

"Then we have Kale," Isabelle told him. "He takes care of intruders, of all kinds."

Jackson had to admit, it was a different world, although a quick glance at the stalwart guard dog everyone was singing the praises of did nothing to instill confidence. Kale was lying on his back by the door, sound asleep with his feet up in the air and his head to one side with his tongue lolling toward the floor.

"That's right, isn't it, big boy?" Wes called out and Kale leapt to his feet with a woof, looking around frantically for the action.

"So, no key then," said Jackson.

"You've got it." Wes grinned. "But I'll bet there's still one by the wood pile, isn't there? Just in case you lock yourself out."

Isabelle nodded. "It has happened but not in a few years. Its hiding place is in the book, but I'll try to remember to show you before I leave. You remember where it is, don't you, Wes dear?"

"I sure do." Wes reached forward and gathered his aunt in his arms. She held him tight. Then he breezed out the door and was gone.

Isabelle walked slowly back to the sink, reached for a towel then stopped. Almost to herself, she said, "I thought I would never see that boy again. Ran out when he was sixteen. Hope he's back for good but I don't know him anymore." She picked up a plate and started drying.

"I figured I would be looking for a new place to stay."

"Nope, you still haven't signed my copies yet, so I need to keep you in my good books." Isabelle laughed. "Good books, get it?"

A weight lifted from his chest, and Jackson groaned at the bad pun.

"It has been ten years since I've him," said Isabelle, "so I don't put any stock in him being here tomorrow or the next day, but I'm hopeful. It would be nice to complete the family again."

Jackson thought about the ease with which Wes had shifted gears, going with the new plan. He wished he could let go of an idea that easily. "He seemed pretty flexible and open to whatever happens."

"Yeah, that about covers it. Whatever." Isabelle shook her head. "I hope I get to know him better. But that's family business. You need to know about here and now. Kale usually spends most of the evening outside unless it's really cold and even then, he has a doghouse and likes to be on guard. You can leave him out, but I always let him in when I go to bed or if I want company. I'm going up to get the last few things ready now. I need to be at the airport at six-thirty. You can drive me over in the Jeep at six."

"What about Wes?

"I'm sure he's exhausted after all his travels." Isabelle spoke casually as she turned and went up the stairs.

Jackson wanted to point out that she hadn't told Wes what time she'd be leaving, but it wasn't his business. "Okay. Good night."

It was still early. Jackson could go to his room and stream a movie or something, but he needed to call his mom to let her know he did indeed arrive alive. He had so much to tell her.

It took three rings before her panicked voice was in his ear. "Eddie? What's wrong?"

Jackson winced. He still needed to tell them he was changing his name. "I'm calling to say I made it."

"Why are you waking us up in the middle of the night?"

What? Was she worried or mad? "It's eight-thirty..." Jackson trailed off, stomach sinking as he remembered the time difference.

"It's eleven-thirty here. We were sound asleep. When the phone rang, I almost went through the ceiling. I thought the police were calling me with bad news."

"Mom, I made it across the country safe. I'm calling to check in. I'm sorry. I forgot about the time change."

"Eddie, I keep telling you to focus. I don't know how you manage anything with that attitude."

"Sorry for waking you. I'll call you later. Bye." Hands shaking, Jackson disconnected before she could say anything else. When would he ever finish a conversation with his mother without feeling like shit? With lightning speed, he turned the ringer off on his phone. She'd call back any moment now, but Jackson could only talk to her again when he felt stronger.

Three hours didn't seem like much when you thought

about it, the sun hadn't gone down here and it was almost midnight there. He should have known that. Instead, he'd hung up on his mother without thanking her for the brownies, never mind telling her about the bears and that he'd changed his name. He knew she loved him but what did he have to do to make her proud of him?

****

Wes slung Shadow onto his back and grabbed the groceries. It was almost dark on the path under the trees, but it didn't matter. His feet remembered. Three steps off the porch and onto the driveway, then over the crunch of the gravel to the packed dirt and finally onto the soft bed of fallen needles. He inhaled the spicy breath of the forest and opened his eyes with a sigh. Wes had spent more time here growing up than at home.

The meeting with Auntie Izzy had gone well. She hadn't kicked him out. How weird was it that Jackson was her house sitter? It had been good to have him there, mostly because it meant Aunt Izzy couldn't roast Wes the way she wanted to with a stranger at the table. Wes was happy not to have to talk about leaving or even coming back because, as ready as he was, he wasn't ready at all. Would he be able to talk to her in April? He moved through the trees, drinking in the scents around him. The rising full moon was bracketed by pines jutting into the darkening sky. He couldn't get enough.

The walk to the Castle was short, a couple of minutes. The trees were taller and the simple lines of the Castle were smaller than in his memory. The red tin roof was faded but sturdy. The logs to build the place came from trees Uncle Jeff felled to make the clearing in which it was now nestled. A small window on either side of the door made the place look like it was smiling at him, welcoming him cheerfully. It felt good.

The door swung open easily. Wes fumbled for the light switch and flipped it on. The room was illuminated by a single bare bulb hanging from the ceiling. Not much had changed. The Castle was a twelve by fifteen-foot cabin with a small loft, accessible by a ladder, and a wood stove. The scarred wooden table with four chairs was the same one they had played checkers and cards on. His younger self had always been convinced that Abby cheated, but the memories of those games made adult Wes smile. The gnarly old pullout couch had been replaced with a flowered monstrosity. The cupboards over the sink were new. Opening them, he was happy to see a pot, a frying pan, and some mismatched dishes. The place was clean with no sign of mice. Aunt Izzy had cleaned here recently. He mentally thanked her for caring so much about this place.

Wes had planned tonight's elaborate meal to both show off his culinary talents and thank her for letting him stay. Since dinner had already on the table, he hadn't been about to cook so he was still left with everything he'd picked up at the store. With a little creativity, he should be able to make the groceries last a few days. He emptied the dry goods into the cupboard and took the fridge stuff outside. On the porch, under a sturdy wooden door, was an old metal cooler buried up to its lid. Food placed in there stayed cool in the summer and froze solid in the winter. Mainly it kept the wildlife out.

There was a double bed in the loft, but Wes knew from experience it would be like an oven up there when the old wood stove got going. Dragging the mattress down to the first floor corner should've been a two-person job, but he managed to dump it over the edge without breaking anything. There was bedding in an old Rubbermaid bin. It would be nice not to rely on his sleeping bag, especially when it got cold enough for the fire. Heating a place like this in the winter with a wood stove was often an exercise in too hot or too cold. It didn't take him long to unpack and arrange his things. He had forgotten to ask Auntie Izzy what time her flight left, so he sat down at the table, pulled out his tablet. A quick google search showed there was only one flight departing Whitehorse the next morning at eight. He groaned. He'd need to get up early. Setting the alarm for six should be good enough. Now that he was here, his longing for family was palpable and he would miss having her around while he said his goodbyes to Uncle Jeff.

The wall lamp and the one on the table had oil in them. He lit them and turned off the lightbulb. The shadows softened. Wes sighed in relief, feeling more at home now than at any point in the last ten years.

Pulling a suede-wrapped bundle from the bottom of his pack he settled on the couch for a bit of carving. He opened the soft leather package on his lap, picking up his chipping knife and the loaf-sized piece of red cedar he'd found in a logged patch on his way here. The shape was already showing itself to be a wind spirit with puffed cheeks and bugged eyes. It had been heavy in his pack but would make a fine gift for Sophie and Nick. Carving had been an escape for him since Uncle Jeff taught him to use a knife. Recently, Wes found he achieved a type of meditation with this work.

Closing his eyes and using his fingertips to feel the rough wood. It almost spoke to him, showing the best places to cut, releasing the figure inside. Then he picked up his knife and allowed the ritual to soothe his battered heart and chase the fear and doubt from his mind.

The wood chips fell rhythmically onto the leather and Wes idly wondered how Jackson was managing in his new environment.

Chapter Five

The following morning was dark and chilly. Jackson shut the front door of the house, still unable to believe there was no need to lock it. "Here, let me take your backpack," he said to Isabelle.

"I've got it." Maybe it was because it was so early in the morning, but Isabelle sounded terse.

Jackson backed off and they walked to the Jeep in silence.

Kale followed them. Isabelle waved him away, telling him to guard the house. Kale walked back to the porch, his head low, turning to look at her as he walked. Did he know she was leaving for a long time?

Jackson slid into the driver's seat and placed the key in the ignition. Isabelle stood by the passenger side, looking over the roof of the Jeep at the property and into the woods. After a few seconds, she gave a quick shake of her head and opened the car door.

The sound of running footsteps echoed in the cold morning and Wes appeared, hurrying down the path. He was out of breath. "I'm sorry." He panted. "I wasn't sure what time you were leaving. Let me drive you."

Isabelle shut the door and moved into Wes's path, opening her arms. He stepped into her embrace. "I wasn't sure you'd come," she said.

"I forgot to ask you when you were leaving." Wes unwrapped her arms and moved out of the hug. "I wouldn't miss this big good bye."

"I'm glad you came but we've got this. Jackson's already got the Jeep started." She reached for him and gave him another hug. They spoke for a moment quietly and hugged tighter. Isabelle broke the embrace and got into the Jeep. "I'm having a hard time leaving now that you're back. I've missed you and I'm so glad you're here. But I really have to go now, or I'll miss my flight." She gestured at Jackson to start driving. "Please be here when I get back," she called through an open window as they pulled out of the lane.

"I'll try." Wes followed the car for a few steps and turned with a wave, heading back in the direction of the Castle.

Jackson wished Wes had come along. He felt out of place taking the beloved auntie to the airport himself.

Isabelle was silent for most of the ride. At the airport, she surprised Jackson with a fierce hug.

Not sure how to respond, he was stiff in her arms.

"You'll do great, don't worry," Isabelle said.

Jackson patted her back. "Thanks. You too. I mean—have a great trip."

Isabelle easily slung the enormous hiker's pack on her back. "See you." She waved and strode into the modern-looking terminal and was gone.

By seven in the morning, Jackson was back at the house. He, Jackson Williams, was responsible for everything here: the house, the dog and chickens, a finicky wood furnace named Bertha, all of Isabelle's worldly possessions, and himself, a half-baked city boy from Ontario. Together, all of them had to move forward successfully. It was daunting but right now, Jackson considered himself almost capable. More importantly, Isabelle had met him and left anyway.

Kale was lying on the porch, head up watching the driveway and Jackson invited him in. The dog appeared to be thinking as he turned and looked back at the drive, then came inside following Jackson to the kitchen.

"Good dog, leaving your post for me. Now I don't have to talk to myself." Jackson ruffled Kale's floppy ears. It would be a good idea to make an appointment for Sunny. He couldn't keep driving Isabelle's Jeep although she told him to. At home, his condo was only a few blocks from the neighborhood where he grew up. He used the same barber, doctor, dentist, and mechanic his parents used. The idea of picking up the phone and making an appointment with a stranger was giving him hives. Well, not actual hives. Absently he scratched his side. Maybe he'd do it later. He could write for a few hours first. It was time for some finishing touches so he could unload this manuscript on his agent, Lorraine, and start thinking about his next book. "Come on, Kale, let's get my stuff from the trunk."

From the car, he grabbed the garment bag and the duffel filled with goodies his mom knew he would need in the wilds of the Yukon. Besides her brownies, which he'd eaten before crossing the border out of Ontario, she'd packed boxes of hot chocolate, a first aid kit with extra Band-Aids, and a ridiculous pile of wool socks. It didn't matter that he told her there were stores in White-horse where he could buy all of this stuff if he needed it, or that the house he would be living in was probably well stocked, she'd fussed and packed it for him. The brown-ies were first rate, though. She really knew how to check his chocolate gene.

Kale followed him out and then in again, taking in the whole process, nails clicking on the plank floor. Jack-son went into the guest room to grab the rest of his stuff. Feeling like a camel loaded to the humps with the pack on his shoulders, suitcase bumping up the stairs, and the garment bag dragging along behind, he laughed at Kale's wide-eyed reaction to the noise and production of the whole thing.

Isabelle's bedroom was in the loft. It was spacious with windows all around, filling it with light. There were heavy black-out curtains for sleeping when they had the midnight sun. That was weird to think about, it being bright all night. Given Jackson would be leaving in April, he probably wouldn't see it.

The trees leaned in, and the mountains beckoned from afar. He searched his writer's brain, looking for words to describe the view. The hope was that it would inspire his writing, not leave him speechless and at a loss. Staggering to the foot of the bed, he dropped his load and took a fresh look around. Isabelle had included the bedroom in her tour, but he hadn't been comfortable enough then to poke through all of her bookshelves. Today he had nothing but time. One shelf held memoirs and nonfiction. Another was devoted to local books describing everything from birds and animals to the char-acters who settled in the north. And there was the romance shelf. Several books by Simone and other authors he respected and read. Next to them were Jackson's, not yet signed. He would do that later. It wasn't much to pay for rent. What a thrill to see them there, though, making their way in the world. On the bottom shelf there were several travel books, including one about South America. Hadn't Wes said he'd spent time in Peru?

There was something about Wes that Jackson couldn't put his finger on. He seemed to have no fear, picking up to cross the country with nothing, not even a vehicle or a bus ticket or a place to stay. Then he walked up to a stranger on the side of the road and fixed his car. He knew how to chop wood, start a fire and care for a variety of animals. The guy was hyper-competent but there was clearly a complicated past lurking beneath the surface. He would make a great leading man with his strong hands, unruly golden curls, piercing blue eyes, and a way of making the world around him feel safe.

Maybe it was safe enough for Jackson to admit to himself that Wes was an attractive man?

A shiver of unease unfurled in his stomach, and his brain shied away from Perry and the last time Jackson had allowed himself to be attracted to a guy. Wes didn't seem like a user and a bully, but Jackson knew any kind of attraction had no place outside his books.

Speaking of his book, it was time to get to work. He'd unpack and make the bed later. Jackson set his laptop on the smooth wooden desk, which was perfectly situated right in front of a window overlooking the mountains, and switched it on. While the computer whirred and settled itself, Kale whined and pushed against Jackson's leg.

"Sorry, I didn't mean to ignore you." He gave Kale a pat and took a step towards his laptop.

Kale moaned.

Jackson turned around to look at him. "What? I don't see you writing my book."

The dog's feathery tail swished on the floor.

"You want out?" Jackson walked to the top of the stairs.

Kale's eyes followed him, but he didn't move.

"Are you feeling abandoned?" Jackson walked back

to the dog, dropped to his knees, and threw his arms around the furry neck. He burrowed his face into Kale's rough coat and hugged him tight. "I'm lonely too."

Kale sighed and let Jackson cuddle him for a few seconds, then he licked Jackson's face pulling away and curling up on a mat between the bed and the desk.

Finally, Jackson could get to work. Sitting down at the computer, he found his place and put his hands to the keys and immersed himself in the scene with his pirate hero on an outlaw ship running ahead of a British Navy frigate, fighting for both his life and the love of a woman in a complicated world of betrayal and intrigue. Soon Jackson was swept away into the magic of his fantasy where beautiful men loved bewitching women, and shy awkward writers didn't wish for things they couldn't have.

A knock at the front door jolted Jackson back to reality. He hurried down the steps and pushed past Kale to open the door. It was Wes. "Hi." Jackson felt strange opening it to Wes, knowing that by rights he should be the one in the house.

"Hey, Jackson."

"Hello." Jackson flushed with embarrassment, remembering his earlier thoughts about Wes. "Do you want to come in?" He opened the door wide, giving Kale the opportunity to push past them and run off in the direction of the creek.

Wes stepped inside. "I noticed you haven't taken Sunny to the shop yet?"

"Yah, I've been pretty busy this morning. Isabelle recommended Mackenzie Auto. I figured I'd give them a call around lunch."

"I know that place, they're solid. But when do you usually eat? It's pushing two and they're not going to be open much longer."

"Two? Crap. I got caught up."

"Yah? What are you writing?"

Jackson's throat went dry. Even though Wes appeared genuinely interested, he would definitely change his tune when he knew the truth. Jackson pretended not to hear the question. "I need to figure out what to do about Sunny."

"If you're going this afternoon, can I come with you? I need to talk to a guy about a job. It won't take long, and then I'll take you to the mechanic. We can walk back. Got to take advantage of the beautiful weather while it lasts."

"What about Kale?"

"It's a decent walk, forty-five minutes to an hour. Wouldn't want to deprive him of a trip to town."

"Okay, a walk sounds good." Jackson was surprised to hear himself agreeing, but Wes was familiar and meeting strangers was less daunting with him.

"I'll get my stuff. Where's Kale's leash? I can get him while I'm at it."

Jackson found a leash behind the door. "I have to check for eggs before we leave."

Their fingers brushed. Jackson yanked his hand back and grabbed a jacket. Avoiding Wes's eyes, he hurried to the small shed.

At the door, Jackson took a deep breath and winced at the sting of ammonia. This would be his first real test. Isabelle had made the whole thing look so easy, casually reaching under the brown hens and pulling out eggs. Maybe it wasn't as invasive as Jackson imagined. Isabelle had said the chickens were wary of strangers and that they would come around when they knew him, so he braced himself, stepping carefully to avoid stepping in poop. Cleaning out the pen would be another test, but he didn't have to worry about that today. He reached tentatively towards the plump bird. It squawked indignantly and pecked him.

"Son of a—!" That hurt! Jackson examined his hand for blood and eyeballed the evil creature who sat glaring at him. Steeling himself and moving in quick, Jackson squeezed his eyes shut and shoved his hand right under, leaving only a sleeve for her to peck. No chicken was getting the better of him. The eggs were smooth and warm in his hand. He withdrew gently, not wanting to damage the precious cargo. The next box was empty and the last one had only one egg and no chicken. Three eggs and no blood. Point to the writer! Grinning, Jackson reveled in his accomplishment of gathering food. This must be how farmers felt providing for their families. He tucked the eggs in a carton in the fridge, then went back outside and found there was no sign of Wes or Kale.

Jackson approached Sunny, walking along her fender stroking her all the way to the door handle. "Start today okay? That way, we can both figure out the lay of the land here." He climbed in, clicked his seatbelt, and turned the key, the engine caught. The rear passenger door thunked open, making him jump.

"Hey, didn't bump your head did you?" said Wes.

Kale clamored into the backseat panting, a big smile on his face.

"I didn't hear you coming," said Jackson.

Wes shut the back door, climbing into the front. "No, you wouldn't have." He buckled up. "You were begging the car again. Feels like this is where I came in." He smirked.

Heat crept up Jackson's cheeks. "She started, didn't she?"

"And you didn't even have to get your hands dirty. That's my kind of mechanical hack."

Jackson started out of the driveway. Wes directed him down the highway to Two Mile Hill and into downtown where they rolled to a stop in front of a place with a neon sign proclaiming *Wily Coyote Eats and Tavern.*

"I'll be twenty minutes," Wes told him. "Meet me back here and we can drop Sunny off."

"Kay, see you."

Wes climbed out of the car.

"Wes?"

He ducked back, sticking his head into the car, "Yeah?"

"Break a leg."

Wes flashed a heart stopping grin, dimples included, and slammed the door.

Jackson watched him disappear inside then eased Sunny into traffic toward Main Street. He passed an old train station that had been converted into offices. Many of the buildings had false fronts and murals painted on them, giving an old timey feel to the modern businesses housed inside. The cumulative effect was a strong impression of the gold rush bustle. Jackson drove slowly as he took in the sights. Twenty minutes flew by. The historian in him longed to dig into the old corners of this town but there would be time for that later.

When he returned, Wes was sitting on the curb waiting. He climbed in and put himself directly in line for Kale to lean over the seat and slurp his ear.

"I got it!" Wes scrubbed the side of his face. "My buddy Nick called yesterday and put in a good word for me. The guy basically showed me around, gave me some info and told me to come back for tomorrow's lunch shift. I've got a menu to memorize."

"Congratulations." Jackson gave him a warm smile.

"My perfect job is one where I can work part time without thinking about it too much, I don't need much to live, especially staying in the Castle."

Jackson got Sunny moving again. He followed the vague gestures Wes made to direct him to the mechanic.

Mackenzie Auto was tucked between the Yukon Brewing Company and the intriguingly named Fireweed Furniture. Jackson parked, leaving Wes and Kale with the car. He took a deep breath and opened the greasy blue door. The cramped office was empty except for a shrill phone ringing. He was about to leave when a door behind the desk opened. A large man in oil stained coveralls walked in. He glanced at the phone, which had gone quiet. "Damn."

"Uh hello?"

"Hi." The dark haired man stared at him.

"I, um." Jackson could feel himself shrinking. "I've got a car that's having some trouble."

"Do you have an appointment?" He cracked his knuckles.

Jackson swallowed hard. "I thought I could show it to you. If you're too busy, no problem, but my umm, Wes said—"

The stony face split into a wide grin "Hey don't worry about it. I was messing with you." He clapped a large hand on Jackson's shoulder.

Jackson flinched.

"Show me your car and tell me what's been going on."

Jackson led the way outside.

Wes was relaxing against the fender, staring into the distance, Kale was leaning against his knees.

"Wesley Palmer?" The large man threw himself at Wes and wrapped his beefy arms around him.

"Kelly!" Wes returned the hug wholeheartedly. "Holy shit. I figured your pop would be here."

"Nah, Pop's slowing down. I'm here most days now." Kelly gave Wes one last thump and stepped back.

Wes turned to Jackson. "Kelly, this is Jackson Williams. He's house-sitting up at Auntie Izzy's while she subdues the continent."

"No kidding! You're helping Izzy? Why didn't you say so? Of course, I can get you in. Pop would smack me upside the head for pulling your leg like that. What's up with your car?"

"Not sure," said Jackson. "I drove her all the way from Ontario and the other day she stalled on the side of the road. Wes said it might be the starter."

Kelly grinned. "Well, if Wes says it, it must be so."

Jackson wasn't sure if Kelly was teasing him, but it didn't feel malicious.

"Stand back, boys, and let a professional have a look." Kelly lifted the hood and began to poke around.

Jackson relaxed a little. "While you're in there, is there anything an Ontario car needs to start on a cold Yukon morning?"

"I'll see what you need," Kelly said. "I can't get to it today but if you leave her with me, I should be able to look tomorrow or Monday. Can I call you at Izzy's number?"

"Yeah," said Jackson. "Thanks."

"So, Wes, where the hell are you staying?" Kelly asked.

"I'm out at the Castle," Wes said.

Kelly let out a low whistle. "That's a blast from the past. That old place is still standing? Have you seen Jimmy yet? We should hang out."

Wes didn't meet Kelly's eyes. "I don't think so. I

don't really party like that anymore."

"Who does?" Kelly shrugged. "We aren't kids any-more."

Wes relaxed. "You and Jimmy? That sounds okay. I don't want to hang with Shane or his crew, though."

Kelly grimaced. "You wouldn't have heard. Shane died in a car accident about four years ago, Malcolm's in jail in BC somewhere, and I think Peter moved to Edmonton to be a lawyer or something. What about Nick Morgan? He says you're responsible for his being here."

"Of course, you'd know Nick. That sounds good."

"How can I get in touch with you?" Kelly asked.

Wes scrawled his email onto a scrap of paper and hugged Kelly one more time.

Kelly pounded him on the back. "So good to see you, man." He turned and offered his hand to Jackson. "Great to meet you, Jackson."

"You too." Jackson doubted his sincerity, but Kelly sure was an interesting character.

They waved goodbye and started walking along the narrow shoulder. Kale trotted beside Wes.

Cool air kept him from overheating and the trees along the way were brilliant with fall yellow, like sun-shine. Wes was quiet, so Jackson enjoyed the mountains in the distance profiled against the blue sky. The walk was all uphill and hard. Jackson was out of shape but pushed himself to the top of the hill. All of a sudden, Jackson was overcome with dizziness and was having trouble standing up. "Wait!" He walked into the dry ditch and plopped down resting his head on his knees. Kale sniffed his face and licked his cheek.

"Jackson? Are you okay?" Wes sounded far away.

"Sorry, I need a minute. I'm fine." What must Wes think of him, literally falling down on the side of the road after twenty minutes of walking?

Wes settled beside him pulling Kale down as well. "You're not fine, is it your head?"

"I forgot to eat." Jackson's face flamed.

"You forgot to eat?"

"Sometimes when I'm writing, I kind of lose track. It's stupid."

"Damn straight it's stupid. What about water?"

Jackson shook his head. He couldn't imagine what Wes must think of him.

Wes reached for the small pack on his back pulling out his beat-up water bottle and a granola bar. "Here."

Jackson scarfed the bar and drank deeply from the water bottle. Wes passed him another bar. He ate it slower.

"You only have one body," said Wes. "You've got to take care of it."

"You sound like my mother." Jackson tried for a light, joking tone.

"This isn't funny. Not eating or drinking all day, then hiking. It's not safe."

"You're right. I should know better. This is why my mother thinks I need a keeper. But when I'm writing, it's like I'm sucked right out of this world and my body doesn't even exist."

"How do you feel now?"

"I'll give it a minute to let it sink in. I'm not dizzy anymore." Jackson passed the water back.

Wes took a long drink himself, then offered it back.

Jackson took another drink, this time aware his mouth was where Wes's had been moments before. He shoved it toward the pack.

Wes put it into his day pack, standing up and brushing the dirt from his backside.

Jackson got back to his feet, making sure not to over-balance, then reached for the leash. "I'll take Kale this time."

Wes regarded him, taking his time, assessing him from top to bottom.

"I'm fine," Jackson snapped.

Wes's lips curled, popping those dimples again. "You sure are." He took Jackson's hand in his and closed it around the leash. Then slung his pack onto his back and started walking.

Jackson followed Kale, clutching the leash, feeling himself being tugged forward.

They walked in silence. Jackson tried to stabilize his crazy pulse. He was no more prepared to be gay now than he had been ten years ago when he'd been shoved in that locker. His counselor's advice for times like these would be to focus on the present. Jackson therefore concentrated on the sun warming his hair and felt grateful for his jacket's protection against the cool breeze. He cut a glance at Wes, appreciating the way the wind ruffled his out-of-control curls.

Their feet crunched rhythmically on the gravel shoulder. Cars whizzed by them. "They go a good clip along this stretch," said Wes. "We'll cut in at the path up ahead, it's a much nicer walk."

"Good, I'd hate to be run over on my second day here." Jackson was taken by the golden leaves of the trees lining the path. "In Ontario," he told Wes, "the leaves put on quite a show with brilliant reds and oranges. People drive from everywhere to see them. This is beautiful, but so different. I feel a long way from home."

"Yah, it's funny I didn't realize I was homesick until I got back. It's in the trees and the mountains and how the air smells." Wes cleared his throat and ran his hand over the back of his neck before slipping it into the pocket of his jacket. "So, how are you settling in?"

"Oh." Jackson kicked a small rock out of his path. "I'm doing okay. I got my stuff unpacked and the chickens—" He shuddered. "The chickens will take some getting used to, but I think I'm making progress." He forced a bright tone, not wanting Wes to know he was dreading the next encounter with the aggressive avians.

They walked on, eventually breaking off onto a wooded trail. Jackson opened his mouth a couple of times to say something, anything, but then he shut it again. The liquid chatter of ravens flying through the trees beside them was soothing. It sounded like they were saying something, and he simply had to listen to catch the meaning. It was easy to let go and walk without thinking about anything. Jackson's foot snagged a root and he stumbled, grabbing the firm flesh of Wes's upper arm through his soft flannel shirt.

"Easy, Turbo." Wes's solid hand on his waist steadied him. Excited, Kale enthusiastically wrapped around their legs.

Jackson's face flamed, couldn't he even stay on his feet? What a day. It was easier to focus on the dog. "Kale!" he scolded and unwound the leash. "Watch where you're going." He raced along the path ahead of Wes, dragging poor Kale behind him.

By the time they got home, feeling every minute of twenty-eight years spent reading and writing instead of pursuing more athletic activities, Jackson turned to Wes. "Okay, for the record, I wouldn't call that walking distance from town. That's a commute. You can't seriously be planning on walking to work every day?"

"Not all the time. Sometimes I'll hitch, and as soon as I get to know some people, I'm sure I'll be able to get rides."

"That's nuts."

"Maybe." Wes waved and aimed for the path to the Castle.

Jackson watched him go. There went an amazing guy, but they were so different. There was no way there could ever be anything between them.

Chapter Six

The following morning dawned sunny but cold. Jackson and Kale took a short walk on paths close to the house. Bears would stay away from the dog, wouldn't they? In between carrying a solid walking stick and talking to Kale out loud, Jackson figured critters could hear them coming. Collecting the eggs had been easier this morning. He got away with nothing worse than the evil eye.

The only snag now was writing. It had gone well enough yesterday but today nothing seemed right. The love scenes felt off. Jackson spent the afternoon hours reading them and tinkering with word placement until his eyes crossed and his shoulders ached. Could he have writers block? It really hadn't happened to him in the past, but today, it was impossible to reproduce the excitement and tingle he usually felt when he wrote. He thought of the sparks in the air around him when Wes handed the leash over to him yesterday, touching his hand for a bare moment. Besides being embarrassed, he'd been overcome by a yearning, something that he'd like to fold into the pages. Usually, it was something that came easily and yet today it just wouldn't land. Maybe it was the northern air. Or maybe he was just rushing the process. Unfortunately, Lorraine wanted the manuscript now. Jackson should have given it to her before he'd left London. Now he wished he had. This was going to be his last book for Hanson's Publishing anyway, at least in this genre. They had been good to him, but it was time to grow up and write something his family could finally be proud of.

Jackson sighed. The sun was starting to set. A break would be a good idea. He closed his computer and headed to the kitchen to feed Kale and himself.

The cupboard was open and filled with boxes and cans, but Jackson wasn't seeing any of them. He was back in the book, turning the last love scene over in his mind. A knock at the front door startled Jackson back to the present.

"Anybody home?" Wes pushed the door open.

Jackson stared at him, trying to pull himself back to reality.

Wes dropped down to his knees to greet Kale, skill-fully avoiding the big tongue and sloppy kisses. Wes raised his eyes. "I have a massive stir fry started. There's more than enough for two. Do you want to come for dinner?"

"I thought your cabin didn't have electricity?" Jackson eyed the fully equipped kitchen that he would barely touch.

"True. I have lights, that's it, but there's an old beaut of a cookstove. Anything you can make over a campfire is way easier on that thing."

"Huh, I guess I never thought of doing a stir fry over a campfire. I mean, it's not like it's on a stick."

"What?" Wes's eyes widened. "Oh yeah, that's funny. You've got a weird sense of humor."

Jackson hadn't been joking. He really wanted to accept Wes's invitation, especially since Wes had talked to Isabelle about learning to cook in some of the best restaurants in Canada, in Whistler Village. But could Jackson get through the meal without making a complete ass of himself? "Sure, I'd like to see the Castle. Let me feed Kale then we'll come over."

"Bring a flashlight, it'll be dark when you head back." Wes gave the dog one last scratch between the ears and headed out the door. "I'll see you in a few minutes."

Jackson scooped kibble into the dish and poured on a teaspoon of olive oil. Isabelle's notes had a comprehensive list of do's and don'ts for Kale when it came to people food.

While he waited for the dog, he found himself in the bathroom staring at the mirror. His hair stuck up and a wet comb didn't help. Jackson gave up on it and focused on the rest. He was wearing his favorite dark red button-down shirt, the one his sister approved of. "It really shows off those incredible brown eyes," she'd gushed when she forced him to buy it. Under that was his *Big*

Damn Heroes T-shirt. It made him feel good when he needed a boost. The beige slacks from this morning were casualties of the chicken coop, so he'd traded them in for a crisp new pair of jeans. It would have to do. When Kale nosed his way into the bathroom, Jackson looked at the time and saw he'd been obsessing about his reflection for almost ten minutes.

"Come on Kale, you can walk me over." Jackson threw on a jacket and headed outside. His growling stomach pushed him down the path.

The Castle door swung open before he could knock, and he was greeted by Wes's bright smile.

Wes was holding a cast iron pan with a worn oven mitt. "You're just in time." He gestured around the small space. "Welcome to my humble abode. Close the door behind you." He took a few steps to a small, square table and began spooning a colorful stir fry onto plates.

Jackson hung his jacket on a peg by the door. The heat in the small room was intense. Wes had stripped down to a white undershirt, faded jeans, and bare feet. The shirt clung to his damp body. Jackson shouldn't be noticing it, but he was. Realizing Wes was waiting for him to say something, he cleared his throat. "It's nice. Cozy." Jackson averted his eyes, gaze landing on the chimney rising from the hot stove up through the loft.

"The chimney distributes the heat up top. At this time of year, it's kind of like sleeping in an oven."

Under the loft was a faded couch with a wooden box coffee table in front of it. A double mattress on the floor with rumpled bedding on it dominated the space. Jackson blushed. Being in the same room as Wes's bed was unbearably intimate. He cleared his throat again. "Smells amazing."

"Thanks, I love to cook. It's even better with an audience. Have a seat." Wes pulled a chair out with a flourish. "Would you like a glass of wine?"

"Wine?"

"Yah, it's a Shiraz. Please tell me you drink wine?"

"I love it. I admit I'm surprised. I kind of pegged you as more of a beer guy."

"A beer guy! I'm offended."

"I'm sorry, I didn't mean—"

"I'm kidding, you're right, I am a beer guy. I wouldn't know a Shiraz if it bit me. My friend Nick gave me three bottles as a housewarming present." Wes filled up two mason jars and handed one to Jackson. He sat down across from him and raised his glass looking him in the eye. "To new friends."

"To new friends," Jackson echoed and took a healthy drink. The first bite was incredible and made it easy to eat rather than worry about awkward silences. He kept stealing glances at Wes, watching the way his long fingers grasped his fork, and how the shadows highlighted the definition in his arms. Jackson gulped more wine.

"So, you're a writer?" Wes put down his fork and gave Jackson his full attention.

Jackson shifted in his chair. He hated discussions that started with "So you write." They inevitably led to, "I've read your mother's literary critiques, what do you write?" Usually best to avoid the whole thing. Before he could change the topic, Wes asked another question.

"Are you published?"

"Yes."

"What have you written?"

"Probably nothing you've read."

"I wouldn't be so sure, try me."

"Lots of stuff. Lately a pirate series. 'The Pirate and the Princess,' and 'The Pirate's Passion'?'"

Wes laughed. "Are you asking me?"

Jackson wasn't used to being teased. His heartbeat throbbed in his cheeks.

"Sounds like hot romance." Wes's voice lowered. "Like, Reginald's throbbing member?"

"Historical Romance actually, and my powers of description are better than that!" Jackson straightened his back. The injustice for the misperceptions of romantic fiction just made him boil.

"You're serious? A romance writer?" Wes grinned, "That's so cool! Wait. Auntie Izzy must have read your stuff. Does she own any?"

Jackson knew where this was going. "I believe she does."

"That's awesome! I'll have to borrow one. It's been ages since I've read anything. Libraries don't like to loan to vagrants like me."

"I'm not sure that's a good idea." If Jackson was going to live on this property all winter with Wes, the last thing he needed was the guy laughing at him every time they met."

The smile slid off his face, "You're right. I don't think I'm one hundred percent welcome to go through her stuff."

"No, I didn't mean she wouldn't want you to look at them—" Jackson took a breath and tried again. "I don't like people to know, okay?"

"Really? Why?"

"They ask questions. I'm not good on the spot. And romance, well you know…"

Wes opened his mouth to speak.

Jackson held up his hand. "People don't think of a guy writing historical romance. It's a voice thing, how can a man speak in a woman's voice or something. You'd hate them." He pushed back from the table, ready to bolt.

Wes grasped Jackson's wrist. "I'm sorry for making this about me. I would love it if you loaned me a book. I'm sorry if some crazy people haven't appreciated what you do. Creativity is a gift. You gotta use it however it shows up."

Jackson thought about his mother's fondest wish that he follow in her footsteps as a literary scholar, not the writer of junk, and gulped. "Coming out here is about changing me, but some things resist my best efforts, and the truth is, I'm not normal, never have been, and apparently that followed me here. Gawd, I always overshare. Why can't I shut up?" He tried to pull his hand free so he could leave.

Wes stroked the skin on his wrist before letting go. "Don't leave. I'd be the last person to judge normal. I guess I'm a little sensitive about my family. I'm working on that. Besides—" the grin was back "—I find you fascinating."

Jackson didn't know how to respond to that, so he sat down and went back to shoveling food into his mouth. A full mouth was a safe mouth.

"Listen, I'm here and I know how to work the place," said Wes. "Let me know if you need anything, okay? Auntie Izzy made it clear I'm not to impose, so I'll stay out of your way but please don't hesitate."

Jackson was grateful for the change of topic. "It's not an imposition. This is nice, thanks for dinner. You can impose anytime and if you need anything, maybe there'll be something I can help with."

Wes's gaze was hot.

Jackson couldn't look away. He was falling into those blazing blue eyes.

"Actually, there is something," said Wes.

Jackson held his breath. What could he possibly do to help Wes?

Wes's expression became concerned. "Are you okay?"

"Fine." Jackson picked up his glass and took another big sip. "You were saying?"

"Well, Uncle Jeff made the cabin with everything except a shower. He built it for a pack of wild children who mostly went home for a bath after being here. I took a creek bath today and don't get me wrong, it was invigorating but I just about ran up the path screaming and begging for a cold shower to warm me up."

Jackson failed at not imagining a frigid Wes running up the path wearing only a small towel.

"Jackson?"

"Yeah?"

"You phased out on me."

"Sorry. My family calls it my writer's brain. You were saying?"

"I was hoping I could use the guest bathroom for showers. I promise, I won't disturb you. You won't know I'm there. Really."

Okay, this was something he could manage. "Door's not locked. I'm using the bathroom upstairs. Anytime." He scraped his plate clean. "This is really good. Thanks."

"I'm glad you like it. Have seconds."

When the plates had been forked clean, Jackson jumped up to collect them and bring them to the counter.

"Don't," said Wes. "I'll take care of them later."

"No, you cooked. I'll do the dishes, I think." Jackson stared at the basin with a blue jug over it. "How does it work?"

Chuckling, Wes retrieved a steaming pot of water from the stove. "Look out." He shouldered in front of Jackson to pour the hot water into the basin, along with a small amount of soap. "It's hot, so use the water from the jug to cool it." He handed over a washcloth and picked up the tea towel ready to dry. Jackson rolled up his sleeves and got to work.

It didn't take long. There wasn't much to clean, thank God, because Wes was standing very close to him. He didn't seem to understand the concept of personal space as he moved in to take a plate from Jackson's soapy hands, then stepped away to put it in the cupboard, then close again. Between the stove and the hot water, Jackson was overheating. His hair was damp at his temples, and a trickle of sweat slid between his shoulder blades. The cool breeze from the open window did nothing to ease his discomfort. He was aware of the strength in Wes's body, the grace with which he moved, and the smell of earth and growing things that surrounded him.

"Leave the glasses," said Wes. "I'll wash 'em in the morning with the breakfast dishes. You can help me finish that bottle of wine for dessert."

"Sounds good." With nothing else to wash, Jackson squeezed the water out of the cloth and ran it over the counter and table.

"Here, you pour the wine and meet me on the couch. I'm going to ditch the gray water." The sink drained into a bucket under the counter. Wes scooped the food bits from the drain and tossed them into the wood stove where they sizzled and popped. Then he grabbed the bucket and slipped on the rubber boots by the door. Not bothering with a jacket, he went outside.

As soon as the door closed, Jackson shed his red overshirt. He was sweltering. Hopefully, Wes wouldn't think it was rude but, given the man was sporting a damp undershirt, it should be fine. A glance assured him he didn't have sweat stains on his T-shirt and a sniff told him his deodorant was still functioning. Jackson emptied the wine between their jars and carried them to the ugly couch, placing Wes's on the crate and taking a fortifying sip of his own. So far, he hadn't ruined everything. Things were going better than expected.

The door burst open, letting in a blessed gust of cool air. "Look who wants to join us."

Kale wormed his way around Wes's legs and came directly to Jackson. His fur was cool and damp, and he had a huge doggy grin on his face.

"You look proud of yourself," said Jackson. "What have you been up to? Scaring the bears away for me?"

Kale tolerated a hug before he settled down at Jackson's feet.

"I love that dog. Auntie Izzy and Uncle Jeff always had a thing for Bernese Mountain dogs. They make great companions and are crazy intelligent." Wes put the bucket away and came over to the couch. His eyes lit up and he pointed to the writing on Jackson's shirt. "Hey, I love that show!"

Jackson followed Wes's gaze. "You know *Firefly*?

"Of course. Have you read the graphic novels?"

"I've got all of them back in London." In his apartment, Jackson had them displayed on shelves in their plastic protecters. At home, he'd hidden under the bed so his mother wouldn't see them.

"Too bad, I'd love to borrow them. I know the series is over now, but some libraries carry old stuff like that. Although in Peru, even if I'd the time to look for them, I'd have been surprised to find any."

"Now you're here, you should be able to catch up."

"You're probably right. I'm not sure how long I'm staying, probably not long enough to get a library card," Wes said.

"I thought you'd said you were here for the winter?"

Wes lifted his wine and took a sip before he answered. "Well, that's the plan at the moment. I need to settle some things with my aunt, so I'm stuck until she comes back. Oh, and there's Nick's baby, so that probably locks me down until I can meet the little booger."

Jackson absently rubbed his foot on Kale's side.

"That sounds like summer to me."

Wes quirked his lips. "It would be nice to pad the bank account before I head out, but I'm not the settling down kind." He tipped back his wine.

"You spent time in Peru. What was that like?"

Wes eyeballed his empty glass and glanced at him. "First, what do you say about opening another bottle?" He popped the cork, and filled both glasses to the brim, settling the bottle on the coffee table.

Jackson's limbs were heavy. Wes was sitting closer, their thighs brushed with his every move. It was distracting.

Wes was vague about his time in Peru. He talked about a Shaman he had worked with, alluding to going through a rough patch and needing the peace of the mountains to get through. His legs were crossed at the ankles and Jackson found himself mesmerized by his feet. They were large and tanned, but something about the delicate bones and the curl of his little toe made them seem vulnerable.

Jackson needed to slow down on the wine but couldn't relax. He was too aware of Wes. The man was unable to sit still. Eventually, Wes hopped up and paced around the small space gesturing with his glass, running his hand through his wild curls and ranting about...something. The commercial exploitation of the Mother for non-renewable resources?

Jackson wasn't really hearing him. He was absorbed by the way Wes's lips formed the words, the curve of his jaw, and those arms. The barely restrained passion bursting from his lean body was magnetic. Jackson had a mental picture of Wes as his pirate, wooing the princess wearing high boots and skin-tight pants. His flowing white shirt would reveal a well-defined chest, flat, tanned nipples, and a light smattering of hair. His imagination was helped by Wes's skinny jeans and damp, practically see-through shirt: it was all right there. Jackson could almost feel strong arms clasped around his back and firm lips at his throat. Wait. It was the princess, not him, in the embrace. Thankfully people couldn't read minds and Wes would never know. Jackson doubled his efforts to keep his breathing under control and focus on Wes's words.

"Besides, Mother Earth is suffering while we dither and exploit her. What sense does it make to wait? Environmentally or financially. Focusing on alternatives now will save billions in the long run, not to mention saving our place on the planet!" Wes flung himself back on the couch, taking up way too much space, waving his glass in Jackson's direction. "Top me up."

Jackson had to lean to reach the bottle on the table. Heat radiated from Wes, and he could smell the salt of his sweat. He jerked the bottle back, sitting straight up, before he did something ridiculous like lean over and rub his cheek against that damp chest.

Jackson poured the wine, surprised to find the bottle empty. He placed it on the floor and tried to settle back. There didn't seem to be anywhere to sit without touching Wes. The safest place was perched on the edge of the couch with their knees knocking together as Wes bounced his leg.

Wes took another drink, setting his cup down, he leaned his head back on the couch. Jackson could see the length of his throat, the golden stubble highlighting his jaw line. He was dizzy with the wine and heat. Not a good combination.

"I can't believe how long you let me go on. Usually I'm a better conversationalist." Wes lifted his head, making eye contact. "You're easy to talk to."

Jackson jolted back to reality. "You think so? I'm not usually."

Wes leaned forward to sit with Jackson and nudged him with his shoulder. "How 'bout you, you got a guy waiting for you in Ontario?"

Their faces were inches apart. He could feel Wes's wine flavored breath on his lips, and he could see a single faint freckle at the corner of his left eye. The urge to touch the soft hair was overwhelming. His fist clenched unconsciously. Then Wes's words sank in.

"What? No!" Jackson sputtered pushing Wes away. He jumped up, lungs constricted.

Kale startled, jumping up with a sharp bark.

Wes stared at him. "What's wrong?"

"I have to go." Jackson shoved his feet into his shoes without bothering to unlace them and grabbed his coat. Slamming the door shut behind him, he flicked on the flashlight and ran, Kale on his heels.

Jackson didn't stop until he flopped down on Isabelle's quilt. He pushed his face into the soft mattress trying to stop his wheezing. Tears were prickling his eyes and his heart was crashing in his chest. He bit his lip, and the sharp metallic taste allowed him to grasp one rational thought. Panic attack. Now that he identified it, his body began moving through the motions, so ingrained after years of therapy. He rolled on his back and sucked his breath in through his nose and forced it out through his pursed lips. In and out. He imagined the clean air rushing into his body and swirling through the poisonous thoughts, a cyclone that blew them right out his mouth. He thought of the anti-anxiety meds in the bathroom. They were there if he needed them. Time to tackle his thoughts. "You're not in danger," he said to himself. "Wes knowing you're gay doesn't mean you're not safe."

Jackson had never been hurt for being gay, not seriously. He'd never been hospitalized or had his life at risk. And yet his anxiety didn't know the difference. In retrospect, Jackson should have been aware that Wes was hitting on him. It had been so many years since he had felt an attraction that he barely recognized it when it happened.

The slow breathing was working. He was relaxing, the tight muscles in his abdomen unclenching, letting his body sink into the bed. Being attracted to someone didn't give them the power to hurt him. Jackson was no longer a child desperate to be liked, and Wes was no school yard bully. He'd figured awkward guys like him didn't get to have relationships, any kind of relationship. It didn't work with women, although Marie had been kind, unlike Perry.

Jackson dragged himself off the bed and shed his clothes in the corner. The panic was subsiding, leaving deep embarrassment in its place. He shouldn't be let out in public.

It was too late to do anything about it now. Might as well get to sleep. He got into his soft Green Lantern pj's and brushed his teeth. Staring in the mirror he could see the logo. Green Lantern was a superhero without superpowers. His ring helped him, sure, but he was a normal guy who lived his life in a powerful way. Taking a breath, Jackson tried to channel his inner superhero. It didn't help. In bed, staring into the dark, he listened to Kale's soft snoring and wondered how he would ever face Wes again.

Chapter Seven

The sheets strangled Jackson all night. At seven a.m., he gave up trying to sleep. He needed some distance from this, some perspective. There was one person he could speak to. Maybe it was sad that his best friend, his only friend, was his younger sister, Corie, but that didn't make it any less true. She could be blunt to a fault and would call him out if she thought he needed it.

Jackson grabbed his phone from where it was plugged in on the bedside table and called. "Hey, Cor, it's me."

"Oh my God." Her usually warm voice was pitched deep. That happened when she was pissed. "You've been gone almost two weeks and I'm just hearing from you now. I can't believe you called Mom first and what, your phone isn't taking calls? Have you blocked me? You said you'd call. You didn't even text. You asshole!"

Jackson smiled, stuffing the extra pillow under his head. Leave it to Corie to call him an asshole and cheer him up. "I'm sorry. You're right."

"Yeah, I know I'm right. So why didn't you call?"

Knowing Corie would say exactly what was on her mind should have been difficult for Jackson's anxiety. But it wasn't, because she said what she meant. No hidden agenda. "I was exhausted and distracted," said Jackson. "But it's no excuse. It's crazy here. There are chickens to feed and there's a fire in the basement to keep the place warm. I'm dealing with it all."

"Chickens and fires? Is that what you said to get Mom all riled up the other night?

"She wouldn't let me get a word in. I spaced on the time-difference thing and woke her up. She wasn't at her best." Jackson sighed. "I was so excited to tell her about my trip I screwed up again."

Corie groaned. "Of course she made a simple misunderstanding sound like a major crime. Anyway, enough about her. Tell me about your trip."

That was another reason Jackson adored his sister. She knew better than anyone when to change the subject. He gave her a brief rundown of his journey until he met Wes. "So, this is the part I need your advice on. There's this guy..." Jackson gave her all the details, right up until last night's disaster.

Corie listened without interrupting, which was unusual for her. Once Jackson finished, she said, "Honestly, I'm still not getting it. You had dinner with this guy. And?"

"And maybe we had a bit too much to drink and I thought about kissing him."

"What! Don't mess with me Ed, Jackson, whoever you are, does this mean what I think it means?"

"It means I had a full-blown panic attack, and I ran out of there without even saying thanks for the meal." He rubbed the tension spot on his forehead.

"Ever since that rat Perry hurt you!"

Jackson winced at the abrupt volume increase. "He didn't hurt me, it was fine, barely a blip."

"He took something from you. Don't minimize it."

"Corie, stop. What I went through was nothing. Some other people have it worse. We hear horror stories all the time. That's not what happened. Thinking about it now, my dignity was hurt."

"You can't compare it, Jackson." Corie's outrage was palpable. "You were young. Perry took advantage of that and it hurt you! He ripped something amazing from you. You are gay, Jackson. That should be a blessing not a curse. You could have spent the last ten years out dancing and having fun making bad choices about men and finding your tribe instead of having a panic attack every time you get a boner!" Corie sniffled.

She must be crying. Jackson kept his tone soft. "Corie, even if I was out and proud, the guy you're describing isn't me."

"Okay, I get that, but why can't you let this Wes guy flirt with you. It doesn't mean you have to do anything about it. Have a little fun. Maybe flirt back. Or make a friend, you deserve it."

"Maybe? I don't know but it doesn't matter anymore,

I blew it."

"I'm sure you didn't blow it. Wait. Did he say you blew it?"

"Of course not! But now I'll have to move to Alaska. It was awful."

"God, Jackson you're such a drama queen! So, you embarrassed yourself, but you've done that before and lived. If this is a person you could actually have feelings for, maybe for once, don't let that win."

Jackson's throat tightened. "You're right."

"What? I didn't hear you. Can you say it again? But this time, include the date and maybe, I, Edward Jackson Williams hereby declare, in front?"

Jackson rolled his eyes.

"That's it, I'm hanging up."

"Before you do, can I tell Mom and Dad you're okay?"

"Sure. Tell them I love the mountains and will get tons of writing done. "

"Really?"

"Yeah."

"Good 'cause it costs extra for me to lie."

Corie had to get back to work and it was past time Jackson should get out of bed, so they said their good-byes and ended the call.

Jackson dropped the phone and sighed, flopping back over the irredeemably messy bed. Fear wasn't over-whelming him now. Embarrassment was. He thought talking to Corie would give him a fresh answer, but in his gut he knew he had to stick with his first choice, to remain quietly gay while fantasizing about Wes from a distance.

****

Wes woke to a cold gray sky. He was too tired to hike to Riverdale, but he could compromise and walk to the bus stop down the road. It would have been a great day to wallow in bed, but he needed to talk to Abby. And what good was living near your best friend if you couldn't drop in for a pick-me-up after being eviscerated by your estranged sister?

Wes felt bad about last night. Flirting with Jackson was a terrible idea and would be a great way to screw up his living situation. He enjoyed the hook-up scene, and he was good at it. Good at keeping things light and sending his partners away satisfied. But generally, Wes avoided hitting on drunk closet cases who lived next door, no matter how much he enjoyed the shy smiles and being looked at like he was something special. He owed Jackson an apology.

Wes scrubbed his eyes, trying to clear the fog from his brain. He'd woken feeling groggy and sluggish. He'd have to watch himself. Less than a week back in town and he'd overdone it with Nick and then again last night. It would be so easy to slip back into old habits. He would need his wits about him with Jackson around. He was like catnip, a combination of weird courage and vulnerability. It was lucky nothing happened. But damn, Jackson was adorable. There was sweetness and naivety that roused Wes's protective instincts and confused the hell out of him. It didn't matter though. This was definitely not a good time for a relationship.

Wes needed to focus on the work he was here to do. In the old days, Uncle Jeff worked a trapline in the valleys and foothills behind their property. He'd stay in a hut for a few days at a time, walking the route of the trap line until he had caught enough small game. The meat fed the family, and the furs were sold to supplement their income. By the time Wes was old enough to join him, it was more of a hobby, but they would go out a few times a year and get back to the land. Getting out there before it snowed to see what kind of shape the old hut was in would be a good way to settle his thoughts. He should have time after his shift tonight.

The bus rumbled to the stop and heaved a great sigh, hunkering down to allow a woman with a cane to disembark. Wes stepped forward offering his arm. With a quick "my pleasure" in response to her thanks, he hopped onto the bus, paid his fare, and settled into a window seat. The bus meandered through the small-town streets of the Yukon Territory's capital city. Too soon it rolled to a stop at the street scribbled on the slip of paper Isabelle had left him.

The house on Alsek Road backed onto treed green space and, behind it, Gray Mountain leaned in protectively. This area would be perfect for his sister. Abby loved the forest almost as much as he did. Whitehorse was one city that allowed its residents the luxury of being near wild areas where animals and Yukoners alike were comfortable with one another. Standing in front of the wooden, one and a half story house with a tree in the front yard, he checked the address yet again. There was a tall wood fence with a gate leading to the backyard with a little pink bicycle leaning against it. Isabelle had mentioned Abby had kids, something he hadn't considered as he only remembered her the way she was that last day. He wondered again who Abby might be after now and how she would react to having him on her doorstep.

He took three steps toward the front door. Fear sat heavy in his limbs, slowing him down. This was harder than going to Isabelle's. Would Abby be willing to talk with him? Would she kick him out? Abby's reaction would play a huge role in his ability to stay through till April. She had far more right to be angry at him than anyone else and forgiveness wouldn't be easy. They needed to talk, and Wes had to apologize. Taking a deep bracing breath, he took the final steps up onto the small porch. Opening the screen door, he raised his hand to knock, then couldn't. Turning, he started back toward the street and paused. This was important. Wes went back up the steps, opened the screen, and knocked, loud and assertive.

The house was silent. There were no sounds or footsteps on the other side of the door. She wasn't home.

Chapter Eight

The lights were out at the main house when Wes arrived home from work. He ignored a twinge of disappointment. It wasn't like he would knock at two in the morning. Besides, the way Jackson had run out didn't give him any reason to think there would be a welcome, despite the offer of the shower. Exhaustion and cold made the Castle icy, but it wasn't worth the trouble to light the stove. Shimmying out of his clothes and into his sleep gear, Wes dove under the covers and quickly fell asleep.

He woke in a fiery nightmare of a car plunging into a ravine. Wes's shirt was drenched with sweat and his heart was pounding. It took a minute to shake off the terror. That was a bad one. He really needed to get a handle on the nightmares before they drove him right out of town without having a chance to settle anything.

Wes finally fell back into a restless sleep until the early light peeked into the cabin. The lack of real rest left him sluggish and negative. There had always been peace when out trapping with Uncle Jeff. Maybe up on the trapline, he would be able to properly grieve the amazing man who'd meant so much to him. Glad he had the time to get there this morning, he rose and packed a small amount of gear and food for the journey into Shadow.

The walk to the hut was familiar and didn't take as long as he'd remembered. Unlatching the door, he stepped into the eight-by-eight space. It was too clean to have been vacant since Jeff died. In the wilderness, places like this one were a haven for hikers. The rule was, "stay, use what you need, and leave it better than you found it."

Tossing his bag in the corner, Wes checked out the old pot belly stove on the other wall that he and Uncle had assembled together. They'd dragged it all the way up here one winter on a toboggan. Wes had strained with the weight of pieces, and his mother had been angry at the heavy work his uncle had given him. But Uncle Jeff had patted him on the back and said, "He's as strong and will-ing as any man I've ever worked with." Wes's heart expanded at the memory of how important he'd felt.

"Oh, Uncle Jeff, I'm sorry." Wes sat on the floor and wept for the time lost. What if he hadn't left? What if he'd stayed to face the implications of his parents' deaths? What if? Such a useless question.

Eventually, his sobs eased and tears stopped. The solid sense of Uncle Jeff that permeated the cabin slowly soothed his soul. Even now, his uncle was here for him. Wes could feel the warmth of his essence and his roots. Time slowed in the face of all this sky and peaceful land. Taking his knife outside, Wes walked to a stand of fir trees not far from the cabin.

Slicing soft boughs from each tree, he thanked them for the warmth they would provide tonight. Arranging them on the sleep platform, he laid out his sleeping bag so it would be ready for him later. Later he set snares and sat meditation in a small grove of trees with a view of the mountains and out of the chilly wind. It was a day of remembrance and connection that he hadn't had while he was traveling. As the dark fell, he had a small meal of trail mix and some strong trail coffee. It wasn't much but out here he didn't need much. As he rolled into his bag that night, he felt nourished. No dreams disturbed his sleep.

The next day, Wes was lucky and snared a rabbit, so he had a stew. He walked the trapline and found memo-ries snagged in the bushes and trees along the path. This time when sitting in meditation, he was protected from the wind by a huge boulder. The voices of the furred and feathered citizens of this place brought his heart back to ground. He could hear the ravens and he knew it had been time for him to come back. That night, he huddled close to the fire with his carving knife, pulling curls of wood away from the figure being released.

Morning came before he was ready. Wes could smell his spicy mattress and the cold in the air. From the warmth of his bag, he could hear rain on the roof. The walk home would be a wet one but right now, he was dry and cozy. Climbing out of the covers and pulling on some clothes, he sparked some kindling to make a small fire to heat up water for coffee.

The clock was ticking. If he wanted to make it home in time to get a shower and make it to work by four for the dinner rush, he'd have to get going soon. But Wes didn't mind. Being up here had worked. No nightmares and he'd woken feeling well-rested. Today, wet or not, anything was possible.

*****

Jackson walked furiously, trying to outpace Lorraine's rejection. He didn't feel the cold and couldn't outrun the sensation of failure.

"Go back to the first draft," she'd said. "It's what Hanson's accepted in the first place. You've changed things too much. Your writing usually exudes emotion, but this poor girl is just calling it in. Does your heroine even like the pirate?"

What the hell was she talking about? Jackson's wounded writer wanted to give up and pursue an entirely different career. After his mom talked him into getting an English degree, he could imagine how she would take him becoming an accountant or a plumber.

If Jackson hadn't met Wes, he wouldn't be so lost. He wouldn't be wondering what it would be like to lose himself totally and passionately to romance, not to a pirate but to someone who would steal his heart.

Kale crisscrossed his path as they worked their way around the perimeter of the property. The dog was carefree and enthusiastic, yet he kept close, often brushing against Jackson's legs.

The stark landscape couldn't hold Jackson's attention. Writing books about romance was usually easy. It was a safe way to feel the emotions of love without complications. Yet everything he had written after that evening with Wes was trite and artificial. Jackson had tried to tuck his newly awakened feelings into the pages of the book, and they had fallen flat.

They approached the Castle and Wes's boots were on the porch. He was back.

Jackson stopped in his tracks. Who was he kidding? He would never be brave enough to make a move on Wes. He couldn't even bring himself to talk to the guy. Jackson veered back to the trail rushing back to the house until Kale stopped directly in front of him, causing him to stumble and instinctively grab the dog's collar. What was that about? Jackson looked around and between the trees, near the water, he spotted what Kale had seen. There was Wes down by the creek, scrubbing himself, wearing only a thin layer of suds.

Rooted to the spot, Jackson watched Wes run his hands over his soapy body and bend to rinse the cloth in the bucket. As Wes lifted the bucket to dump it over himself, Jackson's fingers let go and Kale bounced forward to greet his friend. Jackson turned and ran back to the house.

****

Wes hurried towards the driveway with Kale stuck to his side like a burr. "Kale, no, go lie down. You can't catch the bus with me."

The door opened and Jackson poked his head out. "I wonder if you could check something for me."

Wes threw a glance at the driveway. "I'm running late."

"Can I drive you? That will buy you about forty five minutes, right?" Jackson wasn't making eye contact.

"Right," said Wes. "What do you need?"

"It's been getting kinda cold in here. I followed Isabelle's instructions, but I was hoping you'd check the furnace before I light the match, so I don't smoke myself out."

"Of course. But first I should apologize." Great, now Wes was the one scuffing his toe in the proverbial dirt.

Jackson's eyes widened. "You? What for? I was the one who ran off like a loser without even thanking you for dinner."

"I made you uncomfortable," said Wes. "I'm sorry it won't happen again." Did Jackson look disappointed? Even so, it didn't matter. No good would come from flirting with him.

Jackson backed into the house bumping into the doorframe. "It's uh, getting colder."

Wes stepped forward, trying to look honorable and safe as he walked to the front door. "Yeah, well, you'll need heat tonight for sure."

"True, my keyboarding fingers are getting stiff. Not that it matters." Jackson's voice held a hint of bitterness.

Wes followed him toward the basement. "'Not that it matters'? Did you finish already?"

Jackson scowled. "Well, I thought I was, but apparently my agent says they won't want it."

"I thought it was a done deal?"

"Me too. So now I'm obsessing about it, and I thought I would do something to take my mind off it, take a walk, light the furnace, drive you to town, get drunk."

Wes opened the furnace and looked inside. He turned back to Jackson. "Got Izzy's how-to book?"

Jackson handed it over and Wes flipped through the pages, found the instructions, and checked the damper. "Wow, this is way too much detail, no wonder you're confused. Uncle Jeff and I called this contraption Big Bertha, and you can see why. You've done great. All you need is a match." He gestured to the opening. "Go ahead, light the kindling."

The match caught right away. Jackson lit up too. That kind of joy was totally over the top for lighting a fire. Wes mentally thanked whatever power was responsible for him growing up on the land and not in a big city.

They headed back upstairs, Jackson grabbed his keys, and they walked together to the parking lot.

"Hey, you've got Sunny back," said Wes. "Was Kelly good to her?"

"Not sure," said Jackson. "He dropped her off yesterday and said she was purring like a kitten. But this will be our first trip." He opened the back door and Kale jumped in. "Kelly is kinda, I don't know, intense."

"It's true, Kelly lives in a world of his own. Did he offend you? He usually does that first thing."

"No, really, he was, well..." Jackson thought for a moment. "He played up my car having a name to the point I thought he was making fun of me, you know, saying he gave her a massage, and he kinda made it sound dirty. He may have offended Sunny but I'm good."

Wes shook his head and gave Jackson a wry smile. "Kelly and I go back a long way. His sense of humor gets him into trouble but he always had my back, so I learned to ignore it. He's a darn good mechanic though, so if you can put up with it, I'd keep his number."

"Point taken."

They got in the car and Sunny pointed her nose toward town. The conversation was mostly small talk at first, but when they were on the highway, Wes remembered what he wanted to ask. "You said your agent didn't want your novel, after all that work?"

"She doesn't like the changes I made." Jackson's tone was terse. "She gave me six days to fix it and send it back."

Wes wanted to wipe the look of pain and rejection off Jackson's face, but in a way that was inappropriate. He instead turned to watch the rock walls of Rabbit's Foot Canyon passing the car on their way down the hill. "After you drop me off, you can obsess or take a walk before you get back to writing."

Jackson's smile was lopsided. Silence stretched between them. He cleared his throat. "What's with the bath on the creek bank?" His eyes never left the road, but his ears got red.

"I didn't want to get soap in the creek. You step away from it so the earth can cleanse the water."

"You know that's not what I meant." Jackson's hands tightened on the steering wheel. "You could have had a real hot shower in a warm house, but you decided to freeze your nuts off."

"It was effing cold."

"The other night I said come over, use the shower."

"You weren't supposed to see me."

"Maybe you misunderstood me because I know I can be awkward, but I'm pretty sure I was clear when I told you, you won't bother me. The door is unlocked, you can come in any time, even late, after work. I won't know you're there."

Wes was impressed Jackson was facing the issue head on, even if he was being called out on his avoidance. The conversation was uncomfortable though. "I didn't misunderstand you. I was running late and didn't have time to stop and talk."

Jackson blushed right to the roots of his hair. Wes wanted to touch him to see if he was really as hot as he looked.

"I think you were avoiding me because I overreacted the other night," Jackson said. "I'm sorry too. Please use the shower. I promise not to be weird around you."

"Wow, you're not beating around the bush." Wes flashed him a grin. "Don't take it personally. I'm trying to avoid drama and work my life out, besides I thought I had to walk today. I was gonna be late for work." They parked in front of Wily's, he opened the door and grabbed his bag. "A couple of guys are coming by for drinks when I get off work tonight about ten. Wanna join us?"

Jackson swallowed nervously. "I'll think about it."

"It's just a casual thing, you'll have fun. You can't write all the time." Wes looked at the clock on the dashboard. "Now I really am late."

He slammed the car door and headed into the bar without looking back.

Chapter Nine

If Jackson was going to go to Wily Coyotes, he would need to get everything done before then. The decision to attend a social gathering, even a casual one, was looming large in his mind, but he tried to ignore it. Instead, he followed Wes's advice and took a leisurely walk in the almost winter weather. Things moved so fast here. One day, golden leaves were lighting up the landscape and the next, there was bare trees and snow. Jackson collected the late-day eggs and gave the chickens their dinner. By the time he was finished, he was relaxed enough to face Lorraine's comments on his book. Sitting down at the desk he opened the file and read the feedback with an open mind. Of course, Lorraine was right, she almost always was. His book was solid classic pre-Yukon writing except for the last few chapters. Jackson ignored the new draft, went back to basics, and tried to imagine how his old self would have finished it. Even though he was writing under duress, he fell back into the joy of it and love of his characters.

At one point he got up to avoid cramping his back and he noticed Kale's eager face. Dinner time. He put kibble in the bowl with a dollop of olive oil. Jackson wasn't sure what he was having yet, maybe a sandwich, but there wouldn't be any real treats for the dog's bowl. It didn't matter. Kale wasn't very discriminating with his treats. Olive oil suited him just fine and had the double benefit of being good for his coat.

As Jackson grabbed bread from the box to start his sandwich, an idea came to him. He ran back to the computer to get down the basics of it, promising himself he'd be back in a sec to compose that bit of bread into something edible.

Instead, it was dark when his stomach dragged him away from the manuscript. He rubbed a crick in his neck and checked his phone. Damn, it was almost nine p.m., and had he eaten a sandwich earlier? He wasn't sure.

Downstairs he found Kale snoozing peacefully on his mat, facing the door. He opened one eye, saw Jackson and closed it again. On the kitchen counter, Jackson found two stale slices of bread. So he hadn't eaten. That's why he was hungry. He added butter, mayo, and sliced meat. It wasn't the kind of dinner anyone would approve of, but it worked to take the edge off and had the benefit of tasting great. While he ate, he thought about having to meet up later with Wes and his friends. Jackson had tried not to think about it all evening because it took up way too much brain space and was a terrible idea. The pub was probably a noisy place, anyway. Bad for conversation. He simply wouldn't go.

That decision taken care of, Jackson relaxed and enjoyed his meal. After eating, he lay down on the couch with one of Isabelle's books about life in the early Yukon. He briefly considered lighting the fireplace, but Bertha was pumping out more than enough heat. Despite lying comfortably in a warm room, he found himself completely unable to concentrate on his book. Jackson's mind drifted back to the pub. Yes, it would be noisy, but then, all the noise would probably take the pressure off having to talk. Maybe he could have a beer and try to feel included? He remembered the warmth in Wes's eyes, looking at him like he was interesting. Maybe Jackson could stay for a short time and leave if it was too uncomfortable. Maybe offer Wes a ride home. Jackson had driven across the country to a strange city without knowing anyone. Tonight, at least he would know Wes.

Jackson darted upright, the book falling from his fingers. He would do it. Heart pounding, he dashed upstairs and hit his wardrobe. He tried on every shirt he owned, although nothing offered the right combination of relaxed and casual he was going for. The pants were easy. He only had one pair that hadn't been sacrificed to the chickens. Eventually, he grabbed a blue shirt from the top of the pile, put it on over his t-shirt, buttoned it down and tucked it into his pants. He stepped toward the mirror but changed his mind. Mirrors never made anything easier. He ran downstairs and grabbed his coat. Kale followed him out and curled up on the porch. Jackson headed for

Sunny. She sprang to life like a new car. He sent a flash of gratitude to Kelly for the new fuel pump and everything else that eight hundred bucks must have bought.

Jackson parked the car and walked down the block to Wily Coyote's. His hands were sweaty and his butterflies were going berserk. Even though it was late, the street was busy with people laughing and enjoying the evening. As he reached the door a couple of women pushed their way past him. They were giggling and made kissy lips at him, then stumbled away, roaring with beery laughter.

It was warm inside, and loud with voices raised over music but not too crowded. Wes stepped out from behind the bar. His work uniform consisted of a pair of well-fitted black jeans and a black t-shirt so tight it defined his chest, abs and arms, a little green apron tied around his waist. Then Wes noticed him. His smile lit the whole room.

Now Jackson understood his heroine on the pirate ship. He knew what she was fighting for. It wasn't just for the man she loved, she was fighting for the right to determine her own fate. Where was his pen? Standing at the door, he groped his pocket, sick with the realization that he didn't have his notebook. He'd have to remember for later rather than standing at the entrance like a goof.

Wes didn't seem to notice Jackson's hesitation and directed him to a round table where Kelly sat beside a tall guy with a neat beard and shaved head. "Nick, this is the guy I was telling you about, and Jackson, you remember Kelly?"

Both stood and shook Jackson's hand before sitting back down.

"Pull up a glass." Nick indicated the pitcher of beer on the table.

Maybe Wes had warned them about how awkward Jackson could be, or maybe Nick was good at reading people, but Jackson felt like they gave him space to settle. Wes came and went finishing up the last bit of his shift. Nick kept the conversation focused on catching everyone up but managed to still make Jackson feel included without pressure to be clever. Or maybe it was a first drink grace period because as soon as they poured round two, Nick turned on Jackson.

"So," said Nick, "you're the guy who kicked Wes's sorry ass out to the cabin."

Oh shit, first sentence and Jackson was stopped dead. He stared at Nick's bald head and wondered what he'd got himself into.

"Not kicked me out." Wes jumped in from behind Kelly. "He's the house sitter Aunt Iz brought in to load the furnace and feed the chickens. I only have to keep the Castle's old cook stove chugging when I'm there. Suits me fine." Wes put his hand on Jackson's shoulder and squeezed. "I'm ready to go cash out. You okay till I get back?"

Jackson could see the place was emptier than before and an older guy had taken over behind the bar. He took another sip of beer. "Sure."

Kelly leaned forward to top up Jackson's glass. "Yeah. I'll be good."

Wes looked at him for a long moment and was gone.

"Hey!" Kelly leapt to his feet, "Look who's here."

A guy in loose jeans with unruly hair and a beard arrived at the table.

"Jimmy." Kelly pounded his back like a long lost friend.

"Sorry I'm late guys," said Jimmy, "but I had to take Julie home."

Nick checked his phone. "Kinda early to wrap up a date isn't it? I always figured you single guys were party animals."

Jimmy reached for the pitcher. "Nah, she has a few hours of work left to do tonight and I have to be at work early. We don't party too late." He looked over at Jackson and extended his hand. "Jimmy. I'm the sane one in this group. They probably forget to tell you."

"Jackson." He reached over the table and they shook hands.

Jimmy's clasp was welcoming. "Great to meet you Jackson."

Wes arrived with another pitcher of beer and a bowl of popcorn. "This one's on me." He sat down between Kelly and Jackson. "Whew! I'd forgotten how hard it is to be on your feet all day."

Nick tapped Jackson's shoulder to get his attention. "You picked up our guy and brought him into town. Thanks for that. He must have looked pretty rough with that dilapidated backpack. Most wouldn't have stopped."

"I didn't exactly stop," said Jackson. "My car broke down. He took advantage of me."

Everyone laughed. Jackson was surprised but not embarrassed. They were laughing because he'd been funny, not because he'd made an idiot of himself. The beer had clearly done its work.

"I had to fix the car before I could do any advantage-taking." Wes topped up everyone's drinks.

Kelly examined Jackson gravely at Jackson over his beer. "I hear he had to clobber you on the head to get you to drive him, though."

Jackson relaxed back into his chair and took a deep breath. "He told you that?" Wes talked about him with his friends? It gave him a warm feeling and made the night seem much better than he'd anticipated. He wasn't sitting on the outside yearning to get in. He was a part of this group at this moment and it's possible he was even having fun.

"He tells me everything." Kelly then leaned towards Wes. "You seen Abby yet?"

"Not yet. I tried but missed her." Wes ran his hand through his hair. "Isabelle said she's still pissed as hell."

"Yeah. I bet you're right." Kelly lifted his glass. "I know she's your sister, but you were her one of her biggest supports, besides your aunt and uncle. She was kind of devastated by the way you ran out."

Always the wordsmith, Jackson idly wondered how someone could be kind of devastated, but he was more interested in Wes's reaction to the news.

"Sure." Wes took a sip of his drink. Tension rippled across his shoulders and his jaw clenched.

It was obvious to Jackson that Wes was trying to keep it light with Kelly with minimum success.

"You know she married Thomas what's-his-name from Marsh Lake, you remember, his parents were German and he had to wear those ridiculous leather shorts all summer, in public school."

"No, I don't." Wes was noncommittal.

Emboldened by liquid courage, Jackson decided to jump in and take the focus off Wes. "So, Nick, what do you do?" He cringed inside. It sounded so random, but Nick rolled with it.

"I'm a social worker. I work with at risk youth. How about you?"

"I'm a writer. It's in my genes, my Mom's an English professor." Jackson said it with all the confidence he wished he had.

"So, what do you write?" Kelly asked.

Jackson figured he could say the Bible and Kelly would nod and grunt. "I write historical fiction." He lifted his glass and took a long draw.

"When people say they read 'historical fiction' they usually mean romance novels," Kelly said.

Jackson gulped.

Kelly was on a roll. "Like, ewww ewww and fucking, with tons of misunderstandings drawing the poor suckers through hell for pages?"

Jackson hefted his beer and noticed the glass was empty. "You sound familiar with the genre."

Kelly choked on his beer. Wiped his face and said, "I prefer action/adventure novels."

"Action/adventure? Does it have a woman in it?" Jackson's pulse pounded in his ears.

"Yeah, sometimes."

"Do they kiss?" Jackson leaned in.

Kelly drew his brows together, "Yeah, sometimes. It's part of the action."

"Then it's romance. Do they have sex?"

"That's the adventure, man." Kelly laughed.

"Then it's a hot romance." Jackson hoped this line of banter wouldn't get him punched.

Nick watched with interest. "Wow, Kelly, romance. That totally explains your come-on lines."

Kelly sputtered and turned red.

Nick's phone buzzed. "Sorry guys, I'm gonna take this. Just a sec." His voice lowered and his eyes crinkled as he leaned into the phone. "Hey, babe. I'm on my way out soon. Leave the light on for me. I won't wake you up. Love you."

Kelly snorted and nudged Wes hard. "Look at that. The old ball and chain is calling him home."

Nick put the phone back in his pocket. "Like Jimmy said—" he winked at Jackson "—it's a work night, and just because all of you confirmed bachelors don't have a warm bed to go home to, you don't have to take it out on those of us who do." Nick reached for his glass and swallowed his last beer.

"Twu wuv," Kelly warbled. "The kind that lasts a lifetime." He burst into raucous laughter.

"On the day it happens to you," Nick said, "you'll beg for it and throw away the key and I'll have the last laugh." He pushed back from the table. "Nice to meet you, Jackson. You'll have to come over to the house and meet Sophie. She loves historical fiction."

Wes got up with him. The two friends gripped each other's shoulders for a moment. Jackson could see these two communicated without words. He had a moment of envy. What would it be like to be that close to someone? He couldn't think of anyone, including his sister, who knew him that well. Jackson made a mental note to put something like that in his book. It would be great for adding context and deepening emotional connections.

Nick leaned toward Jackson and spoke over the noise. "Get my number from Wes and call me. It's the best time of year to get to know the Yukon. We'll show you around." He left with a wave.

"He's whipped," Kelly announced as the door shut.

"Shut up, Kell." Jimmy's voice was soft.

Kelly was obnoxious. The things that came out of his mouth were far worse than anything accidentally offensive that Jackson might say. He wondered what Wes saw in Kelly and why they kept inviting him out. There had to be a story there. "How did you and Wes meet?"

Kelly leaned back in his chair, holding his beer. "Grade three." He took another sip and wiped his arm across his lips. "He was tiny and the bigger kids, which was all of them, kept pickin' him up and droppin' him in trash cans, locking him in the janitor closet or stealin' his lunch. He never made me feel stupid because of my big mouth so me 'n my brothers had his back."

Wes grinned. "You guys followed me everywhere."

Kelly nodded. "In high school, things changed. Our boy here learned how to fight. My brothers were gone. I seem to be able to say the wrong thing every time I open my mouth and was getting the crap kicked out of me. That's when Wes took me under his wing. Anyone who had a score to settle with me had to go through the three of us." His wave took in Jimmy, who nodded in agreement. "We still took a pounding every once in a while, but not often. I didn't even mind what other people said about us. We were brothers." He cast a side glance at the others around the table. "Well, it's true, and we still have each other's backs, don't we guys?"

"Yeah we do, Kell, but we're still waiting for you to wedge your foot out of your mouth. It could happen. Pass that pitcher over." Jimmy poured himself another. "Seriously, Wes, I couldn't believe it when Kelly called and said you were back in town. Fucking sight for sore eyes. We thought you were dead. You should have reached out." He was shredding a paper coaster and rolling it tight between his fingers. "It was fucking three years ago, when I was managing the kitchen reno in Nick's place that I figured out he knew you, and you were good." Jimmy gulped his drink not meeting anyone's eyes.

Wes twisted his fingers together, watching his hands. "It was a bad time."

Kelly swung his glance to Jimmy. "Shut up, Jimmy. We got him back now."

"Yeah! I'm just glad you're home." Jimmy reached across and punched Wes's shoulder.

The conversation around the table turned to old times. Jackson refilled his glass and took a sip, listening to the reminiscing. He'd been drinking fast, hoping to relax. Now quick movements blurred his vision. Moving slow and deliberate kept everything almost normal. He wasn't sure if it was the Yukon air, the full body rush he got around Wes, or maybe the beer, but something had shifted. He wasn't counting seconds till a polite moment to leave. Even without really knowing these guys, he felt accepted, like part of something. Jackson wondered if he'd have the nerve to call Nick later, but it didn't matter right now. Exhilaration coursed through him till his cheeks hurt from smiling.

Jackson watched Wes with his friends, guys who had been with him from the beginning. He wondered what it would be like to have people who knew his history and where he came from. He glanced at Kelly. Even someone born saying all the wrong things was safe with them.

Jimmy pushed back from the table. "Okay, I fold. I've got to get some sleep." He stared at Kelly. "And no pussy comments from you." He turned his gaze back to Wes. "Do you guys need a ride home?"

"Hell no," said Jackson. "I missed a whole night of writing to come and pick Wes up. I'm driving."

Kelly and Jimmy looked at Jackson and then at Wes.

"Well, look who's putting his foot in his mouth now." Kelly grinned. "I'm not sure how they do things in Ontario but here, if you walk out the door with that much Yukon Gold in your belly, a nice RCMP officer will relieve you of your car. Take the ride." He got up and put on his coat.

"If you are suggesting that I am drunk, you are seriously mistaken." Jackson enunciated each word carefully, looking at Wes for support.

Wes smiled. "I was working and took it easy. I'll get us home. Thanks." He hugged Jimmy. "Fuck man, it's good to see you guys again." He turned and pounded Kelly on the back. "In case you're wondering, calling Abby to say you had a couple with me tonight could be considered unforgivably inappropriate."

Kelly followed Jimmy to the door, miming zipped lips, then waved.

Wes dropped in his chair. "He can't help himself. He's probably already told her." He pushed a curl out of his face. "I'm glad 'cause although I tried to drop by her house the other day, I haven't had the balls to call yet. Phones make everything harder. I need to look her in the eyes when I say my piece." He sighed and drained his glass. "Time to take you home."

Jackson found his feet and tried to negotiate the arms

of his jacket, surprised at how far down the floor seemed. Steadying himself with a hand on the chair's back, he found his balance, then followed Wes out the door, extremely pleased with himself. He managed the whole evening without stepping in it too deep and he was leaving with Wes.

****

Wes tried very hard not to laugh at Jackson's wobbly yet confident walk to the driver's side of the car. When Jackson began fumbling in his pocket for the keys, Wes crowded against him, pressing close to his body. "Come on, hand them over."

"I can drive, you know." Jackson pushed back. "I told you, I'm not drunk."

Wes wrapped one arm around Jackson's waist and used the other to snatch the keys from his jacket pocket. "Probably, but why take that chance?"

"Because I came to pick you up and I'm a man of my word."

Wes took a deep breath, enjoying the mingled scent of a spicy aftershave and hops. "Point taken, but I've got the keys." He flipped them in the air and caught them deftly. "Get in!"

Jackson, muttering something about evil dictators, moving around to the passenger side.

"Come on, admit it, it's nice to have a chauffeur after a long night though. We could do this again," Wes said.

Jackson flopped back in his seat and waved his hand imperiously. "Make it so!"

Wes laughed. "Not drunk" Jackson was so appealing. There should be laws against being unavailable and that desirable. "I'll keep you in the drink-night loop. You can't hide in the cabin writing all the time." Wes eased Sunny out of the parking spot. He worked hard at watching the road and not Jackson's flushed face and sparkling eyes.

Light snow danced in the headlights. They turned into the driveway, throwing a beam on Kale who got up and shook himself. Wes shut off the engine and took

Jackson's hand, folding the key into his palm. "The keys to your precious."

Jackson leaned forward, his brown eyes wide.

The silence of the car was broken only by the pounding of Wes's heart. He had to get the hell out of there before he did something they'd both regret. Wes scrambled for the handle and pushed the door open while Jackson struggled with his seat belt. The path was clear. All Wes had to do was walk away.

Jackson finally stumbled out the other side of the car. "I don't usually drink. I guess I had a bit too much."

There was no way Wes would leave him to get inside on his own, not when Jackson could barely walk straight. "Hard to prove that by me," said Wes, walking over to him. "This is the second time I've seen you sloppy since we've met."

"If I remember, you were pretty sloppy yourself." Jackson haphazardly flung an arm around Wes's neck.

He braced Jackson and they stumbled up the steps. "Let's get you inside and get some water into you before bed. Don't want you hungover when you're writing tomorrow."

"I'll be fine."

"Sure." Wes opened the front door. Kale was at their heels trying to get his cold nose onto warm skin, almost tripping them.

Jackson laughed. "This whole thing is so weird."

"What do you mean?"

"It's just so strange being at home in a place where I've got to keep a fire burning. And Kale, he gets me." He almost fell trying to hug the dog, then laughed again as Wes readjusted his grip, helping him stand up.

Wes got Jackson onto the sofa. He had to walk away from that appealing bundle of confusion. "I'll check on Bertha." If anything was wrong, the house would be smoky, but Wes needed a second to build his resolve. Things were fine downstairs, as Wes suspected, and he returned to Jackson. "Okay," said Wes. "Everything is set, and the fans are all working. I dropped a couple of logs in and dampened it down."

"Thanks, but I could have done that."

"I know, but I wanted to check. You aren't going to burn the place down on my watch. Will you be okay getting upstairs?"

"I'm not drunk, you know."

"I know, a little muddled maybe. Don't stay up all night making calls to friends back home." Wes headed to the front door.

"Wes?"

He turned around.

Jackson was surprisingly steady as he advanced on him. "I liked your friends, they made me feel like part of the group."

"Yeah, good guys."

Jackson was close enough to touch. Wes clenched both fists at his side, his nails biting into his palms.

Jackson placed his hand on Wes's shoulder.

Wes cleared his throat, stepping back. Jackson didn't look confused or even drunk.

Jackson crowded him against the door. Their lips brushed together. Jackson's fingers tangled in his hair drawing him closer. Wes closed his eyes, letting it happen. Jackson's tongue tentatively slid across his lips.

Kale, eager to join the game, leapt up with a happy woof.

The sound brought Wes back to reality. He untangled Jackson's fingers and gently pushed him away. Jackson's eyes were wide, his breathing uneven. Wes grabbed Kale's collar, opened the front door and let him out on the porch.

"Oh, God." Jackson gasped and stumbled back. "I'm sorry."

Wes couldn't stand the pain in his eyes. "Stop it." His voice was rough. "Don't be sorry."

Jackson leaned in, burying his face against Wes's neck. "I am sorry. I screwed up again; I don't know how to do this."

"It's okay. You've had too much to drink. It doesn't have to mean anything."

"No, you don't understand. This is what I want. I want to touch you. I didn't know before. I want—"

Wes took Jackson's hands and held them tight in

front of him. "Jackson, listen to me. This isn't a good idea. Last week you couldn't even tell me you were gay. I'm not gonna take advantage of you when you're drunk." Wes turned Jackson around and nudged him toward the stairs.

Jackson deflated. "I don't know why—" his voice was muffled "—but I was so sure you wanted this too."

"That could be true, but I don't think it changes anything."

"So you're walking away?"

"If I don't, any principles I have will go out the window."

"What if I tell you I can't make it to bed on my own and I need help." Jackson looked at Wes from under his lashes.

"You're too much. Just take yourself to bed and stop torturing me."

"You want me."

"Yes."

"You've been drinking too."

"Yes."

Jackson lowered his voice. "Then let me take advantage of you." He stepped back into Wes's space, grasped his shoulders, and drew their mouths together. This kiss was firm. Wes opened to him, tasting beer and need, and wrapped his arms around Jackson's back, inserting his thigh between his legs. The door supported their weight as Wes leaned back and Jackson ground their hips together.

A dull ache bloomed in Wes's chest. He didn't deserve this but he wanted it. He sucked Jackson's bottom lip into his mouth savoring the moment then pulled back resting their foreheads together. "We can't do this. I'm not in for a relationship and you're a relationship waiting to happen."

"That's not fair, you don't know what I'm looking for." Jackson nuzzled his jaw.

"I don't do this anymore. No more drunken hookups for me. You don't understand how much I'll hurt you. I'm not some hero in one of your books."

Jackson scoffed. "Don't underestimate me, Wes. My

life is changing. I've spent my life inside a closet so deep my only light was the lamp post. I don't need Prince Charming, I just want to get laid."

Wes searched his face. He talked a good game but couldn't hide the vulnerability in his eyes. "You can't know what you're asking. I probably am underestimating you and for that I'm sorry, but you're not ready for what I want to do to you."

"It's simple, Wes, I'm asking for sex."

"Okay." Wes pushed his hand through his curls. "I'll make you a deal. You sober up and think about this. No sleepovers, no romance, only sex. If that's really what you want, you let me know."

He kissed him hard and hurried away from the warm house, certain Jackson would wake up with a hangover and would avoid him for the foreseeable future.

Wes lay awake for a long time watching the shadows cast by the flickering fire in the wood stove. He'd done the right thing. He was proud of himself for being clear and doing it. Jackson didn't know what he wanted, neither did Wes. Maybe if they'd met another time. He turned over yet again punching his pillow. So if this was the right thing, why did he feel like shit?

Eventually, the crackling of the fire and wind rattling the cabin eventually lulled Wes into a restless sleep. His dreams strangled him, and the sheets wrapped around his body. He dropped deeper into the clutches of the nightmare of flames and heat. A searing pain in his left hand brought him back and he woke with a yell.

It was too dark to see what had happened. By the flickers of the fire, Wes staggered to the door and flipped the light switch. His bed was a mess. A chair was knocked over and his hand was blistered, branded by the edge of the stove. Shit, no matter how bad the nightmares had been, sleepwalking had never been a part of them.

He gritted his teeth against the pain, quickly grabbed a bucket and flashlight, and raced to the creek. Dipping the pail into the icy water, he plunged his hand into it and staggered back indoors. In the light of the cabin, Wes could see a red welt across his palm. He pulled his hand out of the water and headed to the first aid kit. It wasn't easy to do one-handed, but he managed to rub the medicated burn salve on the welt and wrap it in a protective bandage. It looked good, and the stinging had now stopped. Thankfully, the stove hadn't been loaded for the winter cold otherwise the heat could have really hurt him.

There was no way he was going back to sleep. Maybe he could sit and meditate, get his emotions under control. No, Wes was too keyed up for that. He needed to actually do something. Carving often helped pass the dark hours. The bandaged hand shouldn't limit his movements too much. He took out his carving bundle and began to gingerly pull curls off of his block of wood. The face emerging regarded him with a calmness Wes wasn't feeling. He settled in waiting for daylight to come.

Chapter Ten

Jackson sat at the computer, staring at his manuscript. It was finished. He knew it and yet, he couldn't bring himself to hit send. It was stupid. Writing these novels was supposed to be the one thing in his life he was confident about. He would worry about it tomorrow. It was late and he was too tired to think clearly. His chores were done, and he knew he was merely looking for an excuse not to go to bed. Still, he would sit on the manuscript a little longer, just to be sure.

The door opened downstairs, and Kale's nails skittered across the floor as he greeted Wes. Jackson tried to decide if he would pretend to be working too hard to notice Wes's presence, or go downstairs and nonchalantly plant himself on the couch for a few minutes of chat before Wes headed back to the Castle.

Things had been different during the four days since the damn beer had caused him to throw himself at Wes. That kiss had been driving Jackson nuts, and he most definitely wanted more even though he had no idea how to get it. He'd been mulling it over and over, and dammit, how did you approach a guy and say, "I've thought about it and I still want you?"

Wes hadn't brought it up, although he had been not-so-secretly contributing to the wood pile outside the basement door. A token of his affection, perhaps? Right now, Wes was showering in the guest bathroom downstairs, as he did every day now.

The showers were turning out to be a special agony. Jackson kept imagining Wes naked and wet, and he couldn't do anything about it. He pictured Wes's hair darkening with the streaming water, curls straightening and plastering themselves to his head and down his shoulders. Sometimes Jackson even pictured himself assertively striding into the bathroom and offering Wes a hand in a deep confident voice.

Jackson shuddered, pulling himself out of his delusion.

Who was he kidding? It was late and time to move. Maybe warm milk would help him sleep.

Jackson went downstairs to the kitchen, stepping over Kale dozing at the bottom of the stairs. The kitchen was absolutely stifling. A warm drink was the last thing he needed. Jackson shrugged off his sweater and instead went to the living room to pick up a novel from the coffee table.

The sound of splashing water meant Wes was still under the spray, running the soap over his body. Jackson fanned himself with the book. Something must be wrong, it was way too warm. Should he check on Bertha? No, it was best to go to bed. Wes would let him know if something was wrong.

Jackson passed the bathroom on the way to the stairs. He stopped, resting his hand on the closed door. Wes was singing a tuneless song that was almost lost to the sound of the falling water. Jackson strained his hearing, trying to make out the song and judge how close Wes was to finishing. Then he darted back. What was he doing? Was he seriously hanging around, hoping to see Wes when he came out? What would that accomplish? What could Jackson say that wasn't awkward? It was pathetic and so wrong. He was turning into a stalker.

The water turned off. With his heart pounding in his chest, Jackson fled to the bedroom. He shut the door tight, locking in his fantasies so he wouldn't embarrass himself when Wes came out. He heard Wes leave the bathroom and speak to Kale before leaving. The house was deafeningly silent, and Jackson was left to toss and turn for the rest of the night.

****

After a surprisingly brutal lunch shift at work, Shannon, one of the more capable servers, dropped her green apron in the laundry bag. "What a day." She struggled into her winter coat. "Want a ride? You deserve it after that rush."

"Thanks, but I need the walk." Wes put on his coat and hat and searched the pockets for his mitts.

"You're a sucker for punishment. See you next time." She found her keys at the bottom of her pocket and headed down the street.

Wes inhaled the icy air and let the feathery flakes of dry snow settle on his face. Better than the ice pellets of late February. The wind was sharp as it chased itself down the street and over the river. He'd barely started on his walk and his legs were already burning with cold. When had full on winter jumped in?

Wes walked on auto pilot, having had far too little sleep recently. He spent most nights thinking about Jackson, thinking about that kiss, hoping Jackson would want more, and terrified Jackson would want more. At least it was better than having nightmares. He pressed his thumb to his healing burn, and he smiled. Jackson was such a, what? Naïve geek, courageous, terrified blend of emotional contradictions. One moment strong, the next soft, and the whole package was all wrapped up in delectable skin that betrayed his every thought.

Wes didn't deserve a guy like Jackson. Jackson had defied his whole past, moved to what amounted to a strange country, and made a real change in his life. All Wes was capable of was running. Sure, he was trying to slow down but—it wasn't worth thinking about. He wouldn't pursue anything but he couldn't help wishing, in the middle of the night, that Jackson would pursue him.

He found himself on the bridge to Riverdale. That was the way to his sister's house. Well, he sure wasn't doing that today. Wes frowned. Autopilot was failing him. He should be halfway up the hill by now. He was cold, and staring down at the rushing Yukon River did nothing to warm him. He was shivering now and glad Nick and Sophie's place was only a few blocks away.

Wes used the key they'd given him and walked in. He could hear the murmur of a TV somewhere in the house. Shedding his coat, he called out a greeting.

"We're downstairs," Nick called back.

He found the two of them curled up together on the couch, Nick resting his hand on her gently curved belly. A wave of longing washed over Wes. He adjusted his face into a smile. "Hey."

Sophie jumped up and folded him into a hug. "Wesley. We were sitting here thinking of how nice it would be to have a fireplace and some friends to share it."

Nick stood slapping Wes on the back. "Fifty percent of everything we wish for is better 'n average. What brings you to our door this stormy afternoon?"

"I had a crazy shift," said Wes. "I thought I was headed home but my feet had other ideas, so here I am."

Nick raised his eyebrows but said nothing.

"Would you like something to drink?" Sophie stood in front of the bar fridge.

"Just water today," said Wes.

Sophie filled a glass from the small sink. "Will you stay for dinner?"

"If you'll have me." Wes wondered what Jackson would be doing for dinner. Maybe they could eat together again, as friends.

Sophie handed Wes the glass. "I hope you two will excuse me. I must check on dinner."

Wes offered to help, but she insisted he stay and quickly disappeared up the steps.

Nick turned off the TV. "Okay, what's going on? You're always welcome, you know that. But we weren't expecting you, and it is very cold outside for a stroll all the way from downtown."

"Nothing." Wes dropped down on the couch. "Long shift is all."

"Don't hold out on me. I know you as well as anyone and you look like shit."

"Thanks." Wes glared at him. "You don't look so great yourself."

Nick stared him down.

"Fine," said Wes. "I've been having a bit of trouble sleeping. Same old, nothing to tell."

"What's this?" Nick grabbed his hand and turned it over displaying a fading red welt.

Wes pulled back. "Nothing. I got a little too close to the stove when I was making dinner the other night."

"Really?" Nick raised a skeptical eyebrow.

He couldn't fool his best friend. "It was a nightmare

a few days ago." Wes told him about his visit to the trapline to say goodbye to Uncle Jeff.

Nick listened and offered words of sympathy. "But that's not all that's on your mind, is it?"

Wes sighed. Nick was like a dog with a bone. "When you met Sophie... I mean, I know she's from Quebec, but you met her here. You never gave me any details."

"If you want details man, you ask her," said Nick. "She revels in it, fine tunes the story every time, and someday is going to get your friend to handcraft it into a bestselling romance novel."

"Okay, it's not important," said Wes. "It's just that I walked in here you looked, I don't know, in love. I wondered—forget it."

"Really there's not much to tell. I ran into her the first winter I was here at one of the Francophone Association events. I think it was a dinner or some kind of a meeting. Not even sure why I went except I didn't know a soul in town and I was lonesome, so there I was. I saw her across the room, and I knew I had to have her, like forever.

"What did she say when you told her?" asked Wes. He couldn't resist giving Nick a mischievous smirk. "Or did you grab her by the hair and drag her out of there?"

"Nope. I didn't even get to talk to her that night, but I found out her name. Turned out her roommate worked down the hall from me. She thought the whole thing was a hoot and gave me tips about what Soph was up to. I started showing up in places she would be."

"You stalked her?"

"Give me a break, man, I was smitten. In love. It's not stalking if you're in love."

"That, my friend, is exactly what stalking is."

Nick flipped a pillow at Wes. "Eventually she noticed me, and it was love at first sight. She connived, plotted, and set a trap for me. I threw myself on the damned thing. Neither of us had a chance. And now the baby." His eyes lit up and his smile softened. "You should ask her about it one day. It's much better the way she tells it. Why do you ask?"

"No reason. You're just so damned cute together."

Wes fiddled with the corner of the pillow. "Jackson is screwing with my brain. I'm so clear about why I'm here and he keeps blushing in front of me." He glanced at Nick, who was staring at him with his mouth open. "Shut your damn trap."

Nick didn't do anything of the sort. "So why are you here?"

"To be the best damn Uncle Wes your baby will ever have."

Nick narrowed his eyes. "Now the real reason, if you don't mind. The one you were telling yourself before you got here and we told you about the baby."

By the look on his friend's face, Wes knew he could either respond or take his chances out in the snow. "I haven't spoken to my sister in years," said Wes. "I need to make amends with her and Isabelle. I'm having a tough time getting together with Abby and everything about this place, down to the smell of the air, is bringing everything back."

They sat together and somehow Nick wriggled over so their shoulders were touching. "Okay, so for argument's sake, what if Jackson is part of your healing?"

Wes got up and looked down at him. "What are you saying? I'd break him. Remember Ben?"

Nick frowned and shook his head. "That guy had some serious addiction and mental health issues. What happened was not your fault."

Wes's lungs constricted. "I have some serious addiction and mental health issues. I don't want to be Jackson's Ben." His breath was coming in sharp bursts and he clenched his fists. "And what will he say when he finds out who I am, what I've done? What if I give in and he breaks me?" He started for the stairs.

Nick stood and grabbed him by the shoulders pulling him back into a rough hug immobilizing him from behind. "You're not Ben, you will never be him."

Wes gulped for air.

Nick's chin was on his shoulder. His low voice vibrated in his ear. "Take a deep breath, you've got this."

Wes slowed his breathing, letting Nick talk him down, remembering when Nick had been the only link between him and reality. His grounded calm had then taken Wes past the shakes and sweats, one minute at a time, and settled him down now too.

Nick turned him so Wes could see his face. "You keep telling me the Mother provides and there's no such thing as a coincidence, so let go. It's gonna come down the way it's supposed to, and you can't do a thing about it. Don't be afraid to have good things in your life."

Wes nodded.

"Then let's go eat."

Dinner was real French Canadian Tortiere with a big salad and, surprise, the house red. Sophie chatted about this and that, giving Wes time to pull himself together enough to enjoy the meal.

"We've been talking about having a few people over," said Sophie, "probably Kelly and Deidre—"

Nick interrupted with, "Isn't it Ashley this week?"

She glared at him and continued. "—Jimmy and Julie, and you. Would you bring Jackson?"

Wes glared at Nick across the lovely mish mash of dishes that didn't match but went together beautifully.

"Don't look at me like that!" Nick said. "You know I tell her everything, but I haven't had a chance to mention you locking lips with the reclusive writer."

Wes groaned as Sophie's eyes lit up.

"That's perfect." She waved her fork enthusiastically. "Jackson can be your date! Nicholas tells me he will autograph my books."

Wes put his fork down. "We're not dating."

"Then ask him as a friend." Sophie rolled her eyes.

Wes took a deep breath. "He's shy. He'll say no."

"Ask him."

"I don't think I should," said Wes, "it'll just confuse things."

"Give me his number then, I will ask him myself," said Sophie. "You can't keep him to yourself, Wesley."

Wes knew when he was beat. "I'll give you his number. If he wants to come, I'll bring him. And thanks, Soph. I'd love to come to your gathering."

"Bon," said Sophie. "Would you like some dessert?"

"I don't think so," said Wes. "I wonder if I could

bother you for a drive up the hill. I'm not feeling like walking right now."

****

Something had woken Jackson up, but what? The sky was dark and the only sound was Kale's tail slapping the floor. "What's up, Kale?" he muttered. It was probably nothing. Jackson turned over, ready to go back to sleep.

"Jackson?" Wes's voice floated through the dark and up the stairs, along with a sharp knock on the front door. "Hurry downstairs, I've got something you need to see."

"What time was it?" Jackson groggily flipped the bedside lamp on. One-fifteen. What the heck was he doing here so late? Was something wrong? Jackson quickly got out of bed and headed down the stairs to the open front door. "It's late."

"Grab a coat. It's cold out here. I couldn't sleep or I would have missed it. Come on!" Wes waited on the porch practically vibrating with excitement.

Wes's urgency was contagious. All thoughts of sleep fled. Jackson grabbed a coat and shoved his bare feet into his boots. He momentarily thought Wes might laugh at his childish comic book PJ pants, but it was dark out. Further, Wes was not looking at him as he quickly flipped all the lights out, plunging the porch into darkness. He grabbed Jackson's hand, pulling him urgently.

"Quick, it might not last very long." Wes's hand was cold as he led Jackson down the steps.

"Where are we going?"

Jackson tried not to trip. Kale didn't help, scrambling past them.

"Not far, it's a surprise."

As Jackson's eyes got used to the dark, he could see his breath and the shapes of the trees. Kale romped around their feet.

"Are we there yet?" Jackson's voice sounded loud in the quiet night.

"Look up."

The sky was awash with green. White and pink threaded through it. Everything above him throbbed, undulating with color. One minute he had to strain to see it, the next it was as bright as dawn. It was—

"Breathe," said Wes.

Jackson gasped. The sky was an endless ribbon of bright green, muted violet, and soft yellow, stretching wide between the mountains. He used to say he'd seen the Northern Lights in Ontario one time on a drive up north to a friend's cottage, but he had no idea it could be like this. His heart seemed to sync with the beat of the color. Jackson expanded and filled with light. He didn't know how long he was there and motionless, letting the colors wash over him, but the sky abruptly faded to dark, and he could feel the cold soaking into him.

He realized he was still holding Wes's hand and dropped it.

"Thank you," Jackson whispered, afraid his voice would break the spell. "This is more beautiful than I ever thought possible." He felt bold, brave, maybe like someone else was driving his body. Jackson turned toward Wes and pressed his icy lips to Wes's. Heat flooded Jackson's body with joy and embarrassment. He fled before he could ruin it. But at the bottom of the steps, Jackson stopped. He turned to find Wes touching his lips with a faint smile on his face. Jackson found the courage to ask, "Do you want to come in?"

"Not tonight, I've got the fire going and the lamps burning at the Castle."

"Okay. Good night." He climbed the steps with Kale and they watched Wes's shadow disappear down the path, with Jackson wishing he was brave enough to follow. "What do you think of that, Kale?"

Upstairs, he adjusted the quilt over the bed and crawled under the covers. Wes had given him a gift, one Jackson didn't quite understand. He wondered if he would ever sleep again knowing what could be going on in the sky above him.

Chapter Eleven

Jackson spent an enjoyable afternoon procrastinating in the Beringia Center, a place dedicated to the geographical formation of the Yukon. During the time of the Beringia Land Bridge and the ice ages, this had been a very different place. The center was filled with fascinating maps and massive amounts of information about the ancient history of the place in which he was living. Better yet, the Centre was set up to tweak the imagination and Jackson's muse was busy whispering about the possibilities of things he might write when he was done this project.

He stayed until four, closing time, and then drove home. Kale leapt up from the porch and dashed to the car, bouncing with excitement, when he arrived. Giving the big dog a hug, he enjoyed the warm, tail-wagging greeting. He couldn't believe how the sight of Kale's smile filled him with love. "Come on, Kale, let's go inside and get ourselves something to eat."

They'd entered the kitchen when Jackson's phone buzzed in his pocket. He didn't recognize the number, but it was local. "Hello?"

"Hi Jackson, it's Nick!" he yelled over the loud talking and laughter in the background.

"Hi Nick, I can hardly hear you."

"Sorry, I'm in the middle of work, I'll make it fast. Sophie is having the girls over tonight and I'm trying to get an impromptu Euchre game going. Just a second..." There was a muffled conversation and then Nick was back. "So, I'm assuming since you come from Ontario, you know how to play.

"I've played," said Jackson, wondering where this was going.

"Great, I'm looking for a fourth. You in?"

Jackson's stomach sank in a very familiar sensation, but he couldn't always say no to people's invitations. He was here and needed to say yes to new experiences, whether he was in the mood or not. And besides, this was Nick asking. "Sure, what time? Where are you playing?"

"Well, that's the other thing." There was more muffled background noise and Nick raised his voice. "Can you hear me?"

"Yes," said Jackson, raising his voice to match.

"We need a place. Can we come to you? We're all working guys. We won't keep you up late." Nick laughed.

"Ah, sure, but—"

"That's great, don't do anything. See you at seven. I'll bring everything. Gotta run."

Jackson disconnected, staring at the phone in his hand. What had he gone and done? Who was coming? Should he clean up? He glanced around the house. It wasn't too bad since he spent most of his time at the desk in the bedroom, and no one would be going up there. Nick said not to do anything. Jackson would have to trust him. He put together dinner for himself and Kale, then took his plate upstairs to his journal to collect his thoughts and ideas.

One good thing about his brain was, when it was engaged in an idea and he started scribbling, nothing else could occupy his mind. So, it was only when his alarm went off at six-fifty that Jackson surfaced and tried to remember if Nick had given him any details, like what time they'd all be leaving? And what should he wear? For Euchre at home, jeans and a tee would have been fine, especially if it was family, although if he was playing the fourth with his mom and her academic friends, it was a different matter. Probably tonight would be casual. Jackson should have asked, why hadn't he thought of that one stupid thing? He stepped up to the bathroom mirror and checked his hair. Hat head. Darn. He wet his hands and tried to calm down the sticking up bits. He was working up to a critical melt down when Kale nudged his leg.

Jackson laughed. "Thanks, boy. You're right, I'm overthinking things again." Kale woofed, and shortly after there was a knock. Jackson went downstairs and opened the door, only to have Kelly shove his way inside.

"Jackson!" A case of beer was thrust into his arms

and Kelly shed his outdoor stuff in a pile on the floor.

Jackson awkwardly held the beer. "What are you doing here?"

"Cards, man. We're playing Euchre. Nick said he called you and you know how to play. He taught me and Wes way back. We need a fourth."

"Wes is coming?" Jackson hadn't seen him since the northern lights. He thought they'd left things on good terms, but Wes's absence was making him wonder.

"Nick is tracking him down now." Kelly wandered into the kitchen.

Jackson hurried past him, deposited the beer in the fridge, and then cleaned up the packaging of his dinner.

"Big Guy freezer dinner? I love this shit." Kelly tapped the container Jackson was shuffling toward the garbage. "My Pop won't let me eat it, says it'll kill me."

"I'm not much of a cook."

There was a commotion at the door, and Kale ran to greet Wes and Nick.

"Hey, Jackson, thanks for inviting us," said Nick. "I've been craving a good card game and with Sophie entertaining the girls tonight there's no room at my place." Nick clapped him on the back on his way to the table.

Jackson caught Wes's eye, and knew he was blushing by the slow grin spreading over Wes's face. Jackson inhaled the cold pine scent that Wes carried in with him and wished he hadn't been given such telltale skin.

"Hey, Nick, do you need me to rustle up a deck?" Wes asked.

"Nope, brought my own." He extracted a small box from his pocket. "I've been waiting for a chance to use them. Zombie cards."

"Hah! You're such a loser." Kelly's voice was muffled in the cupboard he was digging through. Jackson glanced at Wes in alarm.

"Umm, Kells?" Wes went over and nudged Kelly's foot with his own. "What are you doing?"

"Popcorn maker, can't play without popcorn."

"Here, let me take care of it. You won't find a popcorn maker in this house. We make it the old fashioned way." He shoved Kelly out of the way and found a large pot. He added oil and grabbed the kernels from the freezer.

Nick was glaring at Kelly. "Come check out my cards, Jackson. I know you'll appreciate them."

Jackson sat by Nick and admired the gore on the face cards.

"I call Jackson's partner. Wait!" Wes looked back at him. "You do play Euchre right?"

"Of course," scoffed Jackson. "You are looking at the Williams family champion."

"Great, I call Jackson." Wes went back to shaking his pot on the stove.

The popcorn didn't take long to make. Wes put it on the table, each of them had a beer and the game was moving along. Clearly, they had more experience than Kelly implied. The cards felt familiar in his hands and the action was fast. He didn't have time to worry about saying or doing anything embarrassing.

"Kirk or Picard?" Nick dropped his card on the pile.

"Picard for sure. No question." Jackson threw his card on top and swept them to his corner tossing out a queen.

"How can you say that?" Wes jerked back as if he'd been shot. "In a fight, one on one, no weapons, Kirk would kick Picard's ass. He was a brawler."

"He was skeezy, and his moves—" Jackson paused putting a card down on the table, "—were predictable at best, in a fight or in the bedroom."

"Well." Kelly paused. "Obviously, I don't agree with you but, for the sake of fairness, I need to say that Kirk may have appeared to be a womanizer, but out of seventy-nine episodes, we only have seven possible instances of some kind of relationship and only four of those can count as confirmed." Jackson and Nick both looked at Kelly, eyes wide.

"What?" said Kelly. "I know there's more to life than women and fighting. I don't have to like it, but I am aware."

Laughter rolled around the table. "You're supposed to be on my side, Kell." Wes threw the wadded label he'd scraped off his bottle at him.

"I am on your side," said Kelly. "'Cept when you're wrong!"

"No way." Nick jumped in. "You know what Picard does for the first three seasons? He runs away. Trouble at Far Point? Runs away, first time he meets the Ferengi? He runs away!"

"That's because he's not a raging idiot!" Kelly glared at Nick and Wes. "Did you see how many Red Shirts Kirk got killed? If anyone dies, Picard doesn't count it as a win."

Jackson took the game again. "Our point." He grinned at Nick and Kelly. "Screw Star Trek, we're kicking your ass!"

Nick scowled at them. "You guys are signaling. No way you're that good with someone you've never played with before." His cards hit the table in frustration.

"Oh man, I forgot what a sore loser you are!" Wes laughed. "I was starting to think domestic bliss was making you boring."

"Boring? I'll show you boring." Nick reached for the bowl of popcorn.

Kelly snatched it out of his hands. "Reflexes of a fox." He pumped his fist and moved the popcorn to a safe distance.

Jackson watched the action in delight. This was great. These people were strong Euchre players and the table talk was, well, it was stuff he understood and could participate in. Jackson didn't even feel like he had to censor his words or feelings. It was almost like playing as a kid on Sunday nights in pajamas and house coats with Corie, Mom and Dad, when there were no expectations, and the game was just a game. But when Kelly and Nick were struggling over the popcorn bowl, things got out of hand. "Watch the drinks!" Jackson shouted over the hoopla, grabbing a beer before Nick knocked it over.

Everybody stopped staring at him.

"What?" said Jackson.

"That was loud." Kelly sat down cradling the popcorn.

"Real fucking loud." Wes winked.

"I didn't know you had it in you." Nick picked his cards off the floor.

Jackson rolled his eyes. "Well, I didn't know you were all gigantic nerds." He gathered the cards and began expertly shuffling them. "Captain Malcolm Reynolds or Colonel Jack O'Neill?" He was smiling right down to his toes.

The party broke up around eleven when Nick stood and stretched. "Some of us have to work in the morning. Jackson, my friend, you have to come visit. Sophie's dying to meet you."

"She sounds nice," said Jackson.

Kelly snorted. "That's one way to describe her." He twisted away from Nick's elbow. "What? You know I love Sophie."

"Come on, jackass, let's see if I can't get you home before you put your foot in it." Nick fist bumped Wes and dragged Kelly out to the car, leaving Wes and Jackson alone to tidy up.

Jackson usually found himself worn out by social interaction, eager to get some alone time afterwards to recharge. Tonight, though, he was elated and wide awake. They worked together tucking the empty beer bottles back in the box and washing dishes. When his hands weren't busy, Jackson was watching Wes.

Wes caught him looking and threw a grin his way. "I know it's a bit late, but do you mind if I have a shower before I head out? I work early tomorrow."

"Of course not."

"Thanks." Wes tucked the box of empties next to the blue bin and headed for the bathroom.

Jackson's good mood had given him an idea. "Wes?" Jackson called out, his heart pounding in his chest. This was it, no more hiding, he was going to tell Wes the truth.

Wes glanced back at him.

"Uh." Jackson chickened out. "You don't have to ask, you know, you're welcome anytime."

Did Wes look disappointed? "Okay," he said and disappeared into the bathroom.

"I'm so stupid." Jackson facepalmed. He heard the sink faucet start and his heart sank. How many chances would he let pass him by? He could picture himself ten years from now, writing in his London condo, having dinner at his mom's house three times a week, being berated for writing stories that would rot your brain. That vision was in black and white. Then he thought about vibrant, colorful Wes and kissing him under the northern lights. Jackson's life would never change unless he had the courage to do something about it.

The sound of the water changed from the sink to the shower. This was it. Jackson strode to the bathroom, faking confidence he didn't have, and knocked firmly on the door.

"Just a sec." Wes opened it. He had a towel slung around his trim waist. His chest muscles were firm and lightly defined, with a smattering of gold curls trailing down his sternum. "Jackson?"

"Can I join you?" He was afraid Wes would say no so he kept talking. "I can't help it, Wes. No strings just—" Jackson's voice broke.

Wes held the door wide and stepped back. Ushering Jackson into the steamy room, closing the door behind him. Then then he dropped his towel and stepped behind the curtain.

Jackson was transfixed by the sight of all of Wes's skin in front of him. He didn't think. He simply acted. Undressing he climbed in the tub.

Wes groaned and folded him in a steamy hug drawing him under the pounding water.

Jackson wrapped his arms around Wes's back, rubbing his aching groin against him.

"You're killing me," whispered Wes.

Jackson tangled his fingers through Wes's long wet hair, afraid he would pull back. He thrust his hard length against Wes's slippery cock.

"This is crazy," Wes murmured in his ear.

Jackson wasn't being sent away. He plastered himself against Wes's wet chest.

Wes grasped the bar of soap, sliding it over Jackson's aching body, making soothing noises in the back of his throat. "It's okay." He kissed Jackson's temple and continued to wash him, not missing a square inch of skin. He gently rolled Jackson's balls in his hand sliding his slippery fingers between his cheeks. He grasped Jackson's cock and lined it up with his own, pumping them once, twice, capturing Jackson's cries in his mouth, kissing him deeply.

Nothing in Jackson's life had prepared him for how his body could be hot and cold at the same time, his nerve endings on fire. He slid his hands up and down the muscles of Wes's back, not sure where to put them but not able to stop touching. Lightning started at the base of his spine and coming out his dick as he spilled over both of them not able to hold back. A few more strokes and Wes was coming too.

They supported each other's weight until the fog cleared and Jackson was steady on his feet again.

Wes touched his cheek. "You rinse off while I shampoo."

Jackson let the water run over him, waiting for the embarrassment and shyness to kick in, but they didn't. He moved, letting Wes rinse the shampoo off and when he was finished, Jackson flipped off the tap. Wes reached for him and kissed water droplets from his neck and his shoulders while the blood buzzed through Jackson's veins.

Out of the shower, Wes wrapped him in a towel and massaged him dry.

Jackson relaxed, enjoying the treatment, but he wanted to touch, to make this man his, if only for a moment. He turned to Wes, pulling him close, rubbing his chest, running his fingers over the warm damp skin, lingering on Wes's nipple. He leaned to taste, running his tongue over the hardening nub.

Wes hissed pulling back. "Wait, we should talk before we do that again."

Jackson raised his head, regaining Wes's lips.

Their hands ran over each other's bodies as they migrated, over the sleeping dog, up the stairs, and into the lamp-lit bedroom.

"We should talk," Wes repeated, sitting on the end of the bed.

"Do we have to?" Jackson's eyes were feasting over

Wes's body trying to take everything in at once.

"That was the deal."

Jackson face grew hot and hoped his blush wasn't visible in the dim light. "I did some thinking. I still want you. It wasn't the beer." He fought the urge to hide.

"Nothing's changed, Jackson. I'm not who you want me to be, I don't have anything to offer you."

Jackson sat beside Wes leaning in to trace his cheek. He wasn't going to be talked out of this. There was no way he could live this close to Wes without being able to touch. Not anymore. "This is all I want from you." He pressed his lips to Wes's.

"This is a mistake," Wes murmured into Jackson's mouth.

"Maybe," Jackson allowed, but he was getting hard again.

Wes pushed him back onto the bed, nibbling his lips.

Jackson opened. His body responded. He pulled Wes closer with his legs, wanting friction.

Wes swiped his tongue deep into Jackson's mouth and smoothed his hand down his flank. Their bodies mashed together, the sensation of skin on skin was making Jackson dizzy.

Wes kissed down his neck licking the hollow of his throat and then moving on to his nipples.

Jackson gasped and held Wes's head to his chest, goose bumps covering his skin despite the heat of the room. He loved the feel of Wes's mouth on him and laughed when Wes found his ticklish inner thigh.

And then Wes's mouth engulfed him.

Jackson's body thrashed, grasping for something to ground him.

Wes leaned back. "It's okay, relax."

"I can't," he panted. "I don't know what to do."

"Don't think, touch me." Wes returned to driving him crazy.

Jackson tried to move away, but Wes tightened his lips and kept moving. Jackson clenched his eyes shut and tried to hold back to enjoy the feelings for longer. His hips thrust as if he wasn't in control of his own body. There were fireworks behind his eyelids and he erupted in Wes's hot mouth.

The stars faded from his vision and he became aware of Wes resting his head on Jackson's thigh, stroking himself.

"Wait, let me do that."

"I've got it." Wes's voice was soft.

"I want to. Please?"

"Just touch me." Wes crawled up, drew Jackson's hand down to his straining erection. It was hot, slick with precum. Then Wes wrapped his arms around Jackson's torso, trembling into his neck. Jackson made a tight circle with his fist.

"Harder! Yes, like that." His mouth open, he was panting on Jackson's throat, and then he stiffened, "Jackson!"

Wet heat coated Jackson's hand. He continued to stroke until Wes hissed and pulling back. Jackson held Wes tight and was relieved when Wes raised a hand to his cheek and drew him in for a kiss.

Wes gave him a sleepy smile. "Lie down, I'm coming right back." Wes touched his lips to the tip of Jackson's nose and went into the bathroom, returning with a warm, damp cloth. A few soft strokes cleaned Jackson's hands and body, and he returned to the bathroom to clean himself. When Wes came back, he grabbed the blankets and covered them both up. Wes curled his long body around Jackson and snuggled into the warmth. "I can't stay. Don't let me fall asleep."

"Why not?" Jackson yawned.

"No sleepovers, remember. And I've got an early one tomorrow."

"Okay." Jackson reached over and turned off the lamp, pulling Wes's arms around him tight.

"I mean it, I can't stay."

"I know, maybe a few more minutes, this is nice."

Wes nodded into the back of his neck.

There was probably more to say but Jackson's body was heavy, and speaking was too much effort. He listened as Wes's breathing evened out and let himself drift off.

****

When Wes woke up, the clock said three-fifteen. Shit.

Jackson was wrapped around him and Wes didn't want to wake him. Besides, it was dark and who knew where his clothes were. The wind was moaning around the roof line and Wes didn't relish a naked dash to the cabin. It was as if the universe was telling him to stay. So he did.

Later, Wes surfaced again. The night was peaceful. His heartbeat had slowed to follow Jackson's breathing. He relaxed and shifted his arm to get the blood circulating again.

Jackson moaned and moved, his face now lifted to the starlight. Wes could see every contour. He brushed his lips over Jackson's brow and fell back to sleep.

The next time Wes woke, the clock showed six-fifteen. He couldn't lie there anymore. If he snuck out to go to work, Jackson would get the message that Wes was serious about the no-strings thing. But Jackson had found so much joy last night, and Wes couldn't bring himself to be the one to dim the light in his eyes. Wes kissed the side of Jackson's head. "Time to wake up."

"What time is it? It's dark, go away."

Wes nuzzled Jackson's neck. "It's early I need to get ready for work." He reached out and turned on the lamp.

"Agh!" Jackson squeezed his eyes shut. "I'm awake. Just turn it off."

"I'm opening at work, and I need to be there on time."

"It's early. Come back for another hour. I'll drive you." He shut his eyes and curled even closer to Wes.

Wes sighed. Jackson wasn't making this easy. "That's generous of you but, 'don't bother the writer, Wesley,' was a clear command from Aunt Izzy, remember?"

"I'm the writer. I need to procrastinate today. I'm putting off the inevitable. You're helping."

"You still haven't made up with your agent?"

"Not exactly. I'm doing what she wanted though, so maybe."

Wes rubbed Jackson's shoulder. "You're not much of a morning person, are you?"

"I'm sleeping. I can't talk about it."

"Could you at least pretend to be awake so I can talk to you before I go?"

"Shit. You're persistent." Jackson crawled higher up the bed and into Wes's arms.

"It's your own fault," said Wes. "You were supposed to kick me out last night."

"I'll drive you."

"I need the walk to clear my head. And Big Bertha needs feeding, it's cold in here this morning."

Jackson reddened. "Yeah, I forgot last night, I was— distracted."

"I'll stoke 'er on the way out, but I want to clear a couple of things up." He ran his hand down Jackson's arm. "Nothing's changed. I am not up for a relationship. I hurt people."

"I don't feel hurt except when you talk like this," said Jackson. "I want a say."

"No," said Wes. "I have things to do here, things to make right. Then I'm leaving."

"I've got things to do here too and then I'm leaving, so we're even."

Wes dropped his arms. "We're even? Are you listening to me?"

"I don't see the problem."

Wes rolled his eyes.

"Look, Wes, I don't know what bug crawled up your ass." Jackson raised his eyebrows. "But what do you say we leave it for now. You opened my eyes. Consider yourself my mentor. You teach me everything you know and when we're done, I'll write you a testimonial."

"Jackson, listen to me, you're laughing now, but I can't be who you want."

Jackson moved to the edge of the bed. "We've been thrown together for a reason. Maybe it's to make my books better." He got a dreamy look on his face.

"Oh my gawd, you're crazy. Are you going to write

me into one of your books?"

"Well, only if you help me with the research. We could start now." Jackson tried to tug the covers back over them.

Wes stretched his arms over his head. "I'm gonna sleep at the Castle tonight."

"Do you have to? I have so much to learn."

"Nope, we've done it all."

"No way. There's more."

"How would you know? You're just getting started."

"I can imagine it. I have a good imagination, you know."

"So I've heard. The answer is still no." Wes pushed himself off the bed and out the door before his determination could fail him.

Chapter Twelve

Jackson saved his document and closed his computer with an annoyed sigh. Although Lorraine had been happy when he'd put the old ending back, the book wasn't done. He was sick of struggling with the editors. There were weeks left in the process before *The Pirate's Revenge* could be put to bed. He was eager to be finished with this phase of his career and move on to more serious writing, although he'd miss his Lords and Ladies.

He hadn't seen Wes since their accidental sleepover, although Jackson found evidence he was using the shower when Jackson was out. Hopefully, it was a coincidence and Wes wasn't avoiding him. The house was too quiet. He poked at his phone looking for a playlist to cheer him up. The day of the week and time flashed on the screen. Sunday. The whole family would be home for dinner. He checked the time. He didn't want any more middle of the night surprises. No, it was only eight p.m. in London, perfect time to call.

"Hello, Edward." His mother's voice became muffled as she called out, "It's Eddie," to whoever else was there, and then returned to the phone. "Eddie, where are you?"

"Mom, I told you, I've changed my name. I'm Jackson now, not Eddie."

"What? No, you can't do that. Where are you?"

"I'm here, Whitehorse." Jackson was sure she was aware of exactly where he was. Why did she always have to dig at him?

"Oh, I thought maybe you were home."

"No, Mom, still here, but you can't say no every time I mention it. It's done. I'm Jackson now. I don't want to fight. I thought maybe I could say hi." He walked down the stairs to let Kale in.

"Okay, no fighting. What day is it?"

This felt like a trap. "Sunday?"

"It's true, it is Sunday but more than that, it's Thanksgiving. You should be with your family."

Wait, it was Thanksgiving? But that was in the second weekend of October, and the month had only just started—Jackson quickly checked the date on his phone. Oh no. There was that sinking feeling again, knowing he had disappointed her. Why did she have so much power over his feelings? "Thanksgiving, already? Do you have company?"

"I invited a couple of my students over, they've gone home already." She would do that if there was a student she was particularly proud of who was away from their family. Jackson was never sure if she was trying to rub his face in their success or if she was genuinely being kind. "The table was empty without you here."

"Sorry." He sat on the rocking chair in the living room, fondling Kale's ears while the dog leaned against his legs.

"What are you doing to celebrate?"

"Nothing. I kinda forgot about it."

"Jackson, for heaven's sake, its mid-October. You've moved away from home but you're still in Canada, not the US where it wouldn't happen for a month yet."

"I know that. I said I was sorry."

The next few minutes were spent assuring his mother that yes, he was eating enough, and no, she and his father absolutely did not need to fly all the way to the Yukon to bring him food, and yes, it was cold but he lived in a proper house with real heating, and no, he was not going to cut his foot off while chopping wood.

"Despite what you all think," said Jackson, "I actually am competent."

"Don't be so dramatic," said his mother. "Are you okay? You sound a bit testy."

"I guess I am a little homesick. I'm especially missing your pumpkin pie." It was true. If only he could keep his family in a box and pull them out when he was lonely or needed some extra fussing, but put them away to stand on his own two feet and build a life without their disappointment hanging over him like a dark cloud.

"Oh, sweetie, you could just come home."

"I could, but that's not what I need right now, and besides, Marie might be a little put out if I turn up before she's been in her new sublet for two months."

"Oh, I'm sure she'd take you back."

Jackson sighed. "Mom, pay attention. We never dated, she's a friend and besides, she's not my type. I'm sure there's no woman who would be."

"That's only because you haven't met the right girl. Speaking of Marie, I dropped by the apartment last week and she has a cat. Didn't you say no animals?"

Of course she changed the subject when Jackson even hinted he was gay. "I did, but when I found out Marie was back in town and looking for a place, I changed the rules. She was perfect and I knew her. I hated the idea of a stranger there. And besides, it's her place now, you can't go dropping in as if I still lived there."

"I don't know what happened, I was baking oatmeal raisin cookies the way you like them and suddenly I had four dozen cookies that had to go somewhere. I put them in a tin and took them over. I know it was silly, but she seemed to appreciate them."

"I miss you too, Mom." Jackson couldn't help softening his voice. Despite everything, his mother did genuinely care. "Thanks for the cookies."

"You didn't get them."

"No, but it's the thought that counts. I have to go. Can I quickly talk to Dad?"

"You're so far away, if you got into trouble I would never know."

"I have a couple of friends I'll give your number to. That way if there's an emergency, someone will call you."

"Emergency? What emergency?"

Jackson rubbed his temple. "There's no emergency, Mom. It's just like home here. Really, I'm fine."

"Are you getting out or are you locked in with your books?"

"I am getting lots of writing done but I've met some nice people and I'm having fun. I'm not sure how to say this but I feel like I belong here."

"Eddie, you belong here with your family."

"It's Jackson."

"We'll see about that."

No, he wasn't falling into another trap. "Mom, I'm not explaining myself well. I mean I feel like I'm part of something here. I have friends."

"I'm glad you're happy but don't get too comfortable. I'm expecting you home in the spring, early spring, and you need to call more often."

"The phone goes both ways, Mom. Is Dad around?"

She sighed. "Take care of yourself, eat, and stay warm."

Footsteps sounded down the line. Jackson could hear her walking with the phone and almost see the path from the kitchen to his father's book lined study.

There was a rustling sound and his father took the phone. "Hello, Son."

"Hi, Dad."

"How's life treating you?"

"Very well."

"Are you okay? Is there anything you need from us?"

"No, I'm good."

"Maybe you could call more often, your mother is worried." A man of few words, he was quietly encouraging and understanding but always supported his wife. "Don't upset your mother" was a common theme in his conversations. Jackson sometimes wished his Dad would stand up for him.

They spoke for a few more minutes. Or rather, Jackson told him about his life in the Yukon, and his father murmured noncommittal answers in response. After they said their goodbyes, Jackson's throat was tight.

The quiet in the house was deeper than it had been before the call. Jackson loved his mom's holiday meals. He could almost taste the turkey with his dad's bacon and sausage stuffing, and of course there would have been pumpkin pie. This was the first time he'd ever missed a family holiday.

The computer waiting for him upstairs with plenty of new edits for him to do, but Jackson couldn't face that right now. Fresh air would help. He grabbed his coat and mitts. Kale would be happy to take a walk.

Meandering through the many trails on the property,

Kale's antics in the snow made Jackson laugh, easing the emptiness inside. When they returned home, Jackson was surprised to find they'd been out for over an hour. Kale flopped down in the living room and Jackson resigned himself to a microwave dinner on Thanksgiving. In the meantime, Netflix would keep him company.

When the sun started its descent just after six-thirty, Jackson headed for the chicken coop to check on the girls. On his way back, he saw Wes coming out of the woods with something dangling from his belt and waved to him.

Wes walked up to meet him. "I saw footprints in the snow. You were out for a walk today."

"Yeah, I love the feeling of all the space."

"It's feeling like no other." Wes agreed, walking with him toward the house. He dropped two dead rabbits on the porch.

Jackson stepped back, staring at the carcasses.

Wes didn't seem to notice his discomfort. "I should be showing you around. I don't want you getting lost or hurt out there."

"Kale keeps me in line. Darn dog is uncanny." Jackson's eyes remained on the still bodies.

"Don't walk without him, okay?"

Jackson couldn't keep the annoyance out of his voice. "I notice it doesn't bother you to walk alone." Why did everyone think they could tell him what to do?

"I know these woods like the back of my hand," said Wes. "They haven't changed much since I've been gone. What are you doing for dinner?"

"I was planning to nuke something."

"Well, let me cook for you tonight. I've been shopping in the Mother's store." He nodded to the carcasses.

Jackson didn't cringe and kept his voice steady. "If you know how to unwrap it and cook it, I am pretty sure I can figure out how to eat it."

"Great. There's a butcher block out back. I'll take care of the 'unwrapping,' and come in the back door. Can you toss me out a big bowl?"

"Sure." Jackson turned and headed in with Kale at his heels. After delivering the bowl, he went back inside and washed his dishes from the past few days. He didn't want Wes to see what a slob he could be.

Wes brought the cold smells of winter and blood inside with him. He headed to the sink and washed his hands and a wicked looking knife. He then rinsed the pieces of meat that resembled chicken legs and breast quarters. Kale appeared with a look of intense interest on his face.

Wes found flour, spices and a big pot. Then he opened the fridge. "Three limp carrots and a half a head of elderly cabbage? This looks old enough to be Isabelle's." He shook his head mournfully. "Can you go to the Castle and grab the bag of veg from the cooler?" He returned to the counter and started dredging the pieces of meat in a flour mix.

Jackson grabbed his coat and the flashlight. "Come on Kale."

The dog stood, torn between the kitchen and going out.

"You're here to protect me, not supper," said Jackson, and they stepped outside. Every night it was dark earlier, but it was crisp and beautiful. Snow crunched underfoot and stars glittered above. The path to the cabin was well worn and they were there in no time. Jackson grabbed a fabric bag filled with vegetables from the cooler and followed Kale back to the welcoming warmth of the kitchen.

Wes gave him a bright smile as he took the bag. "Thanks." He chopped up a storm, throwing everything into the pot as it came off the end of his knife.

"No problem," said Jackson. "Can I help?"

"Naw, I was going to make a salad but there is nothing worth putting in a bowl. I'll just super vegetate the stew. Keep me company."

"Okay."

The thump of the knife was the only sound in the room.

"So." Jackson found he had no idea what to say.

Wes tossed a look over his shoulder and grinned as if reading Jackson's mind. "Why don't you tell me how you got into historical romances rather than, say, sci-fi or fantasy?"

"I did try a romantic fantasy once, but it flopped."

Wes stirred the pot, put the lid on and turned, leaning against the counter to face him. "So why romance?"

Whenever anyone asked this question, Jackson would mumble something about strong sales and change the subject. Or he'd leave. But he wanted Wes to know the truth. "In school, I was the freak who would rather read than talk. I was scared of the boys and didn't understand the girls. The school library was my haven. I ran out of stuff to read, and I found a secret stash of Mom's historical romances when I was combing the house. I was about twelve when I started sneaking them out of her closet. I slipped them behind the covers of more 'suitable' choices."

"Twelve?"

"Yup, I was embarrassed but totally hooked. It was another world where everything worked out in the end and no one was alone." He coughed. "Anyway, Corie, that's my sister, found me out and held the whole thing over my head. Said she would tell. She was such a little shit." Jackson laughed. "So, I gave them up. I started to compose them, first in my head and then on paper. It was almost as much fun as reading them. One day, Corie found a manuscript." He trailed off, the sick feeling of being caught still fresh, after all these years. "She held it hostage. I pretended it didn't mean anything. She said she threw it out, but she gave it to Lorraine, a woman from our church who was a literary agent specializing in women's fiction. She actually read it and helped me get my first publishing deal. It was way more work than I thought it would be. My mother was and still is horrified, but these days, if I write constantly, I earn enough to support myself." Jackson started setting the table to have something to do with his hands.

Wes turned from the stove and gave him a broad smile. "That's pretty impressive."

"Ask my parents."

The smile vanished from Wes's face. "Ah, parent's opinions rarely matter when they're trying to live through you."

Jackson stopped and regarded him. There was definitely

a story there. "Yah, I guess. What makes you say that?"

Wes snorted. "I had parents. Not for long, but I had them." He turned back to the stove.

Jackson wanted to ask more questions, but the way Wes's face shuttered made him change the subject. "Kelly left some beer the other night, want one?"

"The stew might benefit from a small addition." Wes poured half of a beer into the bubbling liquid and passed the rest to Jackson. Then he got to work on a bowl full of flour and other ingredients he'd tossed in. Pouring water into it, he started flipping the powder with a fork until a clump formed. "When did you think you'd feed old hungry guts there?"

Jackson checked Kale who was sitting hopefully by the table with a long string of drool hanging from the corner of his mouth. "Ew! Can't you ask like other people?" He jumped up and grabbed the dish off the floor, filling it with kibble. "Have you got a spoonful for him? He won't eat it if I don't stir something in."

"I figure the poor sucker has had pretty lean pickings if he is hoping for handouts from your pot." Wes slopped in a spoonful.

Kale ate enthusiastically.

Watching Wes push the dough into round shapes, kneading, caressing, and patting, forming small balls, a sudden flush of heat hit Jackson's body. Looking away, he put his elbows on his knees to cover his growing erection. God, he had it bad.

Wes placed each ball of dough onto a cookie sheet, leaning each against its neighbor. He slid the pan into the oven then looked at the stew. "This is ready. The biscuits will be done in ten minutes."

Jackson and Wes washed up together and wiped down the counter. While Jackson scooped generous bowls of steaming stew, Wes opened the oven and pulled out twelve, golden-brown mini loafs.

"Wow, my mother is a baker and never made anything so pretty," said Jackson. He carried the bowls to the table.

"I financed my misspent youth in restaurants," said Wes, "but this one's totally home grown. It's a recipe we like to call 'Depression Tea Biscuits', passed down from Aunt Isabelle's grandmother. That woman was a force of nature." Wes followed him with the tray of biscuits. "I tend to prefer serving, it's more social, but you do what you gotta do."

They sat down to eat. Jackson scooped a spoon and blew on it, putting it into his mouth. "It's good."

"What did you expect? You aren't so bothersome that I'm ready to poison you." Wes laughed.

A beat later, Jackson, realizing the joke was on him, relaxed and laughed too. "I mean, I guess all my food has come from the grocery store. It never occurred to me there was food in them there hills. Are you allowed to just take it?"

"Up here, this is how we shop local. Hunting is managed. Not everyone agrees or does it, but it's been a way of life for the First Nations long before we ever showed up. They teach respect for the land and its offerings. The land offers. I accept what is given with gratitude and only take what I'll use."

"That's pretty great." All this was new to Jackson and he filed away the information for possible use in a future book. "I don't want you to think I don't appreciate this. It's probably the best meal I've had since you cooked that stir fry."

Wes's face lit up. "I'm glad you liked it. I know things are very different in the south maybe, but for people up here, it's more than food. If you're gonna live here, you gotta figure it out. I don't think anyone will ask you to hunt unless it's a calling you have, but at many tables you will get to appreciate game, big and small. I'm glad I was able to introduce you to it and impress you with my cooking."

Jackson colored and felt as bold as one of his characters when he replied, "I'm totally dazzled by everything about you."

Wes stopped and then responded, "Don't get carried away. Apparently, you are easily blown away, at least with cooking. I bet I could do that with a hunk of tofu."

"Ew. I doubt that."

"Challenge accepted. Next time, tofu, wild. Maybe

I'll bow hunt it."

Jackson laughed, enjoying the warmth and camaraderie he got from Wes's teasing. It was something he'd hated in school, and yet this was friendly and easy. Hearing Wes making gentle fun of him made him think of the way he and Corie carried on, not wanting to hurt each other but to show feelings that couldn't always be expressed any other way. Somehow it made him feel safe.

Wes showed his dimples. "Just wait until I teach you to skin a block of wild tofu."

"Okay, if you go to all the trouble to track it down and are willing to stand by me when I learn how to use that knife, I'll do my best."

Wes leaned back in his chair. "My uncle showed me how to hunt."

Jackson stopped in the middle of wiping up the last of his stew with a biscuit. Something in Wes's voice had changed.

"He showed me a lot of things. One of my biggest regrets is I wasn't here when Uncle Jeff died."

Now Jackson recognized the change. It was pain. He kept quiet and let Wes speak.

"It was unexpected," said Wes. "He wasn't sick. He went down to stoke Big Bertha and didn't come back upstairs. Aunt Izzy found him. The doctors figure a massive heart attack. I never got to say goodbye or thanks or anything."

"I'm so sorry," Jackson said softly. It was a privilege to have Wes open up to him and he didn't want to screw up. "I can't imagine that."

"Nick heard about it, months later and let me know when it happened. I probably should have called Auntie Izzie, but it was too much to imagine talking her after so long about that, so I chickened out. It's still a shock to be here without him." Wes closed his eyes.

Jackson gave Wes his space. He quickly ate the biscuit, because it was far too good to waste, and began clearing the table.

Wes opened his eyes. "I'm not ready to go back to the Castle."

"Do you want some more stew?" Jackson asked.

"There's plenty left."

"Nah, I'm full. I noticed there are still some old games around. Wanna give me a chance to whoop your ass at checkers?"

They took turns winning and Wes sounded happy again. But the later it got, the harder it was for Jackson to concentrate. He wanted to ask Wes to touch him again, but wasn't sure how to do it in a way that wouldn't make him look like a fool. It should be easier now that they'd done it once already. Maybe Wes would make a move?

At nine, Wes got up. "I've got work tomorrow. Want me to let Kale out for you?"

This was it. Jackson knew he had to do something or miss his chance. "Wait." Jackson stood. "Can I kiss you?"

Wes licked his lower lip and nodded.

Not sure what was going on in Wes's head, he approached slowly, twined his arms around Wes's neck and moved their lips close. Then he hesitated.

Wes pulled against him and cupped his neck, claiming his mouth, completing the kiss.

Jackson moved closer, feeling emboldened. Still kissing he backed them into the shadows of the living room. Gently he pushed Wes onto the couch, straddling him. Jackson's lips landed on the tender skin at the crook of Wes's neck, and he sighed at finally getting what he wanted. His heart slammed in his chest, his body thrummed.

Wes dragged his lips across Jackson's jaw toward his ear.

Jackson drew back resting his forehead against Wes's. "There's something I want to try." He got up and urged Wes to lie across the cushions. Cupping the bulge in Wes's tight jeans, he rubbed the rough fabric.

Wes flexed his hips.

Jackson felt a rush of power. He was in control.

Wes helped him fumble the fly and shove his pants down, dropping them in a pile. His cock lay hard against his stomach. The dim light from the kitchen made it diffi-cult to see, but tonight was about feeling. In one hand he cupped Wes's balls. He dropped to his knees, bending down, inhaling the warm musky scent. He ran his thumb over the tip, smearing precum and bringing it to his mouth. The tangy flavor burst on his tongue. Jackson licked the head. Wes's indrawn breath emboldened him, and he took as much as he could into his mouth. Remembering how good it felt thrusting into Wes's mouth, he went farther and choked.

"Use your hand." Wes's voice was tight. "Feels so good."

Licking and sucking, he pulled Wes in until his lips met his fist. The smell, the feel of the soft skin on his lips and tongue were making him hard. Maybe he could swallow Wes down, steal a piece for himself. He fingered the sensitive skin behind Wes's balls, then stopped. "All right?"

"Oh God, Jackson, don't lose confidence now!"

Wes was his. Jackson licked his lips and slid his mouth back over his beautiful cock, hoping he wouldn't blow before Wes could get another crack at him.

"Jacks." Wes gave a warning growl.

Jackson swallowed him deeper. Wes erupted in his mouth. Jackson let it slide down his throat and spill out his mouth. He moved up Wes's body, wiping his chin on Wes's T-shirt, and eased himself in for a kiss. "Good?"

"Mmm." Wes opened his eyes. "Do you feel a little overdressed?"

Jackson scrambled to get his clothes off.

Wes sat up watching him with a smile. Tugging his own shirt off, he added it to the pile, opening his arms to welcome Jackson back onto his lap. Wes let his hands drift down Jackson's back to cup his butt, pulling him close. "Are you ok with this?"

Jackson rubbed, pushing himself closer, almost into Wes. Still, he squawked in surprise as Wes pressed a fingertip over his tight hole.

"Still okay?" Wes sounded breathless.

Jackson could hardly answer. He hoped his erection, pushing hard between them was reply enough.

Wes's other hand began stroking. Jackson groaned, arching, pushing hard onto the questing finger. His muscles spasmed and Jackson came over them.

Slowly regaining awareness, Jackson could feel his cum sticking them together. He was sure he was crushing Wes but wasn't quite ready to lose the feeling of connection. Reaching his shirt from the floor, Jackson mopped them up and drew Wes down on the couch, putting his head on Wes's shoulder. It was a tight fit, but Wes held him and covered them with the crocheted blanket from the back of the couch.

Jackson found himself tracing abstract pictures on Wes's chest. "I can't get something Kelly said the other night out of my mind."

"What was that?" Wes trapped Jackson's hand with his own.

"He said you guys were such good friends and protected each other so well in school that he didn't mind being thought of as gay. That sounds rough."

Wes's body tensed. "Whitehorse is a pretty small town. I know it's gotten better and there is a larger more open queer community now, but it was never about me. Kids carry their parents' prejudices and a lot of them were just assholes. It was bad, but that was a long time ago. I'm sure it made me stronger, and other than hating bullying of any kind, I don't think it affects me much anymore."

Jackson relaxed, enjoying the feel of Wes's bare skin against his. "It wasn't bad for me because I was gay. I was so introverted that I had no friends. It sounds like you kinda had fun."

Wes choked back a laugh. "Maybe not fun but it sure was great with those guys having my back. It's so good to reconnect with them."

"When it got bad for me, I hid in books or writing."

"Disappearing never felt like an option. First, they hassled me because I was small and then because I was queer. Having Kelly and Jimmy standing with me kept me sane." Wes squeezed Jackson's fingers.

"What was it like being out? Only one guy actually knew about me, and I didn't handle it well."

"I probably wasn't bothered as much as some kids. What I went through at home led me down a darker path. But even that got better, great even because of solid friends. Let's not go there right now."

Jackson could feel him getting ready to move, and knew he had to share something or Wes would blow out of here and maybe not come back. "When I was in grade ten, a guy asked me to cheat for him and I did." He was glad he couldn't see Wes's face as the shame curled through him.

"It must have felt really important to do something so against your nature?"

Tears welled but Jackson held them back. This was the first time he talked about this willingly. He'd had to tell his family and his mom had told the therapist she forced him to see. "Perry was a football player on the junior team. One day, I let my spell of invisibility go for one short second and saw Perry coming down the hall toward me. I couldn't think of anything else for that whole year. I even went to a football game, loaded onto a crowded school bus, and endured the horrors of 'school spirit,' just to watch him run down the field in those tight pants."

Wes stroked Jackson's back and gave him space to speak.

"Somehow, I got sucked into the excitement and I asked a stupid question about football. The whole bus laughed. For the rest of the day, I was the joke. I wanted to die."

Wes's voice was soft in the dark. "That sucks."

"Well, it wasn't a total washout because Perry noticed me, even came over to talk to me. He teased me too, but he noticed me and that's when life got really interesting."

Wes held him closer. "Sometimes it's better not to remember those things."

"Easier said than done," Jackson said with a bitter laugh. "He remembered me when he was failing grade ten Physics. They were going to drop him from the team if he didn't pull up his marks, so he asked me to help him. I thought he was asking to be my study partner. What he meant was, I should do it for him. It made me sick, but I didn't know how to get out of it, and honestly, I kind of liked the attention. I thought he might even kiss me one day. I really thought he liked me." Reliving it brought back all Jackson's humiliation and shame. He'd been so desperate. "When I finally grew a brain and told him I wouldn't, he grabbed me, threw me into my locker and threatened to tell everyone I was perving on him. I was relieved when he passed his exams and didn't need me anymore. I allowed him to torment me and hold me hostage for a year and a half before I confessed to my parents. When it was over, I never wanted to come out of the library again." Jackson listened to Wes's heartbeat in the dark, getting his thoughts together. "I decided it was more about being a socially awkward introvert than being gay, but then hearing Kelly's story brought it back."

"Did you like girls? Maybe you're bi."

"I didn't think about it. I couldn't face being gay, but I couldn't quite bring myself to be straight. I was terrified of both. I stayed out of everyone's way. Whenever I got brave and went out with one of the poor girls my mom forced me to date, I was a perfect gentleman. Once in university, my roommate Marie and I had too much to drink and decided to lose our virginity to each other, but it seemed so ridiculous that we stopped. It wasn't what my books said it should be."

"But that's the fantasy, right? Sex isn't supposed to be like in the books. I've had a lot that wouldn't rate any kind of a story." Wes sounded sad.

"Really? I mean, I think we found out that it is like the books. That it can be, at least. Or is that just me?"

Wes sighed. "No, it's not just you. But that doesn't change anything."

Jackson didn't want to hear more about why this had to be casual, so he went for a lighthearted tone. "Yeah, but I can see now chemistry is real, and that sex isn't tab P inserted in slot V. It's probably the only reason the human race keeps going."

Wes laughed. "Really? Your mind works in the weirdest ways."

"Honestly, if the human race depended on me to procreate, feeling the way I did about the whole thing, it would have died out eons ago."

Wes tickled Jackson's ribs lightly. "Well, if you

intend to keep the human race going, you better stop looking at me."

Jackson laughed and rolled off the couch and out of the range of those feathery fingers. "I am tempted to show you some of my pillow fight moves, but it's late, we should get some sleep." He scooped his clothes off the floor, trying not to look too self-conscious about being naked.

Wes got back into his clothes then hugged Jackson and nuzzled his neck with a chain of soft kisses. "I need to head out. Thank you I had a really good time tonight."

"It'll be freezing in the Castle. You don't have to go."

Wes's smile didn't reach his eyes. "Yes, I do."

Jackson's heart stuttered. He tried not to show his disappointment. "Are you working much over the next few days? I can stop at the store and get some 'real' food so I can invite you over to dinner without embarrassing myself. You have to cook though, or we'll eat frozen pizzas."

"As friends, right?"

Jackson forced a smile, "How about friends with benefits?"

Wes chuckled, kissed him and walked out the door.

Chapter Thirteen

The sun was pinking the horizon when Jackson pushed his way into the chicken coop. The light in the coop was on a timer so the hens would get twelve hours of daylight. They were having their breakfast and chatting companionably. He was getting used to the longer nights but couldn't imagine what it would be like when the sun rose long after he did.

Jackson checked the water tubes, made sure they weren't plugged or frozen, and wiped them clean. He marveled at how simple, even tedious, these chores had become. The chickens were happier with him now that they knew him. They didn't jump up and greet him the way Kale did, but they didn't freak out flapping around the room when he came in anymore either. Rather they continued their soft conversations around him. It sounded like contented purring, music to his ears. Being with them now was easy.

Last night, he had tossed and turned into the morning. Thinking about every detail of the evening before was torture. Had he said too much? Was Wes humoring him?

Jackson returned indoors to have his breakfast. He slowly washed the dishes, his attention outside the window over the sink. It would be tempting to procrastinate all day, following Kale on his daily rounds of the property, but he soon enough found himself at his computer. He quickly reviewed the manuscript and sent what he hoped would be his final version of the book to Lorraine. It was time to think about his next project.

Jackson had been seriously considering setting his next book in the Yukon. More than that, he wanted to write something literary, something respectable. He sifted through all the information he'd accumulated during his time here so far. One folder contained everything he'd collected from the Beringia Centre the other day. Another was filled with notes and photocopies from the local library, which shared space with the Kwanlin Dün Cultural Centre, a place dedicated to the heritage of the Kwanlin Dün First Nation. He'd been struck by the marriage of the distant past and the people impacting that history, and the more recent past, and how the whole mix informed what was going on now. Then there was the town itself. Memories of the Gold Rush were all over this place. There were festivals, museums, and mementos. Could Jackson bring all of it together? And if so, how? There was so much information, but he wasn't sure what he was looking for yet.

Writing was always more than having the pen on the page or sitting at the computer. In this early stage, Jackson needed a vast amount of mental space. He had to let all of the information in his head find its way into a form he could use. This time he was hoping for something non-fiction, literary, or both. Who knew? He'd have to wait, and here he had time. Back home, someone was always clamoring for a piece of that brain space, but here, he should be able to let it happen organically.

Kale woofed and scrambled down the stairs. Jackson followed. When he opened the door, there was a woman standing with her hand raised to knock. The darn dog was uncanny.

She looked at him, eyes wide. "You got eggs?"

"No, I've been giving them to Mrs. Skinner down the road. I'm house-sitting. Isabelle thought that would be easier. You can pick some up there."

She wore a down jacket and a wool toque that barely contained wild blond curls. "Right, I remember her saying something about that." She pushed at the hair escaping her hat into her face. "I shouldn't have bothered you."

There was something about her, something familiar. "I have a few left from yesterday," said Jackson. "Come in, I'll pull them together for you. I know I can manage half a dozen."

"Okay." She walked inside and reached down to pat Kale, who grinned and threw himself on his back for a belly rub.

Jackson shut the door. "Wow, you have a real effect

on the crazy dog. I have to wonder how safe I would be if an ax murderer broke in."

"I think an ax murderer wouldn't get past the front gate." She waited awkwardly at the entrance.

Jackson indicated the couch. "Sit. I'll get the eggs."

She instead followed him to the kitchen, pulling off her hat. Her hair sprang free, giving her a bit of a mad scientist look.

Jackson was unsure of the social requirements for someone picking up eggs. Isabelle had assured him everyone knew and would go to the neighbor for eggs so he wouldn't be disturbed. So far it had worked. "Ummm, can I get you anything?"

The woman was puzzled. "Eggs?" Kale was still grinning at her, rubbing against her legs. She crouched to stroke him. Her voice was almost inaudible as she asked, "Is Wesley here?"

And then Jackson knew. "You're Abby."

She stiffened. "You've been talking about me?" Abby stepped back.

"Not really." Jackson tried to calm his racing thoughts and he gave her what he hoped was a reassuring smile. "Not with Wes, I mean. With Isabelle. When Wes arrived, Isabelle said he'd need to talk to you. You look like him. That's all."

"He's been here since she left? That was weeks ago." Abby swayed and sat hard at the table. "Where is he?"

How much information should Jackson give her? "Um, he's working today. He won't be home for a few more hours. I mean, not home as in here, he doesn't live in the house. He stays in the cabin. Um, I mean, the Castle. You're welcome to wait. I can make you something to eat, although I'm not much of a cook. Or I can give you his number?" Jackson wished he wouldn't ramble. Talking to Abby was important to Wes and he didn't want to scare her off.

Abby leapt up and closed her coat as she started for the door. "Why would I wait for that asshole?" she snapped. "He can find me if he wants." She was shaking, every freckle across her nose standing out in her ashen skin. Her eyes gleamed with unshed tears.

Jackson found himself reaching out for her. "Are you okay?"

"What do you think?" Abby said scornfully. "I find out my brother is back and hasn't bothered to see me. He's seen everyone else in town but hasn't even called or—" She spun around and headed for the door.

She would have been gone if Kale hadn't thrown himself in front of her, wagging, panting and wedging himself between her and the outside.

Jackson swallowed. All these years writing romances and he still couldn't handle real-life conflict. "He's terrified. He's working up the courage to go and talk to you." Jackson prayed Wes wouldn't be too furious with him for saying this. "He thinks you hate him."

"And who the hell are you?"

"I'm his friend." Jackson wrung his hands. "I mean, I wasn't when I came here, I actually came to housesit but then I got to know him. I know he needed to come here to bury some demons. He's scared, like you are." Something about the unfairness of it all loosened his tongue. "He was practically a baby when he left. It can't all be on him."

"Fuck you." Her eyes spilled over, and she tried to push past Kale who was rubbing her with his head but not moving. "How dare you tell me he has feelings or is scared of me or anything else? He deserted me when I needed him. He walked out, stole my car and fifteen hundred dollars. I thought he was dead." Abby managed to break free of Kale and almost fell onto the porch.

She ran down the steps toward a small car parked behind Sunny, then turned around and called back to Jackson. "If you see him, you tell him I was here." Abby opened the door. "No, wait, don't tell him. I want to see how long it takes him to get his sorry ass over to my place." She climbed into the car, started the engine with a roar, and tore out of the laneway.

Jackson shut the door. His hands were shaking. This was not good.

It was impossible to concentrate on writing, so he spent the rest of the day doing chores, the more physical the better. He chopped wood, shoveled snow, and even resorted to doing laundry while he waited for Wes to get back.

Jackson didn't really know much about Wes's issues. He long given up the idea he would be in any danger with Wes around, and yet, car theft and stealing were not small things. Abby was obviously devastated. All Jackson had managed to figure out from listening to Isabelle and the guys was something had happened that made Wes run away and not even talk to his family for ten years. He would have been sixteen at the time. Was it all on him?

Jackson had bared his soul to Wes last night. Maybe one day he would say the exact right thing and Wes would understand how much Jackson meant to him, open up and allow him to heal his wounds. But life wasn't like a romance novel. Jackson had to tell him about Abby's visit. Of course, Jackson being Jackson, he would say the wrong thing and Abby wouldn't be the one to drive Wes out of the territory.

Jackson rolled his aching shoulders. All his muscles ached and his smell alone would encourage Wes to run. It was time for a hot shower.

He dumped his sweaty clothes right in the washer and dashed into the bathroom. Jackson turned the tap as hot as he could stand it and climbed behind the curtain. The pounding water relaxed his body but not his thoughts. Abby's visit was burning a hole in his mind, but he had no idea what to say. Family talk was clearly off limits with Wes.

Abby had said not to say anything, which was tempting. But Jackson had zero confidence in his poker face. He couldn't keep up a lie.

How does a kid disappear for ten years? Shouldn't someone be relieved to see him?

Jackson finished his shower, dressed and came downstairs in time to hear Kale's toenails skitter across the porch.

Wes poked his head around the front door and, seeing Jackson, he came in and closed it behind him. Kale flopped on the rug, apparently worn out from his adventures.

"I just got back," said Wes. "I could clean up and do

some dinner if you're still interested."

Jackson opened his mouth but his voice wouldn't work.

"Jacks, what's going on?" Wes's shoulders crept up towards his ears. "Are you mad for some reason? We have an arrangement, and I don't owe you anything." He abruptly reached for the door.

"Wait! I don't know how to say this."

Wes narrowed his eyes and stuffed both hands in his pockets. He stepped back but didn't turn away. "Spit it out."

"Your sister came to get eggs."

Wes paled. "Abby."

Jackson reached out.

Wes dodged him.

"What did she want?"

"Eggs."

Wes flinched.

"I'm sorry, Wes, I'm not good at this. She wants to see you, she misses you."

"She hates me."

"She is angry, but I'm sure she wants to see you."

"No, she blames me."

"Blames you for what?"

Wes's eyes snapped into sharp focus on Jackson. "Stay the hell out of it!" He turned and stomped out slamming the door behind him.

Jackson stared after him. "That went about as bad as I thought it would."

Kale came and rubbed against his legs like a giant cat. "What are you doing, dumb dog? You should be outside. Wes is the one who needs a hug."

Jackson tried to put himself in Wes's place. No parents, and while Abby must love him to be so angry, she wasn't going to help him. God, that was lonely. He grabbed his parka, checked for the flashlight and gloves in his pocket. "Come on, Kale."

Striding out the door, he almost immediately tripped over Wes sitting on the top step. They scrambled for a moment. Jackson grabbed for the banister, trying to untangle his legs. Wes tried to move out of his way and grasped his waist to keep him from going over. Somehow, Jackson ended up sitting on Wes's lap with his arms pinned to his sides and Wes's sharp chin digging into his shoulder.

"What happened?"

"You're clumsy," Wes told him.

"Am not."

"Okay, how about dexterously challenged?"

"You took off. I thought you'd gone."

"Did you want me gone?"

"No." Jackson stopped struggling and let himself sink into Wes's arms. "I want you to make me dinner."

"Excuse me?"

"Come on, I'm too big to sit in your lap." Jackson leaned over to position his feet back under himself, and then stood up. "Show me how to make something and next time I'll cook for you." He offered his hand to Wes.

Together they made a simple pasta tossed with oil and veg. Wes took Jackson's request to heart and talked him through each step. His eyes were red and he was subdued. Jackson was tempted to bring everything up again at dinner, but it was more important to be with him than to try to fix him. They talked about food and weather until Jackson was wiping the table and Wes was up to his elbows in sudsy water.

"The night my parents died," said Wes, "I snuck home, stole Mom's rainy day fund and took off in Abby's car. I abandoned it in Fort Saint John. I've had no contact with her since. They thought I was dead." Wes's voice was tight. He looked like he might snap.

Jackson reached for the right words, but nothing came. He would rather be silent than make it worse.

For a few moments the only sound was the ticking of the wall clock. They finished cleaning the kitchen together in silence.

Wes put on his coat and boots and brushed Jackson's cheek with his lips. "Good night. I'll see you in the morning."

The door shut behind him and the house was empty. Wes clearly needed his space, and Jackson would give it to him. He snapped his fingers. Kale followed him up to his cold bed.

Chapter Fourteen

Wes didn't sleep much. The past kept him awake. He couldn't think of Abby without being immersed in memories of his final night. Asleep, he experienced it all over again. If he waited until exhaustion took him maybe he wouldn't dream. He kept the fire going all night and curled up in his bed to watch a movie on his tablet. When it was early morning but still dark, he heard a scuffling noise at the door. Rolling out of bed, he flipped the light on and opened the door.

"Hey." It was Jackson, looking cold and miserable.

"Quick, I'm gonna freeze if we don't shut the door." Wes ushered him in. The night had been long and lonely. Simply being around Jackson brought him so much comfort. Wes was giddy with it, or was it the lack of sleep? In the lamplight, he could tell Jackson was upset. Wes hugged him and kissed his cold cheek. "Kinda early for a visit?

Jackson sighed. "I broke the water heater. I'm not sure what I did but there's no hot water. I tried to follow the instructions, but I think I made it worse. Winter hasn't really even started and I'm destroying Isabelle's house."

Wes gave him a reassuring smile. "That's why Izzy let me stay. I helped Jeff build it. It's probably something simple. Let me find some socks and I'll look."

Jackson met Wes's eyes, looking at him like he was a hero. "Thanks. I wasn't sure you'd be here this morning."

Wes cleared his throat looking away. "You head back, I'll be right behind you."

He nodded and slipped out.

Wes got dressed and went in through the basement door, not surprised to find Jackson there in his slippers staring forlornly at Uncle Jeff's contraption, a sheaf of papers clutched in his hands.

"Here's Izzy's notes," said Jackson. "Maybe they'd make sense if I knew what I was looking at."

Wes examined the pipes and connections. After a few minutes, he had an idea what the problem was. He flipped through Aunt Izzie's how-to manual. "Okay, can you grab me a pair of pliers and a wrench?"

There was a pile of dusty cardboard boxes beside the tool bench in the corner. Jackson, eyes fixed on the tools, probably trying to figure out what a wrench was, tripped over the corner of one of them. Tools went flying and he went down.

"Are you okay?" Wes helped him up.

The sheepish grin and the sweeping blush were irresistible. Wes drew him in and nibbled at his lips.

"I'm fine, maybe a bit distracted. Those jeans look— nice on you."

"Nice?" Wes chuckled and pushed him over to the bottom step sitting him down. He kissed his head and ruffled his hair. "You just sit here and stay out of trouble. Let me handle it." He turned, ignoring the raised middle finger.

Jackson made a show of leaning back with his hands behind his head, stretching his long legs out, and crossing them at the ankles. "Run along and fix my heater. I don't pay you to talk."

Wes snorted, enjoying this Jackson more than the cowering guy who dragged him over here this morning. He collected the scattered tools and went to shove the cardboard box further into the corner when he saw his name printed on the side. It didn't make any sense. Why would anything down here have his name on it? He hadn't been part of this family for over ten years.

"Wes?" Jackson put a hand on his back.

He startled. "Sorry, what?" Wes couldn't take his eyes off the box.

"What's wrong?"

"That box."

"It's got your name on it."

"It does."

"Why don't we open it?"

"No! I mean, not yet. Let me fix this first."

Jackson didn't press or ask questions.

Wes worked on the cobbled together pipes. What

could be in the box? Any reminders Wes had wanted, he'd grabbed the night he'd left. He tried to focus on the task at hand, thankful for Jackson's quiet support. "Can you flip the switch for me?" There was a low hum as the pump started. "It'll be a few minutes before you have hot water." Wes took a deep breath and stared at the box.

Jackson came over and put his arm around Wes's shoulders. "Do you want some privacy?"

Wes stroked the warm hand. "Would you open it for me?"

Jackson gave him a squeeze and crouched over the dusty cardboard marked with faded marker. He folded the top open. "Okay, I think this was a book at some point." He handed it over with a look of horror on his face.

Wes turned the thing in his hands. It was an old paperback. The spine was broken and the creases in the cover made it near impossible to read the title. Luckily, he didn't need to read it, he knew it by heart. "*The Forgotten Kingdom*. I can't believe they kept this. It looks like they found it in a puddle." The pages were swollen and wavy from water damage, half covered in a dark stain.

"It looks like it's been through wars. Is it readable?"

"I don't think so. It was my favorite. I took it everywhere with me. This book taught me to love reading." Wes gently put it down. "What else is there?"

"Pictures."

"Not those, I don't want to see them."

Jackson put them beside the box and lifted out a flat wooden case with brass hinges.

"Uncle Jeff's carving knives." Wes took the case and opened it with reverence. The knives were old but well cared for. "Wow, I've only had my chipping knife for the past few years, imagine what I could do with these."

Jackson just sat, watching him.

"Is there anything else?"

"Only the pictures."

"Can you hold onto them? I'm not ready."

"Sure." Jackson put them aside.

It was quiet. Wes debated heading to the Castle to meditate, but lately meditating had been more like chasing useless thoughts. "Do you have any plans for the morning?"

"Not really. It's still early, you want breakfast?"

Wes closed the lid and put the damaged book on top. "Well, I'm not interested in anything you call breakfast but I'll make you an omelet if you like."

"Or." Jackson took his hand and helped him off the cold floor. "We could try out that hot water?"

They headed upstairs.

****

When Jackson pulled up in the driveway, Kale met the car, sniffed hello and went bounding back behind the house on important dog business. Jackson hung the keys on the hook behind the door, stripping off his layers. Wes said Jackson needed to suck it up so he would have stuff left to pile on when it got really cold, but Kelly said Wes was exaggerating. It sure couldn't get much colder than it was.

Dropping Wes off at work, especially after their "breakfast", didn't seem like much of a chore. What a wonderful way to start the day. Rubbing his fingers over his bruised lips, Jackson felt warm deep in his bones, despite the drive and the weather. He'd never experienced the "friends with benefits" thing, but surely this was so much more. He cared for Wes and the sex was incredible. Weren't the best relationships the ones where your lover was your friend? He shook his head to clear the runaway fantasy. This might feel like a relationship, but it clearly wasn't.

The things from the cardboard box were still on the kitchen table. Wes hadn't taken them back to the Castle. Could that mean he would be back after work? Jackson ran his hand over the polished wooden case, allowing himself to imagine Wes carving, his brow furrowed in concentration, his dimple popping with the joy of creation, and his hands, those long skilled fingers, stroking the smooth contours.

Jackson reached for the old paperback. Wes's face had lit up with pure joy when he saw what it was. Jackson had vivid glimpse at the child Wes had been, a guy whom life had since marked. It was so easy to picture young Wes running through the woods, hauling it with him everywhere, climbing trees or reading by the fire. Books were meant to be loved but this one had been loved to death. Too bad it wasn't readable. Favorite books were old friends and Wes could use all the friends he could get right now. Jackson could barely make out the title, but Wes had said it was *The Forgotten Kingdom*. The author's name was illegible. Dashing upstairs, he Googled it and found it for sale at a rare bookstore online. Perfect.

As for the photos, they were sitting on the edge of Jackson's desk where he'd dropped them on the way to their shower. A better place was needed so Wes wouldn't accidentally come across them until he was ready.

There were three photos. The first was of a dour-looking man with his arm around a faded woman. If there was a shadow of Wes in those faces, it was faint. Maybe if they showed an ounce of Wes's spirit it would be more obvious. They had to be his parents.

The next was easier. It was a young laughing Wes being poked in the ribs by a girl who must be Abby. Wes would have been ten or twelve, the same height as his older sister but skinny and all angles. They looked happy.

The last was Wes, an older, gangly kid towering over a weathered man Jackson recognized from Isabelle's photos on the walls. Wes was holding an intricately carved dog in front of him. Jackson thought the guy had to be Jeff. He could imagine Isabelle directing them as she took the picture, bossy but with love.

What brought this happy family to where they were today? Losing both parents so young must have been awful. Jackson thought of the home he'd run from, and the way his mom over mothered him, and yet life permanently without her was unimaginable. He pressed his lips together at the surge of anger. How could Isabelle and Jeff let Wes get away when he needed them most? Despite their faults, his family would never have let him go like that.

Jackson sighed, shuffling through the pictures one

last time before he slipped them between the back pages of his journal.

Chapter Fifteen

Something woke Jackson. The house was dark. The wind was howling outside. He snuggled deeper under the covers and checked the time. Four-fifteen. He had a few more hours to sleep. Jackson shut his eyes, glad he wasn't out there right now. He felt sorry for the bears. Hopefully they were fast asleep in their dens for the winter. The temperature had dropped rapidly last night. It had been very tempting to make sure Wes got home okay, although Nick would pick him up in an instant if his ride bailed. It would be nice if Jackson and Wes had the kind of relationship where he could check up on each other, especially on nights like this. But if Jackson's mom had taught him anything, it was how it felt to be over-mothered. He couldn't go there.

It was so cold, blustery, and nasty that Kale hadn't wanted to go out before bed. Jackson's eyes flew open. That was it. That's what woke him up.

Kale was pacing, his nails clicking on the floor. Jackson turned on the lamp by the bed. The big dog was standing staring at him. He turned to the top of the stairs and then turned back to Jackson, then to the stairs. He walked to the bed and whined, and again headed to the stairs.

"Don't tell me you didn't go. Can't you hold it?"

Kale whined, turned, and ran down the stairs.

"All right, all right, I'm coming." Out from under the covers, Jackson was chilled. He might as well put another log on the fire while the stupid dog did what he was going to do.

The wind pushed a gust of snow and ice in as Kale dashed out the front door. Shaking his head, Jackson headed to the basement and shoved in one, nope, three big logs. He would be hot for the rest of the night, but the heat would cancel the raging wind.

He emerged from the basement to hear Kale barking frantically through the sounds of the wind. Fear flooded

Jackson's body and he raced to open the door. There was Kale, pressing his snowy body against Wes, who was wearing only an undershirt, boxers and bare feet.

"What are you doing?" Jackson jumped out into the storm pulling Wes inside. Kale blew past them on the wind and stood in the middle of the room, shaking snow all over.

Jackson slammed the door and stared at the apparition in front of him. Snow tangled in his hair, skin gray, maybe blue. "Wes, what's wrong?"

Wes was shaking hard. His eyes were unfocused. Jackson didn't know what to do. Hot shower? No, Wes was already soaked and needed warming up. Quick thinking was not Jackson's strong suit, but this was an emergency and there was no one to ask. Making a firm decision, Jackson put an arm around Wes and led him to the stairs. Wes allowed himself to be half carried up to the loft. Breathing hard, Jackson striped Wes's wet things. Then he pushed his robe over Wes's quaking shoulders. Tipping Wes into the bed, Jackson arranged the covers over him, and grabbed the quilt off the old rocker, burying Wes under it for good measure. He crawled into bed and draped himself over Wes's shaking body, trying to sink some of his body heat into him. Throughout the whole process, Jackson talked to Wes, who allowed himself to be moved to bed but didn't respond. It was so weird. What in the world had happened? Jackson chased different scenarios around in his brain until somehow, he dozed.

When Jackson woke, the world had stopped shaking. He was brutally hot, and the room was quiet. It was still dark. That didn't tell him anything. It could be five a.m., ten a.m., or any time in between. He was no longer on top of Wes. In their sleep, they had sorted their bodies so they were tangled together side by side.

Wes's breathing was quiet and rhythmic, in and out. There was music to it, especially when combined with Kale's rumbling breaths. That dog would have a hero's breakfast this morning, with bacon.

Wes mumbled something.

"I beg your pardon?"

"I said, do you have snow tires for Sunny, cause she's not going anywhere till spring without them?"

"Yeah, I do. Kelly hooked me up."

"Good." He stirred. "Jackson? Why am I here?"

That was something Jackson would like to know as well. "What do you remember?"

"I'm not sure." Wes rubbed a hand over his face. "I woke up so cold. I was having the worst nightmare. I couldn't get out of it. I ran and ran. I was lost and now I'm here."

"You went out in the storm dressed in a shirt and boxers. Kale bugged me until I let him out, I think it was around four. He dragged your sorry butt back here. He saved your life."

Jackson sat up and moved some of the blankets out of the way. Those extra logs had done the trick. He flicked on the lamp and turned to Wes. "You okay?"

Wes kicked off the rest of the blankets and inspected himself, wiggling his fingers and toes. "Kale must have come right out after me. I don't know how he knew, but I'm good. Not even frostbite." He was quiet for a moment.

Jackson lay back down, curling around Wes and putting his hand protectively on his chest.

Wes put his arms around him. "Thank you."

"Thank the dog. I would still be sleeping here and—" Jackson choked up, he couldn't go on.

Wes said nothing and was quiet again for so long he appeared asleep. Eventually, he spoke. "I've been having horrible nightmares, worse than usual since I got back. I've been afraid to go to sleep, but last night my body gave out. I dreamed I was driving the car. My parents were arguing, fighting about me, then the car was diving over the embankment. I tried to stop it. I tried to run. I was so cold. I can't do that again."

Jackson shook his head. "You're goddamn right you can't do that again. We're taking you to a doctor. We're going to get you some drugs or something."

Wes struggled to sit up. "If it were that fucking easy, don't you think I would have done something about it? No drugs."

"There must be something?"

"I don't know what it is."

"Let's get some breakfast. I can't think now." Jackson dressed and headed downstairs, leaving Wes to move at his own pace. The implications of what almost happened were so large, he didn't even know how to express himself, let alone struggle over solutions. He let Kale out and flipped a package of bacon into a pan. While it sizzled away, Jackson filled Kale's dish with dog food. Once the bacon was cooked, he roughly chopped every slice and smothered the pile of kibble with it. Jackson let the dog back in and smiled as Kale raced to the kitchen and happily dove into his breakfast treat.

"Good boy, Kale." Jackson ruffled the dog's fur and started on making the humans' food. He put on the coffee and cracked some eggs in the pan. By the time Wes joined him, wearing Jackson's clothes, the table was set.

Wes raised a brow at the scrambled eggs and toast. "You cooked." He sat down. "I'm impressed."

Jackson gave him a wan smile and took his own seat. "Even as a non-cook, I can scramble eggs and make toast. I needed to focus on something other than the voices in my head."

"Thanks. I could have sworn I smelled bacon as well."

"You did."

"You holding out on me?"

"Kale ate it," said Jackson. "My share, your share, his share. My bacon is his bacon for the rest of his life. Yours too, if I have anything to say about it."

"'Kay. I've been considering becoming a vegetarian."

"You have not."

"No, but I could."

They ate in silence. Jackson gathered his courage, and it was only when he was almost finished that he could bring himself to speak. "Listen, Wes, you've got to work this out." Jackson knew he was overstepping but he had to say something. He'd never been so scared for someone.

"Oh shit, why didn't I think about that?" Wes said

sarcastically and dropped his fork onto his plate.

There was silence again. Jackson couldn't think of what to say. His eyes burned and his throat closed up.

"Listen, Jackson, I have lived with this for ten years now. I've tried drugs, I've tried booze, and I've tried running. Now I tried coming back. Nothing works. Nothing."

"Have you tried talking? Have you tried forgiving yourself?"

"Yeah right!" Wes crossed his arms.

Jackson started to get angry. Why couldn't Wes see this was important? "Don't be flippant! Talk to Abby? I don't know."

Wes sucked in a breath and for a moment Jackson thought he'd gone too far.

"No," said Wes, "to be honest I have tried none of those things because I don't know how. What I do best is run."

"But running isn't helping."

"No shit, Sherlock."

Jackson jumped up and collected the dishes, dumping them in the sink with a rattle. He didn't know how to have this conversation. "I've got to go do the chickens."

Wes touched his shoulder softly. It felt like an apology. "I'll head outside with you. I've got to see what shape I left the cabin in."

Luckily, Isabelle kept extra boots and coats by the back door. The path was blown over, leaving no tracks to tell the story of last night's adventure. Kale raced ahead, diving in and out of drifts. The Castle sat in the morning sun waiting for them, the door wide open. They walked inside onto drift caused by last night's swirling wind. Wes grabbed the shovel off the porch and scooped the floor clean. Jackson swept out the last of it, shaking the mat. They pulled the bedding off the mattress and shook it outside.

"Place probably needed a good airing anyway," said Wes.

Jackson regarded him and made a decision. This was worth fighting for. "You're sleeping in the big house from now on."

"With a string around my ankle and some bells?"

Wes gave him a cocky smile that was at odds with his slumped shoulders and limp curls.

"Please stop joking about this. You could have died."

"You're not my keeper and I don't want to disturb you."

"The RCMP looking for your frozen body will disturb me more. Come on, I'm going to help you bring your stuff over." Jackson picked up an empty Shadow from the corner he was propped in.

Wes gave in. "I'll take the guest room."

"No way, then where will I put my guests?"

"Jackson, we've talked about this."

"Yes, we have."

"Look, we've got a pretty good thing happening here and the worst thing for it would be to be living in each other's pockets."

"Right now, I can imagine something worse." Jackson was tired of being afraid to push Wes. This was a matter of life or death. "Look, we're friends, right? This doesn't have to change anything. I won't think you're my boyfriend or ask for more than you can give. But your nightmares are putting you in dangerous situations. And we like sleeping together. If it doesn't work, we'll think of something else." Jackson started stuffing clothes from the bin beside the bed into the battered hiking pack.

"So, what do we do if I keep you awake all night having nightmares?"

Jackson grabbed a handful of socks. "We cope."

"What if you want to stay up all night writing?"

Jackson shoved another handful of socks into the pack. "I'll get you a sleep mask."

Wes gave him a tired smile. "You win, I'm too exhausted to fight about this." He gathered his laundry and wood-working kit.

Jackson finished packing Shadow and waited by the front door. "You scared me," Jackson said softly. "Really scared me. I don't ever want to be that terrified again."

Wes sighed, his shoulders sagging. "Yeah, me too. It's time to get serious about doing my work here. I've gotta talk to Abby."

Chapter Sixteen

Why Jackson thought the events of the last night would slow Wes down, he wasn't sure. But Wes didn't seem to have a care in the world that afternoon, as he casually stated he needed to get some air and Jackson shouldn't wait up. It was so in line with his, "up yours, universe" attitude.

Jackson watched Wes turn his back and walk out, snowshoes and day bag swinging from one hand. Kale flopped back down on the porch at a sharp word from Wes. Jackson wondered if the dog was as bereft and anxious as Jackson. Maybe he shouldn't have let Wes leave, but he couldn't cling to him and watch his every move. For a brief moment, Jackson understood his mother's fear of letting him out on his own, and damn, it was hard to watch him walk off the property heading into the hills. What if something happened?

Jackson squared his shoulders and went upstairs to write. They'd both been freaked out by the effects of the nightmare. He'd gotten Wes's agreement to sleep in the house. That had to be enough. Screaming after him wouldn't even work in fiction.

At his desk, his eyes were drawn past the window to the sun playing in the trees. The screen called him back to work but his heart wasn't in it. Kale moved to the center of the drive and sat, then stood, circled, and sat again. He was restless too. A walk might help them both, and it was a beautiful day. Jackson didn't even feel guilty as he walked away from the computer.

Jackson got his snowshoes off the lean to wall, stepped into them and snugged them up against his boots. He was proud of how comfortably he could walk in them now. A real Yukon man. He chuckled as Kale danced around him. "Come on, buddy, let's see if we can find some mice to scare."

The crisp air cleared Jackson's brain. Putting one foot in front of the other calmed him. It made sense that

Wes did this when he was upset. In his mittens, the tips of his fingers tingled with cold. Jackson shoved them into his pockets and enjoyed Kale's antics. Silly dog was practically doing headstands in the snow. Jackson could imagine legions of mice under the crust running like crazy.

When he and Kale were ready to return, the sun was leaning toward the horizon. Jackson's stomach clenched at the thought of Wes staying out there so late but had to trust his choice. While putting together dinner, Jackson's phone rang with another number he didn't recognize. Maybe someone wanted to organize another Euchre game. "Hello?"

"Hello, is this Jackson?"

"Yes."

"It's Sophie Peltiere. You know my partner, Nick Morgan."

"Oh, of course. You're the one who makes the wine." Jackson flushed at the memories the wine brought to mind.

"Yes, c'est moi." Her smile was so clear in her voice that he smiled too. "We want, Nick and I, to have a bit of a party to celebrate good news with our friends and we thought it would be a perfect time to meet you. I hope you will come?"

Her accent was so appealing he almost missed what she said. "Oh."

"Only a few people are invited," Sophie reassured him. "We asked Wesley already. I feel I know you very well from all Wesley has said about you, and I would love to meet you in person."

Jackson almost dropped the bowl in his hand. "He talked about me?"

"He told us how you met." Her laugh was full and rich. "You must have been surprised to find he would be living so close. He said you are a writer with your head in the clouds. That is something I would very much like to see."

"Well, it's not as clever as you might think."

"He also said you would be reluctant to come because you're shy. I told him I could be very persuasive."

Heat rose in Jackson's neck and cheeks. "Wes is telling all my secrets. Not so much shy as awkward when I don't know people." Damn, his laugh sounded fake as he struggled forward.

"It occurs to me you know our Kelly. You would need to work hard to be so awkward."

"True, I have met him." Knowing that Nick and Wes loved this woman made Jackson comfortable exchanging small talk with her on the phone about something he normally wouldn't consider.

"I think you will know almost everyone there. There will be Jimmy and his girlfriend, and Kelly. He may bring a friend. Then Wesley, you, and us. Only good friends. Please consider it."

"Well, when is it? I'll consult my calendar."

"Please? We would be honored by your authorly presence."

Now she sounded like his sister trying to get the last piece of Halloween candy from him. "I don't want to be there as an author. Just a friend."

"Even better. You'll come then?"

Jackson had "no" fighting to get out of his mouth, but "yes" seemed to be winning. Nick had asked him over more than once to meet the wife he was obviously smitten with. Jackson didn't know too many people in committed relationships. Well, his parents, but they didn't count. Despite Sophie's assurances, he wasn't sure about the kind of a gathering she'd described. It sounded like the parties his mom had, and those were stiff, artificial things. Still, knowing that Kelly would be there actually helped. Jackson might be able to pull it off if he drove there and could leave when he wanted. "When is it again?"

"This Saturday evening."

"Okay I'll come." Jackson held his breath waiting for regret but it wasn't there.

"Oh, wonderful. It's a date then." Her voice was warm, and she sounded delighted.

"What should I bring?" he asked.

"Yourself only. We will be eating around six but

come earlier to visit. See you then, goodbye—oh, Jackson?"

"Yes?"

"This evening, it will be very casual. Just be comfortable."

"Goodbye." He slipped his phone in his pants pocket and whistled. Kale's head popped up. "Well, look at me. I guess I'm going to have a social life after all. You'll have to help me pick the right T-shirt for the big event."

Kale wagged his tail.

Jackson squared his shoulders. He was ready. If his mother told him he was going to a party, he would balk, but this was his decision. New life, new choices.

The rest of his day was uneventful. Later, as the moon came up, Jackson turned the lights off in his room and watched the silver clouds move over the sky. He'd gone out for an evening check on the chickens and it was cold enough to freeze the—no, he didn't want to think about how cold it was. Wes was still out there. He shucked his clothes defiantly onto the floor. No one would see, no one would care. He was too jittery to fold anything right now.

The sheets were not Jackson's friends. They tied him up, wrapping themselves around him. He kicked them off, and was cold, pulled them back on, and he was hot. The clock counted the minutes, mocking him with its blue glow. Jackson wanted to throw his pillow at it. Wes couldn't still be walking around out there. What if he was hurt? He had no phone and there was no service out there anyway. What if a bear attacked him?

A groan from the floor brought Jackson out of his awfulizing. Kale was sleeping peacefully on his back, legs flung every which way. Last night, the dog had woken him up frantically. Wes had to be fine, or Kale would know. Jackson smoothed the sheets and put his head back on the pillow. Kale was relaxed, Wes was fine. The mantra soothed him and he started to drift.

At some point, the bed shifted. Jackson heard Wes pulling off his clothes and rolling under the covers with a sigh.

Jackson didn't move. He wanted to roll over and capture

Wes in his arms, to bury his face in his neck, to bitch at him about the late hour, and to kiss him till he couldn't breathe.

The sheets rustled as Wes settled under the quilt. It was quiet for a few seconds, then he scootched over. Cold hands brushed Jackson's shoulder and then Wes rolled against him. Jackson tried to keep his breathing regular, although his heart skipped in his chest. He shifted, allowing Wes's body to press against him and found his face buried in those curls. Jackson shut his eyes, breathing in the silver of the moon, wood smoke, and something wilder that was pure Wes. He fell asleep.

****

Wes thanked his ride as he climbed out of the car on Saturday afternoon. The shift had gone longer than anticipated and there wasn't much time to get ready for Sophie's get together. He ran into the house, patted Kale on the way, and headed upstairs. Jackson was already in front of the mirror.

Wes dropped a kiss on his neck. "Gotta grab a shower and I'll be ready to go. Sorry I'm so late."

Jackson briefly met his eyes in the mirror and mumbled something.

Wes grabbed a T-shirt and fresh pair of jeans, and headed for the shower. While he soaped himself, he imagined Jackson crowded in with him, rubbing their wet bodies together. His groin tightened. Wes wanted to call him, pull him away from his primping into the steamy water. But Jackson was already nervous about tonight. Doing something that would ultimately make them late would probably not have the effect of taking his mind off things. More than likely, it would only work him up even more.

On the other hand, having a worked-up Jackson scrubbing up with him might not be so bad. Wes grinned to himself and decided to get ready faster. Maybe they'd have some time to remind each other of what they'd come home to. The domesticity of their situation should have bothered Wes more. The thing was, he liked it. While it couldn't last, they were at least both enjoying the benefits.

Wes climbed out of the shower, toweled dry, and quickly dressed. He flipped the towel over the curtain rod and moved to the bedroom, pulling on socks as he went.

Jackson was still standing in front of the mirror. His hair was carefully slicked back, his snow-white shirt buttoned to the top and his khakis looked freshly pressed. Wes took a minute to admire him. The man was so adorable it made his teeth hurt, but something was off. He didn't seem to hear Wes's approach.

"Hey, you." Wes wrapped his arms around Jackson, resting his chin on his shoulder. Their eyes met in the mirror.

"I've changed my mind. I'm staying home tonight."

"Really? You're already dressed. You don't wanna waste that look."

"Don't make fun of me."

"You look great. Want me to prove it to you?" Wes pushed his growing erection against him.

Jackson's eyes widened. His voice was soft. "You know these things are hard for me."

"How can I help?"

"I have been getting dressed since three."

Wes turned to face the bed, which was covered in slacks, jeans, T-shirts, button ups and, was that a tie? Wes picked it up. "Navy stripes. Appropriate for any situation."

Jackson's eyes got bigger. "She said casual, this is what I was going to wear." He picked up a T-shirt that declared *Hello, my name is Inigo Montoya. You killed my father. Prepare to die.* "But I want to look nice. I want them to like me."

"They like you. You've met them all."

"I haven't met the women. Sophie wants to talk about writing. I can't."

"You don't have to do anything you're not comfortable with." That seemed to calm Jackson a little, so Wes took his hand and led him over to the bed. "We're not in a rush, my hair's still wet and no one is making you do anything you don't want to do."

Jackson dropped the T-shirt back on the bed. "I won't be able to talk to anyone if I don't drink."

The non sequitur baffled Wes but he sensed they were getting close to the actual problem. "So drink. They're pushing that wine on everyone right now. Besides, I can hold off tonight and drive us home." Wes stroked his back. "You knew you would be worried. Is that what's speaking right now?"

"I just know *me*. I can't drink. I don't want them to think I need to be wasted to have a decent conversation. You don't understand what a disaster I am."

"I really don't. I remember an evening when you were a little tipsy, and I think it turned out well. I enjoyed meeting that side of you."

"You're different." Jackson leaned on Wes. "You make me feel like my skin fits."

Pleasure rippled through him. "Well, I'll be there. I'm not sending you in alone and Sophie is so excited to meet you because Nick thinks you're awesome. How 'bout we show up for a dinner that someone else cooked for a change. Then we can decide what to do after. If you're uncomfortable, we'll bail."

"I'm not the whiney guy who's going to wreak your evening. If I don't want to be there, I'll take off. No need to ruin your night."

Wes laughed tackling him, knocking him over onto the piles of clothes. "For starters, you're totally whiny. Second, what if I decide I wanna leave early?"

The tight line of Jackson's lips softened as Wes ran the tip of his tongue over them, pushing his hips against him. "Now let's get these clothes off and get you into something a bit more casual." He pulled at the top button watching a flush rise from under Jackson's shirt, up his cheeks till it reached his eyes.

Wes had promised himself that he wouldn't do anything to make Jackson more nervous. But if Jackson was the one pushing Wes back onto the bed, then no promises were being broken, were there?

Half an hour later, Jackson pulled on his Peanuts shirt. "Wait a minute, I have bed head."

Wes shook his head, grabbed Jackson's hand and directed him toward the stairs. "Artfully mussed, very casual. Now hurry. You're making us late!"

****

Sophie put on a great party. The guests were the right combination of people. Jimmy and Julie were there, of course. Kelly brought Ashley, a Gwitch'in woman who was interested in the historical aspects of Jackson's books. The dynamic worked. Jackson was comfortable with them and to be honest, Wes knew he could be himself there too. During dinner, Nick and Sophie got really cute, and all made a toast to a healthy spring baby. Wes joined Sophie in drinking sparkling apple juice instead of the plentiful red wine. He then clapped Nick on the back, hugged Sophie, and was so proud to be part of that little family.

Jackson disappeared just after dinner and Wes found him sitting on a corner of the sofa with Ashley, discussing the gold rush and her perspective of the historical treatment of First Nations by the colonialists of the day. Jackson was listening with intensity and was taking notes. This depth of engagement was what Jackson's family called writer's brain and teased him about, and yet, Wes could see the gears turning. Maybe a story was brewing there. It was thrilling to see although Wes did wonder if he would ever come out of the trance to socialize. He didn't need to worry because Sophie cleared the floor and let Jimmy go on the fiddle. It was a stroke of genius. No one would have danced without it, but Jimmy's music lifted everyone up. Ashley took to the circle and showed everyone a Gwitch'in jig, then invited Jackson to dance. He blushed so hard they had to turn the heat down, but he stomped his way through the jig, laughing. Wes didn't think he'd ever seen anyone so beautiful.

When Jimmy put his fiddle away, the music gave way to a dance mix Nick had put together. Jackson balked at the first slow song. "I don't know how to dance," he said, but Wes pulled him close and convinced him slow dancing was simply cuddling and swaying and so they danced in the dim light of the living room.

"It feels safe. I never had friends like this before,"

Jackson whispered in Wes's ear.

Wes pulled him close, wishing with all his heart that he could be the friend Jackson wanted. It felt right. It would be so easy.

When they left, there was promise in the air. The dancing, the whispers tickling his ear, the stolen kisses, led to an icy race to the car. "I called it," Wes shouted, standing at the driver's side door. "I'm driving."

"I've got the keys, big boy." Jackson held them up and jangled them.

His eyes were full of come-and-get-me, so what could Wes do? Snow flew and their bodies pressed together hard. If Kelly hadn't jeered on his way to his now car, they might still be there now, frozen to death in each other's arms.

Wes's fingers almost froze to the steering wheel and wished he'd worn gloves. "I heard Sophie ask you to read at her book club. I didn't realize that. I thought she just wanted you to sign her books."

"She did have books she wanted me to sign, but she also wanted to ask me if I would do a reading for her romance book club. She was persuasive and I do want to face these demons someday. The publisher would really like me to do so much more than I do." Jackson spoke slowly. "I guess if I was going to break my silence, I would want it to be with people I know."

"Are you considering it?"

"I told her I would but I'm not sure I'm ready yet. I did come out here to make changes though."

"What I don't get—" Wes glanced at Jackson "—is, what's the problem? She loves your writing. They all do. Why don't you want to share it?"

Jackson sighed. "Easy for you to say. Look, all my life I have written. Period. I haven't done readings, I don't blog, I don't make personal appearances. I write. If the readers want more than that, they read Simone's stuff." He put his hand on Wes's arm. "You know, I have never danced with anyone before."

"I haven't either, not like that." Wes glanced over. "You're changing the subject. I know you can do it."

"I did tell Sophie I would. Now I just need to get

used to the idea and figure out what they want, or if it's really me they want to hear."

"What do you mean?"

"Wes, you have whole topics that are off-limits. Can we just say this one is off-limits for me? Please? I don't want to do this. Not now anyway."

"Do what? You write popular historical romances. There are web pages devoted to bringing the mysterious E.J. Williams out of the closet." Wes choked back a laugh. "Although, technically, I seem to be the only one actually doing that."

Jackson glared at him.

The tires crunched as Wes turned onto the driveway and drove Sunny into the parking space. "Tell me what's really going on."

"Okay. I hate it. No serious writer writes romance. I want to write real books. If I go to conferences, blog, meet readers, I'll get pegged there and never have another opportunity to really write. You satisfied now?"

On the porch, Kale stood and stretched.

"You hate it?" Wes couldn't keep the surprise from his voice. "I watch you disappear into your book. I see the smile on your face when you have your characters right where you want them. You don't hate it. You've never hated it. This sounds to me like you're repeating the words of bullies who didn't want you to be who you really are."

"Fuck you." Jackson was out of the car and in the house before Wes opened his door.

Chapter Seventeen

Wes stared after Jackson and sighed. He'd really put his foot in it. Wes pushed the car door shut and plugged in Sunny's space heater so she would start tomorrow and beckoned to Kale, who had shaken a snowman's worth of snow off his thick fur. "Come on in, buddy, looks like you and I are sleeping together."

None of the lights were on when he walked in. He snuck up the stairs into the bathroom where he found his flannel pants and a T-shirt. When he climbed into bed, Jackson was facing the wall. Wes crept as close as he dared. "I'm sorry."

Jackson didn't move. Wes he was sure he was awake, but kept his distance. Lying there he felt sad and lonesome. It had been such a perfect night. Shutting his eyes he waited for sleep but apparently sleep had a night job and wouldn't be by any time soon. Jackson's body relaxed and his breathing softened. Wes crept closer.

This was usually Jackson's position, trying to figure out what the angry guy needed. Not a nice place to be. He spooned Jackson and eventually got close enough to slide his arm under and pull him close. He replayed the evening over and over until his arm fell asleep. Unfortunately, the rest of him still wasn't tired. Another kiss to soft hair. He needed his arm back.

"Oh, for God's sake," said Jackson, "go to sleep."

"I thought you were sleeping."

Jackson turned over. "I was. I mean, I fell asleep but how can I sleep with you tossing and turning and kissing me?"

"Sorry. I thought was being soft."

"I think I overreacted a bit to our conversation on the way home."

"Maybe, but I guess I could let you have some of your stuff on the table too. I seem to take up a lot of space."

"I overreacted. I'm so tired of people trying to fix me."

"I am sorry." Wes tugged Jackson closer. "I hate it

when someone does that to me."

"Apology accepted. Can we change the subject?"

Wes was glad to accommodate him. "What do you want to talk about?"

"Well, after this evening, I was wondering if we could dance more. That was fun. Maybe we could go big and dance with the stars?"

"Maybe, with a bit more practice," Wes told him. "I think it also depends on whether you mean Yukon winter stars or movie stars?"

Jackson rolled onto his elbow. "Well, as an introvert, I'm thinking snowshoe dancing, out in the front yard, with just the two of us and maybe Kale." He leaned close and kissed Wes, a slow, deep kiss. "If I can't sleep and you can't sleep, maybe we could practice some of the close stuff now. We could decide on the other stuff later."

"I'd like that, but I have to be at work by eleven tomorrow."

"I think we'd be done in time to get you there." Jackson pressed closer, rocking their hips together.

Wes flexed his arm and brought their mouths together again. Inhaling deep, he drank the scent from the place between Jackson's mouth and nose. It was pure Jackson. No soap or laundry smells, just his skin. Wes inhaled again. He could get drunk from it.

Jackson fumbled at the waist of his sleep pants and somehow got them around his thighs. He placed Wes's hand on his hip. Wes dragged Jackson on top scraping his teeth across his neck, thrusting against him.

"Wait." Jackson groaned, slowing the frantic drive of his hips. "Can we—? Oh God, fuck me."

"Haven't got the stuff." Wes smoothed his hand down Jackson's back.

It didn't take long. They'd been winding each other up all evening and what the fight took out of them the quiet affection and honesty gave back. They spilled hot and sticky—Wes wasn't sure who went first. He held Jackson while their breathing settled and kissed him slow. Jackson was quiet, not the angry silence from before, but thoughtful. They fell asleep breathing each other's air.

****

The Sunday dinner crowd wasn't busy enough to keep Wes occupied and his thoughts kept drifting to Jackson. Things were getting intense, and sleeping together every night wasn't helping. Wes kept losing track of the reasons he needed to keep his distance, but he had four days off starting now, and he would head to the trapline first thing in the morning. That should give him some distance and time to think about his purpose here.

Wes waved a distracted goodbye to Shannon as she dropped him off and trudged up the path to the door. Kale crowded into him, pushing him, demanding hello. Jackson was standing in the hallway, backlit by the cozy warmth of the house so, with an extra scritch, Wes sent the dog out to dig in the snow.

He leaned in for a quick kiss, but Jackson was tense standing straight, not molding to his body. "Hey, what's up?"

"I want sex," Jackson blurted, brandishing condoms and three bottles of lube.

"Ah." Wes paused unzipping his coat. This was not what he was expecting when he left work.

"Seriously." Jackson clutched his supplies in one hand and tugged Wes's hat off with the other. "Real sex."

"Why, Mrs. Robinson, are you trying to seduce me?" Wes joked.

"Real penetrative sex." His voice was firm.

"Penetration is a heteronormative idea about sex that excludes so many." Wes couldn't help teasing him. He loved assertive-Jackson and wanted more.

Jackson stopped for a moment and stared at him. "That's not making me want it any less.

Wes grinned and took Jackson's trembling hand. "Come here." He tried hugging Jackson again. "Why three bottles?"

"I wasn't sure what to get so I did some research. These had the best ratings." His voice was muffled in Wes's shoulder.

"Research?"

"Mostly online, like I would for a book."

"What do you mean mostly?" Wes tried to imagine what this research looked like, and found the floor appeared to move under him. He tightened his grip on Jackson, who didn't seem to notice.

Jackson's face went red and he buried it in Wes's neck again. "I watched porn and bought a dildo. It was the most embarrassing thing ever. The second most embarrassing, now."

Wes was surprised. "When?"

Jackson pushed himself back. "You work a lot, and before you slept here, you spent lots of time avoiding me or disappearing in the woods. I've had time to practice."

"Practice?" Wes's voice cracked, picturing it.

"I imagined it would hurt. I wanted to see if I could take it before—you know." Jackson plucked the buttons on his shirt staring intently at the floor.

"Take it?" Wes repeated, goose bumps raised across his body his nipples tightened. This man in his arms, this crazy, brave, amazing man. "Goddammit, Jackson. The things you do to me."

Jackson grinned, grabbed his hand, and led him upstairs.

****

Jackson dropped the supplies on the nightstand, Undressing fast he lowered himself on the bed before his nerves got the better of him. He eyed Wes removing his clothes and took in his long firm body. Wes's cock was far more intimidating now that Jackson was thinking of where it was going. He bit his lip and wiped his damp palms on the colorful quilt. "When—" Jackson cleared his throat and tried again. "When was the last time?"

Wes balled his clothes, tossing them on the chair. He met Jackson's eyes. "You mean the last time I had sex with someone not you?" He crawled onto the bed and propped himself on his elbow looking into Jackson's face. "It's been a long time."

Jackson knew the way Wes was stroking him with his eyes didn't mean anything, but the butterflies in his stomach didn't believe it.

Wes touched his hair. "It's okay if you've changed your mind."

"What? No!" Jackson took Wes's hand and drew it to his lips, placing a kiss in the palm. "I'm nervous. I've never had pre-planned sex before."

"Oh really?" Wes slid his body onto Jackson's. "What would you call that night in the shower?"

"Insanity," Jackson sighed into his mouth, drawing their lips together. He craved every sensation. Digging his fingers into the muscles on Wes's back, he wrapped his legs around him, trying to absorb him.

"This won't work if you don't relax." Wes untangled himself shifting his hips and reaching for Jackson.

His fingers tickled Jackson's chest, plucking at his nipples, calluses catching the sensitive skin. Wes's tongue played at the corner of his mouth while one hand smoothed the line of soft hair below his navel. Jackson shivered. The cool bedroom air kissed his heated skin. He could hear the wind rattling the house and feel the hand-stitched quilt beneath him.

"Shit!" Jackson jolted upright, his shoulder knocking Wes's face. "We have to move the quilt!" He scrambled off the bed.

"Ow!" Wes's voice was muffled by the hand protecting his face. His eyes were watering.

"Ohmigod! I'm so sorry. I was worried about Isabelle's quilt! Sorry, is it bleeding?" Jackson leaned over him wringing his hands.

Wes prodded his abused nose. "No blood." He swiped the moisture from his eyes and rolled off the bed. Wes flipped back the blankets and reached for Jackson. "Come 'ere, princess." He wrapped his arms around him.

Jackson willed himself to relax.

Wes kissed him and ran his hands over his back soothing his nerves and fitting their groins together, like pieces of a puzzle.

Jackson pushed Wes down onto the bed climbing on top, bracketing his narrow hips with his knees. He wrapped his fingers in Wes's curls, zeroing in on his beautiful mouth. Wes grabbed his ass in both hands, playing and kneading. Then one of Wes's fingers stroked down his crack to circle his hole. Jackson gasped, releasing Wes's lips to look into his blue eyes.

"Pass the condoms."

Jackson reached for the box, but Wes didn't stop teasing, running his fingers along his taint, cupping his balls. He dropped it beside Wes and thrust back at the pressure that was dissipating rational thought.

"Don't forget the lube." Wes handed a tube to Jackson. "You open it, I'll suit up."

Jackson popped the lid, watching while Wes opened the packet and unrolled the condom. "You've had practice."

Wes winked. "Safety first."

Jackson crawled to the middle of the bed. He felt exposed, but his dick had no qualms. It stood aching between his legs. A cool wet finger spiraled around his opening pressing harder in the middle, dipping in. He gasped and clenched.

"You need to let go." Wes's finger dipped further spreading the slick inside.

Jackson breathed deeply relaxing into Wes's touch.

Wes set up a gliding rhythm going deeper each time, checking in often to make sure Jackson was okay.

The stretch set off a tingle in the pit of his stomach. Jackson pushed into the motion, wanting more. Wes's fingers teased him while his teeth grazed his spine. Jackson gasped when Wes turned his hand and brushed something inside of him. Bright white light exploded behind his eyes and he allowed his arms to collapse, shoving his ass in the air and burying his head in the pillows to muffle his cries. He couldn't come yet. "Hurry!"

"Shhh. I've got you."

The bed creaked as Wes shifted his position. The blunt head of his cock skated across Jackson's opening, once, then twice.

"You're playing with me."

Wes chuckled. "You're so right." The pressure increased as he eased past the tight ring and pressed into him. His arms wrapped tight, grounding Jackson, not letting him fly away. Hot breath in his ear. "We've got it, we're there."

Wes had stopped moving. He shuddered and took great gulping breaths in Jackson's ear.

Jackson's felt each movement deep inside and was filled with a surge of power knowing that Wes was barely holding it together because Jackson was undoing him. Their bodies were fused so tight Jackson could feel Wes's heart racing with his own. He strained his neck to the side; he needed Wes's lips, his taste.

Wes angled their mouths together. The burn eased. He gave an experimental wiggle. Wes hissed, "Don't move."

"I'm ready." Jackson pressed back trying to get Wes deeper.

Wes dragged back and then thrust. Jackson's body thrummed.

They set up a rhythm of slapping flesh and gasping breath. Every time Wes's cock pushed, pleasure rolled over him in waves. He could hear himself babbling nonsense that might have embarrassed him if he weren't peripherally aware of Wes's counter nonsense moaned in his ear. They moved in sync feeling every sensation anticipating every move. Jackson had never been graceful, never been so in tune with another. He sighed as an edge of darkness crept in where there should have been only joy.

Wes sobbed in his ear. "Please, Jacks, grab yourself, you have to come, I can't—"

Jackson wrapped his fist around his cock and pulling hard, releasing over his hand and onto the bed. He clamped down on Wes, who struggled to move another heartbeat before stiffening. It seemed like an eternity before Jackson collapsed grasping the back of Wes's thigh holding him in place, afraid of what would happen if he left.

Heaving breaths and full bodied shudders eased them back to reality. The pillow Jackson was biting was soaked, covered in spit, sweat and tears. There was a twinge when Wes moved away. Wes stroked his shoulder. "Just a minute. I'll take care of you."

Jackson eyes were blurry as he squinted through the

darkness. He could make out the shape of Wes through the open bathroom door, disposing of the condom and washing up. He made his way back, and stroked Jackson's backside with a warm washcloth, easing the physical ache.

"Turn over." Wes gently cleaned him, then he scrubbed ineffectively at the sheets before giving in and covering the wet spot with a towel. Tossing the cloth in the hamper, he crawled back in with Jackson.

The display of tenderness almost pushed Jackson over the edge. Now he got why Wes had been trying to keep his distance. He didn't know how he could be so close and then let Wes go. He was on the edge, torn apart and he couldn't allow himself to lose it in front of Wes. Jackson struggled to sit up. "I need to do the last check on the chickens."

Wes held him tight. "I've got it, let me take care of it tonight."

"Okay." He didn't have the energy to object.

"Jackson?"

"Yes."

"Are we still okay?"

"What? Of course." He tried to sound natural. There was no use grieving when they still had time left. Jackson cupped Wes's cheek, enjoying the scruff beneath his fingers. "That was amazing."

Wes kissed him. "Why don't you sleep?"

"It's still early." It was a weak protest.

"Yah, but you're in the Yukon now, sometimes we hibernate."

****

Wes had a dreamless sleep wrapped in Jackson's arms. When he opened his eyes, he was reluctant to move. Jackson's arm and one leg were thrown over him, as if he was trying to keep him. The thought didn't scare Wes as much as make him sad. Wes had decided to stay until Nick and Sophie's baby was born. But when Aunt Izzy got back, Jackson would leave, and it would hurt. The joy and anguish in Jackson's face had echoed his own. Making love to him had been a mistake. But Wes would do it again, and it would kill him when they had to move on.

Jackson stirred, lazily pressing against his back.

Wes turned in his arms, nose to nose sharing the intimacy of morning breath. "Hey sleepyhead, are you hungry?"

"You making breakfast?" Jackson's voice was thick with sleep.

"Course I am. How are you feeling?"

"Sleepy." Jackson stretched out like a starfish, yawning.

Wes chuckled. He yanked the covers off, making Jackson curl into a ball. "Time's a wastin'. You collect some eggs. I'll make us an omelet."

Jackson glared at him, muttered something about morning people and shivered into his clothes.

It was a lazy day. They spent hours exploring the curves and secret places of their bodies. When Kale protested about his lock up, they found coats and scarves, heading out into the cold. They walked the path to Porter Creek with Kale romping in the snow. Wes led them to the Hilltop Coffee Shop where they grabbed hot chocolate and headed home into the teeth of the wind, clutching their cardboard cups. Wes dragged them off the highway into the shelter of the trees. They teased and talked about nothing until they hit the warmth of the house and each other's arms.

The next morning, Wes woke to Jackson nuzzling his neck. For a moment, he luxuriated in the perfection of being buried under heavy covers, knowing he had no place to go and nothing to do. Jackson ran to the barn to check on the ladies while Wes stirred a waffle batter and made fruit sauce.

Jackson's eyes widened when he saw the feast. "You expect me to eat that for breakfast? I'll get fat."

"I have to nourish you so you can get back to work. I sense some procrastination happening."

Jackson moved to the table and sat down. "It's an essential tool of the trade. Besides, I'm more in the research phase right now." He took a bite. "Oh God, this is heaven on a plate."

Wes took a bite. "Whipping cream, that's what we need."

"Whipping cream?" Jackson raised his eyebrows. "Sounds messy."

Wes rolled his eyes.

****

After breakfast, Jackson sat on the couch reading Pierre Burton's, *Klondike Fever*. Wes grabbed the newspaper and settled beside him. Jackson twisted around until he was lying with his head on Wes's lap. "Listen to this," Jackson said. "Did you know the guys coming up here to find gold had to bring a literal tonne—and I mean the metric tonne, one thousand kilograms—of supplies or the RCMP wouldn't let them into Canada. That was to keep them from starving the first winter."

Wes loved Jackson's excitement. "They spoon-feed us this gold rush stuff from birth up here. Tidbits on the radio, every school field trip, plays, productions and museums. When I first met Nick, I was so shocked he didn't know anything about it."

It was so quiet they could hear the furnace pipes expanding and snow thumping off the roof. The weather was cold outside, but the sun was shining and they had been inside long enough. The energy was building in Wes's body. He knew what he needed, but how would Jackson take it? "I'm going to head into the bush."

Jackson sat up and tossed the book on the table. "It's minus thirty out, you can't mean today?"

"There's no bad weather, just bad clothing choices," Wes joked, hoping Jackson would smile.

He didn't.

Wes could feel the defiance welling up, along with the childish urge to yell "you can't tell me what to do" and storm out.

"When are you coming back?" Jackson asked quietly.

"Don't know." Wes ran frustrated fingers through his hair. "I don't work till Friday, so before then."

"What if you sleepwalk? There's not enough bacon

in the Yukon to help Kale find you when you're so far away."

That took the wind out of his sails. Jackson shouldn't have to worry while Wes was out there.

Wes put an arm over Jackson's shoulders. "You have to believe me when I tell you there are two times I am not having nightmares, when I'm sleeping with you—" he nuzzled Jackson's cheek "—and when I'm on the land."

Jackson looked skeptical. "What do you do out there?"

Wes stared at the distant mountains through the window and tried to gather his thoughts. "When I was a kid, my family didn't have any kind of a religion that made sense to me, and yet Uncle Jeff introduced me to the land. There's something there. I don't know how to explain it. When I was sick and lost after Nick and I split up, I wound up in Peru. An Andean shaman took me into his hut, took care of me, and when I knew the language, he started to teach me about the Mother. They call her Pachamama, and I came close to the spirit I found here. I was content to stay there and study with him, but he knew until this part of my journey was done, I couldn't commit myself to that part. Since I've been back here, going out there sometimes takes me to the times before. The times Uncle Jeff and I were out there, sitting, watching an elk walk across a clearing. We would be so quiet you could hear the mountains breathe. It's there I understand my place in the world and that's what I was missing when I was away. Coming back to it has been—I don't know— it's been redeeming. I feel like I am where I need to be and believe me, even in Peru I didn't feel this sane." Wes got up from the couch and stretched. "I go out there to meditate, looking for answers about my role here on earth and how to find peace." He threw Jackson a wry smile. "Maybe this time, I'll get an answer on how to deal with Abby." With that, Wes headed to the bedroom.

"That sounds important." Jackson followed Wes upstairs. "But what if something happens? What if you get hurt or eaten by a grizzly?"

Wes shoved a few long-sleeved shirts into Shadow. "My own mother didn't worry this much about me."

"Yeah well I'm not your mother, I'm your lover." Jackson averted his eyes, his cheeks growing pink.

Wes froze, surprised how good it felt to hear that, then raised his eyebrows and grinned. "Until further notice, anyway. "The first rule of outdoor safety is, make sure someone knows where you are at all times when you're out there. So, you're right. I'll write down the coordinates. If I'm not back by Thursday evening, call Kelly or Jimmy. They can find me."

Wes quickly finished packing and filled his water bottle in the kitchen. He could see that Jackson was pale. Setting the bottle by the sink and urged Jackson into his arms. "Come here."

Jackson's body relaxed against his. "I shouldn't have called you my lover."

"It's fine." Wes found he really meant it. "It's been a long time since I had one of those. I won't take it lightly."

"Me neither." Jackson wrapped his arms around Wes. "What if you finish your work out there and decide not to come back?"

"I promise not to leave the Yukon without telling you, okay?"

"I promise too."

"I'll be back for supper the night before my shift. You okay with cooking?"

Jackson nodded against Wes's neck then kissed him and stepped back. He picked up Shadow while Wes got dressed in his layers of outdoor gear. They embraced once more and Wes left, shutting the door behind him, feeling Jackson's eyes following his every step.

Chapter Eighteen

By Thursday, Jackson was restless. He'd spent time at the McBride Museum, looking at artifacts from the Gold Rush and having a lively conversation with an employee named Alyse. After that, he'd pawed through the history section at the library, and then picked up all the groceries for dinner when Wes came home. Jackson even got a few extra things in case he burned or otherwise defiled the food. The rejects could go to the chickens, since they loved kitchen scraps. Wes would get whatever turned out the best.

For the salad dressing, he crushed garlic into olive oil to let the flavors marry—Wes's words, not his. He covered everything and packed it back into the fridge. There was water on the stove ready to boil and drop the fusilli in. All of that was done and it was barely past lunch.

The temperature had finally gone up to a balmy minus twenty-six Celsius, so he headed outside to strap on the snowshoes leaning against the wall on the front porch and invited Kale for a long walk. The afternoon shadows were lengthening by the time Jackson got back to the couch. He grabbed his latest library find about Yukon history and tucked a pillow behind his head. It didn't take long until the words blurred and holding the book was too much effort. It fell onto his chest and Jackson dozed.

Sometime later, something brushed Jackson's face. "G'way, Kale." He opened his eyes when he heard the responding snort.

Wes was leaning over him. "I could take issue at you thinking I'm the dog, or maybe I need a shower."

Jackson's arms rose to capture him. He took a deep breath filling his lungs with Wes: the wood smoke, pine, and fresh air scent. "Umm, I love the smell of you. Let me up, I've got dinner almost ready."

Wes kissed him. "Okay, you finish dinner. I'll clean

up." He returned to find the table set and food ready. "Jackson, this looks amazing!" Wes took a bite of the pasta. "It's perfect. Your cooking skills have gone up exponentially."

Jackson beamed at him. Their conversation was mostly light, with some boisterous laughter in between. They lingered over the meal, but it was only much later that night, when they tangled together, that Jackson dared to ask the question. "Did you find what you needed?" He curled a lock of Wes's hair around his finger.

"Maybe."

"You want to tell me about it?"

"Ummm." He moved his lips to Jackson's neck. "You know when you blush, this bit of skin gets warm and I love my lips right here."

Jackson blushed.

"See what I mean? To answer your question, I started another carving. I was getting tired of watching that wood spirit's angst."

"It is kind of snarly. Maybe we can tuck it into the trees for unsuspecting hikers to run across."

"Sure." Wes swallowed and the humor left his face. "It's time for me to talk to Abby."

"Are you ready?"

"No."

"It'll help."

Wes nodded. "It's the right thing. I should have done it years ago."

"Wes, you were a baby." Jackson stroked Wes's arm. "You weren't ready then."

"Still not sure I'm ready now." Wes drew a deep breath. "I work until three all weekend. I can set something up after work one day."

"At her place? Or here?"

"Whatever she wants."

"Then I'll be with you, whatever she choose. I'm not letting you deal with it by yourself."

Wes leaned onto his elbow and looked down at Jackson. "It's something I need to do alone."

"I get it, but I'm doing it anyway. You have support. You're not alone."

Wes sighed. "For a socially awkward introvert, you sure make a lot of demands."

"Yeah? Well, shut up and kiss me."

****

By Sunday afternoon, Wes's skin felt too small for him and the urge to run was keen. Abby and her husband, Thomas, would be here any second.

There was a brisk knock at the door and Wes leapt up from the couch. He swallowed, wiped his sweaty palms on his pants and walked into the hallway.

Jackson was there ahead of him and answered the door. "Hi, welcome—"

Abby pushed past him, trailed by a tall, sandy-haired man. She stopped directly in front of Wes, her chest heaving like she'd run a marathon.

"Abby," Thomas said in a low tone.

Wes knew he needed to say something, but he couldn't. Looking at his big sister for the first time in ten years, his throat clogged with tears he struggled not to shed. She hadn't changed and yet she was so different.

"Well?" she bit out. "You wanted to see me?" Her eyes were swimming as she shook Thomas's hand off her shoulder.

Wes cleared his throat, "I'm so sorry."

"Sorry? You're sorry. That's all you've got. FUCK YOU!" Tears were streaming down her face. "I can't do this, Thomas." She wheeled around and headed for the door with Thomas following.

Wes took a step forward, her scream still ringing in his ears, but Thomas shook his head. "We'll try another time," he told Jackson, barely looking at Wes.

On the porch, Thomas put an arm around her heaving shoulders and led her to the car.

****

Jackson gulped and gently pushed the door closed. Someone had to say something. He couldn't stand there watching Wes crumble. "That could have gone better."

Wes startled, as if he'd forgotten his presence.

Jackson reached for him. "I didn't expect...well, any of it."

Wes flinched and turned for the stairs. Jackson followed. After the heat of the kitchen, the bedroom was cool. Wes robotically stripped down, not making eye contact. Jackson wracked his brain. If he were a character in his book, he would say the perfect thing. Wes climbed into bed without saying a word. He turned away, dragging the covers over his head.

Jackson tugged his clothes off and climbed in. The force of Wes wrapping around him told him he was on the right track. Tucked in their cocoon under the heavy pile of blankets, it was hot and dark. Jackson could feel Wes's shoulders heaving. At times he was still as if holding his breath but then spasms would shake his body. Jackson was sure if Wes bolted now, he would never see him again.

Their cave grew humid and Jackson lost the feeling in his right arm. The leg coiled around his softened a bit. Jackson eased onto his back, settling Wes into the crook of his arm and pulling the quilt down, allowing a sweet draft to caress their faces. When he was sure Wes was asleep, he pressed his lips to Wes's sweaty curls. And whispered, "I love you." Jackson had never felt this way about anyone before. What was he going to do with his heightened awareness? Of course, Jackson was clear he could never say anything to Wes but damn it, his heart knew and it would cling to the swell of emotions as long as possible.

* * * *

Wes knew Jackson was being careful, tiptoeing around as if he was made of glass, trying to be extra thoughtful and give him space. But it was also incredibly aggravating, for reasons Wes didn't fully understand. He wanted to rage and lash out, but Jackson was the one in the line of fire, and he didn't deserve that. So Wes left. He called his boss and begged him for every available shift for the next few days. Then he called Nick and

Sophie for a place to stay. "I'll be working late every night. I won't even see you."

And he didn't. Wes didn't see anyone. He worked in the kitchen, behind the bar, and serving. His smile was pasted on and his movements were automatic. His tips weren't bad for a guy who wasn't there. Wes texted Jackson to confirm he was fine. But they never spoke.

Wes's gut was a war zone and his appetite almost non-existent. Food was a no go, booze not so much either, but it was his mind he wished he could lose. Why was he working? He should have gone out on the land.

He was glad to creep into the house long after Nick and Sophie were in bed. He didn't want to talk. He wanted to run away, leave town. He wanted to climb back up the hill into Jackson's arms. He wanted to have his sister back. He wanted a lot of things he just couldn't have.

Somehow, the week passed. Friday night, he stayed late helping the other servers with their clean-up. When it looked like closing time, he walked into the kitchen. Len, the owner, followed him. "Listen, Palmer, Shannon called in, she's back from her vacation and needs some bucks desperately. I told her she could have your shifts. You've put in so many extra hours this week I can't afford you. Take off and enjoy your weekend. I don't want you back till Wednesday for lunch. Got that? Go home and sort your shit."

"I—thanks." Wes didn't know whether to laugh or cry. Even Len could see through him.

Wes walked the empty streets to Nick's. A light was on in the living room lamp. Damn! The door was unlocked and the warmth when he walked in made his cold cheeks burn. The house was quiet. Sophie was curled on the corner of the couch, knitting.

Even if there was a physical way to avoid Sophie, there was no way Wes could be that crass. "What are you doing up?"

"Mon petit peanut is giving me indigestion, already taking over my life. Nick was tired. I don't want to wake him with my restlessness." Sophie's needles clicked rhythmically as she talked.

Wes moved toward her, watching her hands. "What are you making?"

"This is a sweater. I want to make hats, booties and a shawl for myself. All the things I won't have time to make when mon petit arrives." Sophie took her eyes off the knitting and patted the couch by her side. "Sit with me, I haven't seen you at all this week. You've been avoiding us."

"It's been a long week." Wes sat gently onto the couch, not wanting to jostle her. "I haven't been fit company."

"We're not company, we're family."

"I'm going to get a beer. Do you want something?"

She indicated a steaming cup beside her. "Tranquility tea."

He popped a beer open and joined her back on the couch.

She said nothing, only focused on her knitting and waited.

"I talked to Abby."

"Ah."

Sophie's soft exhalation made him think she understood, and maybe she did. Wes was sure Nick shared everything with her. Somehow, knowing she knew his deepest shame and was still willing to allow him to be part of their lives, their baby's life, comforted him.

Wes played with the label on the bottle. "She was so mad she couldn't even talk to me."

Sophie put her warm hand on his knee. "I'm sorry."

"I deserved it, expected it, anyway. She didn't let me explain myself, but honestly, what could I say?"

"Abby might not forgive you, but it's something you need to do, I think."

"But if she won't talk to me—"

"It is a long time for her to be so angry." Sophie set her knitting down. "Abby must have been very hurt. You can only do the best you can and hope for some resolution, good or bad."

"Maybe that was my only chance."

Sophie tipped her head slightly to the side. "Do you believe that?"

Wes took a long drink of beer, considering. "No, I need to try again. I need her to hear me before she decides. This time I'm not going to run because things are tough."

The quiet enveloped them. Wes drank his beer as Sophie knitted. The clicking of her needles was hypnotic. He was warming up and his body felt lighter than it had for days.

Sophie counted stitches under her breath. Once she was satisfied, she asked, "Where has Jackson been this week?"

Wes sighed. "I was a coward."

"What do you mean?"

"I was such a mess. I couldn't stand him seeing me that way. He thinks I'm something I'm not, maybe one of the heroes in his books, and if he finds out who I really am—" Wes couldn't finish. Saying it out loud twisted the breath in his chest.

The rainbow sweater continued taking form under Sophie's hands. "It must be exhausting caring for someone you don't trust to see you through your 'ugly.' I am so glad Nick and I can let those feelings flow honestly. It would be too hard otherwise."

Wes gave her a wan smile and set the beer on the coffee table. "You and Nick make it look so easy."

"It is a negotiation. We treat each other with respect and move from there."

Wes leaned over and clasped his hands on his knees. "I don't think I've always been respectful with Jackson."

Sophie regarded him gravely over her yarn. "Do you not respect him?"

"No, I do. He doesn't see how strong he is. It's hard to tell him sometimes."

"Bon, then what is it you need to make this easier?"

"Maybe I need him to understand I'm not right for him before I get too attached. I seem to be the one getting all the benefits from knowing him. I'm not sure what he sees in me."

Sophie put her knitting down again and moved right into his space. "I am so sad to hear that. We all love you, Wesley. You must learn to love yourself and then you can give yourself freely." She looked down at her belly. "Ah, my peanut is asleep. I need to do the same."

"It was so nice to see you." Wes got up and helped her to her feet, accepting her hug. "I hope sleep comes and finds you. Thanks."

Sophie started toward the bedroom and turned. "Will we see you in the morning? Nick will make waffles."

"His breakfasts are the best but…"

Sophie nodded to the kitchen. "If you need a phone, mine is charging over there."

"Sophie, you're going to be a wonderful mother."

"I hope so. It is so hard to imagine."

"You will, believe me."

She smiled and left him in silence.

Wes squared his shoulders and walked into the kitchen. The clock on the wall said it was two-forty eight. He picked up Sophie's phone and dialed.

Jackson answered up on the first ring. "Is everything okay?"

"Not sure," said Wes. "Can you come and get me?"

"I'll be right there."

"I'm sorry to wake you. I've been a dick."

"I'm on my way."

Wes put his bottle in the blue bin and Sophie's mug in the dishwasher, found paper and a pen by the phone, and scribbled a note. *Thanks for everything. Gone home. Talk soon.*

He was shivering in the cold by the door when Jackson arrived.

Chapter Nineteen

It was finally happening. Jackson's reading for Sophie's book club. He had been half dreading and half excited about it, ever since he agreed almost a month ago. Somehow, mid-November had arrived with his barely noticing the days passing and tonight was the night.

Lorraine, his agent, had been thrilled and mailed all kinds of swag, posters, and books. They sat in a massive cardboard box by the front door. Did all of Hanson's authors get this level of attention when doing their promotions? Or was it because he'd never done anything like it before and Lorraine was pulling out all the stops? Sophie had phoned with countless details about the afternoon meeting, trying to involve him, but Jackson begged told her to stop. It was impossible to concentrate on anything else with his growing anxiety. His inner voices were mixed. Half of them were telling him to change his mind and change his phone number. The other half were more confident, declaring it was going to be exciting and would help him in the long run. The funny thing was, the positive voices were a little louder than usual. They reminded him this wasn't his mother's academic group. This book club specifically focused on historical romance, which meant not one of them would think Jackson was wasting his life. Besides, they were all friends of Sophie's, and she'd been nothing but kind to him. Still, this could be one of those things that seemed like a good idea at the time, but then you regretted for years after.

Wes stuck his head into the bathroom. "I'll drive. I know you can handle it, but a big author like you should have a chauffeur."

Tension rippled across Jackson's shoulders. "Fine. You drive."

"Great. We'll get you settled in, then Nick and I will disappear. And if you need a last minute blow job to help you relax, I'll be in shouting distance."

Jackson tripped; he wasn't sure on what since he was

standing still. "Dammit, Wes! You can't say stuff like that. We'll be late."

Wes's grin was wicked. "Hey, my job is to distract you and I think it's working."

Jackson rolled his eyes and took one last look in the mirror. Wes had insisted he keep the top button of his shirt open and his hair tousled, claiming Jackson needed to look a little rakish to sell his book.

Jackson thought he looked mildly untidy more than anything else, but it was too late to change.

Wes kissed his cheek and groped his butt. "Come on, stud, it's time. I'll go warm up Sunny."

They left Kale outside. It was cold but he preferred watching the driveway when they were gone and he would be fine until they got home. The past weeks had flown by in a haze of stress and preparation for this meeting. Wes saved Jackson by being available to take his mind off things. There was still a wall Jackson couldn't get past, but Wes was so sweet and attentive that Jackson could quietly pretend they were in love, that this was their house, their dog, and their forever.

Sophie was absolutely thrilled with Lorraine's box of goodies. Digging in like a kid at Christmas, she found a poster for Jackson's pirate trilogy. "Mon Dieu, look at all of this, it is amazing." She unrolled it reverently to view the half-clad pirate holding the barely contained princess in his muscled arms. Her eyes shone.

"Wow," said Wes. "That guy is really built."

Nick rolled his eyes. "Come on, Wes, let's figure out what we want to watch later, or would you rather go to a movie?" With that, they left the room.

Sophie kept pulling things out of the box. There were a lot of books by Hanson's writers. Some were by Simone De Bravé and others were by newer, unknown writers. There were a few of Jackson's earlier books too. "Oh, Jackson, this is wonderful. Thank you."

"Don't thank me until after." Jackson laughed nervously. "I still don't know what I'm going to say."

"Don't worry. I have it all arranged. The ladies will come in, we will have a glass of wine, or beer if you want?"

"I don't want to drink too much. That would be worse than awkward."

Sophie hugged him. "You are too hard on yourself. You will be fine."

Despite all the reassurance, Jackson was worried. There was a lot riding on this, at least in his mind. It might not make much difference to the larger world, but what if he really couldn't do it? After all these years of telling himself he wasn't capable, he was scared to prove the voices right.

"Have you picked out a piece to read? Sophie asked.

"Yes, Hanson's said I could read a couple scenes from *The Pirate's Revenge*. They even gave me a code to get your group advance copies."

"Oh, Jackson, you are the best! Once you are finished, I have told the women they can ask you a few questions.

Jackson's stomach did a dive, but he kept the smile on his face. She thought he could do it. She made it fail proof. He could do it, he hoped. Crossing his fingers was a bit immature, but the pressure between his knuckles was grounding and made him smile.

Sophie put wine glasses, cookies and a roll of masking tape on the counter. "Let's get that poster up."

They taped the pirate to his place on the wall. It was pretty impressive. Seeing Jackson's name in big letters at the bottom of the poster along with the book title gave him a little boost.

The doorbell rang. "Why don't you go to the kitchen and wait there until everyone arrives," Sophie said. "I will introduce you to them all at once."

Wes was in the kitchen, sneaking a cookie and waiting for him. "You look like you're on your way to an execution. That greenish gray is not your color." He brushed Jackson's cheek. "Let me get you a glass of wine?"

"Don't you dare. When I drink, I get way too loose. This way I'll be able to focus and do a good job."

"You'd look sophisticated with the glass in your hand. Authorly. You don't need to drink it, but it would give you something to do with your hands."

Jackson considered. "Well, I could have water, or I

could just sip, and not slam it. That's where I get in the most trouble."

The doorbell rang twice more in rapid succession. Wes pulled him into a hard embrace. His whisper tickled against Jackson's ear. "Your words hold their own, babe. Don't listen to the voices in your head, listen to me." His lips brushed Jackson's ear, neck and then he captured his mouth in a spine tingling kiss. Wes let his hand drift over Jackson's back and gave his butt a firm squeeze before heading downstairs.

Great, now Jackson didn't have to worry about looking like an idiot, just a pervert. He adjusted his pants and poured himself a glass of wine. He could hear Sophie greeting guests. She was amazing and would fit perfectly as an intrepid woman of the Gold Rush. The thought made Jackson smile and he was still writing in his head when Sophie's fingers on his shoulder startled him back to reality.

Sophie directed him to a chair facing the group and Jackson saw Jimmy's girlfriend, Julie. She waved to him, and he gave her a wave back. Then he saw another familiar face. It was Alyse from the McBride Museum.

"Jackson!" Alyse said. "What a surprise. I knew you were researching the Gold Rush but I had no idea that you were you."

"It's really nice to see you again," said Jackson. "Hope you have fun tonight." That sounded a bit generic but she gave him a pleased smile in response.

Jackson sat down and gazed at the circle of women around him, each with a glass of wine, munching on oatmeal cookies. He sipped his wine and took a calming breath.

Sophie stood beside him smiling, her hand resting on her barely visible bump. "Ladies, welcome. We are so lucky to have tonight's guest. He is on a writing retreat in our city this winter and has agreed to talk to us. I would like you to welcome, Mr. E.J. Williams."

Jackson sat red-faced while they clapped, sweat trickling down his back.

"Why don't we start with the reading from your upcoming book?" Sophie handed him a copy of the book with his passages marked.

Jackson had a moment of gratitude for her. Sophie had thought of everything. Then, aware of the group waiting for him, he cleared his throat and started at the part where Nicholas Rycroft, the gentleman pirate, had to face that his undying love for feisty Kiana would never be. Fate had decreed their love would hang forever in limbo. By the time Jackson finished, his hands had stopped shaking.

Jackson snapped the book closed to a surprising ripple of applause.

"Who has the first question?" Sophie looked around.

A woman in purple yoga pants raised her hand. "Mr. Williams, my name is Jana. I'd like to know why you write?"

Jackson could hear the clock ticking in the kitchen. Ten sets of eyes focused on him. Surely they could hear the sweat pooling in the waist of his boxers. Taking a sip of wine to moisturize his dry mouth, he tried to say what was in his heart while not listening to his head. "I wrote my first novel when I was fourteen. My characters brought me to places I could never go in real life." He stopped, catching the eyes of Jana across the circle. "It's possible I write them for the same reason you read them."

There was a collective sigh. Sophie smiled.

Jackson was doing okay. He really was. He wasn't sure where the time went. As he answered questions his heart rate slowed, then he actually enjoyed himself. When Sophie stood to thank him, Jackson was startled at how the two hours had flown by. He'd survived. And he was pretty sure, if the right circumstance presented itself, he'd do something like this again.

****

The next day, Wes had to leave before Jackson was awake to work an early shift. Their shared elation from the previous night's success carried Wes through the day, and he found himself humming as he worked. Jackson's relief at making it through the evening had been overridden by his surprise that it had gone so well. Wes wasn't sure if Jackson had been certain he would fail, but knew Jackson hadn't expected to succeed so wildly. Sophie had also been thrilled and carried herself with the confidence of someone who'd been proven right. Jackson had been euphoric on the ride home and as much as said he'd be looking for another event along the same lines soon. Of course, Wes had known Jackson would be fine but, his opinion didn't count, only Jackson's.

Wes was, however, amazed at his immense pride in someone who wasn't even his boyfriend and sang under his breath as he sorted receipts.

Len caught his eye and gave him an amused smile. "Good to see you sorted your shit, Palmer."

After work, one of the Wily's servers had been heading out to the hot springs after her shift and had offered to drop him off at home. Bonus. Even better, Wes walked in to find dinner on the table. The chicken was a little dry and the potatoes had a light crunch, but the salad was fresh with a tasty vinaigrette Jackson had made himself.

"This is fantastic!" Wes took another bite of the chicken, which wasn't really dry now that he thought about it. It was great to have Jackson thinking about food without prompting and to have him trying more complex meals than scrambled eggs. Wes leaned in and enjoyed his food.

In contrast, Jackson was not present. His body was, and his hand was shoving food around his plate, but his eyes were far away.

Wes nudged him. "What's up?"

"I talked to my dad today. I had some overflow courage from last night and decided to properly come out to them. Before that, I mostly just implied and hinted, and they ignored it. Mom wasn't home. I wasn't sure about talking just to Dad. He's pretty quiet and really follows Mom's lead on a lot of things. I was gonna wait till she got home but, I figured I wouldn't be able to later so—" He dropped the fork and pressed his lips together.

Wes leaned in to rub comforting circles on his back. "So what happened?"

"He wasn't surprised." Jackson grimaced. "I guess I wasn't as subtle about Perry as I thought. What really hurts is if they suspected, couldn't they have done any-thing to show it was okay? I spent so long absolutely con-vinced that gay wasn't an option, and going out with those girls to keep Mom off my back just reinforced the idea that anything else was unacceptable. I'm furious. How dare she put so much energy into convincing me I wasn't okay as I was. I don't think I can talk to her again till I work this out." Jackson jumped up and started angrily stacking dishes. Then he sighed, shaking his arms like he was trying to shake off the anger. He glanced back at Wes. "What was it like when you came out?"

Wes shrugged. "I guess I never really came out. I mean, it felt like everyone in town knew. I never really talked to my parents about it. I think my mom was depressed and my dad was a mean drunk. I don't remem-ber him much when I was young but when I hit high school, the old man seemed to need to show the world who was boss, and it wasn't me."

For a moment, Wes was a child again, realizing that not all families were like his. He had loved all the times his mom would put them in the car and drop them with Izzy and Jeff, just for the day. Now he wondered how she had coped, but at the time he hadn't cared.

Wes put down his glass and clenched his hands in his lap. He was aware of Jackson moving closer. Wes proba-bly needed to stop but the words forced themselves out of him. "When Dad was drunk, he didn't notice the more he pushed me, the less time I spent at home and the more I, um, self-medicated. Those days, it was mostly weed and what I found in the medicine cabinet. I spent more time high than sober and avoiding the family at all costs. Mom was mostly in a fog, so she never noticed. I had to stay away from Izzy and Jeff when I was like that. They wouldn't have put up with it. Things came to a head at a family party. We were at a hall in one of the small com-munities, Carcross I think, celebrating some stupid thing, probably an anniversary or birthday. Dad the gall to have one of his women there and was practically fucking her on the dance floor, in front of everyone. Mom, family friends, literally everyone."

Wes knew he was on the edge of yelling his words,

so he took another breath. He so vividly remembered his outrage when he saw his mom sitting at a table, watching and crying. "I was pissed and embarrassed."

It was an avalanche. Once Wes started talking, he couldn't stop. "I got him in the coat room and told him to straighten up. We fought, first verbally and then I got so disgusted and mad that this time I threw the first punch, right in his face. He punched me back. He was bigger than I was. He hit me hard, but I let him have everything that had been building in me for years. I was screaming at him that he was a waste of skin and he could do us all a favor by going out and driving off a cliff."

Jackson was standing beside him awkwardly, as the words poured, unbidden from Wes's body.

"Mom must have heard us. It was the first time I ever saw her challenge him. She was between us, screaming at me to get away. I did. I left them there and headed out back with Shane, a stoner friend, and got high, or maybe higher. I didn't even know they'd left until Aunt Izzy gathered us to say there had been an accident. By then, I was wasted."

Without any conscious thought, Wes was moving toward the door. "They crashed over a cliff on the way home and didn't survive. When I understood what had happened, I ran. It wasn't long after my sixteenth birthday." He turned, needing to get out of there.

Jackson followed, grabbing his shoulder. "Wes, it's not your—"

"Please, don't." Wes wasn't ashamed to beg. "Please." He took Jackson's hand in his but didn't meet his eyes. "I'm sorry. I can't be here right now." Wes dropped his hand and turned away.

"I'll be here when you're ready to come home." Jackson's voice was soft and full of tenderness.

Wes pushed open the door and walked out, trying to hold Jackson's words in his heart.

Chapter Twenty

Jackson didn't have time to brood about Wes's departure because Sophie called an hour later and she was bubbling over with a new plan.

She'd been out to her favorite hangout, the local used bookstore. Since yesterday had been such a success, Sophie wanted to introduce him to the owner. "A couple of people were had already in there raving about you, and she wants to talk to you about doing an event for her."

Jackson gulped. Yes, he wanted to stretch himself in that area, but geez, give a guy space to enjoy his previous success, can't you. "Wow! That's nice of you," said Jackson. "But you don't have to go to any trouble on my account."

"Oh, I'm not doing it for you," Sophie said with a mischievous giggle. "I was promised a discount on my favorite authors in return for bringing you. So really, you are doing me a favor."

Jackson couldn't help laughing. "Then how can I refuse? I'm free most afternoons this week. When would you like to go?"

They settled on three days from now and chatted for a few minutes. Jackson was in a better mood after the call. He was really doing this! His thoughts immediately returned to Wes. Should he be out there all alone right now? While Wes got sustenance from the land, which was what he needed in this moment, thinking about him hurt Jackson with a pain that was almost physical.

If that was the case, then he simply wouldn't think about him. Besides, Jackson functioned best if he didn't think too deeply about his emotions and the time would pass faster if he kept busy. Wes would come back when he wanted to.

As it turned out, Wes only spent a night at the trapline. He came back late the following day and in a decent mood. Jackson wondered if his cheer was a little forced and thought he could detect a brittle edge to Wes, one that hadn't been there before the confession about his family. Jackson didn't ask about anything. He had told Wes he would be there until he was ready and Jackson could wait.

In the meantime, Jackson had a meeting with a bookstore owner to worry about. He tried to subdue his terror by digging into the powerful feeling he'd had the other day when sharing his writing with people who knew his work and appreciated it for what it was.

The day arrived and Sophie and Jackson pushed their way out of the cold into the cozy house on 4th Avenue, home of the bookstore Wayword Words. Jackson unwrapped his scarf and stuffed his hat in his pocket. He wanted this, he really did. Heck, hadn't he actually wished for it on his high after he met her book club? When Sophie got an idea in her head, she would see it through and make it happen. It actually reminded him a bit of his mother. So why did it feel like support when Sophie did it, and smothering when his mother did it? Maybe it was because she had faith in him and his mom had very little belief in anything he did.

"Jackson, this is Barb Finstead," said Sophie, introducing them with a flourish. "She owns this amazing place. Barb, this is my friend E.J. Williams."

"Call me Jackson." He clasped Barb's hand, feeling thrilled that Sophie introduced him as her friend.

"Welcome to my store, Jackson. Let's sit down." Barb led him to a group of armchairs and called out to a woman standing behind the cash register. "Violet, come over and meet Mr. Williams."

Violet shuffled over. She was wearing a deep blue apron emblazoned with the phrase, *Don't get lost in Wayword Words.*

Jackson laughed. "I'm always getting lost in wayward words." He shook Violet's hand as she mumbled a greeting. Her long hair hid most of her face. She peered through it, investigating him from behind a dark curtain of hair. Jackson was surprised at her reaction. Was she nervous about meeting *him*?

"Sophie tells me you did quite a presentation at her book club," said Barb.

Violet ducked back behind the counter.

"Um, I did *a* presentation..." Jackson didn't know how to finish the sentence.

"I'd be thrilled if you'd consider doing one here," said Barb.

"I—" Jackson's face heated. He tried to say yes, or something close to it, but the words wouldn't come out.

Barb gave an understanding nod. "You don't do many public appearances."

"None!" Had he yelled that? Jackson swallowed. "No, Sophie's was the first." The ground could swallow him now.

"Five of the eight people who were there have been here telling me I have to meet you," said Barb. "We don't get too many authors because we're mostly a used book-store. I'd like you to come in soon. I'll put your books out, you can do a reading, then answer a few questions like you did at Sophie's." Barb snapped her fingers. "You know what, I'm getting ahead of myself. I should show you around first. Let you get a feel for the place. We're now in the children's section. Over there we have New Age and occult."

The store was comfortable with wide windowsills, easy chairs, and a Christmas tree festooned with decorative pens and colorful notebooks. Garlands surrounded the children's books around him. The other rooms were filled with stacks and shelves and Christmas music played softly throughout the building. It was a great store, more like his grandmother's living room than a place of business, and Jackson loved it.

He stopped in the Canadian Literature section and gestured at a shelf dedicated to new books by Yukon writers. "You really support your own here."

"Of course," said Barb. "We have an amazing and diverse group of artists in the territory. Many are the First Peoples, and they have a perspective that's worth paying attention to." She led him into a side room, proba-bly at one time a formal dining room. It was wall-to-wall romance novels. "And this is where you live." She waved to a shelf that was all E.J. Williams.

Jackson's jaw dropped. Those were all his? "I don't

think I've ever seen so many of my books all in the same place before." He gently ran a hand over the spines, unable to stop smiling.

"There's probably three copies of each, except for the first. We can't seem to get that one."

"I should check with my agent. She may know why."

"It could be that people don't want to part with it," said Barb. "Some books never come unstuck from readers who love them."

Strolling past shelves and shelves of loved books made Jackson feel as if anything was possible. "How many people would you expect at a book signing?"

"Thirty or forty, max. It's all we can hold. I sell tickets for a nominal price, usually five dollars, and we give it to the Food Bank."

"You'd sell tickets?" Jackson was taken aback.

Barb's face filled with surprise, and perhaps even mild shock. "Mr. Williams. Jackson. You must realize you'd be a big draw here."

Jackson gave her a self-deprecating smile. "Most of the people I know who read my books hide them under the covers at night."

Sophie muttered something under her breath behind him.

Barb regarded him closely. "Jackson, you are a gifted, prolific writer of Historical Romantic fiction. Is it possible you're ashamed of your work?"

Jackson's flush started at his toes. "It's complicated. I love writing them. I get lost in them. I've never been given much respect for my work."

"From whom?" Barb asked. "You've got a huge fan following."

"Well, my mother is an English professor at the University of Western Ontario. She publishes literary critiques as part of her job. I guess most of our family friends are part of her academic circle. Even people outside that group tend to snicker and mock."

She harrumphed back to the cash register with Jackson following meekly behind. "Violet, what books do we get the most of?"

"Romance."

"And what books pay the rent here?"

"Romance again."

"And at the risk of repeating myself, what is the most active book club here?"

"Romance."

Barb spun to face him. "Romance makes people feel good and many people read them. I have a good selection of every genre, but a great story with a happy ending, that's what people want, so, yes, I will have a sellout crowd. And your family won't be here. The question is, will you be able to handle it?"

"I'm not sure," Jackson said honestly. "But I'm willing to try."

The bells over the door jingled and a couple of customers walked in, bringing a swoosh of cold with them.

"How about a Sunday afternoon?" said Barb.

"That sounds fine." Oh God, Jackson was talking like he was saying yes. "It'll take some time for me to get material from Hanson's."

"You'll do it then. Terrific! How about the beginning of January? I'll start advertising and get tickets printed right away. That gives us almost five weeks to get ready and will liven up the place in the dead zone after the holidays."

Sophie put her arm around Jackson. The smile she directed at him was warm and soft, but the look she flashed Barb was a high five.

Jackson finalized the final details with Barb and headed out into the cold with Sophie. "Oh my God, I can't believe I agreed to that!"

She looped her arm through his and patted his hand. "You were phenomenal! And do not worry, you have lots of time to prepare. I will help."

Jackson sighed, trying to push back the creeping dread. "Having lots of time to prepare might be worse. That's five weeks to psych myself out."

The city put Christmas lights on every tree push and lamppost. His mom would call it tacky but he enjoyed how it brightened the dark afternoon while they walked back to his car.

"Don't worry," said Sophie. "There will be lots to

keep your mind busy. Christmas is coming up and I had another idea of something you could do."

"Wait, did you say another idea? Let me get used to this one."

"Don't forget, this one was your idea. The only thing I did was put you in the right place at the right time."

"Fine." Jackson pulled her along to the car. "Tell me now. I'd rather be prepared." He unlocked the passenger door for her.

Sophie dropped down into the seat, pulled the door shut and buckled her seat belt around her belly. "Actually, this was not my idea, but Wesley's. He thinks it would be good for you to teach a class for people who want to write."

Jackson started the engine. "No way. I could never do that." It was too much. His brain was full now. He needed time to process.

"You also thought you couldn't talk to my book club, remember? You were stunning. And I have surveyed the people in our Romance Readers Club. Almost half would pay for something like that. Maybe six weeks. I have checked with the university and if you send a proposal, it is almost certain they would run a course in the fall semester, or Barb would give you her program room for a small fee." Sophie's smile was blinding.

Jackson pressed his lips together and stared at the steering wheel. "I will be gone by fall."

"Oh yes, I understand, but it wouldn't hurt to check it out."

As much as Jackson appreciated her faith in him, he was feeling completely overwhelmed. "Please, Sophie, let me survive the bookstore first. I don't have room for anything else."

"But of course. Nick has told me I sometimes get too excited for people. I only want you to know that I know you could do it, and there are a lot of people who would be happy to support your writing."

They drove the rest of the way to Sophie's house silently while Jackson fought to get his mixed emotions under control. He'd made a decision today to take another step outside his comfort zone. He had a friend who believed in him. He could focus on those things to keep the doubt at bay.

When they arrived, Jackson walked in the door, not even taking his jacket off. He was ready to get out of there. This must be how Wes felt when he needed to get back on the land. All Jackson needed was Isabelle's cozy living room to cocoon till his heart stopped pounding. He leaned down the stairs. "Wes, come on, I'm ready to go."

"Hey, you're back." Nick raced up the stairs and pushed past him to swoop Sophie into his arms. "I missed you."

"You missed supper on the table," Sophie teased. "You could have started it yourself."

"Aw, sorry, Wes and I got caught up," said Nick. "Do you mind getting started? We're just finishing up."

Sophie laughed. "Jackson, will you stay for dinner?"

Jackson gave her a tight smile. "Sorry, Wes has dinner in the slow cooker."

Wes came up the steps, pulling his jacket on.

. "Yeah, I have a stew going but it will be fine for a bit."

"All right, we will catch up later." Sophie waved goodbye and headed to the kitchen.

"So," said Wes. "Nick and I have been talking about a project. He needs your help."

Jackson tossed Wes the car keys. He was sure he didn't have the energy left to even drive.

"I already told Jimmy I would help in his backroom when he's ready, so I hope you don't need walls torn down."

"It's not that." Nick looked at Jackson. "I'm not sure where to start, so I guess I'll try the beginning. You know those kids I work with? There's a group that meets after school three days a week. It keeps them out of trouble. We play some games and shoot the shit. I keep looking for different things for them to do."

"Yeah, you mentioned it when we were skiing. You took them out once, right?" Jackson's heart sank, wondering what this had to do with him.

"Right, they loved it but there's no funding for that kind of thing and it comes right out of my pocket," said

Nick. "None of these kids are really in trouble yet. I keep thinking if they could find some way to express themselves, art or something, they would be set. I asked Wes to come and give them some carving lessons, but—"

Jackson glanced at Wes. "I can think of a few problems with that."

Wes chuckled. "Yeah, like giving them all sharp knives." He pulled on his boots.

Nick rolled his eyes. "I can picture it now, me trying to explain how they all have infected tattoos carved on their bodies."

Wes shook his head. "I thought they might carve each other up, but tattoos didn't occur to me."

"As a general rule," said Nick, "as long as there are no drugs or alcohol involved, they like each other pretty well."

Jackson watched their banter but felt like crying. He knew what was coming.

Nick him a friendly smile. "I was hoping you'd come and talk to them, you know, about being a writer."

"I'm sorry I can't." Jackson reached for the door. It was time to leave now.

Wes didn't move. "Just hear him out."

Nick glanced between him and Wes. "Nothing formal, maybe you sitting with them talking, maybe about telling their stories. They have things to say, and they don't know where to start."

"Nick, I just can't," Jackson pleaded.

"It's okay, Jackson, I understand." Nick held up his hands and backed off.

"Just think about it," Wes pushed. "You don't have to decide right now."

"I said no!" Jackson snapped and fled out the door.

****

Wes was right behind Jackson. What happened here? He wasn't used to feeling so wrong-footed. He quickly unlocked the car and got behind the wheel. Jackson did up his seatbelt and laid his head back as if he was too tired to hold it up any longer.

"So how did it go at the bookstore?" Wes put the car in gear.

"It was great." Jackson sounded defeated. "They love my work and want me to come in the New Year to do a reading. Barb thinks she can sell tickets."

Wes eased the car along the slippery streets. "That's a good thing, right?"

"It was great, it felt really good. For a few minutes I actually thought I could do it."

"Of course you can do it." Why would Jackson think otherwise? Wes must be missing something. He'd been moody and short-tempered since he brought up all those memories of his parents. But Wes was self-aware enough to know his current annoyance with Jackson was probably unjustified.

Jackson stared away from him out the window. "You told Sophie I would teach a writing class. I don't know the first thing about teaching!"

"Don't sell yourself short. I think most people want to know how you write a story. It would inspire them."

"Yeah, maybe and that might hold them for an hour but it would wear pretty thin after a week or two. It might work better if I was a real writer."

Wes saw red. He wanted to strangle whoever had done such a number on Jackson. "You're published! Your books are available in great bookstores everywhere, you have a huge following. What the hell does it take in your eyes to be a real writer?"

Jackson bit his lip.

Wes ran a frustrated hand through his hair. "You're an acclaimed writer. Why doesn't that count?"

Jackson shook his head, "It doesn't." He hurried on. "I love it. Work isn't supposed to be fun, things worth having are hard. They take sweat and blood, and you can be proud of them. People create amazing things in the face of adversity, I've never faced anything in my life!"

Jaw clenched, Wes eased Sunny around the Sternwheeler corner, up the street, and through the traffic circle before he let his breath out. "Why is it so damned hard for you to respect yourself? I respect what you do. That should mean something to you."

"Of course it does, but you're twisting things. You make it sound like if I don't agree with you, I don't respect you."

Wes slumped behind the wheel. "I don't understand why you only believe the bad things people say and never the good. You're doing amazing things with your life and bringing millions of people joy."

"Millions is a gross exaggeration."

"That's not the point." Wes focused on the road and stomped on the gas pedal.

"Stop it! Don't take your anger with me out on Sunny."

The rest of the drive was heavy with silence. Once home, Jackson tumbled into the darkness of the yard. "I'm sorry I'm not who you want me to be," he bit out over his shoulder and stormed to the barn.

Wes went inside and checked on the stew. The house could be warmer, so Wes laid a fire in the living room grate. He turned out the lights, immersed in the flickering of the flames. How had this afternoon gone so bad? He'd only wanted to help. Playing everything through a loop in his mind, it finally clicked. Wes hadn't been listening. Jackson had been overwhelmed and rather than trying to understand, Wes had given in to his emotions in the moment and tried to fix things by yelling that Jackson shouldn't feel how he felt. Hopefully Jackson wouldn't be long. Wes owed him an apology.

The front door opened and Jackson ducked in with the chill, hung his jacket, washed his hands and sat down beside Wes. "The stew okay?"

"Yeah, I wasn't feeling very hungry."

"Me neither." Jackson slumped on the couch.

"I'm sorry, Jackson, I can't tell you how to feel. I want so badly for you to see yourself the way I do. But I realized I'm trying to bully you into it, and that makes me no better than the voices in your head."

"I'm sorry too. I had too much in my brain. I just told the bookstore that I would do their thing and was having very mixed feelings about it when Sophie hit me up about teaching writing. Then Nick and his kids. It felt like everyone was lurking waiting to pounce." Jackson reached for his hand.

Wes grasped it, holding it tight. "Wow, bad timing. And then I piled on the pressure."

"You're right, though."

"I am?" Wes was surprised.

"About me, about it being easier to believe the negative things." Jackson grimaced. "Every once in a while, I catch a glimpse of the person I could be if I weren't so scared to fail. I want that."

"And I want that for you too, but please keep reminding me to give you space to find it for yourself. I hate it when people tell me what's so obvious to them about me. You've been really great about giving me space to deal with my feelings. I owe you the same respect."

Jackson leaned his head onto Wes's shoulder. "You know what the worst part is?"

"What?"

"Nick and Sophie were thinking about me and trying to help me and I said no. Practically threw it in their face. This is why I don't have any friends. I'm really not good at it."

"Jackson." Wes softened his voice. "Their friendship isn't conditional. They like you for you, and respecting your boundaries is part of that. It's easy to screw up with someone you care about especially when you want to help them. Hopefully you can forgive them and me."

Jackson craned his neck to look at Wes without relinquishing the spot on his shoulder. "There's nothing to forgive. I'm not up for teaching writing at the university but talking to Nick's kids sounded important. I would like to help someday if I can."

"You don't have to decide anything right now. This has to be on your terms. You know how to reach Nick if you change your mind." They sat together in the dark listening to the snap of the fire and the dog's soft snores. "You hungry now?"

"You could talk me into it."

"Yeah, me too. Let's eat." Wes got up but didn't let go of Jackson's hand. "If you did decide to help Nick, I don't think you'll be sorry."

"You might be. It'll be you who gets to pick up the

pieces if they break me."

Wes hugged him. "I have a feeling you are made of tougher stuff than you think."

Chapter Twenty-one

Wes didn't have to go to work today. He had been looking forward to a long afternoon walk with Kale and Jackson to help Jackson work out some of his jitters about then upcoming book signing.

Then Thomas called to say he and Abby were ready to visit, and could they come over today?

Now Jackson was the one calming Wes down. It hadn't gone well last time, and Wes had no illusions about this time. His stomach was cramping, and his breathing was shallow. He both wasn't ready to face this and more than ready to have it done with, no matter what it meant in the big picture. If only he had gone to the land today and hadn't been here for the call! That would have been so much easier.

Jackson watched Wes pace back and forth. "What can I do?" he asked softly, his face serious.

"This isn't your crap. It's mine." Wes ran his fingers through his hair, letting the curls snag and pull.

"Maybe, but you don't have to go through it alone."

Wes swallowed. "Could you hold me?"

Jackson intercepted Wes's pacing and pulled him down on the couch.

Wes let himself be wrapped in Jackson's arms. "I'm glad you're here. You can do something for me."

Jackson quietly stroked Wes's back. "Whatever you need," he murmured.

"When they get here, will you get Thomas out of the way? Last time, he dragged Abby out before we got anywhere. This is going to hurt us both but we need to figure it out. She may chew me up and spit me out, but I have you to put the pieces back."

Jackson hugged him tighter.

"Careful," Wes gasped, "you'll strangle me before she gets her chance at me."

Jackson chuckled loosening his hold.

"Do you think you can do it?"

"Yes," said Jackson. "I'll offer him a drink and take him to the kitchen."

"Not far enough away," said Wes. "Go to the Castle. The fire is laid, you strike a match, you'll be warm there. Don't come back too soon."

Jackson didn't immediately reply. He took a shaky breath and said. "Sure."

He could feel Jackson's heart beating along the length of his chest where their bodies touched.

They sat in each other's arms. The sun moved across the floor and the clock ticked. Then Kale jumped up and started to pace back and forth at the door, nails clicking on the wood.

"Showtime." Wes got up.

Jackson put on his coat and hat. When the knock came, he opened the door. "Um, hi."

Abby ignored him as she stepped inside. Thomas followed her and gave Jackson a nod. Kale was alert, intently watching everyone.

"Wesley." Abby spat the name.

"Hi, Abby." Wes spoke quietly. "Thanks for coming over."

Abby crossed her arms. "You have something to say to me?"

"I am sorry. I'm sorry for leaving, for everything. I was a coward. I ran."

"You!" Abby charged across the room. "You left me all alone to deal with everything by myself. I was eighteen years old! I thought my baby brother was dead." Her face was red and blotchy.

Wes thought she would hit him. Then she was crying, collapsing under the weight of her tears. He grabbed her before she hit the floor, wrapping his arms around her easing her down, rocking her back and forth. Wes realized he was crying too, and his tears were falling on her. "Oh Abby, I'm sorry, I'm so sorry."

Kale sniffed at Abby and licked her cheek. He gave a huge sigh and lay down, his body pressed against them both.

From the corner of Wes's eye, he saw Jackson gently set a tissue box next to them. He heard Jackson ask

Thomas if he'd like to take a walk with him. There were soft footsteps and the door closed.

Only when they were alone did Wes speak. "Abby, please, Abby. I'm so sorry."

Abby's sobs started to subside. "I needed you so bad, but you were gone, you had my car and Mom's run-away money. Why didn't you take me with you?" She was hiccupping with tears.

Wes stroked her hair. "I couldn't take you, I knew you would hate me the minute you found out what I did."

"How could I hate you? You're my brother." She leaned back and grabbed some tissues, passing him one before mopping her face.

"I killed them." He crumpled the tissue in his hand and wiped his face on his shoulder.

Abby scrambled to her feet, startling Kale. "What do you mean you killed them? I killed them." She gestured to Wes. "Come on, let's sit in there. The floor hurts and it's freezing."

Wes let her pull him toward the living room. "Not possible. You didn't kill them, I did."

Abby deflated into the couch. "Isn't that just like you, trying to take this away from me too." She looked despondent, as if all the fight had gone out of her.

A chill went up Wes's spine. He sat next to her and reached out for her hand. "Tell me."

Abby grasped his hand back. "Dad was always an asshole, pushing you around constantly and making you feel less than human." She shuddered. "He always reeked of whiskey. I still can't stomach the smell. Thomas can only drink beer, anything harder and I throw up."

She started shaking and Wes put his arms around her.

"Dad went from a drunken asshole to an insane drunken asshole. I thought I could protect you from him but I was afraid of what he'd do to you." Abby resumed sobbing.

Wes guided her head onto his shoulder and stroked her kinky hair.

"I should have stopped him. He wasn't violent with me, not like he was with you. I was afraid he'd kill you one day." Abby drew a shuddery breath as her sobs came to a halt. She started playing with the edge of his shirt. "It doesn't matter. The point is, it's my fault they're dead, not yours."

Wes shook his head. "No. I told him he should do us all a favor and kill himself. I didn't know he'd take Mom with him. She shoved herself between us. I thought she was protecting him, after everything." Wes held his breath waiting for the recriminations.

"You're such a jerk, Wesley." Abby sat up straight and glared at him. "You need to grow up. This isn't all about you. If you'd stuck around for ten more seconds, you'd know what I know."

Wes waited, wiping his eyes on his wet shoulder, and blowing his nose on a crumpled tissue.

"I was scared of Dad," said Abby. "I was afraid to sleep, afraid to be in the house with him, never sure when he would go off. I hated his guts. I wished him dead. I prayed for him to die. Mom was broken, I couldn't talk to her. She had no control of the situation and there was no point saying anything to her." Abby's voice was firm, but she was avoiding his eyes. "We went to the party. He was trying to get into that woman's pants. When you and he headed into the coat room, you looked so miserable, I couldn't keep quiet anymore. I found Mom and told her he was hurting you. I screamed at her to do something or I was going to kill him. She dragged him out and loaded him in the car. He was totally wasted. She was behind the wheel when they crashed."

The room was quiet. Kale was lying at their feet watching them. Abby reached down and wound her fingers in his fur. "God, I love this dog."

Wes found he'd been unconsciously holding his breath throughout Abby's story. He exhaled, still trying to process what he'd heard. "I thought he crashed the car."

"You would have known if you'd stayed long enough for the funeral. Of course, there would have been no funeral if I hadn't laid down the law."

Wes gripped her hand. "You don't know that."

"She was so mad," Abby whispered. "I'd never seen her like that. She was in no shape to drive."

"No." Wes looked around the darkening room, a sense of detachment falling over him. "I had my learner's permit. I was supposed to drive that day. Our parents were drinking, thinking they had a safe ride home, and I got high anyway."

"When my youngest was born, Thomas talked me into going for counseling. I was a horrible mother and wife, hell, a horrible person. The counselor said it wasn't my fault."

"Good, because it wasn't."

"No, it was her. Mom killed them both."

Wes gasped and stared at her in shock.

"It took a lot of counseling before I could believe that she did it and I wasn't responsible." Abby laughed, soft at first and then rising in volume until she was shaking with laughter and tears. Her breath was jagged. "I named him Wesley."

"What?"

"My baby. His name is Wesley. He reminds me of you."

His sister had named her son Wesley. It was more than he could take. He cried, harder than before, and kept crying until there was nothing left. Wes felt Abby's sobs in return as she leaned into his arms. Kale pushed against their knees, holding their grief until they ran out of tears and sat quietly holding each other.

The stove light came on and they blinked at the sudden glare. Squinting over the counter into the kitchen, they watched as Jackson and Thomas snuck around, trying to be quiet. Jackson pulled things out of the fridge. He poured soup into a pot and turned on the burner. Thomas placed four beers he'd brought up from the basement on the counter.

Jackson glanced over and his brows rose in surprise. "Sorry! I didn't want to disturb you, but it's getting late and I thought you guys could use sustenance."

As if reading each other's minds, Wes and Abby rose together, with Wes keeping his arm firmly around his sister. Wes gave Jackson what he hoped was a cheerful grin. "Don't tell me you're cooking?"

"More like reheating," said Jackson with a mischievous glance. "I'm leaving the hard work to you."

Abby gulped and snickered. "Thomas, I think it's time you formally meet my brother, Wes, and Auntie Izzy's house sitter, Jackson."

Thomas raised one of the bottles of beer to Jackson. "We're old drinking buddies." Thomas set down the bottle and said to Wes, "Well, little brother. I never thought I'd meet you alive. Figured you'd come with your head on a platter." He put out his hand. Wes shook it, grateful for both the humor in the comment and the compassion in Thomas's eyes.

Jackson invited them to stay for dinner, and Abby and Thomas agreed. Wes was so glad. There was no way he could just let Abby walk out the door after they'd found each other again. He felt like he was floating as he headed to the kitchen to make personally sure Kale was given an extra treat with his kibble. Kale had saved Wes yet again.

The conversation was a bit strained as they wound their way through things they still had in common. Both Thomas and Abby were enthusiastic parents and Wes thought he might recognize his niece, Samantha, and her young brother, his namesake, if he met them on the street. He tried to absorb every little detail as they spoke. He had missed so much. Finally, after ten years, he was in the same room as Abby. There would be plenty of time to get to know her, and her family, during his stay in the Yukon.

Abby loaded a biscuit with butter, popped it in her mouth and rolled her eyes up in her head. "These are amazing. They are almost as good as Izzy's. You make them?" She looked at Jackson.

"Naw, they're leftovers from last night," said Jackson. "Wes handles the complex stuff. "I keep to the basics, like can-opening and dishwashing."

"Wes, this is fantastic." Abby's smile was genuine.

"Yeah, well, when you're a kid on the road, you either plant trees or work in a kitchen," Wes replied. "I did both. I'm a better cook, though."

While Jackson and Thomas cleared the dishes, Wes took the opportunity to stay authentic with his sister.

"Abby, I have ruined every relationship I've had by running. I've hurt everyone who crossed my path. You're the only person in the world who can possibly understand." He reached for her hand and held it.

Wes thought he heard Jackson gasp, but immediately forgot about it when Abby briefly squeezed his hand back and they walked to the door, their hands clasped, while Jackson stayed in the kitchen scrubbing the counter. At the door, Wes hugged Abby one last time, then shook Thomas's hand. "Thanks for giving me a chance."

As they stepped off the porch Abby turned. "Let's get together. I'll phone you and set a time."

"Yes," Wes called back. He waved at them enthusiastically as they drove off, happy beyond belief at how things had worked out. Once they were out of sight, he came back to the kitchen to find it empty. Where was Jackson? Wes's gaze immediately went to the stairs. His guess, and he was a pretty good guesser, was Jackson needed some alone time. All right, Wes would grant him that.

He puttered around, finishing the evening chores. He wanted to sing at the top of his voice and dance around the room. If only Jackson was here to celebrate with him.

Once Wes was satisfied with his work, he headed upstairs. The room was dark, and Jackson was face down on the bed. Wes stroked his back until he stirred. "I did the chickens and loaded the fire. Can we talk?"

Jackson raised his head. "That was intense. Are you okay? "

"I think so, I'm hopeful, but that's not what I wanted to talk about."

"No?"

"No. So, does this sound weird? Sometimes when I look at you, I can kinda hear your thoughts. Remember the first night I walked in, you were making plans to rent a place in town 'cause you thought Isabelle didn't need you?"

"Yeah?"

"And remember after you smashed your head so hard all you could see was stars, you saw me and thought, that is the hottest guy I have ever seen, I could use him in one of my porno books?"

Jackson turned over. "No way did I ever think a word of that."

"So you say. Anyway tonight, when I told Abby she is the only person who understands me, you looked like I sucker punched you."

"I did? I mean, it makes sense, right?"

"Yeah. But I think you're worried now that I've talked to Abby, I'll leave. Maybe I haven't been clear with you. You've gotta know, I'm not done." Wes curled up next to him on the bed and cupped his cheek. "Abby might understand what we went through as kids and the fallout from that, but you're helping me face who I am now. I'm a bad risk, but today I feel hopeful. I don't know if I can be who you deserve, but goddammit—?"

Jackson watched him expectantly.

"Don't give up on me. I can't promise to give you what you need but—"

"Shut up." Jackson gave him a soft kiss. "No promises. I never asked for that."

Chapter Twenty-two

A week later, Wes found himself jogging down the icy street for an early morning meeting with Abby at the donut shop. It was cold outside and still dark, but he had a song in his heart just bursting to get out. He was going to see Abby! He grinned to himself. For years, he couldn't imagine this happening.

In the warm donut shop, he joined the line and waved to Abby, who was sitting at a table in the back. He picked up his order and sat down at her table, shoving a honey cruller towards her and then cradled his coffee to warm his fingers. "Hey."

"Hey yourself." Abby glared at the cruller softening her gaze to look at him. "Sorry it's so early, Tom was willing to get the kiddos to daycare today so we could do this before work." She poked at the donut. "Thanks for this, but I get up really early so I can sit by myself for a bit. I ate then." She shoved it back at him.

Wes broke off a piece, popping it in his mouth, letting the sweetness energize him even further. "You didn't get me up. I'm a morning person."

She arched an eyebrow.

"That was a long time ago. I've changed, and besides, I'm pretty sure there are studies proving teenagers need more sleep than babies."

"Maybe. My kids don't seem to sleep, ever."

"We talked about the kids a bit at dinner the other night but tell me more. I still can't believe I have a niece and nephew." How could Wes not know these kids, her babies?

"You're going to regret that." Abby laughed and turned to her photos on her phone. "The two of them remind me so much of me and you. Samantha is the oldest. She just had a birthday and is four. She's headed for Junior Kindergarten next year and here's Wesley, he'll be two after Christmas but, he's acting like a full on two-year-old already. Here they are at swimming lessons when Wesley was a baby. See how Samantha won't leave him alone? I remember mothering you like that."

"I remember that too. You always wanted to have one hand on me, even when I was in high school."

Abby laughed. "That's when you needed it most. Oh man, you were a handful. Here look at this one. It's more recent, taken just after the first snow. Samantha let Wesley bury her in a drift. He kept saying he was building a snow sister. It was so cute."

There were more. Picture after picture of adorable kids who were blonder than he remembered Abby being, but really did look a lot like her with curls and dimples. It took his breath away. "So, when do I get to meet them?"

She lowered her eyes and sipped her coffee.

Wes knew that look. It meant Abby didn't want to say what she was thinking. Ten years may have passed but some things don't change. He took a breath. "You don't want me to meet your kids?"

She sipped again, raising her eyes over the cup. "It's not really like that, Wesley. I don't really know you anymore. Although I never stopped loving you, these are my babies and they are my priority. How long are you planning to stay?"

"I'm not sure. Till I'm ready to leave, I guess."

"Then what? Kids get attached."

"I don't know. I've been wanting to reconnect with you and the family, but I honestly haven't thought that far ahead."

Abby reached for his hands but he kept them clenched around his hot cup, trying to listen to what she was saying, not what he was hearing.

"It's not just that. Dad fucked us both up." Abby pulled her hands back, "What kind of help are you getting? I'm seeing a great therapist. I didn't even realize how much I was poisoning my family until her. Maybe I can get you in?"

"I don't need therapy!" What was going on? First Jackson, now his sister wanting him to see someone. "Jesus, Abby. I'm working through it my own way."

"Well, I'd argue what you're doing isn't working. It's been ten years."

"I'm here, aren't I?"

Abby softened her tone. "Yes, and please don't think that doesn't mean everything to me. But I need to know you have legitimate intentions to build a relationship with them before you meet the kids." She took his hand. "I guess I need more time to get to know Wes the man. I have trust issues, baby brother. I'm not blaming you, but I'm afraid you're going to disappear again and break my heart all over. I might be able to handle it, but I'm not going to ask my kids to go through that." She glanced at her phone. "Give me time to work on that and then we can talk about meeting the kiddos." She shifted and pulled her coat back on. "I have to get a move on, or I'll be late."

When they stood, Abby grabbed him and hugged him tight. "We'll do this again soon. I promise." She smiled and then was gone through the crowd and out the door.

Relief flooded Wes as she walked out. He needed time to think. She didn't want him in their lives, that much was clear. Or was it? Abby had only said she needed to work on it. But her demands of him were over the top. A therapist? Was that really her place? Wes took his time bundling up and he headed out.

Jackson had tried to force Sunny on him this morning, but Wes had been so excited, he'd figured some walking and taking the bus would be good for him. Now he was glad he couldn't just slam the door and drive away. The familiar urge to give up and run was far too strong. Wes needed this walk.

He cut over to the river path heading toward the bus park. Without the shelter of buildings, the wind whipped his breath away, but the reality of it eased his claustrophobia. God, he needed Jackson's presence right now. Screw the bus. He'd walk up the hill and maybe hitch a ride if it got too cold.

****

Jackson traced the crystalline feathers across the living room window, icy cracks melting under his fingers. Outside, Kale was holed up under the porch. He came out frequently to run the property. The silence, or rather the scraping of the knife on wood, was getting to Jackson.

Wes was in the rocker leaning over a small tarp, doing the same thing he'd done all week. At least he didn't have one foot out the door. Since the first breakfast meeting with Abby, Wes had been moody. He went to work and came home, barely spoke, went to bed long after Jackson was asleep, and stomped around. He'd gotten together with her for breakfast a couple of times, and they were getting to know each other, but she was standing firm on her decision and he hadn't met the kids. The Christmas season was swirling around them, and Wes also had an allergy to the holidays. Every time Jackson suggested hanging decorations, Wes's response would be a rant about commercialization and wasted resources.

This afternoon, the energy in the house was making it impossible for Jackson to concentrate on the books he had from the library. Wes was stuck, and Jackson wondered if there was anything he could do. "Listen Wes, this isn't working. I know you need space to work it out but, it's almost Christmas. Sometimes magic happens at this time of year. Why don't you try making yourself available to it? Go shopping, get her a card, do something, anything."

"Magic?" Wes gave him a long look and then disappeared into the basement.

Jackson sighed. Maybe he'd try something else later and went back to his notes. Hours later, Wes hadn't reappeared so Jackson went down to check. He found Wes carving a piece of wood with a smile on his face. The mood had shifted. Maybe it was magic.

By Saturday, something was taking shape.

"It's a toy for the kids," said Wes. "Something we can bring by Christmas morning on the way to Nick's. She won't refuse a gift for them."

Jackson shook his head. "Who is this 'we' you refer to? I've said I'll support you through this, but that sounds like a plan doomed to fail. If you go against your sister's wishes and try to force something on her, I'll go in later and clean up the mess."

Wes glared at him, but then nodded. "Yeah, I guess I

know that. Then again, I'm loving imagining them playing with it, so with your permission, oh wise one, I will keep going with the fantasy and hope some of your so called magic will present a better idea." He rubbed the back of his neck. "I guess old habits die hard."

Working side by side with Wes was nice. The quiet in the room wasn't empty but creative and, at times, it was even energizing. But today Jackson was finding Wes's hyper focus on carving to be almost as bad. It was distracting. Bits of wood flying everywhere all the time. Not that Jackson was having much luck with his own work. He was trying to put together an outline for his new book, but his characters weren't cooperating. Rather than explaining the colonial aspects of the decisions made in the territory as the gold rushers swarmed over the land, in a respectable consideration of history, his characters were bent on hooking up. Jackson sighed heavily and shoved at the pile of papers sitting next to him on the couch.

Wes paused putting his carving down. "What's up?"

"Nothing." Simply having Wes acknowledge that they were working in the same space was grounding. Jackson picked up his notes and scanned through them again. He squared his shoulders. He was a writer, he could do this. He tackled the writing with new determination and focused on the rest of the story. There were other characters to flesh out and so many real-life elements to incorporate. Jackson fell into his familiar state of immersion, where there was nothing but him and the page.

They were sitting for almost an hour in silence when the house phone rang. Neither jumped to answer it. Wes glanced at him. "It could be important."

Jackson shrugged. "I'm buried in paper, they'll leave a message."

"Lazy." Wes cast a pointed look at him, shook the curls of wood off his jeans, and headed for the phone. "Hello?"

There was something in the silence that followed that made Jackson look up.

"Okay... No... Sure... I understand... Okay. That'll be fine. No, I'm not working. I'm glad too. I was worried that you wouldn't... No, I do understand. See you then. Bye." Wes put the phone down and walked to the couch, looking dazed.

Jackson frowned. "What's wrong?"

"Nothing." Wes swallowed. "That was Abby." He broke into a huge smile. "Do you want to go with me to dinner at her house on Christmas Eve?"

Jackson's mouth dropped open. "You're invited to dinner? I thought you couldn't meet the kids yet?"

"I guess she's feeling bad, nostalgic or something. She invited us for dinner Christmas Eve."

"Great, now we don't have to do a stealth present drop." Jackson grasped Wes's hand and the tension run out of him.

Wes played with his fingers. "I guess that is what you would call Christmas magic."

Jackson squeezed his hand.

"You know what we should do?" Wes stood and headed for the basement door. "Go with the flow."

Jackson followed him, despite his confusion. "What?"

"There's a box marked X-mas in the basement. Let's see what's in it. Maybe we can spruce this place up a bit?"

Jackson smiled. "Deal."

****

It didn't seem long until it was Christmas Eve. They climbed into the car on the frosty evening and drove down the hill to Abby's house. Whitehorse was all dressed up for the holiday with lights strung everywhere. Even the old paddle wheeler was decorated. Abby greeted them with a hug in the small hall and Thomas shook their hands, then he took their coats and bag, and offered mulled cider.

Wes tugged uncomfortably at his collar, catching Jackson's smirk. Jackson was not going to let him forget the scene in the bedroom this afternoon, where he'd had a very Jackson-like meltdown over what to wear.

Abby led them to a comfortable room with a huge

Christmas tree piled with presents. Two small children sat next to the tree, recreating the Christmas story with the ceramic and stuffed toy characters in a small nativity scene.

His niece and nephew.

"Hey." Wes crouched to their level. "Who's this?"

The girl turned her face away, squeezing her eyes shut. The boy stared curiously at him.

Abby crouched behind them and adjusted a bow slipping from the girl's tangled blonde curls. "This is Samantha. Samantha, this is your Uncle Wesley. He's my brother."

Samantha opened her eyes, which looked so much like her mother's, and gave Wes a half smile.

"And this is Wesley." Abby rested her hand on his small shoulder. "Wesley, say hello to your uncle. He has the same name as you do."

Little Wesley gave him a soft, "Hello."

"Hello," said Wes. Tears sprang to his eyes. "I'm so happy to meet you both."

It didn't take long before the children enlisted him in their game, insisting he play the part of the sheep and make the requisite noises. On the other side of the room, Jackson sipped hot cider, chatting with Thomas about his research.

Wes was overcome by a wash of love and wonder. It was Christmas Eve and he was surrounded by his family. He was in Abby's house, with her kids jumping in and out of his arms, treating him like he was someone they'd known all their lives. The moment was more than he could have wished for, or even imagined, a few months ago.

During a lull in the game, Wes ducked back to the hall and took out a package from their bag. He returned to the living room. "We brought a present for the kids," he announced as placed it under the tree.

"What is it?" Samantha asked, crouching down and peering under the branches.

"It's a surprise," said Wes.

Abby shot him a wink. "What do you think about letting them open it tonight while you're here?"

Wes was both thrilled and overcome with emotion. In their family, presents had stayed firmly under the tree until their mom got home from her shift in the kitchen at the hospital, giving all the patients their Christmas dinners. The hours of waiting, when they weren't allowed to even look into the living room, were grueling and long. Abby really was working hard not to repeat their parents' mistakes.

"But," Abby added, "only if you're okay with it and of course if the kids want to."

"Please Uncle Wesley, say yes, say yes, say yes!" chanted Samantha while little Wesley danced at her side.

"I would love that." Wes put the shoebox-sized package into Wesley's small hands. The two kids sat and unwrapped it taking unusual time and care with the paper. Kids usually ripped and tore, didn't they? Wes certainly had. He still would if given the chance.

The kids opened the box, dug through wadded newspaper and Samantha held a wooden bear in her hand, her eyes sparkling.

"Look." Wesley held up another smaller bear.

Samantha dug out a baby bear. "It's the three bears. Maybe there's a—"

Little Wesley found Goldilocks. There were interlocking walls and a roof for a little cabin. Samantha figured out how to set the building up and in no time, they had mama bear making porridge.

Abby wiped tears from her eyes. "This is beautiful. Just as good as anything Uncle Jeff made. Thank you, Wes."

They had pizza for dinner, and Abby explained the menu was the kids' choice on Christmas Eve. After dinner, Abby and Thomas got ready for church and placed Jackson and Wes on babysitting duty. The kids' antics were thoroughly adorable, and Wes even distracted little Wesley from wanting to open another present by promising to show him how to carve wood when he was older.

All of them left the house together in a swirl of laughter and good wishes. Abby hugged Wes tighter than she ever had before and whispered, "Merry Christmas. Let's do this again in the New Year."

****

Wes opened his eyes. Jackson's face was inches away, visible in the moonlit room. Their sleepy breath mingled, legs tangled together, hands curled between them. As Wes's brain caught up to his body, he realized it was Christmas morning. When was the last time he'd looked forward to the holidays? It was cozy and warm in bed, but he was eager to start the day. He ran a gentle finger down Jackson's nose and brushed his lips. "Wake up, sleepyhead."

Jackson swatted his hand away and dug himself further under the blankets. "It's still dark. You kept me up too late last night."

"Excuse me? Who kept who up? I couldn't have done that by myself! Come on, I got you a present." Wes rolled over and flipped on the bedside lamp.

"My eyes! A little warning?" Jackson pulled the blanket over his head.

Wes dragged the blanket from Jackson's face and pressed their lips together. "Merry Christmas."

"I've got to pee," Jackson announced. "Why don't you let the dog out on your way to heat up Bertha. Let's meet back here in ten for presents."

"Deal." Wes threw on a robe and hurried through the cool house to the basement.

By the time Wes finished, Kale was outside bounding gleefully through the snow. "Brr." Wes dove back into bed trying to reclaim his warmth.

Jackson laughed and snuggled deeper. "Remember the time I forgot to stoke the fire and we could practically see our breath the next morning?"

Wes burrowed under Jackson. "Your point?"

"Suck it up!"

Wes glared and shoved his icy feet between Jackson's warm calves.

Jackson pushed him away and headed for the edge of the bed. Hanging himself over and reaching under his side of the bed without losing the covers, he came up with a flat festive package. "Here, open mine first."

Wes sat up and crossed his legs arranging the blankets. Jackson piled the pillows behind him and watched him tear through the paper to find a small stack of cellophane encased graphic novels.

"It's the Serenity collection." Wes smoothed the slight wrinkle in the plastic over Mal's face. "This is amazing."

Jackson's cheeks pinked, "I had Corie mail them a few weeks ago. I hope you like them."

Wes caught his hand. "Thank you, I can't wait to read them." He pressed his lips to Jackson's fingertips, then passed him the cloth bag from the drawer on his side of the bed.

Jackson opened it to find a well-loved copy of *The Alchemist* by Paolo Coelho.

"It's one of my favorites." Wes wiped his damp palms on the rumpled sheet. "I hope you like it."

"I've always meant to read this." Jackson flipped open the book and went still reading the inscription.

This book saved my life; I want it to be part of yours. Your friend always, Wes.

The back of Wes's neck heated up. "I should—"

Jackson threw himself over Wes in a full body hug, kissing him deeply.

The phone rang.

"Crap! Is it nine already? I made Mom promise not to call too early." Jacks rolled off him and grabbed the phone.

Wes dressed and went down to start the coffee, giving Jackson some privacy with his family. Wes took a moment to file this perfect morning in his memory. He didn't know what he'd be doing next year at this time, but it wouldn't be with Jackson.

Chapter Twenty-three

A week and a half later, Wes was working the Sunday shift and he could not stop checking the clock. Today was the day Jackson was reading and signing books at Wayword Books. Wes had wanted to be there for him, to help Jackson through the manifold wardrobe choices or make sure he ate breakfast or lunch. Of course, Wes knew Jackson could do it, but there was still the intense desire to step in and help. It was good he had hiked down to work early and left Jackson and Kale to do what had to be done. Was it even sane that he'd wanted to call all day, just to see what was going on? Probably not.

Finally, it was time for him to knock off. Wes dropped his apron into the laundry bag at the back, grabbed his coat and stepped out into the cold but not unreasonable weather. Instead of heading home, he was walking over to the bookstore to hitch a ride with Jackson. It was almost four-thirty and already dark. Jackson would probably be eager to go and recharge. Wes hurried into the warm store and the first thing he noticed was the remnants of Christmas. The tree and garlands were still up, and the place smelled like coffee and, something else, gingerbread? Ah yes, there was a pile of gingerbread cookies next to the counter. Wes grabbed one and then he noticed the store was still filled with people, and all those people were waiting for Jackson.

Jackson was seated at a table, surrounded by copies of his books and laughing women. He had a pen in his hand and looked like he was having fun. Barb Finstead was standing at the cash register, bagging books and looking very pleased.

Wes found a space where he could watch without disturbing Jackson and sighed with relief. He should never get caught up in Jackson's anxiety about these things. Sometimes Jackson forgot who he was, and it was Wes's job to remind him. Or was it?

Jackson was talking to a woman, looking animated.

"Writing—" he held his pen up for emphasis "—is an inexpensive hobby, whether you're getting feelings down in a journal or penning an essay, novel, or poetry. You just need a pen, an imagination, and a table."

The woman nodded and handed Jackson a couple of his books to sign along with a thick book on writing. "Could you sign this one too?" she asked. "It's not one of yours but, if you could write down what you just said, I could use it to inspire me."

Jackson enthusiastically agreed and Wes shook his head in admiration. It was as if Jackson could bring out a different person for these public events. Wes wanted to go over, grab him, and kiss him, right now, in the middle of the store, although it probably wasn't the right time. Maybe later.

By five-fifteen, the line-up had thinned at last and Barb turned off the lights in the back. Wes helped her move the dishes to the kitchen and snuck another gingerbread cookie. It was almost five-thirty when he and Jackson walked out to the car.

Jackson threw the keys at him and sank deep into his seat, shutting his eyes. "Home, James," he said, his voice a little hoarse.

Wes started the car. "It looked like it went well. What do you think?

"Good, better than expected. Fantastic even, but I'm running on fumes right now."

"When we get home, I'll get you something to eat." Wes pulled out of the parking lot. "It won't take me long to heat some stew and make biscuits."

Jackson opened his eyes. "No offence, but I don't think I have the energy to eat right now. Maybe a hot bath, though."

Wes puzzled for a minute. "You looked like you enjoyed it. Was it that hard on you?"

"No. It scared me though, but new stuff often does. I was nervous to start but once I got going, it was amazing. When I read, people listened and when I was signing books, the stories they shared with me were stunning. I couldn't believe it. I knew that my introverted self would need some serious recharging though... Look, my battery is totally empty." He slumped in his seat.

"We need to get plugged in, then." It was an interesting concept. He was glad Jackson understood himself well enough to do the right thing.

When they got home, Jackson took a bottle of Nick's wine and a glass up the stairs. "Bath. I'm gonna go soak and prune up," was all he said.

Wes fed Kale, checked the chickens, and filled Big Bertha for the night. Then put together a tray filled with finger foods: sliced apples, grapes, hunks of cheese and meats, and a couple of thick ends of homemade bread slathered in butter. Grabbing a glass, he climbed the stairs, and set up the tray within reach of the tub.

Jackson mumbled a greeting but kept his eyes closed.

Wes started to undress.

Jackson opened his eyes. "What are you doing?"

"You've been in there for a while now." Wes pulled off his jeans. "I'm hoping you're ready for a bit of company and food. I could join you for dinner if you're up for it."

Jackson looked him up and down. "Yes, if you don't make me think about anything, I'd love to have you. Did you bring a glass?" He held up the bottle of wine.

Wes presented his glass and climbed into the hot water pushing his way in behind Jackson, sitting down with his legs around him and his arms pulling him in close. "I want to prune up a bit too." He nuzzled the back of his neck and Jackson melted against his body. "Here." He popped a piece of cheddar between Jackson's lips.

The piece of cheese disappeared quickly. "I guess I am a bit hungry." Jackson reached for a slice of apple. "Thanks, this is wonderful."

Wes liked it too. They could hear the logs of the house cracking in the cold. It made their steamy retreat even cozier.

Jackson drifted against him. "I've been thinking. Nick has been so good to me, always accepting me without judgement. I'd like to do something to give back."

Inwardly, Wes leapt with joy. Outwardly, Wes waited and let him finish.

"I think I'll give him some pointers about writing he

can share with the kids," said Jackson. "I could maybe even go over one afternoon after school and answer some questions, maybe be his assistant for a couple of weeks. He'd be there, doing the work. It would be easier than today."

Wes held him close. "I'm sure he'd appreciate any help."

Jackson pushed his weight against him. "Would you scrub my back?"

Wes rubbed his evening scruff onto the wet shoulder in front of him. "Sure."

Jackson laughed. "Not like that!"

"Okay, okay, Mr. Picky." Wes grabbed a washcloth, soaped it up and pushed the relaxed body away from him so he could reach all over. He swirled the cloth in circles, starting at Jackson's shoulders and working his way down, with care not to miss one piece of skin.

Later, when Jackson was sound asleep, Wes watched the light of the stars travel across the blanket, feeling a sense of something he couldn't define. Contentment? He hadn't felt this way in a long time, maybe never. Possibly when he was little Wesley's age but that was long gone. He liked it. He wanted more of it. Was it even possible? Best not to ask for too much and not be disappointed.

Chapter Twenty-four

Wes shook his head as he scraped his last mouthful of omelet from his plate. Jackson had barely been present for breakfast, eating robotically and staring into space.

Naturally, Wes couldn't resist teasing him. "I'll have to scrub the elephant while it's still light out. Are you up for helping me?"

"Uh huh."

"Can you bring a big box to empty the pockets first?" This was hysterical. Wes was feeling an overload of affection for the distracted writer.

"Uh huh."

"I could get you to do or sign anything in this state." Wes got up from the table and wrapped his arms around Jackson's neck.

"Okay." Jackson blinked and frowned. "Wait, what do you need me to sign?"

Wes laughed. "How do you make it through life in this condition?"

Jackson's eyes briefly focused and he accepted the kiss dropped on his lips. "Sorry, you were saying something?"

"Yeah, I was bitching about being left at the table alone with a breathing corpse."

"Sorry, say again, I am paying attention."

"No, go upstairs, write it out, I'll clean up here." Wes didn't mind. He liked it, actually. Care and feeding of the writer was essential and important. It was good to be needed. He grabbed a cloth, happy that there wasn't much to clean up. When the house phone rang, he tucked it between his shoulder and ear so he could continue washing dishes. "Hello?"

"Wesley?"

Wes put down the washcloth. He didn't recognize the voice. "Yes?"

"It's Corie."

"Corie? Jackson's little sister?"

"Ahh, I see you've heard of me." She sounded pleased. "All lies, I assure you."

"Umm, good to know. Are you looking for Jackson?" Why hadn't she called Jackson's cell?

"No, I actually called for you. Do you know what today is?"

Wes thought for a moment. "The anniversary of the Eagles being inducted into the Rock and Roll Hall of Fame?"

There was a long pause. "Awesome, you and my brother are made for each other. It's Jackson's twenty-ninth birthday. Dammit! He promised he would tell someone so he wasn't celebrating alone!"

"He's not alone. He's got me, and friends." Wes moved on to sweep the toast crumbs off the counter.

"Well, don't invite them."

"Don't invite them?"

She made an exasperated sound. "You should know how much he hates being the center of attention!"

"He's really been stretching himself in that area lately."

"I heard. I know he gets something out of those things, but they aren't exactly relaxing for him. I was hoping you could acknowledge today is special."

"Of course. A little more notice would have been nice."

"Sorry about that, I believed him when he told me he would let someone know. I only just remembered this morning that I actually know him, and that promise was bullshit."

Wes laughed. He too was familiar with Jackson's carefully worded promises. "What's his favorite cake?"

"Brownies," she said without hesitation, "the more chocolate the better."

"Thanks for the heads up."

"No problem, Wesley. It's good to finally meet you, but fair warning, if you hurt my brother they won't find a piece big enough to bury. Talk later." She disconnected.

Wes stared at the phone in his hand, not quite sure what just happened.

Jackson called out from the top of the stairs. "I heard

the phone?"

"Really? I didn't think you could hear anything."

Jackson grinned, his eyebrows raised. "Anything important?"

"Nah, junk call. Back to work, you procrastinator."

****

January was colder than December. By four o'clock, the sun already down. It was also getting noticeably brighter every day and by June, the midnight sun would be shining. Jackson didn't want to think about it. The more light he saw, the closer it was to Isabelle's homecoming and his leaving. He had spent all morning in a fog with his characters fighting for space in his head. Somehow, gradually, thoughts of the future got a toehold and pushed their way in until he found himself staring blankly at the computer screen. Time to bring in the big guns and put this stuff out into the universe. He punched Corie's number into his phone and luckily caught her on a study break.

"Did you call so I could say happy birthday?" Corie asked.

"Oh. No, I forgot." Jackson normally didn't have much love for birthdays. Every year had been another reminder that he wasn't living the life his parents wanted for him. But this year he was living a life of his choosing, and it felt pretty good. Maybe he should celebrate.

"Well, happy birthday anyway."

There was the socially accepted way to get into a call, talking about the weather and other things a person wasn't interested in, but Jackson was too restless to play the game. "Do you want to know the reason I called?

"Sure, what is it?"

"Well, the other day I did a book reading and signing at a local bookstore and now I've volunteered to help a friend with his youth group, maybe once, maybe more."

"That's wild! It doesn't sound like you at all. How was it?"

He stopped her there. "It sounds exactly like me, just not like Eddie."

"Jackson, you rock! Although I could remind you that Eddie is you too, but let's not ruin the moment."

"Anyway—" Did she always interrupt him like this? Probably but he knew what he wanted to say "—It made me think. That's why I'm calling. I need to run something by you. I'm thinking I might do more of that." Jackson took a deep breath. "And I'm staying here longer. I like it. I have friends here. Other than you, I have nothing to come home to."

"Holy shit." Corie's voice fell to a whisper. "Jackson."

"Yeah!" He grinned. So it wasn't just him thinking this, it really was a big deal. "I was hoping you and I could talk about a way I could present it to Mom so she doesn't go ballistic."

"Do you really think she'll be relaxed enough to simply be ballistic?" Corie laughed. "You're the big time writer, surely there's a word that would better describe her real reaction. On the other hand, at heart I think she does want what's best for you, and if that's it, she'll accept it—in the end."

"I've been thinking and planning. I wouldn't just drop the family, I miss you guys too much, but I think I might sell more books if I start doing more events. Lorraine keeps bugging me about it, and at the reading, we pretty much sold out the whole stock of E.J. Williams. Maybe she's right." Jackson got up and walked to the window where he could see the mountain range in front of him, steady and grounded. It slowed the adrenaline shooting through him as he said out loud the thoughts that had been with him for the past few days. This wasn't a crazy idea. "If I'm making more money, I could fly south and visit occasionally."

"What about Wes? Didn't you say he was leaving soon?"

"He is." Jackson sat down at the desk and put the phone on speaker.

Corie's voice filled the room. "Could you be there without him?"

"I'm not gonna lie, that's gonna be hard, but this is about me. I'm done living my life through other people, so I'll cross that bridge when I get to it. There are people here who like me and respect me. I have nothing like it at home."

"If you'd stepped up here the way you have there, you could have had it."

"Maybe, but, I'm up to my ears in this new book. I've got to be here for that."

She was quiet.

"Are you crying?" he asked.

"No! Well, maybe a bit, but only because this essay has me on edge. I'm so happy for you. Let me know when you want to talk to Mom, I'll have your back."

They were about to end the call when Corie chose to share some big news. "So, I have a boyfriend and it's getting pretty serious."

"What!" Jackson leapt out of his seat. "Since when? Why haven't I heard about this before? What the heck, Corie? Why are you holding out on me?"

Laughing, Corie said, "You're being pretty directive."

"That's how we show we love each other in the Williams family. We make sure to tell our family members how we would live their lives."

The next fifteen minutes were spent listening to Corie rave about her amazing boyfriend, Mark, and the struggles of juggling school and a serious relationship. When Jackson finally put the phone down, he had mixed feelings. He was happy for her sure, but he wanted to be there, meet this Mark guy, and hug the heck out of Corie. Soon, he thought. He'd need to have all these conversations and a trip back might be called for, maybe in the fall.

It didn't scare him as much as he thought it would have a few months ago. The Jackson of today reached across his imagination to Eddie and held him in his heart. It would take both of them to get through the next few months but he was up for it. Yes! It was his birthday and the beginning of his very own new year. Anything was possible.

Jackson tucked the phone into his pocket and headed down the stairs. There was no sign of Wes on the main floor. He grabbed his keys and put on his coat and hat, calling at the top of the basement stairs, "Wes, you down there?"

"Yeah." Wes appeared at the bottom, dusty with a curl of wood in his hair.

Jackson wanted to race down and brush it out, replacing it with his fingers, but he held back. "Got an email from the library. The books I ordered from Dawson City are in. I'm going to run down and grab them.

"Okay. Have fun." Wes blew him a kiss.

There was no way Jackson could resist. He ran down the stairs and into Wes's arms. "You have such a bad aim, that one went right past me, you owe me another." He claimed his kiss and headed out.

****

Wes shook his head. Jackson didn't even mention his birthday. It was going to be up to Wes to make sure he got a proper celebration. First, the brownies. Remembering what Corie had said, he doubled the chocolate. That meant more sugar, which would definitely get Jackson's approval. The guy did not care one bit what he put in his mouth. A smile curved Wes's lips at the images that brought to mind.

Despite being made in a hurry, the brownies turned out pretty well. Wes set them on a cooling rack, loosely covered them with baking paper, and hid them on a shelf under his workbench in the basement. Even a focused Jackson wouldn't find it there. Now it was time for the next part of the surprise.

Wes had been carving this piece of wood for some time now. He'd always intended it to be a gift for Jackson. There wasn't much left to finish and if he rushed, he could finish today. The last bit was mainly sanding and then, using the lightest pressure with Uncle Jeff's finest knife, he applied the final yet intricate touches. It was tedious and yet so relaxing. Wes was so absorbed in his work that he was only alerted to Jackson's return by footsteps directly above him.

"Hey." Jackson's voice drifted down the stairs. "Are

you still there?"

"Yeah," Wes yelled back as he flipped the board he was working on so only the flat backside showed.

Jackson came crashing down the steps, red-cheeked, bringing the fresh smell of the crisp air outside down with him. "I got the books. Hey, whatcha baking? It smells like cookies."

"Cookies?" Wes thought he feigned innocence pretty well. "No, it must be something burning in the oven. I turned it on to roast some veg for the stew tonight."

"Stew?"

"Yes, stew. If you are going to be a kept man, you can't complain about the food."

Jackson colored. "I would never complain. I'm so grateful to you for cooking."

"I heard you say 'stew' and it sounded like 'Ewww' and it registered with the complaints department."

"It's just that we had stew last night and my stomach thought cookies."

"I can honestly say no cookies today or any time in the near future I'm afraid." Wes picked up the carving knife, hoping Jackson would get the hint and go.

He didn't. "What are you doing?"

"Waiting for this board to tell me what it wants to be."

Jackson raised his eyebrows. "You're waiting to hear the woody voice of Mr. Chips?"

"No, the chippy voice of Mr. Wood. Don't you have a hero to rescue or a lady to ravish?"

"Probably, I'm kind of procrastinating. I'm restless and I don't know, I'm feeling kinda high."

"Ha, that's it, you're almost glowing. It looks good on you. But I'm trying to work here. I hate to spoil the mood, but do you need to do it here?" For a moment Wes felt mean, but what the heck, all for a good end.

"I guess not."

"Good, I can't hear Mr. Chips with all of the noise my head is making with you here, especially looking the way you look this afternoon."

Jackson turned and walked up the stairs much slower than he had come down.

When he was sure Jackson was really gone, Wes took an old rag and dipped it into a stain to darken the fine details of the piece giving it shadow and life. He viewed the work with a critical eye. It was pretty good. He turned it back over to carve his initials. Maybe he should put, "Love Wes," or maybe not. He wouldn't hesitate if it was for Nick or even Kelly. For Jackson, he finally decided on "WP" and the year.

Wes swept up and then checked the brownies. They were cool enough to ice. He left them in their hiding place and headed upstairs.

Butter, icing sugar and chocolate spun under his beaters and sauce burbled on the stove. Wes should be able to finish before Jackson figured it out. He could be pretty vacant when he was in a book. Wes pictured the noise that must go on in Jackson's head with all the characters yelling out their stories. It was a miracle he was sane. Well, most of the time.

Jackson came into the kitchen and yelled over the beaters. "What are you making? Is that chocolate?"

"You said you wanted cookies."

"Really?" Jackson beamed with delight. "You're making cookies for me? What did I do? Are you trying to poison me? 'Cause that would totally work. Can I taste the batter?" He was really upbeat for someone who had forgotten his birthday.

Wes tried to glare at him but it morphed into a smile. "Aren't you supposed to be writing or something?"

"Yup but nothing's happening. I'm listening for the voice of the wood."

"You're going to make me sorry I said that, aren't you?"

"Maybe? I'm surprised how much the process of wood carving is like writing. Where are your cookie sheets? I'll grease them. Hey, shouldn't the oven be on?"

Wes put his hands on Jackson's shoulders. It was clear he needed to be firm. "Jackson. Go. Please. Take Kale for a walk, then do the chickens. By the time you get back, I'll have dinner ready. We'll eat early and then maybe watch TV or something."

The second he left, Wes raced downstairs, grabbed

the brownies and the carving then headed back up. He wrapped the carving in a clean tea towel and spread icing on the brownies, cutting them into generous squares. Those he arranged on a plate and pushed them to the back of the cupboard.

By the time Jackson opened the door with a whoosh of winter air, the table was set with Aunt Izzie's good china and candles bathed the room in a flickering light.

Kale raced to his dish and stared mournfully at it. Wes scooped a bit of sauce into the bottom and then some kibble. "Bon appétit, pup."

Jackson stared. "Wow, who's coming over?"

"Count the spots, this is a party for two."

Wes raised a glass of wine. "Happy Birthday."

Jackson's eyes widened. "How did you know?"

Wes smiled. "A little bird told me. Sit and eat, tell me what you think."

Jackson put pasta on his plate and doused it with sauce. He ate a bite and then put his fork down. "This sauce is fabulous."

"Family recipe, I used the last of that ground moose. I have to talk to Kelly to see if we can get more."

"I hope you can, this is incredible." Jackson pushed more pasta onto his fork but paused to ask a question. "Who was the little bird?"

"It was your sister."

"Seriously?" Jackson's mouth dropped open. "That sneaky little—when I talked to her today, she didn't say a word!"

"Obviously you and she are related, you didn't say a word either."

"I'm not one of the birthday-inclined. I can take them or leave them, but with food like this, I might change my mind. This sauce is incredible. You definitely nailed my pasta gene."

"Maybe we're related 'cause I have a weakness in that area too."

As they ate, Jackson raved about the meal. He complimented everything, from the richness of the sauce to the tenderness of the meat. When they were done, Wes topped up their wine and raised his glass. "To your last year as a twenty-something."

"I'll drink to that." Jackson sipped. "This goes down way too easily."

"I'm counting on that." Wes lowered his voice to a whisper, devouring Jackson with his eyes.

Jackson flashed him a "come and get me" look and pushed back his chair.

"No, that's for later. You stay there. I'll get the next part of your present." Wes quickly cleared the table and grabbed the plate of brownies from the cupboard, serving them on top of his towel-wrapped gift. He cleared his throat and began to sing Happy Birthday.

Halfway through Jackson joined in.

"You're not supposed to sing," Wes told him.

"I couldn't let you carry it alone—oh my gawd, are those chocolate brownies?" Jackson was practically vibrating in delight. "The little snitch really did spill the beans."

"If you don't want them?" Wes pretended to carry the plate away.

Jackson immediately snatched one. "Oh no, set them down right here." He took a bite and moaned. "I thought the sauce was good. These are incredible. So sweet."

When was the last time someone had appreciated Wes this way? It felt so good and normal, like being held. "Let's go sit in the living room."

"Can the brownies come?"

"Sure, what you aren't carrying in your mouth I'll bring on the plate."

Jackson licked the icing off his lips.

Wes's eyes were riveted to those lips. He wanted them all chocolate covered just like that, but first things first.

They sat close together and put the plate on the coffee table in front of them. There didn't seem to be any right time or way to do it, so Wes shoved the wrapped board over to Jackson.

"What's this?" Jackson gave him a hopeful look. "More brownies?"

"Look at it."

Jackson pulled off the towel. He ran his fingers over

the carved board showing a frigate under full sail tossed on a stormy sea. The name on the hull was *Revenge*. His eyes were bright. "Thank you. It's—it's alive. I can hear the wind flapping in the sails. Wes, I love—" he cast his eyes down, and then started again, his cheeks flushed pink "—this. It's too much." Holding the carving in one hand he threw himself against Wes. "I've never had anything like it. I don't know what to say."

"You talk a lot for someone who's speechless." Wes pulled him close and buried his face in Jackson's hair.

Chapter Twenty-five

They fell into a routine. Jackson did the chickens while Wes made breakfast. After, if Wes wasn't working, he walked Kale while Jackson wrote. Later, Wes would pull him out of his chair and feed him.

Sometimes they played, exploring each other, finding new ways their bodies fit together. Some days they chopped wood or shoveled. Other times they'd walk holding hands and talking. Wes showed him his childhood haunts and taught him to appreciate wood craft from a safe distance.

In the evenings, they had dinner and watched a movie, or Wes carved in the basement while Jackson wrote in the bedroom. Jackson needed alone time. He didn't think Wes minded because he needed space too. But Jackson loved the support he was getting. It left him free to write or research or simply get lost in his thoughts. His story was coming together but not without some surprises. He struggled to force it into a shape, but it seemed to have its own ideas. With the amount of research he was doing, he might qualify for a doctorate in local history when he finished and yet, something was morphing. He sent an email to Lorraine explaining it and wondering, what if anything, she would have to say?

Jackson's social life was changing too. Wes's friends were rapidly becoming his friends and family too. The whole gang came together to help Nick and Sophie paint their nursery. The airline made a fortune bringing Ikea baby furniture from Vancouver to Whitehorse, which then needed a deft hand to put together. Sophie's body started to make some real changes and it was funny to see Kelly treating her like a princess, carrying a foot stool to raise her swollen feet and giving Nick a hard time about not taking better care of her. Jackson's whole life was shifting in a way that made him feel needed and content. It brought him peace in so many ways he couldn't even express.

One morning, after a plate of bacon, eggs and fried potatoes mixed with broccoli and mushrooms, Wes said, "I have a few days off, so I thought I'd take a walk up to the cabin, check the trapline. It's been too long."

"When do you think you'll be back?"

"Abby said she would check on the chickens and see that the pipes don't freeze." Wes stopped and took a breath. "I was hoping you would come with me."

"Really?"

"I want you to come with me, but it doesn't have to be now if you're too busy."

Jackson didn't have to think. "I'd love to come. I'm so ready for a break."

Wes grinned. "Great, eat up, I want to get moving and you still need to pack."

****

Jackson pushed the sunglasses up his nose. It had been early and overcast when they left. Now the sun glared bright off the drifts. At one point, they stopped to watch Kale race through the snow, plowing his nose into places where there might be a mouse. Kale stood tense, glaring at a drift then pounced into it, head first. His tail high in the air waved back and forth furiously. Finally, he pulled himself out, shook hard, saw them watching, and pranced off.

Jackson laughed. "Crazy dog."

Wes shook his head, smiling broadly. "And to think, that's the hero who saved me." He brushed his cold cheek against Jackson's. "Come on. We're almost there."

They kept putting one snowshoe in front of the other, going higher and higher. Every once in a while Wes would stop, turn and smile, causing Jackson's heart to skip a beat. Sometimes Wes pointed out tracks, hare, grouse, or a place where mule deer had bedded down. The path eventually opened up into a clearing, and there was a shack buried on three sides by snow.

Wes grabbed a long stick leaning against the wall and whacked the drift of snow over the door. It fell with a muffled thump to the ground. "You have no idea how many times that's fallen down the back of my jacket when I try to get in." He opened the door.

Jackson laughed, following him inside. The cabin was small and dark, the only light coming from the open door and a dusty window. If possible, the still air inside was colder than the brisk, sunny outside. There was a wood stove in the corner, a handmade table and bench as well as a raised platform that didn't look comfortable for sleeping but couldn't possibly be for anything else. Two shelves on the wall by the table had candles and a couple of books on them.

"Cozy yet sparse," said Jackson.

"It's pretty luxurious for a trapper's cabin. They're usually only for sleeping and small to retain body heat, but Uncle Jeff and I were always up here together, so we built it a bit bigger than usual and dropped in the stove. In the summer your living room is outside."

Wes started the fire. "I'm going to do a bit of housework and fix it so you can sit to write if you want to."

"Let me help you. I can write later." Jackson loved seeing Wes's smile. The skin around his eyes crinkled, lighting up his whole face. It was worth freezing for.

"I want to bring in enough wood to keep the fire going all night and some boughs for our bed, then I'll show you around."

"Boughs for our bed?"

Wes gave him a roguish smile. "You'll see." He dragged an old wooden toboggan down from the eaves and led Jackson to a snow-covered wood pile between two trees. They brushed off the snow and stacked a load onto the toboggan, which they then hauled to the door.

Jackson's job was to keep the wood on the sled, which was not happening. He was laughing by the time they got to the door. "How do you do this by yourself?"

"I carry them one at a time. It's the work that's important, not the speed."

"Really?"

"I'm here to calm my soul." Wes shrugged. "Unless it's really freaking cold, then I get it done as fast as I can."

"What are you here for this time? I don't mind carting

one at a time if it's what you need."

"This time I am here for you," Wes said softly. "It's different. It was different when I was here with Uncle Jeff too. I guess he was here for his own reasons as well. The land answers so many questions." Wes reached out his mittened hand. "Come on. Are you up for walking some more? I'll let you break trail."

The wind-swept snow was crusty, and they were able to mostly walk on top, until they reached the summit looking down into the valley below.

Jackson drew in a sharp breath. "Ohh." Never had he seen such a winter view, green and white mingling to create this soft palette of serenity. "Okay, I get it. I understand your belief in the Mother. How could you not believe when you've seen this?"

They stood for moments, or maybe hours, then Wes kissed him. "Sometimes I think this is me."

"It is you. When you've been here, you smell like this." Jackson lowered his eyes.

Wes laughed. "I love the way your mind works." He held him tighter.

Jackson unwrapped himself from Wes's arms. He had something to say, and he couldn't keep it in any longer. He gazed at Wes, who was standing out here in his element, and knew it was the right time. "Wes, I love you." Jackson's words tumbled out in a rush, not wanting Wes to get a word in before he finished. "I know it's not part of our arrangement, and maybe you don't want to hear it, but it's true and I don't think it's fair to either of us to keep it to myself."

Wes didn't move. His eyes were wide, and he was completely still.

"It's okay, you don't have to say it back," Jackson hurried to reassure him. "You don't even need to feel the same way. It's just that I've been thinking a lot about staying past Isabelle's return. I know you have your own plans, and you shouldn't change them, but I want you to know where I'm coming from."

Now Wes moved. He blinked. "You're staying for me?"

"Of course not, I'm staying for myself." Jackson said

the words gently, not wanting to cause offense. "I've tried to imagine life without you here. I've gotta admit even my writer's brain doesn't have the scope to envision it. I'll miss you big time, but I have work to do here and I know I can do it without you. On the other hand, if you were staying… Well, let's just say—" he gulped "—I'd be okay with that."

Wes swallowed. "There hasn't been any good time to tell you, but I don't think we can go forward without you knowing about Ben."

"Any time you want to talk about your past, I'm here."

"You're right, Ben is the past, long past, but he still has a hold on me in some ways." Wes reached for Jackson's mittened hand as they walked along the valley edge and he told him the whole story.

Wes had met Ben when he arrived in Vancouver, after running away. Ben had almost immediately taken Wes under his wing. He knew the ropes and could find booze or drugs even on days when there was no money for food. His independence and confidence were almost addictive, and Wes fell for him hard.

Then Wes met Nick, who helped Wes get clean. Ben wanted to keep using, so Wes broke up with him and left with Nick to plant trees for the summer.

"In the fall Nick and I got jobs in Whistler." Wes stared out over the valley. "Somehow Ben tracked me down. He told me he'd changed, and it was just to be with me. I was flattered. He had changed his whole life for me. We stayed together most of that winter, but I couldn't ignore his erratic mood swings and other things. The longer we were together, the more jealous he was of Nick. I should have known he was still using. I finally broke up with him and…" Wes pressed his lips together. "And he OD'd three days later. I'll never know if it was on purpose or if he just got some bad stuff. In my brain, I know it wasn't my fault, but that was the end, no more serious relationships for me. I'm working hard to not allow my past to keep affecting our present, but it'll always be there."

Jackson waited, making sure Wes was finished. He

gave him a nod. "Okay."

Wes raised his brows. "Okay? That's it?"

"That's it. I mean, any time you want to talk about it, that's fine but, okay." Jackson moved close, almost close enough to kiss him but not quite. "I told you, I love you. That isn't going to change. I said I didn't need you to say it. All I want is for you to know that no matter what, that's what's going on. We've both had lives before now. I want to know about your past and what has shaped you, but it won't change how I feel."

Wes smiled. "Okay."

They took the toboggan to a long sweeping hill and rode it all the way down. Jackson couldn't remember ever having so much fun. Sliding, laughing, kissing; oh, the kissing.

The afternoon dusk was falling as they got back to the cabin, Wes pulled out his knife and showed Jackson how to pick the softest boughs from several fir to make the wooden platform softer and fragrant. Jackson watched quietly while Wes thanked the trees and the earth for the gifts they would be using for their comfort. They each carried an armful of them to the door.

The little cabin was warm when they came in and made up the bed. Once all the housework was done, Jackson fed Kale outside. He ate with gusto then bounded off again into the snow. Wes heated soup on the stove for their dinner and served it into travel bowls.

Jackson wasn't ready to eat just yet. "I have something else to tell you. No big deal but I've decided about my writing."

"Yeah?" Wes threw him a quick glance as he took a quick sip of his soup. "What did you decide?"

Why was Jackson so nervous? He knew Wes would support anything he came up with. "It's just that I've been, you know, trying to write a serious work. I've done the research."

"Oh man, have you done the research." Wes scooped more soup into his mouth.

"But the book wasn't coming together. There was something missing. Remember the piece of wood? You said you were waiting for it to tell you what it wanted to be?"

"Mm hmm."

"Well, that's what happened with my book. It wanted to be a romance. It wouldn't be anything else. I sent a rough outline to Lorraine the other day and she says Hanson's will take it."

Wes grabbed Jackson into a happy dance stumbling around the small space. "Congratulations! How long have you known?"

"I found out yesterday." Jackson broke into a giant smile. "It's official, I'm a romance writer."

"I knew it!" Wes stepped back and pounded him on the back. "You've been wandering around the house in love with your characters for weeks now. I was so sure but was waiting for you to say something."

"You knew?"

"I wasn't sure, and I almost asked you last week but I figured you'd come clean sometime. The question is, how do you feel?"

"Me? Good, goofy. I mean, how could I be so stupid?"

"Don't be so hard on yourself. You got to find the grain in the wood yourself, no one can show you."

"Being here has helped me claim it."

"I'm so glad. You shine when you write." Wes nuzzled Jackson's cheek. "I knew you'd get there." Wes wrapped his arm around him.

Jackson's entire being suffused with warmth. "I don't think anyone has believed in me that way before."

"It's because I love you," said Wes. "I can see you."

Jackson gasped at the confession.

Wes appeared surprised he'd said the words but didn't look away.

Jackson pressed his lips to Wes's. The salt of the soup and the wild tang of fresh air combined into an intoxicating taste Jackson couldn't get enough of. He pulled Wes closer. "Not hungry. Touch me."

Wes pushed them a safe distance away from the table. "I carried that soup a long way for you."

"I'll make it worth your while." Jackson's lips found the pulse in the hollow of his neck. The surge of life under his mouth immediately became the sexiest thing in the world. He untangled himself from the bench and Wes's arms to stand on shaky legs. "Come."

The look on Wes's face as he followed him to the sleeping platform would stay with Jackson for a long time. He sank down and slipped his fingers into Wes's waistband, tugging at the laces of his camp pants. They loosened and slipped down exposing his boxers, an erection pushing at the fabric. Jackson kneaded Wes's muscular ass pulling him close, nuzzling him through his boxers. He inhaled deep, breathing him in. "To think I was in doubt about where I fit in the world," Jackson whispered, tugging down Wes's boxers. He rubbed his face into Wes's groin, kissing his inner thighs, running his tongue, cheeks and lips over warm skin.

Wes stilled him with a hand on his shoulder. "We are definitely overdressed." He stepped back and they shucked their clothes. He dropped to the platform beside Jackson. Wes's hands, lips and tongue took over where Jackson's left off, leaving shivery trails of wet on his hot skin.

"Here." Wes tugged a corner of the sleeping bag, making space for them to climb in together. Wes reached under the pillow bringing his hand back with a small bag of supplies.

Jackson reached for the lube, kissing Wes with all the emotions the day had brought him.

"Let me take care of you this time." His hand traced down Wes's back, over his hips, between his cheeks, fingers reaching, cool and wet finding their way to his opening, sliding and stretching. "Okay?"

"Please."

Jackson rolled on the condom and positioned himself at Wes's slick entrance, pushing, gentle at first, listening to Wes's encouragement, and then harder. And then he was deep inside, his body thrumming with impossible joy as he became one with the man he loved.

They moved together, their breath, their hearts, the blood in their veins. Jackson reached between them to close his hand around Wes. They rocked as one until he flew apart. Wes followed with a full body shudder. He spooned Wes, keeping him safe in his arms weaving their fingers together over his pounding heart. "Someone's gonna have to sleep on the wet spot."

They rolled together holding each other, warm under the covers.

Slivers of firelight played on the ceiling. Wes's light snores tickled the back of his neck. The timbers cracked as they expanded to accommodate the heat inside. There was a peace here that couldn't be found anywhere else.

Chapter Twenty-six

They brought some of the peace of the cabin back with them and it stayed for a whole week. Then Nick called, barely able to speak. All he could say was something was wrong and could they please, please come over.

They raced to the house, Wes pushing the car past the legal limits to get there.

At the door, Nick grabbed Wes in a tight hug. "It's the baby," he choked out.

Wes gripped him tightly back.

No one spoke.

Eventually, Nick relaxed his hold. "Sophie's on the phone with her mom. Let's go downstairs."

Wes kept a hand on Nick's back and made sure he sat down. He looked so pale. "Jackson," Wes said quietly, "can you get him a glass of water?"

Jackson moved to the bar fridge and filled a glass from a pitcher of water on the shelf. He brought it back to them, carefully guiding the glass to Nick's hand.

Nick grasped the glass but only took a sip when Wes made him. He swallowed and spoke. "At the doctor's appointment this morning, she said Sophie has an incompetent cervix."

"What does that mean?" Wes was scared, picturing worst case scenarios in his head.

Nick's face crumpled, as if was about to cry. "The best I can understand is, Sophie's cervix isn't strong enough and the baby might fall out. It's too early."

Wes was lightheaded. This baby was already loved by so many. "Can they do anything?"

"The doctor tried to put it in a good light. She said Sophie needed to go to bed and not do anything till her due date. If that doesn't work, she'll have to go to the hospital and maybe have some other things done."

"That's gotta be—" Wes counted mentally "—at least six weeks, more even. How will Soph handle that?"

"For the baby, anything, but what if it doesn't work?"

Wes tried to project a confidence he didn't feel. "You said the doctor wasn't worried."

"What if they say stuff like that to make us feel better? I couldn't stand to lose her."

"Nick, it's not the dark ages. Trust the medical system. They've done this before. She'll be fine."

"She will," said Jackson, speaking for the first time. "Some of my mother's friends had pregnancy complications. One even had an emergency C-section. The teams did a great job, and everyone is doing well today."

"Really?" said Nick, looking less pale.

"Really." Jackson gave him a reassuring smile.

"A worse problem as I see it," said Wes, "is how you're going to keep Sophie in bed and off her feet for six weeks. Six hours I could see but six weeks, man, I don't envy you." Sophie believed only boring people got bored and lived her life accordingly.

"I'm going to have to take time off work," said Nick. "I can take over her share of the housework and cooking, but how will I keep her from going crazy? You can only read in bed for so long."

Once again, Jackson surprised Wes. "Don't worry about anything. We've got you covered."

****

When they got home, Wes made a list of everyone he knew, split it with Jackson, and they both got on the phone. Jackson hated calling people, even people he knew well. Most of these folks he didn't know at all, or maybe had seen them from a distance at best. But for Sophie, he could swallow his discomfort. She would do this and more for him. Everyone was willing to help. No one even hesitated.

Barb Finstead said she would provide enough reading material. Jackson would work on his novel by Sophie's bedside whenever Nick was at work. Wes said he would be there when he wasn't at work. People volunteered frozen dinners, and help with shopping, laundry, and other household tasks. Jackson and Wes took notes and the next day, they presented Nick and Sophie with a schedule of on-call help.

Tears ran down Sophie's face. "This is the best gift. Thank you."

Nick could barely speak, he was so choked up. "I—this—thank you."

Sophie lifted her head from the pillow face to face Nick. "You won't need to take time off now." She brushed away the tears. "You can save those hours for when our peanut comes home and I really need you." Sophie gave Jackson an impish smile. "And I'll get to see the great E.J. Williams, hard at work!"

Jackson laughed. "More like you'll see me procrastinating." He and Sophie joked some more, and even Nick was smiling at their antics.

But on the drive home, Jackson was quiet.

"What's up?" Wes asked.

Jackson took a few seconds to answer. "I'm overwhelmed. My mind almost can't take in the community support, the family they've built here, that you've brought me into."

"And this is a good thing?"

"It's the best. I feel like I belong to something so big and rich, I almost can't believe it." Jackson smiled. "Thank you."

****

Jackson faithfully visited Sophie every day for the next two weeks, even if the two of them mostly chatted and he didn't get much as much writing done as he'd like. Today, though, one of Sophie's neighbors was keeping her company, so Jackson was typing furiously away at Isabelle's kitchen table. Ever since he'd accepted his characters falling in love, the words flowed easily. Jackson was so immersed in the pictures flickering through his mind that when he lifted his phone to his ear to stop the incessant ringing, he was surprised to hear someone on the other end.

"Jackson? It's Marie. I'm so sorry to bother you."

He hadn't heard from Marie all winter aside from the rent she transferred to his bank account. Hopefully there wasn't an issue with his condo. "Hi! What's up?"

"When are you coming home?" Her voice wavered.

"Home?" Oh, home. "Not for a while, why?"

"Because—" She hesitated. "Your mom called me and told me to pack up my stuff and be out by the end of March. I'm looking for a place but I'm not sure I can be out by then."

"She *what*?" Jackson's family had done some outlandish things, but this was way too far. "No, you can definitely stay. I won't be making any decisions about my condo until the end of summer at least. You're a great tenant."

"Really? She sounded so excited about you coming back."

"She hasn't talked to me yet, obviously," said Jackson wryly. "I've been meaning to call you, but I'm in a story right now and forgot."

"You're staying there?"

"Yeah, I've really found my place."

"Isn't it cold?"

"There's no bad weather, only bad clothing choices." Jackson felt like a real Yukoner saying that. "The days are getting longer and, in a few months, I'll get to see the midnight sun."

"I could never leave London," Marie said with a laugh. "I'm a city girl."

"I thought so too, but Whitehorse is different. Anyway, listen, you stay as long as you want. I'll give you plenty of notice before I ask you to leave, and I'll call my mother to make sure she doesn't bother you again."

"Thanks. I'm taking good care of the place for you."

"I knew you would. Thanks. Bye."

Jackson sighed heavily. He really did not want to make this call.

His mother picked up on the first ring. "Eddie, I was just thinking about you."

"Jackson, Mom, I am going by Jackson now."

"Of course, dear. I'm sitting here setting up the guest list.

"Guest list?"

She laughed. "For your coming home party, of course."

"I don't do parties." As soon as the words left Jackson's mouth, he realized they weren't completely true. Yukon parties were fine. But he wasn't going to tell his mother that.

"Just because you haven't enjoyed them before doesn't mean you won't like this one. I'm inviting the neighbors. You like Jim and Patty. They ask about you every time I see them, and of course Corie will be there with her new beau. You'll like him."

Jackson wouldn't let himself be sidetracked. "Mom, I am not going to a party. I've decided I'm not coming home. At least, not yet."

"What do you mean, not coming home?"

"I'm staying on after Isabelle gets back. I'm in the middle of a project and my main research material is here." The words were coming out all wrong but Jackson couldn't help it. "I'm going to spend the summer in Dawson City where I'll have access to the Gold Rush Archives, and I promised to speak at a book club while I'm there."

Her laugh was shrill. "You bad boy. I thought you were serious for a moment. Stop teasing me."

That wasn't the response Jackson expected. "What?"

"I know you don't speak in front of people. That's preposterous. I'll extend the party date till you get home."

"I've done quite a few speaking engagements now. You know that." Jackson pushed on. "I've met someone. I need to stay here and see how everything goes. I'm in love." Saying the words out loud made his heart skip a beat.

"Oh, darling, that is wonderful. Eddie, I am so excited. Bring her with you. Dad and I had almost given up on the thought of you crawling out of your fantasy world long enough to meet anyone."

Not again. "I'll bring my boyfriend—" Jackson made sure to emphasize the first part of the word "—home to meet the family. Just not right now."

"Boyfriend?"

"Yes."

"You're gay?"

"Come on, Mom!" Jackson threw his hand into the air. "You've known this for years. I've talked to Dad about it so don't act surprised now! I've always wondered why you pushed those women at me. Is it because you can't stand the idea of me being gay? Or is it because you can't handle the real me?" Jackson didn't know if he was going to yell or cry.

The line went quiet.

"Mom?"

"It was a phase!" his mother shouted. "After the incident in high school, you never brought it up again! I only wanted you to be happy. Too many changes. I want my Eddie back. Come home, we can introduce you to a nice boy."

It was as if she didn't even hear him. Jackson's anger seeped away, leaving him feeling defeated. "Mom, listen to me, I'm happy here. I have friends. I have a purpose and I have Wesley. I'm different now. Your Eddie doesn't exist anymore, he never did."

"You think this is all about you," she spat. "What about your family? We're important too, more important than you gallivanting across the country trying to find yourself. You belong right here."

The line was quiet again. Was she crying? He didn't want to leave things this way but nothing was being resolved here.

The door opened and Wes's broad smile filled him with resolve. Jackson gestured to the phone. Wes tiptoed toward the stairs, trailing his hand across Jackson's back on the way. Jackson tried to look relaxed, but it must have come off shaky because suddenly Wes was on one side of him, and Kale was pressed against his legs.

"You're right, Mom, I'm only thinking of myself. Maybe when Isabelle gets home, I'll arrange to fly back for a visit so you can meet Wes before we head to Dawson?"

"Well, I guess if you decide to cut us out of your life, we'll take the scraps we're offered, won't we?"

"Come on, I'm not cutting you out. You know that." Jackson held back an exasperated sigh. "Can I say hi to Dad?"

"No. He's busy."

"Okay, give him a hug for me. And Mom? If you have something to say to my tenant, let me know and I'll contact her. Please don't upset her like that again."

"Well, if you called me more like a good son we wouldn't have these misunderstandings, would we?"

"No, you're right. I should have called sooner. Goodbye." Jackson disconnected, dropped the phone on the counter and leaned into Wes.

"That sounded fun," said Wes, holding him tightly back.

"She's still having trouble getting used to me being out here. When she's so disappointed in me, it can be hard to remember how much she loves me."

"That sucks." Wes nuzzled his neck. "What can I do to make it better?"

"Remind me how happy I am."

"I intend to. Should I remind you now or after I make you dinner?"

"Both."

Jackson was staying, and nothing or no one could change his mind.

Chapter Twenty-seven

Ringing tickled at Wes's subconscious, working its way into his dreams. It didn't sound like the house phone. Wasn't that Jackson's ringtone? Wes fumbled on the nightstand and brought the phone to his ear. "'Lo?" his voice croaked with sleep, and beside him, Jackson stirred.

"Jackson?" A woman gasped over chaotic background noise of sirens and shouts. The clock radio read almost four in the morning. "Jackson, it's your father."

"Just a second." Wes pressed the phone into Jackson's hand then wiggled over to flick on the lamp.

"Mom?" Jackson's voice wavered. "Slow down, Mom, what happened?"

Wes could hear her talking but couldn't make out the words. His eyes adjusted. Jackson pushed himself up, the blankets pooled around his waist. He was pale, his eyes large and dark. Wes pressed himself against Jackson's back, trying to ground him, offer some warmth.

"Okay, Mom... No, it's okay, I'll get there as soon as I can." Jackson caught Wes's eye, making a writing motion with his free hand. "Mom, can you put Corie on?"

Wes grabbed a pen and paper from the desk, handing them over. He turned on Jackson's laptop and settled into the cold leather chair to pull up the flight schedule.

The early morning air was cool on Wes's body and the dread in the pit of his stomach didn't do anything to warm him.

"Don't worry, Corie... No, I'll take care of it. I'll let you know when I figure out my flights... I can rent a car... Sure that's nice of him to offer but... All right, have Mark pick me up at the airport." He grimaced. "I'll make sure my cell is on and fully charged. Keep me updated. I love you."

The instant Jackson ended the call, Wes returned to the bed, wrapping Jackson in his arms and stroking his hair.

Jackson was trembling.

"They think it's his heart, they're all at the hospital." Jackson tried to push away. "I've got to get moving."

Wes tightened his arms. "It'll be okay, we'll make a plan." He kissed Jackson's clammy forehead. "There are two flights that leave before eight. One of them should have space. We'll connect in Vancouver—"

"We?" Jackson asked.

"You don't think I'd let you go through this alone?"

"I didn't, but you can't come."

The dread burbling in Wes's stomach solidified to physical pain. "You don't want me?"

"It's not that. I don't know how long this will take and you can't leave Nick and Sophie now."

Wes shook his head. "Shit, you're right. Sophie has a doctor's appointment at eleven. I promised to drive her."

"They both need you." Jackson freed himself from Wes's arms. "You're the only one Nick actually opens up to. You are doing so much for them right now and it's the final push. The baby will be here in three weeks. You can't leave now. You need to stay and be strong for our family here. I'll go and be strong for my Ontario family and get back as soon as I can."

"I don't want you to have to do this on your own."

"I can handle it. What I need is to know is you're here keeping our family safe for when I get back."

What if you don't come back? Wes didn't say that out loud. "Okay." He kissed him again and stood up. "You start packing, I'll book the flights."

"Card's in my wallet. Book me the earliest one."

Wes picked up the jeans his lover had peeled off only hours before and slipped the brown wallet out of the back pocket. "It's going to set you back a lot."

"I don't care." Jackson kept shoving clothes into a large suitcase. "I'll worry about money later."

Wes printed out the ticket. "You've got enough time for a shower. But we need to be leaving the house by five."

Jackson came to him, leaning into him wrapped his arms tight around Wes burrowing against his neck. "What if I lose him? Mom keeps us together but he's the lighthouse. I—"

Wes blinked back tears pulling Jackson close. "He'll be fine. Heart attacks, if they're caught fast, are almost totally reversible these days." He squeezed him tighter. "If you need me just say the word, I'll be there. Promise you won't do this alone?"

"I love you," Jackson whispered.

"Okay, shower, I'll get food and coffee going, and pack you something for the plane. I'll meet you downstairs."

Wes needed to get out of there before he lost it.

****

Unlike the rest of his family, Jackson never had a problem with waiting, whether it was in line at the grocery store or in traffic. He'd simply drift into his imagination and plot his latest story. Waiting for his dad to wake up from emergency heart surgery was very different. Jackson sat on a hard plastic chair in a white-walled room. He'd tried flipping through the magazines spread out on the coffee table, but it was impossible to focus on the words.

On his left sat his mother, Natalie. Her face was drawn, and her curly hair seemed far grayer than when Jackson had seen her last. Dark circles framed her eyes. Her usual composed and refined posture had disappeared. It had been replaced with slumped shoulders and hands that could not stop fidgeting.

Jackson's phone chimed and he pulled it out of his jacket pocket.

"How can you be playing about with your phone at a time like this?" his mother snapped.

"Someone messaged me, Mom," said Jackson.

"Your friends need to be more respectful!" His mother pursed her lips and glared at him.

Jackson didn't respond. He knew her frustration wasn't about him. The text message was from Wes: *Thinking of you. Sophie and Nick send their love. Sophie is totally cheating at cards. I'm pretending not to notice, that's the only reason she's winning.*

The message made Jackson smile. It soothed his

spirit to know life was continuing as normal in the Yukon. He wrote back: *Totally believe you, that's the only reason. Thank you, love back. Still no news. Even if Dad wakes up soon, it might be hours before anyone is allowed to see him. Will keep you updated.*

Jackson's mother sniffed in disapproval as he slipped his phone back into his pocket.

Corie sat on the other side of Jackson and had been surreptitiously texting her boyfriend the entire time. She'd been getting away with it by allowing her long, dark hair to cover her face as she held the phone close to her side. Their mother hadn't noticed a thing.

Everyone sat in silence for a few more minutes until their mother muttered, "This is getting ridiculous."

"They warned us it could be a long time," said Jackson, keeping his voice gentle. "Why don't you go home and get some rest? Corie can take you. I'll wait here and call you the instant anything changes."

His mother glared at him. "Oh, you'd like that, wouldn't you?"

Jackson stared at her. "For my father to wake up? Yes, I would like that. What are you talking about?"

She waved an impatient hand at him and pushed herself out of her chair. "I'm going to find out what's going on."

Jackson stood up as well. "They're going to tell you what they said the last two times. The surgery went fine and he has to wake naturally. Come on, sit back down, I'll get you a drink—"

But his mother was already out the door.

Jackson and Corie raced after her as she strode to the nurses' station.

No one was there and their mother tapped repeatedly on the bell. "Hello, where is everyone? I demand to know what's happening with my husband!" Her strident voice echoed through the hall.

Jackson's face burned. It must be flaming red. This was never the way the Williams family behaved. "Keep unwanted attention away from yourself at all times" had been his mother's motto for as long as he could remember. He briefly locked eyes with Corie, who looked as embarrassed as he felt. "Come on, Mom, let's go back to the waiting room." He put a hand on her arm.

"I will not!" His mother jerked her arm away. "Not until they tell me what's happening to your father!"

A harried-looking nurse popped her head out of a door. "One moment, please," she said, and she ducked back into the room.

"Everything's fine," Corie called out to her. "My mother's just tired of waiting."

"Don't speak for me," their mother snapped.

"I'm not speaking for you, Mom," said Corie. "I'm just—"

The nurse came running up. "What do you need?"

Natalie Williams drew herself up. "I need to see my husband!"

The nurse frowned. "Ma'am, please keep your voice down. We have patients recuperating here. And as I've already told you, it might be a while before you can see your husband. It's best if you go home and get some rest."

An unnatural red flushed over his mother's face. "How dare you speak to me that way. You will not keep me from my husband. Who knows what you people are doing to him in there—"

Without thinking, Jackson dove in between his mother and the nurse. "Mom, that's enough!" Too late, he remembered he was supposed to keep his voice down. "You've been awake for too long and haven't had anything to eat. Corie is going to take you home right now." Jackson gently but firmly turned his mother around to face his sister. "No more arguing. Go. Don't make the nurses call security on you."

Corie's eyes were wide with shock as she put an arm around her mother. "Come on, Mom, let's go. We won't be long, I promise." Over her mother's shoulder, she mouthed at Jackson, "Who are you?"

It was a very good question, but Jackson didn't have time to consider it. Once his mother and sister were out of earshot, he turned to the nurse. "I'm so sorry, she's not normally like that. It's been a stressful couple of days. I know you're doing all you can for my father."

The nurse gave him a tired smile. "Thanks. I appreciate it. I'll come and get you the instant there's news from the doctor, okay?"

"Sounds good," said Jackson. "By the way, do you have a brand of chest pillow you can recommend? I want to get my dad a couple. He doesn't laugh a lot, so it'll probably be mostly for sleeping and riding in the car. And what about information on the kind of exercises he'll need to do during recuperation? Oh, and should we get him a reclining bed, in case he has trouble lying down?"

The nurse's eyes sparkled. "You're a nursing student, aren't you?"

"Nope, just a writer," said Jackson. "I'm used to doing research for books and sitting here with too much time on my hands, it was helping keep me sane."

"Oh, what kind of books do you write?"

It wasn't long ago that Jackson would have stuttered and tried to find a way out of the conversation. This time, he acknowledged his discomfort but set it aside. "Historical Romance."

"Romance... Wait, your surname is Williams?" She looked at him in surprise. "As in, E.J. Williams?"

"That's me."

Her jaw dropped. "I can't believe it! I've got all your books."

They chatted for a few minutes until she was called to help a colleague. Jackson promised to sign a book for her and returned to the waiting room.

It was only when he sat down that he realized he'd yelled at his mother. If his hands were shaking, he told himself it was because he hadn't had anything to eat. At that precise moment, a text message from Wes arrived:

I know it's officially after lunch, but I'm betting you haven't had any, so make sure you eat something!

* * * *

The week went faster than expected when every second in the hospital dragged by like goo. The surgery had been a success. Jackson's dad would need to do lots of healing and make a major diet shift, but all that seemed easy considering everything they'd been through. The hospital was doing a few more routine things and the doctor assured them Edward Williams would be ready to leave the next morning at eleven o'clock, just in time to be home for a light, fat-reduced lunch. Natalie Williams had insisted on getting the *Recovering from a Heart Attack Diet* book, and several shopping trips had been managed to make sure they were well provisioned for the welcome home event.

When Jackson and his mom were in the same room, they walked around each other lightly. He was sure she hadn't forgotten he yelled at her in the hospital. But now her time was taken up with preparations for her husband's homecoming, and she didn't have much time to do more than snipe at her son. It was irritating but Jackson understood. The stress had been getting to all of them. Having his dad here would make things so much more relaxed, or he hoped it would.

Wes's call came right as Jackson's mother made a snide comment about his time in the Yukon. When his phone rang, she gave him a withering glance and left, shutting the door in a move just short of a slam. Jackson snuck down the stairs and into the back yard to talk. "Perfect timing. Please tell me you have something to say that isn't critical."

"I do," said Wes. "Congratulations, Uncle Jackson."

"Oh my God!" A broad grin spread over Jackson's face and he bounced on the spot. "Sophie had the baby? When, what time? Oh no, I need to be there. Tell me everything."

"I'm trying to," Wes said with a little laugh, "but I can't get a word in."

"Okay, okay, go ahead."

"They called me at five this morning. She was born at three-thirty."

"She's a girl." Jackson gulped the humid spring air, trying not to cry.

"They weren't expecting her for a couple of weeks but she's perfect. Almost seven pounds. I'm going to see her after dinner."

Jackson sighed. "You lucky dog. Have they figured

out a name yet?

"Of course. Margarite after Sophie's Mom, Elizabeth after Nick's grandmother, Peltier Morgan."

"Big name for her to fit into."

"I think they're going to call her Maggie, or whatever the heck she wants, 'cause Nick is already hopelessly in love and that girl is going to trump even Sophie."

Jackson rubbed a hand over his face. "I can't believe it, one moment there were two of them and now there are three. It's magic."

"Yeah, magic." Wes drew an audible breath. "I was talking to Nick. They aren't going to need people helping as much. He and Sophie are looking forward to taking Maggie home and shutting the doors behind them for a few weeks, regrouping and forming their family. I talked to my boss. I can take some time off work and come to be with you."

The giddiness subsided. Jackson leaned back against the wall. "I would love that. I miss you so much, but at this point it would be crazy. We need to save our money. Dad will be out of the hospital tomorrow. I just need to see him settled. I'll be home soon."

"If you're sure," Wes said, although he didn't sound convinced.

"I'm sure," said Jackson, injecting as much confidence into his voice as he could. "A week or two at most, then I'm back."

Chapter Twenty-eight

Two weeks later, Jackson was still in London and Wes tried so hard to hide his disappointment. It wasn't Jackson's fault. His dad was home with orders not to lie in bed or sit in a chair all day. Healing meant movement. There were endless physiotherapy appointments he needed to be driven to, new foods he had to consider, and the pain that never seemed to leave him. Chest surgery was very invasive. Wes knew better than anyone that recovery time was unique to the individual, and it would take as long as it took.

He and Jackson had settled into a daily routine of speaking on the phone at four p.m. Yukon time. Wes had given up trying to call Jackson after work because the time difference meant he woke Jackson every time. Now he spent his afternoon breaks on Len's phone in Wily's cramped office. Wes smiled when his call was answered on the first ring. "Hey, I wasn't sure I would catch you."

"Are you kidding, I live for this." Despite Jackson's enthusiasm, his voice was ragged.

Wes wanted so much to hold him in his arms. "Tough day?"

"Ugh, yeah." Jackson paused and the sound of a door clicking shut came down the line. "Things have been rough with Mom, but I keep trying to remember something dad told me a few months ago, that controlling us is how she handles her anxiety. Thinking about it through that lens makes it easier for me to understand but man, is she pushing it. I am going crazy with her haranguing me to stay. Trying to help her see my position and be strong all the time is wearing."

"She's still trying to keep you there?" Wes's heart sank, even though wasn't surprised.

"Nothing different from her conversations ever since I left, but it's harder to handle in person." Jackson spent a few minutes talking about the other things bothering him, namely his father being so belligerent about every aspect of his care that Jackson despaired he'd ever return to the Yukon.

Wes kept his tone light yet sympathetic. "But at least he's getting better, right?"

"Stronger every day." Jackson was quiet but his breathing was slightly on the rapid side.

Wes decided it was time to change the subject. "I went swimming with Abby and the kids today."

"That's great." Jackson's voice was soft but his smile came through.

"And even better, I got to spend two hours holding Maggie while Sophie took a nap."

"Please." Now Jackson sounded more animated than ever. "Tell me you've got pictures. I need to see that."

"I'll send them as soon as I get home." Wes could hear Len calling him to the front. "I've got to go. Len needs me or his office. I miss you."

"I love you. Goodnight."

"Goodnight, I love you too." Wes got back to work, the elation at having hear Jackson's voice tempered by the melancholy of not knowing when he'd return.

With Jackson away, the only way to deal with the ragged hole in his life was to keep busy. Now that Sophie and Nick didn't need him as much, Wes took as many shifts as Len would give him. On the days he didn't have to be at work, which were few and far between, he puttered around with Uncle Jeff's tools on projects his uncle had carefully drawn out in the workshop notebook. Kale knew something was off and stayed closer to Wes than usual. Spring's return would be slow, but every day the sun disappeared later as the world moved toward the midnight sun. It was no longer dark when he got home from afternoon shifts, so he had started ripping up the Castle's floor to install pipes for warm water generated by the stove. It wasn't much but it would afford the residents a short, hot shower if the cook stove was fired up. Uncle Jeff's home-drawn plan was ingenious and shouldn't take long for Wes to implement. Maybe he'd even be done by the time Jackson got back.

****

Wes's days ran together into a blur of work, watching the baby grow, walks, and restless sleep. Now that Jackson's dad was home, and their whole family was under one roof, phone calls were getting more difficult to schedule. It had been almost a month and their tolerance for being apart was wearing them thin. Conversations were getting harder.

Wes sighed. "Do you need me to tell you how hard it is here so that you feel okay with how awful it is there?"

"Maybe. I miss you. I just want to be home."

"So come home. Your dad's out of the hospital now."

"He is, but with Mom and Corie both back at the university trying to finish the semester, and me alone with dad, trying to get him to eat the right, apparently boring food, and get out of his chair onto his feet, along with endless laundry and housework, it's just—it's complicated."

"Of course, it is." Wes couldn't help the bitterness dripping from his voice.

"I'm the only one here most days and it seems like Dad doesn't want to get better." Jackson took a breath and started right back in. "Corie and I are supposed to be working together, but Corie is finishing her finals and her thesis paper to graduate. She deserves the support, although I think she's spending all her spare time at Mark's house and totally MIA."

"That sucks. I get it, and maybe I'm being selfish but—"

"Yes, you are being selfish," Jackson snapped.

Wes felt as if he'd been punched in the gut. For a moment, he couldn't breathe.

Being on the phone, Jackson didn't even notice and plowed ahead. "They need my help! For maybe the first time in my life, I can step up and do something substantial for my family. The bigger thing is, I don't know how much longer I'll have my dad."

Wes wanted to lash out at something. None of that was fair. But he couldn't spend their precious moments fighting. He swallowed down his pain. "How about we change the subject? Sophie loved the gift box you ordered. Maggie is so cute in the little wolf hat. If she hasn't done it yet, you better get ready to be bombarded with pictures."

"She has." Jackson sounded calmer now. "I get at least a hundred of them every day. I have to smile every time I see the rattle you carved, propped up against the poor kid. It will be months before she can hold it up without popping herself in the bean."

"Sophie's humoring me. She loves that I made it with my own two hands, but you're right, it's still kinda big for Maggie."

"Oh, I have a bit of news." There was a rustling sound, as if Jackson was shuffling paper. "I asked Lorraine to set me up for some exposure while I'm here. I figure worrying about presentations will keep me from obsessing about not being with you. And since I need to be here, I might as well. She's set up a meet and greet at one of the bookstores in town for tomorrow, and a talk for a university study group at the end of the week. That'll be harder, I mean what do I know about the theory of romance." Jackson gave a self-deprecating laugh. "I'll need you to remind me I can do it."

Wes's heart sunk. "This is starting to sound like you're working."

"Not working." Jackson sounded a little defensive, at least to Wes's ears. "I'm trying so hard to think of it as walking into Sophie's living room, filled with friends. It's not work, and I can't believe I suggested it."

"I didn't mean that." Wes rubbed his temple. Why was this so difficult? "I meant, it sounds like you're building a life for yourself there, without me."

"No." Jackson sounded shocked. "How can you even think that? I can't even do this without your support."

"Of course I support you." What else could Wes say? "We both know you'll do great. Take some deep breaths and don't worry about it now." Were relationships always this hard? Wes wanted to reach through the phone and touch him. "Speaking of university, I have some news too." He took a deep breath of his own. "I'm not going back to Peru. I'm staying here. Even after Aunt Izzie gets back." And he told Jackson the whole story.

Life in Peru had been solitary and rigorous, but it had been what Wes thought he'd wanted when coming back to make amends had been an impossibility. Now he knew life in Peru had given him the space he needed to make the important decisions. The Yukon was where Wes needed to be, and his path forward had become clear. Having not completed grade eleven, the route he was choosing had seemed unlikely. Once again, Nick had come to his rescue. He was friends with the dean of Environmental Studies at Yukon University and set up a meeting. The dean had been friendly and encouraged Wes to apply, saying they were open to students with Wes's life experience. It was weird applying without talking to Jackson first, but he hadn't had any real hope of being accepted.

And now he had a letter of acceptance in his hand, his ticket to start a program of studies next fall. "I can serve the Mother, Pachamama, from this place right here," said Wes. "It's what I'm meant to do and I can't wait to start, but I need your blessing first."

"Really, you want me to weigh in on something this big?" Jackson sounded bewildered. "Why? Congratulations, but this is you. It's what you're meant to do."

Wes wasn't sure how to respond. Wasn't it obvious? He struggled for the words. "I think now that we're an official couple, I wanted to know what you think. It's a huge commitment. I've always made my own decisions. I never had anyone who I cared to ask or share with. What do you want to do? I don't want to be tied to the full program if you need to be in London. I want this to be about us, not just me."

Jackson was quiet for a moment. "To be honest Wes, I just need to jump through the phone and hug you so hard but I can't. I do need to be here for the next couple of weeks, maybe even a month—"

Wes clenched his jaw.

"—but you know I can't stay here. The Yukon has my heart now. I have you. I have friends, I even feel like I have a little person who's going to need some Uncle

Jackson pretty soon and honestly, writing can be done anywhere."

Wes relaxed and let go of the breath he didn't know he'd been holding. "Parts of this course can and will be done online, but so much of it needs to be done in person. If you're sure, I'm going to send in the first payment."

"I am so sure." Jackson told him with so much feeling it felt like an all-encompassing hug. "I promise I'll be home soon. I only need to see Dad come back to himself. Then I'll be on a plane so fast, it'll feel like, 'Beam me up Scotty,' and I'll shimmer into existence right in front of your eyes."

Wes laughed. "I love how your mind works. Goodnight. I love you."

"Love you too."

Wes did love him, and he was sure Jackson loved him right back. Love wasn't enough to keep people together, though, not when they had somewhere else to be. Maybe Jackson would return soon. Maybe he wouldn't. Maybe his family would need him for much longer than a month. Still, Jackson had given his blessing, and it was what Wes needed to move forward with his life. Even if he ended up doing so on his own.

Chapter Twenty-nine

A week later, Isabelle arrived home in a flurry. Kale was ecstatic and couldn't stop bouncing around her. While Wes was happy she was back, he also wasn't ready for her to be there. In his mind, he had conflated Isabelle's arrival with Jackson's departure. Jackson had been gone for weeks, but he had assured Wes that he would "shimmer" in as soon as humanly possible. Wes was sure Jackson wanted to be there, but would he be able to break free? The urge to go and help was high, but Wes was staying put, because that's what Jackson wanted, maybe even needed.

With Wes's work schedule and Isabelle's need to sleep off her jet lag, it was a few days before they were able to spend any time together. He started by showing her his work on Jeff's projects. Isabelle was both thrilled and impressed, declaring she could hardly wait to try out the shower at the Castle. On the next cold day, Wes knew she would be down there, lighting the old cook stove.

From there, they headed to the porch, with their conversation turning to Jeff for a brief moment.

Wes sat in one of the wooden chairs. "I spent lots of time at the trapline cabin this winter. I felt close to him there."

"You did?" said Isabelle as she took a seat in the other.

"I was pretty messed up when I got back. I didn't know what to do with myself. I was glad to have Jackson's company, he was amazing. He anchored me."

They were quiet as they watched Kale dash about the front yard.

"You love him." It wasn't a question.

Wes smiled at her. "I thought anyone who really knew me wouldn't want anything to do with me, and here's this guy who..." The smile fell away. He couldn't talk about it. Not now. Not till Jackson was sitting beside him. Wes waited for the weight in his heart to go, for it to start beating again.

Isabelle went inside and returned with two cold beers, handing him one as she sat down. Birds chirped and flew between the trees. It was almost ten o'clock and the sun was still high. Neither of them spoke. Isabelle held the silence, letting him know without words she'd listen whenever he was ready, no matter how long it took.

Wes was almost halfway through his beer when the words made themselves known. "I didn't know how much help I needed to process my feelings about being back here, and Jackson was this quiet presence in the background, never leaving me alone and supporting me through my roller coaster of emotions."

Isabelle's voice was soft. "Your father did a real number on you."

Wes stopped mid-swig and lowered his bottle. "Yes."

Now it was Isabelle who unleashed the words she'd kept inside for so long. Her eyes were firmly focused on the tree line as she talked about Wes's dad, her brother. A man so in love with his wife and children in the beginning, but life happens. There was an accident at the mine, his back was ruined and the drugs he took for pain didn't help. He couldn't work and spent too much time alone. When the drugs were gone, he turned to alcohol. "Men of the day were not able to ask for help. Even if he had, there would have been nothing available. He had to be a man. I think the addiction became a monster he couldn't control." Isabelle frowned, searching for the right words. "Did he want help? I don't know. In the beginning, we offered but we gave up because he got so angry, and we were afraid he would stop us from seeing you and Abby."

This was a whole story Wes hadn't known. He shuddered, thinking about his own experience with addiction. Shame could so easily destroy a person.

Isabelle set the bottle next to her chair, still not looking at Wes. "I wish we'd done more but those days were different. You didn't interfere with other people's children. We did what we could, but we had no idea how bad it was until it was too late."

"You did plenty." Wes rested his hand on her shoulder. "All my memories of family have you and Jeff in them."

"My brother..." Isabelle sighed, releasing resignation and regret in one exhale. "He was such a mess." At long last, she met Wes's gaze and gave him a warm smile that reached her eyes. "But sitting here with you now, after thinking you were gone, I feel so damn grateful. Now, you're not moving back into the Castle, young man."

The abrupt change of topic threw Wes for a moment. "What do you mean?"

"Ha! You think I don't know the real reason you installed those hot water pipes? No, you're staying with me. I need another heartbeat in the house, and I know you want to be near the phone since you're too stubborn to get a cell." Isabelle stifled a yawn. "You and Jackson can move into the Castle when he gets back, and not a second sooner."

The last thing Wes wanted to do was discuss his doubts about Jackson ever returning at all. "Sounds good. Thank you."

Isabelle patted his hand and pushed herself out of the chair. "Time for me to get some sleep. What about you?"

"Sounds like a good idea," Wes said, getting to his feet.

Isabelle whistled for Kale, who came bounding up the steps. He snuffled at Wes's hand and then followed Isabelle inside, wagging his tail in delight.

Wes spent a few meditative minutes tidying the kitchen and headed to the guest room. He picked up his tablet to find a message from Jackson:

Hey, I tried to call to say goodnight but no answer. I'm going to bed to try and sleep. Big day tomorrow. Wish you were here to tell me I'm up for it. Talk soon <3

Wes headed for the house phone and yes, there was a message. His toes curled when he heard Jackson's voice low and whispery: "Everyone is sleeping here. I just wanted to hear your voice. Goodnight. I miss you. I love you."

It was too late to call back. Maybe Wes would get lucky. He carried his tablet to bed and sent a message back:

You still up? Don't worry, you'll be amazing. You always are.

Wes snuggled under the blankets waiting for a response. Oh, how he hoped for a response. He'd only now started to process Isabelle's revelations. A little of the anger Wes had always held toward his father had dissipated. For the first time in his life, Wes understood him. All these years of running, hiding, and searching for answers, and all it had taken was a short, honest conversation with his aunt. There was no forgiveness, and there might never be. But there was some compassion for why his father had turned out the way he did, and that was something Wes had never thought would happen.

The fear remained, though. Would Wes become him? He had become his father for a time, numbing his pain with drugs, lashing out and hurting others in the hope it would erase his own hurt. Unlike his father, Wes had sought out and accepted help. But knowing where he came from, understanding his family history, how could Wes be sure he wasn't doomed to repeat it? All these things and more he so desperately wanted to discuss with Jackson, but there was still no reply. Wes had to concede that Jackson was asleep, and it was time for him to do the same.

It took a lot of tossing and turning, but Wes's ruminating thoughts eventually succumbed to his exhaustion and he drifted into a deep, dreamless sleep.

Chapter Thirty

Rain sluiced down the windowpanes and lightning jagged across the sky. It would be a perfect morning to spend in a blanket fort with Wes. Since he wasn't here, Jackson would have to settle for a phone call this afternoon. Except that for the past four days, Jackson had been missing him every time he called.

Messaging wasn't enough. Hearing Wes's rich, warm voice while the phone pressed against Jackson's ear, his five o'clock shadow scraping against the edge, had been keeping him sane. Those calls reminded Jackson who he was while his family tried to force him back into the box he'd occupied for too many years.

Today was Wes's birthday. Jackson should have been stepping off the plane into his arms. Instead, he was here. Maybe he should pack up and go. But maybe it was too soon to leave. How could Jackson know when it was the right time? The heart attack had hit both of his parents hard. They needed him. What if his father fell in the shower when no one was around? What if he had another heart attack while his mother was teaching? Jackson was the only who could reliably be home for much of the day. Corie was spending every free minute with Mark and couldn't be counted on if things got hairy.

Jackson's fingers lingered over the phone screen. It was still too early to call. He didn't want to risk waking Isabelle. Instead, he turned on his laptop to review his presentation this afternoon. Without warning, a wave of panic raced over him like a freight train. It was impossible to breathe. What were the instructions again? It had been so long since his last panic attack. The voice of his therapist filtered through the haze and Jackson quickly put his head between his knees and battled through the panic, waiting till the tremors subsided. Slowly, he came back to himself. When was the last time he ate? Probably at dinner last night. Wes was always reminding him to eat and it helped. Jackson headed to the kitchen to see what he could find.

Unfortunately, he found his mother. She had a teaching assistant in the classroom and didn't need to be at the university every day. She was baking again. Ever since he could remember, when she was stressed she put out an endless stream of cookies, cinnamon rolls, pies, and more. None of them were on his father's strict new diet. The freezer was full, and the counters were stacked high. "Eddie, what in heaven's name?"

Jackson had stopped correcting her. His pleas to use Jackson were completely ignored every time. He knew she needed something to stay the same, but it irked him just the same. "I need some juice and I should get myself some breakfast."

"You haven't eaten yet? You're worse than a child. Let me get you something."

"Mom, I'm just a bit nervous, that's all. I can get my own breakfast."

"You didn't eat a proper meal last night either. Don't think I'm not watching." She opened a drawer. "This is just like that time you fainted in high school, you are never going to do anything if I'm not there to do it for you!"

Okay, that was just too much. He could be kind, had been kind, but where did it end? Nowhere if he didn't stop it. "I see what's going on now. Things are sure back to normal. Poor little Eddie can't take care of himself! Well, if I'm such a burden when you need to be occupied with Dad, then it's time for me to go home!" He grabbed a green apple and bit into it. The sour juice of regret washed through his mouth. He'd gone too far and resorted to her level of sniping instead of standing up for himself.

Her lower lip trembled and his mother folded into herself. "I thought this was your home." Tears poured down her cheeks.

Jackson's anger melted away. "Aw, Mom, come here." He rested tentative hands on her shoulders and leaned his cheek on her graying hair. He'd gotten used to hugging Wes and being mauled by Sophie, but touching was not encouraged in this house. "This will always be home."

Jackson's heart cracked wider. How could he go when they still needed him? And yet, how could he stay when his soul was drying up and blowing away? He thought of Wes, celebrating his birthday alone when he'd gone to such incredible lengths to make Jackson's big day special. No, he just couldn't drop the subject. "But I have a second home now. The semester ends this week, Corie will be around more and your workload will be easier. I'm going to start looking into tickets back to the Yukon."

She blinked in surprise and opened her mouth to speak but stopped. With a rough jerk of her shoulders, she pulled away and went back to her mixing bowls. Her back was turned. Jackson had been dismissed.

He took his apple and went to help his father with his morning exercises. If there ever had been a test of Jackson's patience, it was dealing with a petulant and ill parent who was not allowed to go outdoors because of the storm. Nothing was good enough for his father that morning. Everything was too hot, too small, too itchy, too far away, too tiring. Jackson spent most of the time biting his tongue. How did nurses do this kind of work? When it was time for his father's afternoon nap, Jackson convinced his mother to take one also. The storm was still raging outside his bedroom window. If he didn't call now, he'd risk missing Wes's birthday all together.

The phone rang, once, twice, three times. What if no one was home? Isabelle was back from her trip but she wasn't one to sit around the house all day. What if Jackson didn't get another chance to call? What if Wes thought Jackson didn't love him anymore and—

Then the phone clicked. "Hello?" said Isabelle.

Relief made Jackson weak at the knees and he fell onto the bed. "Hi, Isabelle. It's Jackson. Is Wes there?"

"No, he had to work today."

"When will he get back?"

"I don't know. There's a party at Sophie and Nick's tonight. It'll probably be late."

At least Wes wouldn't be alone on his birthday. "Could you do me a favor and give him my present? I wrapped it and dug it deep into the back of your closet months ago."

"I'll find it and get it to him." Isabelle's voice was filled with warmth. "Don't worry, I've been conspiring with Sophie, and we'll make sure he has a great birthday and doesn't miss you too much. Best present will be when you get here, though."

Jackson felt small and bruised, he could barely speak. He needed to hug Wes and see the look on his face when he opened the gift. He just needed to touch him. But he couldn't. Jackson's goodbye was short.

Isabelle left him with prayers for the family.

****

Wes gathered his energy and sat on his depression. Nick and Sophie's living room appeared as if a dollar store had exploded in it. There were balloons, ribbons and a banner that burst with *Happy Birthday*. Kelly had a brunette on his arm, and Jimmy was making eyes at Julie. Isabelle was sitting in a rocking chair, tickling Maggie and hoping for smiles, and Abby was in the kitchen directing the action. It was probably the only reason Sophie wasn't overdoing it.

Everyone was animated but the noise of Jackson's absence was thundering in his ears.

Nick and Thomas barbecued ribs and fixings out in the backyard as Samantha and Wesley roared over and under the picnic table. Once everything was cooked, the full meal was laid out on the dining room table and everyone dug in, bringing their plates back to balance on their knees in the living room. The food had to be great, although Wes only poked at it and hoped no one would notice he couldn't eat a bite. Later they brought out the cake and all bellowed "Happy Birthday" out of key as he blew out the candles and made his wish. Nick and Sophie gave him a block of African mahogany that weighed a ton. It was beautiful. Wes traced the grain imagining the shape inside. Jimmy, Julie, and Kelly had gone together to get him a set of knives like the local totem carvers used.

Sophie came and sat beside Wes, with Nick settled at

her feet. The room went silent. Sophie held up an envelope but didn't give it to him. "Happy birthday, Wesley. Nick and I, all of us really, want you to know how much we love you." She stopped and gulped. "We couldn't have made it through these last months without your support. When Jackson had to leave, you should have gone with him, but you stayed, to help us. That choice was hard and we appreciated it. We want you to have this." She handed him the envelope. "We took a collection."

All his friends were smiling at him.

"There should be enough for plane tickets to Ontario—" she stumbled "—or to spend for school or whatever you need. We love you."

Wes didn't know what to say. His feelings of depression vanished. Tears pricked his eyes. He didn't know how much was in the envelope but it had to be a lot. How could he accept such a huge gift? But also, how could he reject it? Everyone he loved wanted this for him. They wanted for him what he wanted for himself. "Thank you." Wes stood and wiped his eyes. "Thank you, everyone. I… I don't know what to say."

They clapped and cheered. Wes hugged everyone within reach, giddy with happiness. This was his wild, crazy family, now and forever. If it wasn't too late, maybe he could call Jackson and tell him how nuts their friends were. Maybe book a flight as well.

Isabelle came to sit beside him. "Sophie can really throw a party."

"Yeah, I think she lives for this stuff. I'm glad Abby helped her. I'm sure she's doing too much."

"Probably, but I think having Maggie is only making her stronger." Isabelle reached into her bag and brought out one last small package wrapped in newspaper. "Jackson called this morning to talk to you. He wanted me to give you this."

Wes turned it over in his hands, then tugged the tape off the wrapping to find a copy of *The Forgotten Kingdom* by Norman Power. This book had been his refuge when he was in public school, from the moment he turned ten. Even in high school he'd read it over and over again. The water-ruined copy was still on his night table. The note on the inside cover of this one read, "Never let the magic disappear. Love, Jackson."

Wes raised the book to his nose. The last person to touch it was Jackson. He only detected the smell of words. His friends were busy being busy, but Sophie was watching him. Wes pulled his hand across his eyes. "Can I borrow a phone?"

Sophie gestured to the bedroom. "Of course."

He went into the bedroom and sat on the bed keying in the number. It went straight to voicemail. "You've reached Jackson, leave a message. If this is Wes, happy birthday. I love you."

Wes smiled. "Hey, great message. I love the present. Call me back."

He should rejoin his friends. It was his birthday party, after all. But all he wanted for his birthday was to talk to Jackson. It was even what he'd wished for when blowing out the candles.

Inspiration struck. Hadn't Jackson given him a list of numbers months ago, in case of emergency but mainly to ease his mother's anxiety? The piece of paper was still tucked in Wes's wallet and he couldn't help smiling at the sight of Jackson's neat handwriting. He thought for a moment about calling Cori's number. She'd sounded fun, even if their conversation had been brief. But Jackson was more likely to be at his parents' place, so that was the number he dialed.

The phone was answered on the second ring by an older woman. "Hello?"

That must be Jackson's mother. "Hello, Mrs. Williams?"

"Yes." Her tone was clipped and terse.

Wes turned on the charm. "Hi, I'm sorry to be calling so late. This is Wesley Palmer. I'm a friend of Jackson's."

"I am well aware of who you are." Not even midwinter in the Yukon was as frosty as her tone.

Wes was completely bewildered. She sounded nothing like either of her children. Was she really that mad about a ten p.m. phone call? "Oh, uh, could I please speak to Jackson? I promise I'll make it quick."

"No. He isn't here."

"He isn't? Can I talk to Corie?"

"She isn't here either, but to be frank Mr. Palmer, even if they were here, I would not let you talk to them." Her voice was low but vicious. "I am glad, however, to have an opportunity to speak to you. I want you to hang up this phone and never call it again. You're not welcome here. I want you to stay away from my children. Jackson had his little fling. He's back with his family now where he belongs. This is where he will stay. Am I being clear?"

Wes couldn't breathe.

"Mr. Palmer?"

"Yes."

"Good, I thought I had lost you. Did you hear me?"

"Yes, ma'am."

She disconnected with an echoing finality.

Chapter Thirty-one

There was no time to worry about this afternoon's presentation because Jackson was going to do something truly daring. He was going to attempt to convince his father to go for a walk in the rain.

Walking in the rain used to be a special treat for Jackson when he was younger. His dad had worked long hours and wasn't home often, but sometimes when it was wet out, Dad would say, "Do you want to go for a walk?" And of course, Jackson did because neither Corie nor his mom would want to get damp. The two of them would suit up in rain gear and walk, mainly in silence. It had been nice, just the two of them. His dad had been so distracted and cranky lately that Jackson felt stupid even thinking of it, but he brought their raincoats and stashed them in the car, just in case.

When they came out of the physio appointment, his father looked drawn and tired. Jackson almost didn't ask but gathered his courage. "I've always wanted to explore the park near here. What do you say to a walk in the rain? Like the old days?"

His father shook his head. "No. I want to go home."

Jackson swallowed and hoped he'd kept the disappointment from his face. "Okay. Sure."

But instead of heading with him to the car, his father remained in place. "It's not a bad idea, son. But we don't have our raincoats."

A smile slowly spread across Jackson's face. "Actually, we do. Want me to get them?"

For the first time in weeks, his father's expression softened. "Go ahead. I'll wait here." He stood under the awning of the physio building, out of the rain.

Jackson dashed to the car and back. They donned their bright yellow raincoats—his mother had insisted on yellow for visibility—and headed to the park.

It was a slow stroll to the first bench. They sat in silence. The rain was light and fell with the softest of patters.

His dad was the first to speak. "Jackson, this was a good idea. I've wanted to talk to you since you've been here, and we haven't had much of a chance to do that."

Jackson only nodded, giving his father a chance to say what was on his mind.

"I wanted to say that in the months you've been away, you've matured, come into yourself. You look like a man with a purpose. We're both so very proud of you."

Jackson's brow shot up in surprise. "You are? But Mom—"

"Your mother has a lot on her mind, and she may not show it the way she should, but never doubt that she loves you."

Jackson was shocked. His father never talked to him like this. He wanted to say something big to match his father's words, but nothing came. "Thank you." He leaned over and put his hand on his father's knee.

His dad took it and held it, turning to look in Jackson's eyes. "The other thing I wanted to say is, you look like you've lost your best friend, son." He gripped his hand tighter. "And I haven't seen you write a thing in days. In all my life, I have not seen you without a pen or a story brewing in you, even before you were old enough to write. It's disturbing and makes me think something is terribly wrong."

Jackson had so much to say that nothing came out. It was true. He hadn't written or even thought of writing since he got here. Jackson considered his words, knowing he had to tread carefully. His dad was improving a lot, but how much could he take? "Well, I've been worried about you. You look like you've lost your will to live."

His dad shook his head. "I have been a bit of a lout, haven't I. I was so discouraged and depressed. I felt like my life was over, but my doctor says it's pretty normal and I feel like a fog is lifting. I'm trying to take it day by day."

"That's great. I'm really glad." Jackson took a deep breath. "There's more. I'm in love, Dad. I haven't seen Wes in weeks and I miss him so much. Before I got here, I thought I had my life on track for the first time ever. I was making my own choices and acing them. Now, I feel like I'm being shoved back into Eddie's old room, his old clothes and his old life. I can't do it anymore because I'm not that guy anymore. I'm really not. Maybe I never was. I do know I need to get back to Wes and back to writing."

His dad sat with rain dripping from his wide brimmed hat. "I'm sorry, Jackson. I've not been the best patient and none of us have thought about what we've asked you to give up."

"I did it happily, Dad, for you, for my family. But things are going better and I'm booking my ticket home when I get back from the university today."

His dad grinned, probably for the first time since Jackson had been home. "Well, thank heavens. Let's get that pen back in your hand and your beau back on your arm. We can't take the world's number one writer of historical fiction out of commission any longer. We'll be fine. It's bad enough I was willing to give up my life. We really don't want you giving up yours."

Jackson was stunned. As always, he'd forgotten that when he took the time to talk to his dad, he really understood him. Jackson should do it more often.

****

Wes had been right again. Jackson's presentation was amazing. The audience was a friendly bunch of university staff members celebrating the break between the spring and summer semesters. The reading and question period was as relaxed as Sophie's book club had been, minus the wine. Meeting his readers one-on-one and signing their books was delightful, and they'd all cheered when Jackson gave them the special link for a discount on Hanson's website. Why had he ever thought he would hate doing this kind of promotion? The day got even better when one of the women, a professor, told him the English department would be hosting a new course exploring the romance genre next fall. Romance at university. The idea of it would blow his mom's socks off. The professor asked if he would consider coming to London in the fall to speak and then asked for his card. Jackson didn't have a card. The memory of Wes calling him a big-time author, in need of a chauffeur, flashed through Jackson's mind. Maybe he didn't need a driver but, really, a card would be so simple. He would think about that when he was back in the north.

Jackson had already decided what he was going to do. The high after his talk at the university helped clarify things even further. All he needed was to talk to Wes and let him know what was going on, but no one was answering their phones.

****

After dinner, Jackson went to his computer and purchased a ticket home. The only thing left was telling his mother. He tucked his phone in his pocket in case Wes tried to get back to him. Time to face the music. He knocked on Corie's door and poked his head in. "It's time. You ready?"

Corie pushed away from her desk and stood up. "Are you?" She hadn't been really surprised but still couldn't believe Jackson booked his flight for the next morning, although they could both see the wisdom of not giving Mom time to stew about it.

Jackson smiled at her. "Actually, yeah, I am. Talking to Dad went so well this morning, and he's probably already prepared her. Still glad I've got you to back me up."

"Always." Corie gave him a quick hug. "But let's get this over with before Mark comes. If it goes south, he'll help calm her down." Corie was waiting for Mark to drop by and spend a bit of time with her that evening before bed. The whole family liked Mark. He and Corie were in sync, they communicated well and complemented each other. Jackson didn't really want to compare them to him and Wes, but really, what other relationships could he look to with any experience?

They headed down to the living room where their parents were reading.

"Um, hi, if I can have your attention, please?" When they looked up, Jackson outlined his plan to leave early and have Corie be the one who got up at the crack of dawn to get him to the airport. He explained that he knew it was sudden, but he really needed to return to the Yukon, and not to worry because there would be plenty of phone calls and visits.

His mother said nothing but Jackson was so sure she would accept this decision that when she rose from her chair, he thought she was coming to hug him, to thank him for all he'd done. Then he took a better look at her in the lamp light. Her face was a study of lines and bitter creases.

Dad leaned from his chair and reached for her. "Natalie. Don't say something you might regret later."

She ignored her husband. "Eddie, you don't know what you're talking about."

"Yes, I do." Jackson was firm. "Life is settling down here, you don't need me anymore, and it's time for me to go home to Wes."

"Wes?" She spat the name. "You're giving your family up for some guy you found on the road?"

Jackson started back at the viciousness of her words, but it made him more determined to have his say. "He's my future and I need to be back there."

A familiar voice spoke behind him. "God, it's good to hear you say that!"

Jackson spun around.

There, behind Mark in the doorway, stood Wes with Shadow slung over his shoulder.

"Oh fuck," Jackson breathed. "You're here." He lunged forward and found himself wrapped safe in strong arms. He inhaled the scent of home. The room faded. All that existed was Wes and his tight embrace. Jackson's pulse synchronized with Wes's heart for the first time in forever.

The spell was broken by Jackson's mother. "Eddie, don't be rude. Introduce your friend," she snapped.

Jackson turned in Wes's arms, which remained loosely enveloped around him. "Mom, Dad, this is Wesley."

"And I'm his sister." Corie did a mock curtsy. "Finally, the great Wesley Palmer in person. Did you meet Mark?"

Wes gave her an amused glance. "Yes, he let me in."

"So, Wesley." Mom moved closer. "You certainly picked an interesting time to arrive. Jackson was telling us he is leaving tomorrow at some ridiculous hour, all because of you. So what are you doing here?"

"Tomorrow?" Wes's brow rose in surprise. "It does seem like weird timing, doesn't it. But our friends knew how much we were missing each other and bought me a plane ticket for this grand romantic gesture." He beamed at Jackson.

Natalie was shaking. Red-faced, she approached Wes and shook a finger at him. "You are not welcome in our home Mr. Palmer. Get out!"

Wes blanched and looked at Jackson.

Jackson's stomach churned. "Mom?" Never before had she spoken to a guest like that. It was another one of her rules to be a gracious host, no matter the circumstances.

"You heard me!" His mother's kept her focus on Wes, her face twisted into someone unrecognizable. "Get. Out!"

Not believing his ears, Jackson grabbed Wes's hand. He couldn't even look at his mother. "I'm already packed," he said to Wes in a low voice. "I just need to get my bags, then we can go."

Corie stepped in front of their mother. "Don't worry about your bags," she said to Jackson, her face pale and expression somber. "I'll bring them to you. Call me later."

His father walked to them, shaky after a long day. He reached for Wes's hand and gave Jackson a hug. "Don't worry, son, she'll be okay."

"Don't speak for me, Edward." His mother was vibrating in rage. "Leave then, all of you, just leave." She burst into tears.

Jackson took one last look at her. Could he do anything to make it better? No, not at this moment, if ever. He clutched Wes's hand tightly as they walked out, stunned at the turn things had taken. He could hear Corie's voice raised behind the closed door, asking her mother what she was even thinking.

"What do we do now?" Wes asked as they stepped off the porch onto the dark, tree-lined street.

"I guess we find a hotel maybe near the airport." Jackson pulled out his phone to get an Uber.

"Wait!" someone called out, and they turned to see Mark hurrying up behind them. "Come back to my place, Corie will be over when they're done in there. She'll want to talk to you."

****

Mark's place was an old but well maintained apartment building overlooking London's Victoria Park. He showed them to the guest room, where Wes set Shadow down, and ushered them into the kitchen for grilled cheese sandwiches. "Airline food isn't known for its sustaining power." He dropped bread and cheese slices on the pan.

Wes put his arm around Jackson. "That was quite the welcome."

Jackson was still shaken but apologized on behalf of his mother. "I'm really sorry. That wasn't like her at all. She's always been controlling but it's like she's lost her mind. She would always welcome someone to our home, whether she liked them or not."

Mark nodded as he turned the sandwiches over. "She likes her rules, but I've never seen her that angry."

"She's been so intense lately," said Jackson, "but I chalked it up to Dad's close call."

Wes pulled him close. "She's under a huge amount of stress and I come waltzing in to steal her baby. You said yourself she handles her anxiety by controlling everything around her. I kind of get it."

"Don't defend her," said Jackson. "That was over-the-top rude. I don't know how I can forgive her."

"We'll figure it out together," said Wes. "We're both tired, let's just get home and then see how we can tackle her. I can be pretty darned charming when I get going."

Jackson snorted. "Don't I know it. But I don't think it'll work on her."

Mark flipped two golden brown sandwiches onto

plates with a huge dollop of ketchup on the side. "Enjoy."

"Food hasn't tasted this good in weeks." Jackson all but inhaled his sandwich.

"In my professional opinion," said Wes, "these are the best grilled cheese sandwiches I've ever had." He took another large bite and a thumbs up as Mark beamed at him.

Corie came in with Jackson's bags right as they'd finished cleaning up. She gave Mark a quick kiss hello and pulled a chair up beside him. "Well, that sucked. I've never heard Dad talk to Mom like that. He let her have it for treating a guest in our home that way. Then he came right out and asked her if her intention was to drive you so far away you never came back. She was crying. He said he knew things weren't easy on her and he felt like he had let her down. Sounds like he insisted on counselling, couples and individual. That's a first. I left when he took her up to bed." Corie bit her lip. "She seemed genuinely sorry."

Wes was leaning against Jackson, eyes half closed, but suddenly he shifted and sat up straight. "She's going to need to see you, Jackson. The two of you need to talk or this will fester between both of you."

Jackson stared at him in disbelief. "I can't believe you're ready to forgive her!"

"That's not my place," said Wes. "You've still got family. If you lose them, they're gone." There was no judgment in his voice, only pain and regret.

Now the ache in Jackson's heart was for Wes. "What are you suggesting?" he asked softly.

"Let her know you're willing to talk," said Wes. "I didn't know what I'd find here. I left my ticket open ended. I can book it for tomorrow and leave with you, or maybe you can change yours and we can go back later in the week. That gives us some leeway, some time to let her make amends."

"I could do that if you're up for it." The stress of the whole evening was starting to pull at Jackson's eyelids.

"I'm here for you and with you, no matter what you decide," said Wes.

"I'm still angry," said Jackson. "But..." He turned to

Corie and gave her his most pleading look. "Can you tell Mom I'll be here for a few more days if she wants to talk?"

"Of course," said Corie. No teasing, no giving her brother a hard time. Just a simple agreement to help. She fished her car keys out of her pocket. "I probably should get going, anyway."

Mark offered to let Wes and Jackson stay in his guest room as long as they wanted and use it as a command center, then he told Corie he would walk her to her car. They still hadn't made the leap to sleepovers in their relationship.

"When you live under Mom and Dad's roof, you follow their rules," Corie told them ruefully as she hugged them both, and then followed Mark into the corridor.

Jackson's thumbs traveled quickly over his phone to change his flight, trying to ignore how much it cost. "There, it's done. We're heading back on Thursday, no matter what."

Wes gave him a tired smile. "Great. Now, come with me." He grabbed Jackson's hand and pulled him through the kitchen to the bathroom. "I don't know about you, but I've been on an airplane since seven-thirty this morning. I need a shower. Join me?" He reached for his buttons.

Jackson stilled Wes's hand. "You're exhausted. Let me do that." He didn't linger over the undressing. Wes was nearly asleep on his feet. Jackson got them into the shower with the hot water sluicing over tired muscles. He moved the soapy washcloth over Wes's skin before bringing them off together, shuddering into each other's mouths. It wasn't the frantic passion he'd imagined these last weeks. That would come, but right now they needed to touch and be mindful of being guests in Mark's place.

The bed was soft. Jackson lay on Wes's chest. Long days and sleepless nights covered them like a warm quilt.

"I don't want to shut my eyes." Wes shifted Jackson into the crook of his shoulder. "If I'm dreaming, I don't want to wake up without you."

"I'll sleep if you sleep, then we can only have good dreams."

"Sounds good," said Wes. "You know, I haven't had

a nightmare in weeks. Months maybe.”

“That’s amazing! You worked so hard to make that happen. I’m thrilled for you. I’ll help you keep them away however I can.” Jackson pressed a kiss to Wes’s neck. “Wes?”

“Yeah?”

“I’m so sorry my Mom treated you like that.”

“We’ve been over this already, I get it.” Wes rubbed his cheek on Jackson’s hair.

“She wasn’t always like that. There was this one time, before she started trying to fix me. She took us to this fancy hotel downtown for tea. She and Corie wore white gloves and she put a red bowtie on me. It's funny, I can’t remember if Dad was with us. She told us to pretend we were visiting the Queen. It was so fancy.”

“You don’t have to stop loving her or remembering the good times.”

“I won’t.” Jackson looked up to meet his eyes. “I still can’t believe you’re here.”

Wes kissed him on the lips. “You can thank Sophie and Nick and the whole gang, they all chipped in. I was stuck in limbo, ready to start our life together but missing one crucial element.” He tightened his grip. “Never again, Jackson Williams. I go where you go, and you come with me.”

Jackson kissed the soft skin of Wes’s ear. “That’s so romantic. I think the next book will be all about you.”

Wes sighed. “I accept that. Every book from now on can be about me, as long as I’m the one reminding you to eat your vegetables.”

“Mmmm.”

They fell asleep to the sound of London traffic on the street below. Jackson woke up before Wes. Their bodies were wrapped together. This was where Jackson belonged. He wasn’t going to move, not one inch. Sure, he had promised Lorraine he’d set up a blog so he could promote his books. But he could do that from this position. Everything he wanted, he could do from here.

Including answering a call from Corie. “What do you want?” Jackson whispered into the phone. “Wes is on Yukon time and is still sleeping. I’m not even sure if

Mark is awake."

"'m up." grumbled Wes moving closer and rubbing himself against Jackson.

Jackson rolled his hips against Wes's erection.

"I've already talked to Mark," said Corie. "I've got a plan."

Wes wrapped his arm around Jackson playing with his chest hair and teasing his nipples. Jackson stifled a groan.

"Mom's willing to talk. It would be nice to meet on neutral territory so poor Wes doesn't have to come back here. I figured we'll invite them over to Mark's for a late lunch, if you're ready to see her. Mark and I will stop off and get some take out, Chinese maybe."

"Wait, Wes cooks." He moved Wes's roving hands away, finding the conversation very hard to follow. "You'd cook, right, Wes?"

"Sure." Wes looked up for a moment then leaned back to continue his delectable, distracting behavior.

"That sounds good, if he's sure," said Corie. "We can help. Have Wes check the kitchen and see what he needs."

"Let me know what time you're coming," Jackson said, his finger hovering over the end button.

"I'm on my way shortly. I'll have all the details by then. And Jackson, you're not as subtle as you think you are. Tell Wes good morning for me. See you soon." Laughing, she hung up.

Jackson set his phone on the night table. "I can't believe you! Do you know how hard it was to talk to her with you doing that?" He gasped as Wes moved his lips and tongue across his shoulder nibbling and licking down his spine. Jackson gulped for air, his heart pounding. "Hey, let me go and empty my bladder or you'll get more than you bargained for."

"I always get more than I bargained for from you." Wes slapped his thigh. "Hurry up or I'll finish without you."

Jackson pulled on his sleep pants and walked across the hall to the bathroom. He ran into Mark as he was leaving for a jog.

"Corie's filled me in on everything," said Mark. "I've got the day off, so whenever you want lunch is fine with me. I'll be back in about an hour, we'll talk about it then?"

"Sounds good," said Jackson, and seconds later, he was back in the bedroom, diving onto Wes and relishing the full body contact. Wes wrapped him tight, his lips against Jackson's neck raising goose bumps all over.

In between kisses, Wes said, "I heard you say we're eating lunch here."

Jackson took a deep breath. "Yes."

"You said I'm cooking." He grabbed Jackson by the wrists, wrestled him to the bed, rubbing his whole body. "Well then, time to pay up, I don't cook for free." He feasted on Jackson's lips as if he'd been starved for days.

Coherent thought gone, Jackson's world narrowed to sweat, skin gliding hot, hard, and nothing else mattered. Slick fingers sliding and stretching, hearts beating, and mutual possession. Jackson came and Wes followed, heat splashing between their bodies. They held each other though the shaking and tears.

"You okay?" Wes whispered.

"You're here. I'm superb."

"Then it was definitely worth the trip."

"I was on my way home, you know. It took longer than I wanted, but I had it handled."

Wes looked at him. "I had no doubt you would be back, but I couldn't wait. You complete me in a way no one or nothing ever has, Jackson. Even the land didn't have the same appeal without you there. I meant what I said earlier. I don't want to do life without you right now, whatever that means."

They hugged one last time and took a quick shower before starting the day. Wes had just started searching the cupboards for what he might need to make a simple but satisfying lunch when Corie arrived, Mark close behind.

"Okay, I have my menu." Wes waved a piece of paper. "Where did you say the store was? Driver!" Wes joked, snapping his fingers at Jackson.

Jackson responded with a kiss. "Right here."

****

At one-thirty, there was a knock on the door. Natalie and Edward Williams had arrived. Wes straightened his shoulders and moved toward the door. He was nervous about how things would go, not for himself but for Jackson.

Edward shook hands all around, giving Wes an extra warm smile. Natalie was pale but held her head high. She gave Wes a cool greeting without meeting his eyes.

Wes was fine with that.

There was an air of apprehension in the room, but nothing unpleasant happened. Mr. Williams tried hard to keep up his end of the conversation, but exhaustion showed on his furrowed forehead. Mrs. Williams used what appeared to be her best "polite company" attitude, avoiding topics that could cause trouble and only talking about things like the weather and the food. Wes had made quiche with a green salad and a sharp, sweet dressing. The French Beaujolais brought out the flavors of both. She may not have liked him, but she raved about the food, asked for the recipe, and drew him into a conversation about how life led him to cook. Wes figured it was her way of apologizing.

When the meal was over, Wes started stacking the dirty dishes.

"No way." Corie stopped him. "You shopped, you cooked, and you chose the best wine I've had in ages. We'll do the cleaning. Go relax."

"Jackson chose the wine," said Wes. "It all tastes the same to me."

Corie didn't care. "Go!"

Jackson, Corie, their mother, and Mark were laughing as they chatted and scraped the dishes. Wes wondered when the other shoe would drop. Maybe that's why they didn't want him in the way. The exile didn't seem fair but Corie had been adamant. Wes took one last look at the group and made his way past Mr. Williams dozing in the living room, slid the patio door open, and walked out onto the wide balcony.

The May day was bright and sunny, the air fragrant with lilacs and heavy with humidity. Wes broke out into an instant sweat. The Yukon rarely experienced this kind of heat. Hot, yes. Humid, not so much. Wes leaned on the railing and watched people below snaking beneath the trees. A scraping noise made him look up.

Jackson's mother closed the patio door behind her. She came and leaned beside him, her back to the view.

Wes tried to call Jackson to his side mentally. "Mrs. Williams."

"Call me Natalie. I owe you an apology. Well, perhaps two apologies."

Wes kept his tone noncommittal. "Okay."

Natalie drew in a shaky breath. "You didn't tell him."

Wes furrowed his brow. "Excuse me?"

"You didn't tell Jackson about our little conversation the other night."

"No." Wes shook his head. "I spent a long time estranged from my family. I won't come between him and his."

She looked at him. "Aren't you?"

Wes met her gaze calmly. "Look, Natalie, you will always be welcome in our home. Any estrangement will not be our choice."

Her shoulders slumped slightly. "I guess I deserve that. I'm sorry."

"That Jackson loves me?" Wes wondered if he'd gone too far but he refused to look away.

"I'm sorry I was such a bitch."

The word grated in the air between them.

"I was hoping it was just a fling," Natalie said, "that you would give up or that he would. I was wrong. I was scared. I don't handle change well. But that's no excuse for my behavior. He loves you and you clearly love him."

"Yeah." Wes gave her a wry smile. "Sorry about that."

"Oh, Wesley, I'm not. Mothers worry, and Ed—Jackson, was different than my friend's children. Even as an adult, he didn't seem to know what he wanted. You've changed him."

"I don't think he's changed. The Yukon gave him the space to be who he is. By the time I met him, he was already Jackson. He inspired me by being himself."

Her smile was tremulous. "I'm very happy to hear that. But the Yukon... It's so far away."

"I understand being too far away from the people you love. I'll remind him to call and we'll visit. Next summer we'll have a place with a guest room. Come, I'll take you and Mr. Williams down the river to a spot where you can watch eagles."

"I'll do the best I can." She moved to the door.

"Natalie, wait."

She turned to look at him. Wes stepped across the space between them and gathered her into his arms. Natalie stood stiff and then relaxed, putting her arms tentatively around him.

Natalie didn't push him away but looked up at him. "Thanks." She tightened her arms and then released him, heading back to the living room toward Jackson.

Jackson raised his eyebrows as she stopped in front of him. "Everything okay, Mom?"

"Yes." Natalie took hold of her son's hand. "Jackson, I am so sorry. I was way out of line. I don't want you so far away, but I think you have done amazing things with your life. I've always been proud of you, although I know I don't show it well." She glanced back at Wes. "And Wesley tells me I can visit."

Jackson's eyes widened. He opened his arms and she walked into them with very little awkwardness. "It's all I want, Mom. I'm so glad." He held her for a moment looking at Wes over her shoulder, eyes wide.

"There's something else I've been meaning to talk to you about since you arrived, there just hasn't space in the chaos." Natalie made no move to leave his embrace. "This spring I formed a team of likeminded professors and teaching assistants at the University. Our purpose is to explore the impact that romance writing has had on women since its inception. This information will become a certificate course, with credits toward an English degree. Academia is slow to change, but it gets there." Natalie pulled back to meet her son's eyes, but remained within his clasp. "There will be several E.J. Williams novels on the syllabus. My ask is twofold. I would like your input on authors and stories we should be using in our course material. I was also hopeful you would come and speak to our students in our inaugural semester next fall, although I can understand why you may choose to say no, especially now. No need to commit to anything at this moment. I am very aware that kind of thing gives you the shakes, but I have it on good authority that you are very good at it." She gave him one more quick hug then moved away toward the living room. "I love you, Jackson. I don't think I've said it to you enough."

Were those tears shimmering in her eyes? Wes couldn't tell, his own eyes were so wet as he watched Jackson absorb the words he'd been longing to hear. Jackson came onto the patio and moved to the space his mother had vacated at the railing not that long ago. Wes slipped his arm around Jackson's waist, and they stood together, listening as Natalie woke her husband.

****

They almost missed their flight. After a couple of crazy days touring Jackson's childhood haunts, trying to see everything, spend time with Mom and Dad, and ending the long days with nights at Mark's place laughing with Corie and Mark, it was hard to pull away the covers and untangle their limbs to say goodbye. Now sitting on the plane, Jackson could finally relax. He turned his eyes away from the prairies far below his window to the man slumbering peacefully by his side. Wes snored a light snore, one that invited kissing. Jackson resisted the temptation, for now. He was grateful Wes had ignored his wishes and come to London. Yes, Jackson had been on his way home but having Wes there completed the circle of both their journeys. Everything was going to be alright. Everyone had promised to visit soon, and Jackson was looking forward to it, to all of it.

He was ready to go back to tackle a future that scared the heck out of him. Jackson knew he and Wes could accomplish anything together, no matter what it was: his new romance story about gay gold rushers, uncle-ing, Wes's schooling, talks, blog posts, or even the big party Sophie was bound to throw when they got back. They were up for it.

Wes opened his eyes and smiled. Jackson was finally home.

Acknowledgments

Thanks to the tag team of muses that sat on our beds and woke us up to fill us in on details of plot, always keeping in mind what our characters wanted and needed. We didn't get much sleep but, how cool is that? We'd also like to thank our families who put up with our "writers' brains," and "what? I'm listening," when we were clearly in another place. You rock and we couldn't have done it without your support. We'd love to mention our pups, Cauli and Jayne for being there and reminding us of Kale and how much he loves winter. Thank you too, to Patty Schramm of Flashpoint Publications who believed in us and gave us space to bring this story out of the woods and into the light of day. Mostly we want to thank our amazing editor, Zee Ahmad (Two Marshmallows) who took the time and babied us along. She understood our vision and seemed so tuned in to our wavelength it was uncanny and magical. We had the story, but Zee brought the wardrobe and makeup. The book was fine when we started working with her and she helped us make it what it is. And thanks to you for reading it and helping make our dreams come true.

Grandma's Tea Biscuits

"Wow, my mother is a baker and never made anything so pretty," said Jackson. He carried the bowls to the table.

"I financed my misspent youth in restaurants," said Wes, "but this one's totally home grown. It's a recipe we like to call 'Depression Tea Biscuits', passed down from Aunt Isabelle's grandmother. That woman was a force of nature."

- Yukon Winter, Chapter Twelve

Ingredients

- 2 cups sifted flour
- 4 tablespoons lard
- 4 teaspoons baking powder
- ¾ cup water (if too dry add up to 1 cup more)
- ½ teaspoon salt
- Flour for kneading

Directions

1. Preheat the oven to 450 degrees Fahrenheit. Be grateful that you have a thermostat and not a wood stove as Grandma had.

2. Sift together flour, baking powder and salt.

3. Cut in the lard coarsely (it should resemble the size of a small pea).

4. Make a well in the center, turn water in all at once, stir lightly with a knife.

5. Turn out on floured board, gather batter into a ball, kneed gently for 20 counts.

6. Press dough down with the heel of your hand to about ½ an inch thick and cut with a cookie cutter or small can at one end.

7. Place biscuits so they are touching one another on a cookie sheet. Bake in hot oven.

8. Serve warm from the over with butter if you have it, just dip in soup or stew or use preserves. Yields 12.

Notes:

· When biscuits touch each other on the pan, they rise higher and evenly.

· Don't over kneed. Those peas of lard make the finished product so flaky.

· If you don't have a cookie cutter, form 12 small balls with your hands.

· Dumplings for stew can be made from this dough by increasing water from ¾ cup to 1½ cups, to increase the moisture content so that dumplings drop from the end of an oiled spoon and form islands in your simmering stew.

Wes's notes: Today we would use butter and the milk of your choice. My great-grandma lived in the wilderness. She would have had lard from the pig they'd killed that fall, and sometimes they would have milk from the old cow, but usually water was their choice. Sometimes she would fry this batter in her cast iron pan over a fire and it would make a very acceptable fry bread. The recipe is flexible, leaving room for what they had or didn't have at the time, but I like to do it the way she did it. It connects me to her and my roots in surprising ways. When I was on the road, it gave me something of home.

For more recipes from Yukon Winter, please visit our website: https://northernlightslove.com

Bringing rainbow stories to life.

Flashpoint Publications welcomes submissions from writers of every color and books featuring characters of every color. In addition, Flashpoint Publications encourages job applicants of every color whenever a staff position becomes available. We believe that EVERYONE is entitled to a seat at our table.

www.flashpointpublications.com